Praise for Val McDermid's Kate Brannigan Series

"Kate Brannigan is a sparky, funny and much to be welcomed entrant into the still tiny profession of the female private eye."
—*Times* (UK), on *Dead Beat*

"Kate Brannigan deserves promotion to the top rank, alongside Kinsey Millhone and V.I. Warshawski."
—*Sunday Telegraph* (UK), on *Kick Back*

"At long last, this is a genre heroine with a big heart, witty tongue and an understanding of modern youth."
—*Evening Standard* (UK), on *Kick Back*

"McDermid's heroine is as likeable as they come—she's tough and tender in equal measures and has a lovely way with witty one liners."   —*Liverpool Daily Post* (UK), on *Crack Down*

"Manchester's answer to Thomas Harris."
—*Guardian* (UK), on *Star Struck*

"Kate's wit has the bite of Fran Leibowitz's."
—*Kirkus Reviews*, on *Kick Back*

"Kate Brannigan is truly welcome. Hot on one-liners, Chinese food, tabloid papers and Thai boxing, she is refreshingly funny."
—*Daily Mail* (UK), on *Kick Back*

"This Manchester-set series is among the best with a slangy, wise-cracking heroine; good plots and a great cast of characters. A sure winner."   —*MLB News*, on *Clean Break*

BLUE GENES

AND

STAR STRUCK

Also by Val McDermid

A Place of Execution
Killing the Shadows
The Grave Tattoo
A Darker Domain
Trick of the Dark
The Vanishing Point
Northanger Abbey

TONY HILL/CAROL JORDAN NOVELS

The Mermaids Singing
The Wire in the Blood
The Last Temptation
The Torment of Others
Beneath the Bleeding
Fever of the Bone
The Retribution
Cross and Burn
Insidious Intent

KAREN PIRIE NOVELS

The Distant Echo
A Darker Domain
The Skeleton Road
Out of Bounds

KATE BRANNIGAN NOVELS

Dead Beat
Kick Back
Crack Down
Clean Break

LINDSAY GORDON NOVELS

Report for Murder
Common Murder
Final Edition
Union Jack
Booked for Murder
Hostage to Murder

SHORT STORY COLLECTIONS

The Writing on the Wall and Other Stories
Stranded
Christmas is Murder (ebook only)
Gunpowder Plots (ebook only)

NON FICTION

A Suitable Job for a Woman
Forensics

VAL McDERMID

BLUE GENES

AND

STAR STRUCK

Grove Press
New York

Blue Genes first published in Great Britain in 1996 by HarperCollins Publishers. First published in the United States in 1996 by Scribner.

Star Struck first published in Great Britain in 1998 by HarperCollins Publishers. First published in the United States in 2004 by Spinster Ink Books.

Printed in the United States of America
Simultaneously published in Canada

First Grove Atlantic edition: July 2018

This book was designed by Norman Tuttle at Alpha Design & Composition

This book was set in 11.5 point Bembo by Alpha Design & Composition of Pittsfield, NH

Library of Congress Cataloging-in-Publication data is available for this title.

ISBN 978-0-8021-2831-7
eISBN 978-0-8021-6576-3

Grove Press
an imprint of Grove Atlantic
154 West 14th Street
New York, NY 10011

Distributed by Publishers Group West

groveatlantic.com

18 19 20 21   10 9 8 7 6 5 4 3 2 1

INTRODUCTION
TO THE GROVE EDITION

When I started writing crime fiction, I planned to write a trilogy because the book I really wanted to write was the third one, but I couldn't figure out how to get there without writing the first two. And so my first series character, Lindsay Gordon, was born.

I'd always known that I'd move on to something different after those first three books. And what really tempted me was the private eye novel. Sara Paretsky, Sue Grafton, Barbara Wilson and their American feminist sisters had taken that genre by the scruff of the neck and remade it in our image. And I was desperate to see whether I could make that work in the UK, with our different laws and social mores.

Kate Brannigan was the result of that desire. I had three main aims with the Brannigan books. The first—and probably the most important—was that I wanted to stretch myself as a writer. Fledgling writers are often told to write what they know. I took that injunction literally and started my career with a protagonist whose life mirrored my own in many respects. Our personalities were very different, but the superficialities were broadly similar. Ethnicity, gender, occupation, politics.

The question I asked of myself was whether I could create a credible character whose experience of the world was very different from my own. An imaginary best friend rather than an alter ego, I suppose. Because it was important to me that I liked her. If she was going to be a series character, I had to be sure I'd want to come back to her again and again.

So I considered my friends. What was it about them I liked and respected? But equally, what was it about them that drove me nuts? Because Brannigan had to be human, not some goody two-shoes who would make me feel perpetually inadequate.

The Kate Brannigan I ended up with grew up in Oxford. Not the dreaming spires of academe—the working class row houses where the workers at the car plant lived. Unlike Lindsay, we know what she looks like—petite, red-headed, a fit kickboxer with an Irish granny. She has a boyfriend, Richard, a rock journalist. Kate knows them both well enough not to live directly with him. They're next-door neighbours whose adjoining houses are linked by a conservatory that runs along the back of both homes.

She's a law school dropout who became an accidental PI. She starts out as the junior partner in Mortensen and Brannigan but eventually becomes her own boss. She has a social conscience but what really drives her is the desire to figure out what is going on. As with most PI novels, we hear the story in the first person. We see things through Kate's eyes and hear her whip-smart wisecracks in real time. Because she always gets to come up with the smart retort that most of us only think of two days later in real life.

There were some tropes of the PI novel I was less comfortable with. For a start, civilians absolutely don't have access to guns in the UK. So I did not have available to me Raymond Chandler's solution to the problem of what to do next: 'Have a man walk through the door with a gun in his hand.' I had to get my kicks in other ways. Literally. With the Thai kickboxing.

More importantly, I felt the new wave feminist crime writers from the US had missed a trick. Most of their protagonists were loners. They maybe let one or two people close but that was the limit. To me, this seemed at odds with my experience of the way women connected. I myself had a nexus of close friends with different backgrounds and skills; we all weighed in and provided help and support both practically and emotionally when needed. This was a pattern I saw all around me. I was determined to reflect that in my work so I gave Kate a network and a significant other. It made the storytelling a damn sight easier too!

The Lindsay Gordon novels had been published originally by a small feminist publishing house, The Women's Press. The advances were small and so were the sales. My second aim was to become a full-time writer of fiction and I knew that to achieve that I had to find a home with a more commercial publisher. So while I didn't tailor my writing to the market place, I knew that the decisions I'd made in giving Kate her personal attributes would mean she'd appeal to a wider audience. I also felt very strongly that I didn't want to live in a ghetto or write in a ghetto. I wanted to embrace the wider world that I inhabited. Kate allowed me to do that, and by giving her a lesbian best friend, I could be inclusive too.

My third goal was political subversion. I've been addicted to crime fiction since childhood. I know how crime lovers read. When we find a new author we like, we search out their backlist and devour that too. What better way to persuade people to read Lindsay Gordon than to give her a seductive sister under the skin? It worked—every time a new Brannigan appeared, there would be a spike in those Lindsay Gordon sales.

The one thing I didn't foresee when I started writing the Brannigan novels was how important their setting would become. The six Brannigan novels are as much a social history of Manchester and the North of England in the 1990s as they are mystery novels. This decade was a fascinating time to live and work there. A former industrial city known in the nineteenth century as Cottonopolis, it had been hollowed out and brought to its knees by the economic policies of Margaret Thatcher's government. But Mancunians don't give up easily. They gritted their teeth and set about reinventing the city throughout the decade. Football, music, financial services and sheer bloody-mindedness produced a reinvigoration and reinvention of the city. Watching that and writing about it was one of the greatest pleasures of writing this series.

I hope reading them gives you as much pleasure.

Val McDermid, 2018

BLUE GENES

For Fairy, Lesley and all the other lesbian mothers who prove that moulds are there to be broken. And for Robyn and Andrew and Jack.

ACKNOWLEDGEMENTS

What is outlined in this novel is entirely within the realms of possible science. Somebody somewhere is almost certainly carrying out these procedures, probably for very large sums of money.

I'm grateful to Dr Gill Lockwood for most of my medical and scientific information, and to David Hartshorn of Cellmark Diagnostics for background on DNA testing. For other matters, I'm indebted to Lee D'Courcy, Diana Cooper, Yvonne Twiby, Jai Penna, Paula Tyler, Brigid Baillie and the press office of the Human Fertilisation and Embryology Authority.

1

The day Richard's death announcement appeared in the *Manchester Evening Chronicle*, I knew I couldn't postpone clearing up the mess any longer. But there was something I had to do first. I stood in the doorway of the living room of the man who'd been my lover for three years, Polaroid in hand, surveying the chaos. Slowly, I swept the camera lens round the room, carefully recording every detail of the shambles, section by section. This was one time I wasn't prepared to rely on memory. Richard might be gone, but that didn't mean I was going to take any unnecessary risks. Private eyes who do that have as much chance of collecting their pensions as a Robert Maxwell employee.

Once I had a complete chronicle of exactly how things had been left in the room that was a mirror image of my own bungalow next door, I started my mammoth task. First, I sorted things into piles: books, magazines, CDs, tapes, promo videos, the detritus of a rock journalist's life. Then I arranged them. Books, alphabetically, on the shelf unit. CDs ditto. The tapes I stacked in the storage unit Richard had bought for the purpose one Sunday when I'd managed to drag him round Ikea, the 1990s equivalent of buying an engagement ring. I'd even put the cabinet together for him, but he'd never got into the habit of using it, preferring the haphazard stacks and heaps strewn all over the floor. I buried the surge of emotion that came with the memory and carried on doggedly. The magazines I shoved out of sight in the conservatory that runs along the back of both our houses, linking them together more firmly than we'd ever been prepared to do in any formal sense with our lives.

I leaned against the wall and looked around the room. When people say, "It's a dirty job, but somebody's got to do it," how come we never really believe we'll be the ones left clutching the sticky end? I sighed and forced myself on. I emptied ashtrays of the roaches left from Richard's joints, gathered together pens and pencils and stuffed them into the sawn-off Sapporo beer can he'd used for the purpose for as long as I'd known him. I picked up the assorted notepads, sheets of scrap paper and envelopes where he'd scribbled down vital phone numbers and quotes, careful not to render them any more disordered than they were already, and took them through to the room he used as his office when it wasn't occupied by his nine-year-old son Davy on one of his regular visits. I dumped them on the desk on top of a remarkably similar-looking pile already there.

Back in the living room, I was amazed by the effect. It almost looked like a room I could sit comfortably in. Cleared of the usual junk, it was possible to see the pattern on the elderly Moroccan rug that covered most of the floor and the sofas could for once accommodate the five people they were designed for. I realized for the first time that the coffee table had a central panel of glass. I'd been trying for ages to get him to put the room into something approaching a civilized state, but he'd always resisted me. Even though I'd finally got my own way, I can't say it made me happy. But then, I couldn't get out of my mind the reason behind what I was doing here, and what lay ahead. The announcement of Richard's death was only the beginning of a chain of events that would be a hell of a lot more testing than tidying a room.

I thought about brushing the rug, but I figured that was probably gilding the lily, the kind of activity that people found

a little bizarre after the death of a lover. And bizarre was not
the impression I wanted to give. I went back through to my
house and changed from the sweat pants and T-shirt I'd worn
to do the cleaning into something more appropriate for a grieving relict. A charcoal wool wraparound skirt from the French
Connection sale and a black lamb's-wool turtleneck I'd chosen
for the one and only reason that it made me look like death.
There are times in a private eye's working life when looking
like she's about to keel over is an image preferable to that of
Wonder Woman on whizz.

I was about to close the conservatory door behind me as
I returned to Richard's house when his doorbell belted out
an inappropriate blast of the guitar riff from Eric Clapton's
"Layla." "Shit," I muttered. No matter how careful you are,
there's always something you forget. I couldn't remember what
the other choices were on Richard's "Twenty Great Rock Riffs"
doorbell, but I was sure there must be something more fitting than Clapton's wailing guitar. Maybe something from the
Smiths, I thought vaguely as I tried to compose my face into
a suitable expression for a woman who's just lost her partner.
Just how was I supposed to look, I found a second to wonder.
What's the well-bereft woman wearing on her face this season?
You can't even go for the mascara tracks down the cheeks in
these days of lash tints.

I took a deep breath, hoped for the best and opened the
door. The crime correspondent of the *Manchester Evening Chronicle* stood on the step, her black hair even more like an explosion
in a wig factory than usual. "Kate," my best friend Alexis said,
stepping forward and pulling me into a hug. "I can't believe
it," she added, a catch in her voice. She moved back to look at
me, tears in her eyes. So much for the hard-bitten newshound.
"Why didn't you call us? When I saw it in the paper . . . Kate,
what the hell happened?"

I looked past her. All quiet in the street outside. I put my
arm round her shoulders and firmly drew her inside, closing the

door behind her. "Nothing. Richard's fine," I said, leading the way down the hall.

"Do what?" Alexis demanded, stopping and frowning at me. "If he's fine, how come I just read he's dead in tonight's paper? And if he's fine, how come you're doing the 'Baby's in Black' number when you know that's the one colour that makes you look like the Bride of Frankenstein?"

"If you'd let me get a word in edgeways, I'll explain," I said, going through to the living room. "Take my word for it, Richard is absolutely OK."

Alexis stopped dead on the threshold, taking in the pristine tidiness of the room. "Oh no, he's not," she said, suspicion running through her heavy Scouse accent like the stripe in the toothpaste. "He's not fine if he's left his living room looking like this. At the very least, he's having a nervous breakdown. What the hell's going on here, KB?"

"I can't believe you read the death notices," I said, throwing myself down on the nearest sofa.

"I don't normally," Alexis admitted, subsiding on the sofa opposite me. "I was down Moss Side nick waiting for a statement from the duty inspector about a little bit of aggravation involving an Uzi and a dead Rottweiler, and they were taking so long about it I'd read everything else in the paper except the ads for the dinner dances. And it's just as well I did. What's going on? If he's not dead, who's he upset enough to get heavy-metal hassle like this?" She stabbed the paper she carried with a nicotine-stained index finger.

"It was me who put the announcement in," I said.

"That's one way of telling him it's over," Alexis interrupted before I could continue. "I thought you two had got things sorted?"

"We have," I said through clenched teeth. Ironing out the problems in my relationship with Richard would have taken the entire staff of an industrial laundry a month. It had taken us rather longer.

"So what's going on?" Alexis demanded belligerently. "What's so important that you have to give everybody a heart attack thinking me laddo's popped his clogs?"

"Can't you resist the journalistic exaggeration for once?" I sighed. "You know and I know that nobody under sixty routinely reads the deaths column. I had to use a real name and address, and I figured with Richard out of town till the end of the week, nobody's going to be any the wiser if I used his," I explained. "And he won't be, unless you tell him."

"That depends on whether you tell me what this is all in aid of," Alexis said cunningly, her outrage at having wasted her sympathy a distant memory now she had the scent of a possible story in her nostrils. "I mean, I think he's going to notice something's going on," she added, sweeping an eloquent arm through the air. "I don't think he knows that carpet has a pattern."

"I took Polaroids before I started," I told her. "When I'm finished, I'll put it back the way it was before. He won't notice a thing."

"He will when I show him the cutting," Alexis countered. "Spill, KB. What're you playing at? What's with the grieving widow number?" She leaned back and lit a cigarette. So much for my clean ashtrays.

"Can't tell you," I said sweetly. "Client confidentiality."

"Bollocks," Alexis scoffed. "It's me you're talking to, KB, not the bizzies. Come on, give. Or else the first thing Richard sees when he comes home is . . ."

I closed my eyes and muttered an old gypsy curse under my breath. It's not that I speak Romany; it's just that I've refused to buy lucky white heather once too often. Believe me, I know exactly what those old gypsies say. I weighed up my options. I could always call her bluff and hope she wouldn't tell Richard, on the basis that the two of them maintain this pretence of despising each other's area of professional expertise and extend that into the personal arena at every possible opportunity. On the other hand, the prospect of explaining to Richard that I was responsible for the report of his death didn't appeal either. I gave in. "It's got to be off the record, then," I said ungraciously.

"Why?" Alexis demanded.

"Because with a bit of luck it will be sub judice in a day or two. And if you blow it before then, the bad guys will be out of town on the next train and we'll never nail them."

"Anybody ever tell you you've got melodramatic tendencies, KB?" Alexis asked with a grin.

"A bit rich, coming from a woman who started today's story with, 'Undercover police swooped on a top drug dealer's love nest in a dawn raid this morning,' when we both know that all that happened was a couple of guys from the Drugs Squad turned over some two-bit dealer's girlfriend's bedsit," I commented.

"Yeah, well, you gotta give it a bit of topspin or the boy racers on the newsdesk kill it. But that's not what we're talking about. I want to know why Richard's supposed to be dead."

"It's a long and complicated story," I started in a last attempt to lose her interest.

Alexis grinned and blew a long stream of smoke down her nostrils. Puff the Magic Dragon would have signed up for a training course on the spot. "Great," she enthused. "My favourite kind."

"The client's a firm of monumental masons," I said. "They're the biggest provider of stone memorials in South Manchester. They came to us because they've been getting a string of complaints from people saying they've paid for gravestones that haven't turned up."

"Somebody's been nicking *gravestones*?"

"Worse than that," I said, meaning it. Far as I was concerned, I was dealing with total scumbags on this one. "My clients are the incidental victims of a really nasty scam. From what I've managed to find out so far, there are at least two people involved, a man and a woman. They turn up on the doorsteps of the recently bereaved and claim to be representing my client's firm. They produce these business cards which have the name of my clients, complete with address and phone number, all absolutely kosher. The only thing wrong with them is that the names on the cards are completely unknown to my client. They're not using the names of his staff. But this pair are smart. They always come in the evening, out of business hours, so anyone who's a bit suspicious can't ring my client's office and check up on them. And they come single-handed. Nothing heavy. Where it's a woman who's died, it's the woman who shows up. Where it's a man, it's the bloke."

"So what's the pitch?" Alexis asked.

"They do the tea-and-sympathy routine, then they explain that they're adopting the new practice of visiting people in their homes because it's a more personal approach to choosing an appropriate memorial. Then they go into a special-offer routine, just like they were selling double glazing or something. You know the sort of thing—unique opportunity, special shipment of Italian marble or Aberdeen granite, you could be one of the people we use for testimonial purposes, limited period offer."

"Yeah, yeah, yeah," Alexis groaned. "And if they don't sign up tonight, they've lost the opportunity, am I right, or am I right?"

"You're right. So these poor sods whose lives are already in bits because they've just lost their partner or husband or wife, or mother or father, or son or daughter get done up like a kipper just so some smart bastard can go out and buy another designer suit or a mobile bloody phone," I said angrily. I know all the rules about never letting yourself get emotionally involved with the jobs, but there are times when staying cool and disinterested would be the mark of inhumanity rather than good sense. This was one of them.

Alexis lit another cigarette, shaking her head. "Pure gobshites," she said in disgust. "Twenty-four-carat shysters. So they take the cash and disappear into the night, leaving your clients to pick up the pieces when the headstone remains a ghostly presence?"

"Something like that. They really are a pair of unscrupulous bastards. I've been interviewing some of the people who have been had over, and a couple of them have told me the woman has actually driven them to holes in the wall to get money for a cash deposit." I shook my head, remembering the faces of the victims again. They showed a procession of emotions, each more painful to watch than the last. There was grief revisited in the setting of the scene for me, then anger as they recalled how they'd been stung, then a mixture of shame and resentment that they'd fallen for it. "And there's no point in me telling them that in their shoes even a streetwise old cynic like me would probably have fallen for it. Because I probably would have done, that's the worst of it," I added bitterly.

"Grief gets you like that," Alexis agreed. "The last thing you're expecting is to be taken for a ride. Look at how many families end up not speaking to each other for years because someone has done something outrageous in the immediate aftermath of death, when everyone's staggering round feeling like their brain's in the food processor along with their emotions. After my Uncle Jos's second wife Theresa wore my gran's fur coat to the old dear's funeral, she might as well have been dead too. My dad wouldn't even let my mum send them a Christmas card for about ten years. Until Uncle Jos got cancer himself, poor sod."

"Yeah, well, us knowing these people haven't been particularly gullible doesn't make it any easier for them. The only thing that might help them would be for me to nail the bastards responsible."

"What about the bizzies? Haven't they reported it to them?"

I shrugged. "Only one or two of them. Most of them left it at phoning my client. It's pride, isn't it? People don't want everybody thinking they can't cope just because they've lost somebody. Especially if they're getting on a bit. So all Officer Dibble has to go on is a few isolated incidents." I didn't need to tell a crime correspondent that it wasn't something that was going to assume a high priority for a police force struggling to deal with an epidemic of crack and guns that seemed to claim fresh victims every week in spite of an alleged truce between the gangs.

Alexis gave a cynical smile. "Not exactly the kind of glamorous case the CID's glory boys are dying to take on, either. The only way they'd have started to take proper notice would have been if some journo like me had stumbled across the story and given it some headlines. Then they'd have had to get their finger out."

"Too late for that now," I said firmly.

"Toerags," Alexis said. "So you've put Richard's death notice in to try and flush them out?"

"Seemed like the only way to get a fix on them," I said. "It's clear from what the victims have said that they operate by using the deaths column. Richard's out of town on the road with some band, so I thought I'd get it done and dusted while he's not around to object to having his name taken in vain. If everything goes according to plan, someone should be here within the next half-hour."

"Nice thinking," Alexis said approvingly. "Hope it works. So why didn't you use Bill's name and address? He's still in Australia, isn't he?"

I shook my head. "I would have done, except he was flying in this afternoon." Bill Mortensen, the senior partner of Mortensen and Brannigan, Private Investigators and Security Consultants, had been in Australia for the last three weeks, his second trip Down Under in the past six months, an occurrence that was starting to feel a lot like double trouble to me. "He'll be using his house as a jet-lag recovery zone. So that left Richard. Sorry you had a wasted journey of condolence. And I'm sorry if it upset you," I added.

"You're all right. I don't think I really believed he was dead, you know? I figured it must be some sick puppy's idea of a joke, on account of I couldn't work out how come you hadn't told me he'd kicked it. If you see what I mean. Anyway, it wasn't a wasted journey. I was coming round anyway. There's something I wanted to tell you."

For some reason, Alexis had suddenly stopped meeting my eye. She was looking vaguely round the room, as if Richard's walls were the source of all inspiration. Then she dragged her eyes away from the no longer brilliant white emulsion and started rootling round in a handbag so vast it makes mine look like an evening purse. "So tell me," I said impatiently after a silence long enough for Alexis to unearth a fresh packet of cigarettes, unwrap them and light one.

"It's Chris," she exhaled ominously. More silence. Chris, Alexis's partner, is an architect in a community practice. It feels like they've been together longer than Mickey and Minnie. The pair of them had just finished building their dream home beyond the borders of civilization as we know it, part of a self-build scheme. And now Alexis was using the tone of voice that BBC announcers adopt when a member of the Royal family has died or separated from a spouse.

"What about Chris?" I asked nervously.

Alexis ran a hand through her hair then looked up at me from under her eyebrows. "She's pregnant."

Before I could say anything, the doorbell blasted out the riff from "Layla" again.

2

I looked at her and she looked at me. What I saw was genuine happiness accompanied by a faint flicker of apprehension. What Alexis saw, I suspect, was every piece of dental work I've ever had done. Before I could get my vocal cords unjammed Alexis was on her feet and heading for the conservatory. "That'll be your scam merchant. I'd better leg it," she said. "I'll let myself out through your house. Give me a bell later," she added to her slipstream.

Feeling stunned enough to resemble someone whose entire family has been wiped out by a freak accident, I walked to the front door in a bewildered daze. The guy on the other side of it looked like a high-class undertaker's apprentice. Dark suit, white shirt that gleamed in the streetlights like an advert for soap powder, plain dark tie. Even his hair was a gleaming black that matched his shoeshine. The only incongruity was that instead of a graveyard pallor, his skin had the kind of light tan most of us can't afford in April. "Mrs Barclay?" he asked, his voice deep and dignified.

"That's right," I said, trying for tremulous.

A hand snaked into his top pocket and came out with a business card. "Will Allen, Mrs Barclay. I'm very sorry for your loss," he said, not yet offering the card.

"Are you a friend of Richard's? Someone he works
—*worked*—with?"

"I'm afraid not, Mrs Barclay. I didn't have the good fortune to know your late husband. No, I'm with Greenhalgh and
Edwards." He handed the card over with a small flourish. "I
wonder if I might have a quiet word with you?"

I looked at the card. I recognized it right away as one of
the ones that come out of machines at the motorway-service
areas. The ones on the M6 at Hilton Park are the best; they've
got really smart textured card. Drop three quid in the slot,
choose a logo, type in the text and you get sixty instant business cards. No questions asked. One of the great mysteries of
the universe is how villains catch on to the potential of new
technology way ahead of the straight community. While most
punters were still eyeing the business card machines warily on
their way to the toilets, the bad guys were queuing up to arm
themselves with bullshit IDs. This particular piece of fiction
told me Will Allen was Senior Bereavement Consultant with
Greenhalgh and Edwards, Monumental Masons, The Garth,
Cheadle Hulme. "You'd better come in," I said tonelessly and
stepped back to let him pass me. As I closed the door, I noticed
Alexis emerging from my house with a cheery wave in my
direction.

Allen was moving tentatively towards the living room, the
one open door off the hallway. I'd drawn the line at cleaning the
whole house. "Come on through," I said, ushering him in and
pointing him at the sofa Alexis had just vacated. He sat down,
carefully hitching up his trousers at the knees. In the light, the
charcoal grey suit looked more like Jasper Conran than Marks
and Spencer; ripping off widows was clearly a profitable business.

"Thanks for agreeing to see me, Mrs Barclay," Allen said,
concern dripping from his warm voice. He was clean cut and
clean shaven, with a disturbing resemblance to John Cusack at
his most disarming. "Was your husband's death very sudden?"
he asked, his eyebrows wrinkling in concern.

"Car accident," I said, gulping back a sob. Hard work, acting. Almost convinces you Kevin Costner earns every dollar of
the millions he gets for a movie.

"Tragic," he intoned. "To lose him in his prime. Tragic."
Much more of this and I wasn't going to be acting. I was going
to be weeping for real. And not from sorrow.

I made a point of looking at his business card again. "I don't
understand, Mr Allen. What is it you're here about?"

"My company is in the business of providing high-quality
memorials for loved ones who pass away. The quality element
is especially important for someone like yourself, losing a loved
one so young. You'll want to be certain that whatever you
choose to remember him by will more than stand the test of
time." His solemn smile was close to passing the sincerity test.
If I really was a grief-stricken widow, I'd have been half in love
with him by now.

"But the undertaker said he'd get that all sorted out for
me," I said, going for the sensible-but-confused line.

"Traditionally, we have relied on funeral directors to refer
people on to us, but we've found that this doesn't really lead
to a satisfactory conclusion," Allen said confidentially. "When
you're making the arrangements for a funeral, there are so many
different matters to consider. It's hard under those circumstances
to give a memorial the undivided attention it deserves."

I nodded. "I know what you mean," I said wearily. "It all
starts to blur into one after a while."

"And that's exactly why we decided that a radical rethink
was needed. A memorial is something that lasts, and it's important for those of us left behind that it symbolizes the love and
respect we have for the person we have lost. We at Greenhalgh
and Edwards feel that the crucial issue here is that you make
the decision about how to commemorate your dear husband in
the peace of your own home, uncluttered by thoughts of the
various elements that will make up the funeral."

"I see," I said. "It sounds sensible, I suppose."

"We think so. Tell me, Mrs Barclay, have you opted for interment or cremation?"

"Not cremation," I said very firmly. "A proper burial, that's what Richard would have wanted." But only after he was actually dead, I added mentally.

He snapped open the locks on the slim black briefcase he'd placed next to him on the sofa. "An excellent choice, if I may say so, Mrs Barclay. It's important to have a place where you can mourn properly, a focus for the communication I'm sure you'll feel between yourself and Mr Barclay for a long time to come. Now, because we're still in the trial period of this new way of communicating with our customers, we are able to offer our high-quality memorials at a significant discount of twenty per cent less than the prices quoted on our behalf by funeral directors. So that means you get much better value for your money; a memorial that previously might have seemed out of your price range suddenly becomes affordable. Because, of course, we all want the very best for our loved ones," he added, his voice oozing sympathy.

I bit back the overwhelming desire to rip his testicles off and have them nickel-plated as a memorial to his crass opportunism and nodded weakly. "I suppose," I said.

"I wonder if I might take this opportunity to show you our range?" The briefcase was as open as the expression on his face. How could I refuse?

"I don't know . . ."

"There's absolutely no obligation, though obviously it would be in your best interests to go down the road that offers you the best value for money." He was on his feet and across the room to sit next to me in one fluid movement, a display file from his briefcase in his hand as if by magic. Sleight of hand like his, he could have been the new David Copperfield if he'd gone straight.

He flipped the book open in front of me. I stared at a modest granite slab, letters stuck on it like Letraset rather than incised in the stone. "This is the most basic model we offer," he said. "But even that is finest Scottish granite, quarried by traditional methods and hand-finished by our own craftsmen." He quoted a price that made my daily rate seem like buttons. He placed the file on my lap.

"Is that with or without the discount?" I asked.

"We always quote prices without discount, Mrs Barclay. So you're looking at a price that is twenty per cent less than that. And if you want to go ahead and you're prepared to pay a cash deposit plus cheque for the full amount tonight, I am authorized to offer you a further five per cent discount, making a total of one quarter less than the quoted price." His hand had moved to cover mine, gently patting it.

That was when the front door crashed open. "Careful with that bag, it's got the hot and sour soup in it," I heard a familiar voice shout. I closed my eyes momentarily. Now I knew how Mary Magdalene felt on Easter Sunday.

"Kate? You in here?" Richard's voice beat him into the room by a couple of seconds. He arrived in the doorway clutching a fragrant plastic carrier bag, a smoking spliff in his other hand. He looked around his living room incredulously. "What the hell's going on? What have you done to the place?"

He stepped into the room, followed by a pair of burly neopunks, each with a familiar Chinese takeaway carrier bag. It was the only remotely normal thing about them. Each wore heavy black work boots laced halfway up their calves, ragged black leggings and heavy tartan knee-length kilts. Above the waist, they had black granddad shirts with strategic rips held together by kilt pins and Celtic brooches. Across their chests, each had a diagonal tartan sash of the kind worn on television on Hogmanay by the dancers on those terrible ethnic fantasias the Scottish TV companies broadcast to warm the cockles of their exiles' hearts and make the rest of us throw up into our champagne. The one on Richard's left had bright red hair left long and floppy on top. The sides of his head were stubbled.

The other had a permed, rainbow striped Mohican. Each was big enough to merit his own postcode. They looked like Rob Roy dressed by Vivienne Westwood. Will Allen goggled at the three of them, aghast.

Richard dropped the bag of Chinese food and his jaw as the transformation to the room really sank in. "Jesus, Brannigan, I turn my back for five minutes and you trash the place. And who the hell are you?" he demanded, glowering at Allen.

Allen reassembled his face into something approaching a smile. "I'm Will Allen. From Greenhalgh and Edwards, the monumental masons. About Mr Barclay's memorial?"

Richard frowned. "Mr Barclay's memorial? You mean, as in gravestone?"

Allen nodded. "That's not the term we prefer to use, but yes, as in gravestone."

"Mr Richard Barclay, would that be?"

"That's right."

Richard shook his head in disbelief. He stuck his hand into the inside pocket of his leather jacket and pulled out a press card with his photograph on it. He thrust it towards Allen. "Do I look dead to you?"

Allen was on his feet, his folder pulled out of my grasp. He threw it into the briefcase, grabbed it and shouldered past Richard and the two Celtic warriors. "Ah shit," I swore, jumping to my feet and pushing through the doorway in Allen's wake.

"Come back here, Brannigan, you've got some explaining to do," I heard Richard yell as I reached the door. Allen was sprinting down the path towards the car-parking area. I didn't have my car keys on me; the last thing I'd anticipated was a chase. But Allen was my only lead and he was getting away. I had to do something. I ran down the path after him, glad that the only respectable pair of black shoes in my wardrobe had been flat pumps. As he approached a silver Mazda saloon, the lights flashed and I heard the doors unlock. Allen jumped into the car. The engine started first time. Another one of the joys of modern technology that makes life simpler for the bad guys. He reversed in a scream of tyres and engine, threw the car into a three-point turn and swept out of the cul-de-sac where I live. Anyone seeing him burn rubber as he swung on to the main drag would only mark him down as one of the local car thieves being a little indiscreet.

Dispirited, I sighed and walked back to the house. I'd got the number of his car, but I had a funny feeling that wasn't going to take me a whole lot further forward. These people were too professional for that. At least I had the whole thing on tape, I reminded myself. I stopped in my tracks. Oh no, I didn't. In the confusion of Alexis's visit and the fallout from her shock announcement, I'd forgotten to switch on the radio mikes I'd planted in Richard's living room. The whole operation was a bust.

Not only that, but I was going to have to deal with an irate and very much alive Richard, who was by now standing on his doorstep, arms folded, face scowling. Swallowing a sigh, I walked towards him. If I'd been wearing heels, I'd have been dragging them. "I know you think being on the road with a neopunk band is a fate worse than death, but it doesn't actually call for a tombstone," Richard said sarcastically as I approached.

"It was work," I said wearily.

"Am I supposed to be *grateful* for that? There's a man in my living room—at least, I *thought* it was my living room, but looking at it, I'm not so sure any more. Maybe I walked into the wrong house by mistake? Anyway, there's some smooth bastard in *my* living room, sitting on *my* settee discussing *my* gravestone with *my* so-called girlfriend—"

"Partner," I interjected. "Twenty-nine, remember? Not a girl any more."

He ignored me and steamrollered on. "Presumably because I'm supposedly dead. And I'm supposed to be calm and laid back about it because it was *work*?" he yelled.

"Are you going to let me in, or shall I sell tickets?" I asked calmly, gesturing over my shoulder with my thumb at the rest of the close. I didn't have to look to know that half a dozen windows would be occupied by now. TV drama's been so dire lately that the locals have taken up competitive Neighbourhood Watching.

"Let you in? Why? Are we expecting the undertaker next? Coffin due to be delivered, is it?" Richard demanded, thrusting his head forward so we were practically nose to nose. I could smell the sweetness of the marijuana on his breath, see the specks of gold in his hazel eyes. Good technique for dealing with anger, focusing on small details of your environment.

I pushed him in the chest. Not hard, just enough to make him back off. "I'll explain inside," I said, lips tight against my teeth.

"Well, big fat hairy deal," Richard muttered, turning on his heel and pushing past the two neopunks who were leaning against the wall behind him, desperately trying to pretend they were far too cool to be interested in the war raging around them.

I followed him back into the living room and returned to my seat. Richard sat opposite me, the coffee table between us. He started emptying the contents of the three carrier bags on to the table. "You'll find bowls and chopsticks in the kitchen," he said to his giant Gaelic gargoyles. "First on the right down the hall. That's if she hasn't emptied it as well." The redhead left in search of eating implements. "This had better be good, Brannigan," Richard added threateningly.

"It *smells* good," I said brightly. "Yang Sing, is it?"

"Never mind the bloody Chinese!" I waited for the jolt while the world stopped turning. Never mind the bloody Chinese? From the man who thinks it's not food if it doesn't have soy sauce in it? "What was that creep doing here?" Richard persisted.

"Pitching me into a gravestone," I said as the redhead returned and dumped bowls, chopsticks and serving spoons in front of us. I grabbed a carton of hot and sour soup and a spoon.

"I realized *that*. But why here? And why *my* gravestone?" Richard almost howled.

The punk with the Mohican exchanged apprehensive looks with his mate. The redhead nodded. "Look," the Mohican said. "This mebbe isnae a good time for this, Richard, know what ah mean, but?" The Glasgow accent was so strong you could have built a bridge with it and known it would outlast the civilization that spawned it. Once I'd deciphered his sentiment, I couldn't help agreeing with him.

"We could come back another time, by the way," the redhead chipped in, accent matching. Like aural bookends.

"Never mind coming back, you're here now," Richard said. "Get stuck in. She loves an audience, don't you, Brannigan?" He piled his bowl with fried noodles and beansprouts, added some chunks of aromatic stuffed duck and balanced a couple of prawn wontons on top, then leaned back in his seat to munch. "So why am I dead?"

He always does it to me. As soon as there's the remotest chance of me getting my fair share of a Chinese takeaway, Richard asks the kind of questions that require long and complicated answers. He knows perfectly well that my mother has rendered me incapable of speaking with my mouth full. Some injunctions you can rebel against; others are in the grain. Between mouthfuls of hot and sour soup so powerful it steam-cleaned my sinuses, I filled him in on the scam.

Then, Richard being too busy with his chopsticks to comment, I went on the offensive. "And it would all have gone off perfectly if you hadn't come blundering through the door and blowing my cover sky-high. Two days early, I might point out. You're supposed to be in Milton Keynes with some band that sounds like it was chosen at random from the Neanderthal's dictionary of grunts. What was it? Blurt? Grope? Fart?"

"Prole," Richard mumbled through the Singapore vermicelli. He swallowed. "But we're not talking about me coming back early to my own house. We're talking about this mess," he said, waving his chopsticks in the air.

"It's cleaner and tidier than it's ever been," I said firmly.

"Bad news, but," the Mohican muttered. "Hey, missus, have you thought about getting your chakras balanced? Your energy flow's well blocked in your third."

"Shut up, Lice. Not everybody's into being enlightened and that," the redhead said, giving him a dig in the side that would have left most people with three cracked ribs. Lice only grunted.

"You still haven't said why you came home early," I pointed out.

"It was two things really. Though looking at what I've come home to, I don't know why I bothered about one of them," Richard said, as if that were some kind of explanation.

"Do I have to guess? Animal, vegetable or mineral?"

"I'd got all the material I needed for the pieces I've got lined up on Prole, and then I bumped into the lads here. Boys, meet Kate Brannigan, who, in spite of appearances to the contrary, is a private investigator. Kate, meet Dan Druff, front man with Glasgow's top nouveau punk band, Dan Druff and the Scabby Heided Bairns." The redhead nodded gravely and sketched a salute with his chopsticks. "And Lice, the band's drummer." Lice looked up from his bowl and nodded. I found a moment to wonder if their guitar players were called Al O'Pecia and Nits.

"Delighted to make your acquaintance," I said. "Richard, pleased though I am to be sharing my evening with Dan and Lice, why exactly have you brought them home?" My subtlety, good manners and discretion had passed their sell-by date. Besides, Dan and Lice didn't look like the kind who'd notice anyone being offensive until the half-bricks started swinging.

"My good deed for the year," he said nonchalantly. "They need a private eye, and I've never seen you turn down a case."

"A paying case," I muttered.

"We'll pay you," Dan said.

"Something," Lice added ominously.

"For your trouble," Dan added, even more ominously.

"Why do you need a private eye?" I asked. It wouldn't be the first time Richard's dropped me in it, and this time I was determined that if I agreed, it was going to be an informed decision.

"Somebody's trying to see us off," Dan said bluntly.

"You mean . . . ?" I asked.

"How plain do you need it?" Lice demanded. "They're trying to wipe us off the map. Finish us. Render us history. Consign us to our next karmic state."

There didn't seem to be two ways of taking Lice's words. I was hooked, no question.

3

This was definitely a lot more interesting than rehashing the cockup of my gravestone inquiries. There would be plenty of time for me to beat myself up about that later. Dealing with the seriously menaced, even if they were barely comprehensible Glaswegian musicians, has always seemed a better way of passing the time than contemplating my failures. "You've had death threats?" I asked.

Lice looked at Dan, shaking his head pityingly. Dan looked at Richard, his eyebrows steepling in a demand for help. "Not as such," Richard explained. "When Lice talks about being wiped out, he means metaphorically."

"That's right," Lice confirmed. "Poetic licence and that." My interest was dropping faster than a gun barrel faced with Clint Eastwood.

"Somebody's out to get us *professionally* is what we're trying to say," Dan butted in. "We're getting stuffed tighter than a red pudding."

"What's a red pudding?" Richard demanded. I was glad about that; we private eyes never like to display our ignorance.

"For fuck's sake," Lice groaned.

"What do you expect from a country where the fish and chip shops only sell fish and chips?" Dan said. "It's like a sausage only it's red and it's got oatmeal in it and you deep-fry it, OK? In batter," he added for the benefit of us Sassenachs.

I wasn't about to ask any more. I still hadn't recovered from the shock of asking for a pizza in a Scottish chip shop. I'd watched in horrified amazement as the fryer expertly folded it in half and dumped it in the deep fat. No, I didn't eat it. I fed it to the seagulls and watched them plummet into the waves afterwards, their ability to defeat gravity wiped out in one meal. "So this metaphorical, poetically licensed professional stitch-up consists of what, exactly?"

"Essentially, the boys are being sabotaged," Richard said.

"Every time we're doing a gig around the town, some bastard covers all our posters up," Dan said. "Somebody's been phoning the promoters and telling them not to sell any more tickets for our gigs because they're already sold out. And then we get to a gig and there's hardly any genuine fans there."

"But there's always a busload of Nazis on super lager that tear the place to bits and close the gig down," Lice kicked in bitterly. "Now we've been barred from half the decent venues in the north and we're getting tarred with the same brush as they fascist bastards that are wrecking our gigs. The punters are starting to mutter that if these guys follow us around from place to place, it must be because there's something in our music that appeals to brainless racists."

"And actually, the boys' lyrics are quite the opposite of that." Richard with the truly crucial information as usual. "Even the most PC of your friends would be hard pressed to take offence."

"The only PC friend I've got is the one next door with the Pentium processor," I snapped. To my surprise, Dan and Lice guffawed.

"Nice one," Dan said. "Anyway, last night put the tin lid on it. We were doing this gig in Bedford, and while we were inside watching the usual wrecking crew smashing the place up, some total toerag torched our Transit."

"Have you talked to the police about this?" I said. Silly me. The boys scowled and shook their heads. Richard cast his eyes heavenwards and sighed deeply. I tried again. "This sounds like a campaign of systematic harassment to me. They've got the resources to pursue something like that properly. And they're free," I added.

"I thought you said she knew her arse from a hole in the ground?" Lice demanded of Richard. "'Have you talked to the police about this,'" he mimicked cruelly. The last time I felt that mimsy I was nine years old and forced to wear my cousin's cast-off party frock in lemon nylon with blue roses, complete with crackling petticoat, to my best friend's birthday party. "For fuck's sake, look at us. If we walked into the local nick, they'd arrest us. If we told them we were being harassed, they'd piss themselves laughing. I don't think that's the answer, missus."

Dan picked up the last salt and pepper rib and stood up. "Come on, Lice," he said. "I don't want to embarrass the woman. Richard, I know you meant well, but hey, your missus obviously isnae up to it. You know what they're like, women today. They cannae bring themselves to admit there are things that are way beyond them."

That did it. Through clenched teeth, I said, "I am nobody's missus and I am more than capable of sorting out any of the assorted scumbags that have doubtless got their own very good reasons for having it in for Dan Druff and the Scabby Heided Bairns. You want this sorting, I'll sort it. No messing."

When I saw the smile of complicity that flashed between Richard and Dan, I nearly decked the pair of them with the flying sweep kick I'd been perfecting down the Thai boxing gym. But there's no point in petulance once you've been well and truly had over. "I think that little routine makes us quits," I told Richard. He grinned. "I'm going to need a lot more details."

Dan sat down again. "It all started with the flyposting," he said, stretching his long legs out in front of him. I had the feeling it was going to be a long story.

It was just after midnight when Dan and Lice left Richard and me staring across the coffee table at each other. It had taken a while to get the whole story, what with Lice's digressions into the relationship between rock music and politics, with particular reference to right-wing racists and the oppression of the Scots. The one clear thread in their story that seemed impossible to deny was that someone was definitely out to get them. Any single incident in the Scabby Heided Bairns's catalogue of disaster could have been explained away, but not the accumulation of cockups that had characterized the last few weeks in the band's career.

They'd moved down to Manchester, supposedly the alternative music capital of the UK, from their native Glasgow in a bid to climb on to the next rung of the ladder that would lead them to becoming the Bay City Rollers of the nineties. Now, the boys were days away from throwing in the towel and heading north again. Bewildered that they could have made so serious an enemy so quickly, they wanted me to find out who was behind the campaign. Then, I suspected, it would be a matter of summoning their friends and having the Tartan Army march on some poor unsuspecting Manchester villain. I wasn't entirely sure whose side I was on here.

"You are going to sort it out for them?" Richard asked.

I shrugged. "If they've got the money, I've got the time."

"This isn't just about money. You owe me, Brannigan, and these lads are kicking. They deserve a break."

"So give them a good write-up in all those magazines you contribute to," I told him.

"They need more than that. They need word of mouth, a following. Without that, they're not exactly an attractive proposition to a record company."

"It would take more fans than Elvis to make Dan Druff and his team attractive to me," I muttered. "And besides, I don't owe you. It was you and your merry men who screwed up my job earlier tonight, if you remember."

Richard looked astonished, his big tortoiseshell glasses slipping down his nose faster than Eddie the Eagle on a ski jump. "And what about this place?" he wailed, waving his arm at the neat and tidy room.

"Out of the goodness of my heart, I'm not going to demand the ten quid an hour that good industrial cleaners get," I said sweetly, getting up and tossing the empty tinfoil containers into plastic bags.

"What about killing me off?" he demanded, his voice rising like a Bee Gee. "How do you think I felt, coming home to find my partner sitting discussing my gravestone with a complete stranger? And while we're on the subject, I hope you weren't going to settle for some cheap crap," he added indignantly.

I finished what I was doing and moved across to the sofa. "Richard, behave," I said, slipping my legs over his, straddling him.

"It's not very nice, being dead," he muttered as my mouth descended on his.

Eventually, I moved my lips along his jaw, tongue flickering against the angle of the bone. "Maybe not," I said softly, tickling his ear. "But isn't resurrection fun?"

≈✧≈

Richard barely stirred when I left his bed next morning just after seven. I scribbled, "Gone 2 work, C U 2night?" on a Post-it note and stuck it on the forearm that was flung out across the pillow. I used to write messages straight on to his arm with a felt-tip pen until he complained it ruined his street cred to have "Buy milk" stencilled indelibly across his wrist. Nothing if not sensitive to people's needs, I switched to Post-its.

Back in my own home, I stood under the shower, taking my first opportunity to consider Alexis's ballistic missile. I knew that having a baby had climbed to the top of her and Chris's partnership agenda now that they had put the finishing touches to their house on the edge of the Pennines, but somehow I hadn't realized parenthood was quite so imminent a project. I'd had this mental picture of it being something that would rumble on for ages before anything actually happened, given that it's such a complicated business for lesbian couples to arrange.

First they've got to decide whether they want an anonymous donor, in which case their baby could end up having the same father as half the children of lesbians in the Greater Manchester area, with all the potential horrors that lines up for the future.

But if they decide to go for a donor they know, they've got to be careful that everyone agrees in advance what his relationship to the child is going to be. Then they've got to wait while he has two AIDS tests with a gap of at least six months in between. Finally, they've got to juggle things so that sperm and womb are in the same place at the optimum moment. According to Alexis, it's not like a straight couple where the woman can take her temperature every five minutes till the time is right then seize her bloke by the appropriate body part and demand sex. So I'd been banking on a breathing space to get used to the idea of Chris and Alexis as parents.

I've never been smitten with the maternal urge, which means I always feel a bit bemused when my friends get sandbagged by their hormones and turn from perfectly normal women into monomaniacs desperate to pass their genes on to a waiting world. Maybe it's because my biological clock has still got a way to go before anything in my universe starts turning pumpkin-shaped. Or maybe, as Richard suggests when he's in sentimental father mode, it's because I'm a cold-hearted bastard with all the emotional warmth of RoboCop. Either way, I didn't want a child and I never knew if I was saying the right thing to those who did.

Selfishly, my first thought was for the difference it was going to make to my life. Alexis is my best friend. We go shopping for clothes together. We play seriously competitive and acrimonious Scrabble games together. When Chris and Richard aren't there to complain about the results, we concoct exotic and bizarre snacks (oatcakes with French mayonnaise and strawberry jam; green banana, coconut and chicken curry . . .) and wash them down with copious amounts of good vodka. We pick each other's brains and exploit each other's contacts. Most of all, we're there for each other when it counts.

As the hot water cascaded over me, I felt like I was already in mourning for the friendship. Nothing was ever going to be the same again. Alexis would have responsibilities. When Chris's commitments as a partner in a firm of community architects took her out of town, Alexis would be shackled without time off for good behaviour. Instead of hanging out with me after work, she'd be rushing home for bath time and nursery tea. Her conversation would shrink to the latest exploits of the incredible child. And it would be incredible, no two ways about it. They always are. There would be endless photographs to pore over. Instead of calling me to say, "Get down here, girl, I've just found a fabulous silk shirt in your size in Kendals' sale," Alexis would be putting the child on the phone to say, "Wo, gay," and claiming it as "Hello, Kate." Worst of all, I had this horrible suspicion I was going to become Auntie Kate. Even Richard's son Davy has never tried to do that to me.

I rinsed the last of the shampoo out of my auburn hair and stepped out of the shower. At least I didn't have to live under the same roof as it, I thought as I towelled my head. Besides, I told myself, nothing healthy stays the same. Friendships change and grow, they shift their emphases and sometimes they even die. "Everything must change," I said out loud. Then I noticed a grey hair. So much for healthy change.

I brushed my hair into the neat bob I've opted for recently. Time to get my brain into gear. I knew where I needed to go next on Dan and Lice's problem, but that was a source that might

take a little time and a lot of deviousness to tap. More straightforward was a visit to the dark side of the moon.

～❖～

Gizmo is one of my silver linings. The cloud was a Telecom
engineer that I'd had a brief fling with. He'd caught me at one
of those weak moments when you kid yourself into believing a
nice smile and cute bum are a reasonable basis for a meaningful
relationship. After all, if it's a good enough principle for most of
the male population . . . His lectures on telephone technology
had been mildly interesting the first time round. After a month
of them, there wasn't a court in the land that would have convicted me of anything other than self-defence if I'd succumbed
to the temptation of burying a meat cleaver in his skull. But he
had introduced me to Gizmo, which gave me something good
to remember him by.

If Judy Garland was born in a trunk, Gizmo was born
in an anorak. In spite of having the soul of a nerd, he had too
much attitude for the passivity of trainspotting. So he became a
computer whizz. That was back in the steam age of computers,
when the most powerful of machines took so long to scroll to
the end of a ten-page document that you could go off and drip
a pot of filter coffee without missing a thing. When 99.99 per
cent of the population still thought bulletin boards were things
you found on office walls, Gizmo was on line to people all over
the world. The teenagers who invented phone phreaking and
hacking into the Pentagon were close personal friends of his.
He'd never met them, you understand, just spent his nights typ-
ing his end of conversations with them and like-minded nutters
all over the planet.

When the FBI started arresting hackers and phreakers on
the grounds that America has never known what to do with
nonconformists, and the British police started to take an interest, Gizmo decided it was time to stop playing Butch Cassidy

and the Sundance Kid and come out into the sunlit uplands. So he started working for Telecom. And he manages to keep his face straight when he tells people that he's a computer systems manager there. Which is another way of saying he actually gets paid to keep abreast of all the information technology that allows him to remain king of the darkside hackers. Gizmo's like Bruce Wayne in reverse. When darkness falls on Gotham City, instead of donning mask and cape and taking on the bad guys, Gizmo goes on line and becomes one of the growing army who see cyberspace as the ultimate subversive, anarchic community. And Telecom still haven't noticed that their northern systems manager is a renegade. It's no wonder none of Gizmo's friends have Telecom shares.

If I had to pick one thing that demonstrates the key difference between the UK and the USA, it would be their attitudes to information. Americans get everything unless there's a damn good reason why not. Brits get nothing unless a High Court judge and an Act of Parliament have said there's a damn good reason why we should. And private eyes are just like ordinary citizens in that respect. We don't have any privileges. What we have are sources. They fall into two groups: the ones who are motivated by money and the ones who are driven by principle. Gizmo's belief that information is born free but everywhere is in chains has saved my clients a small fortune. Police records, driver and vehicle licensing information, credit ratings: they're all there at his fingertips and, for a small donation to Gizmo's Hardware Upgrade Fund, at mine. The only information he won't pass on to me is anything relating to BT phone bills or numbers. That would be a breach of confidence. Or something equally arbitrary. We all have to draw the line somewhere.

I draw it at passing Gizmo's info on to clients. I use him either when I've hit a dead end or I know he can get something a lot faster than I can by official routes, which means the client saves money. I know I can be trusted not to abuse that information. I can't say the same about the people who hire me, so I don't tell them. I've had people waving wads of dosh under my nose for an ex-directory phone number or the address that goes with a car licence plate. Call me a control freak, but I won't do that kind of work. I know there are agencies who do, but that doesn't keep me awake at night. The only conscience I can afford to worry about is my own.

Gizmo had recently moved from a bedsit in the busiest red-light street in Whalley Range to a two-bedroomed flat above a shop in Levenshulme, a stretch of bandit country grouped around Stockport Road. The shop sells reconditioned vacuum cleaners. If you've ever wondered where Hoovers go when they die, this is the place. I've never seen a customer enter or leave the place, though there's so much grime on the windows they could be running live sex shows in there and nobody would be any the wiser. And Gizmo reckons he's moved up in the world.

I was going against the traffic flow on the busy arterial road, so it didn't take me long to drive the short distance to Levenshulme and find a parking space on a side street of red-brick terraces. I pressed the bell and waited, contemplating a front door so coated with inner-city pollution that it was no longer possible to tell what colour it had originally been. The only clean part of the door was the glass on the spyhole. After about thirty seconds, I pressed the bell again. This time, there was a thunder of clattering feet, a brief pause and then the door opened a cautious couple of inches. "Kate," Gizmo said, showing no inclination to invite me in. His skin looked grey in the harsh morning light, his eyes red-rimmed like a laboratory white rat.

"All right, Giz?"

"No, since you ask." He rubbed a hand along his stubbled jaw and scratched behind one ear with the knuckle of his index finger.

"What's the problem? Trouble with the Dibble?"

His lips twisted in the kind of smile dogs give before they remove your liver without benefit of anaesthetic. "No way. I'm

always well ahead of the woodentops. No, this is serious. I've
got the bullet."

"From Telecom?"

"Who else?"

I was taken aback. The only thing I could think of was
that someone had got wise to Gizmo's extra-curricular activities.
"They catch you with your hand in somebody's digital traffic?"

"Get real," he said indignantly. "Staff cuts. The section
head doesn't like the fact that I know more than anybody else in
the section, including him. So it's goodnight Vienna, Gizmo."

"You'll get another job," I said. I would have found it easier
to convince myself if I hadn't been looking at him as I spoke.
As well as the red-rimmed eyes and the stubble, a prospective
employer had to contend with a haircut that looked like Edward
Scissorhands on a bad hair day, and a dress sense that would
embarrass a jumble sale.

"I'm too old."

"How old?"

"Thirty-two," he mumbled with a suspicious scowl, as if
he thought I was going to laugh. I didn't have enough years on
him for that.

"You're winding me up," I said.

"The guys who do the hiring are in their forties and scared
shitless that they're going to get the tin handshake any day
now, and they know nothing about computer systems except
that someone told them it's a young man's game. If you're over
twenty-five, twenty-seven if you've got a PhD, they won't even
look at your CV. Believe me, Kate, I'm too old."

"What a bummer," I said, meaning it.

"Yeah, well. Shit happens. But it's nicer when it happens
to somebody else. So what did you come round for? Last orders
before I have to put my rates up?"

I handed him the piece of paper where I'd noted Will
Allen's licence plate. "The name and address that goes with
the car."

He didn't even look at it. He just said, "Some time this afternoon," then started to close the door.

"Hey, Giz?" He paused. "I'm really sorry," I said. He nodded and shut the door.

I walked back towards the street where I'd parked the zippy Rover 216 that Mortensen and Brannigan had bought for me a couple of months before. Until then, I'd been driving a top-of-the-range sports coupé that we'd taken in part payment for a long and complicated car-finance fraud case, but I'd known in my heart of hearts it was far too conspicuous a set of wheels for the kind of work I do. Given how much I enjoy driving, it had been a wrench to part with it, but I'd learned to love the Rover. Especially after my mate Handbrake had done something double wicked to the engine which made it nippier than any of its German siblings from BMW.

As I rounded the corner, I couldn't believe what I saw. There was a spray of glittering glass chunks like hundreds of tiny mosaic tiles all over the pavement by the driver's door of the Rover. The car was twenty yards from the main road, it was half past eight in the morning and I'd been gone less than ten minutes, but someone had had it away on their toes with my stereo.

4

It took me an hour and a half round at Handbrake's backstreet garage to get a new window and stereo cassette. I knew the window had come from a scrapyard, but it would have been bad manners to ask about the origins of the cassette. I wouldn't have been entirely surprised if my own deck had arrived in the bike pannier of one of the young lads who supply Handbrake with spare parts as an alternative to drug-running round Moss Side, but it clearly wasn't my lucky day and I had to settle for a less sophisticated machine. While that might increase the shelf life of my new driver's-door window, it wouldn't improve the quality of my life in Manchester's orbital motorway traffic jams, so I wasn't in the best of moods when I finally staggered through the door of the office just after ten.

I knew at once that something was badly wrong. Shelley, our office manager, made no comment about my lateness. In all the years I've been working with her, she'd never before missed the opportunity to whip me into line like one of her two teenage kids. I'd once found her son Donovan, a six-foot three-inch basketball player, engineering student and occasional rapper with a local band, having to give up a weekend to paint my office because he hadn't come home till four in the morning. After that, I'd always had a good excuse for being late into work. But this morning, she scarcely glanced up from her screen when I walked in. "Bill's in," was all she said.

Worrying. "Already? I thought he only flew in yesterday afternoon?"

Shelley's lips pursed. "That's right," she said stiffly. "He said to tell you he needs a word," she added, gesturing with her head towards the closed door of my partner's office. Even more worrying. Shelley is Bill's biggest fan. Normally when he returns from one of his foreign security consultancy trips, we all sit around in the outside office and schmooze the morning away over coffee, catching up. Bill's a friendly soul; I'd never known him to hide behind a closed door unless he needed absolute peace and quiet to work out some thorny computer problem.

I tapped on the door but didn't wait for an answer before I opened it and walked in on the sort of scene that would have been more appropriate in the new Dancehouse Theatre a few doors down Oxford Road. Bill Mortensen, a bearded blond giant of a man, was standing behind his desk, leaning over a dark woman whose body was curved back under his in an arc that would have had my spine screaming for mercy. One of Bill's bunch-of-bananas hands supported the small of her back, the other her shoulders. Unlike at the ballet, however, their lips were welded together. I cleared my throat.

Bill jumped, his mouth leaving the woman's with a nauseating smack as he straightened and half turned, releasing his grip on the woman. Just as well her arms were wrapped round his neck or she'd have been on the fast track to quadriplegia. "Kate," Bill gasped. His face did a double act, the mouth smiling, the eyes panicking.

"Welcome back, Bill. I wasn't expecting to see you this morning," I said calmly, closing the door behind me and making for my usual perch on the table that runs along one wall.

Bill stuttered something about wanting to see me while the woman disentangled herself from him. She was a good six inches taller than my five feet and three inches. Strike one. Her hair was as dark as Bill's was blond, cut in the sort of spiky urchin cut I'd recently abandoned when even I'd noticed it was getting a bit passé. On her, it looked terrific. Strike two. Her skin was burnished bronze, an impossible dream for those of us with the skin that matches auburn hair. Strike three. I didn't have the faintest idea who Bill's latest companion was, but I hated her already. She grinned and moved towards me, hand stuck out in front of her with all the enthusiasm of an extrovert teenager who hasn't been put down yet. "Kate, it's great to meet you," she announced in an Australian accent that made Crocodile Dundee sound like a BBC newsreader. "Bill's told me so much about you, I feel like I know you already." I tentatively put out a hand, which she gripped fervently and pumped up and down. "I just know we're going to be mates," she added, clapping her other hand on my shoulder.

I looked past her at Bill, my eyebrows raised. He moved towards us and the woman released my hand to slip hers into his. "Kate," he finally said. "This is Sheila." His eyes warned me not to laugh.

"Don't tell me, let me guess," I said. "You met in Australia."

Sheila roared with laughter. I could feel her excessive response thrusting me into the role of repressed Englishwoman. "God, Kate, he was right about your sense of humour," she said. I forced my lips into what I seemed to remember was a smile. "Hey, Bill, you better tell her the news."

Bill stood chewing his beard for a moment, then said, "Sheila and I are getting married."

To say I was gobsmacked would be like saying Tom Hanks can act a bit. It's not that Bill doesn't like women. He does. Lots of them. He also likes variety. As a serial monogamist, he makes Casanova and Don Juan look like absolute beginners. But he'd always been choosy about who he hung out with. While he preferred his girlfriends good-looking, brains and ambition had always been just as high on his agenda. So while Sheila might appear more of a bimbo than anyone I'd ever seen Bill with, I

wasn't about to make a snap judgement on the basis of what I'd
seen so far. "Congratulations," I managed without tripping over
too many of the syllables.

"Thanks, Kate," Sheila said warmly. "It's big of you to be
generous about losing your partner."

I looked at Bill. He looked like he'd swallowed an ice
cube. "I thought that in these situations one said something
like, 'Not so much losing a partner as gaining a secretary,'" I
said ominously. "I have this feeling that there's something you
haven't got round to telling me yet, William."

"Sheila, Kate and I need to have boring business talks.
Why don't you get Shelley to point you in the direction of all
the best clothes shops? You can come back at lunch time and
we'll all go to the Brasserie?" Bill said desperately, one eye on
the toe I was tapping on the floor.

"No problems, Billy boy," Sheila said, planting a kiss smack
on his lips. On her way past me, she sketched a wave. "Can't
wait to get to know you better, Kate."

When the door closed behind her, there was a long silence.
"'Why don't you get Shelley to point you in the direction of
the clothes shops?'" I mimicked as cruelly as I could manage.

"She owns three dress shops in Sydney," Bill said mildly.
I might have known. That explained the tailored black dress
she'd almost been wearing.

"This is not a good way to start the day, Bill," I said. "What
does she mean, I'll be losing a partner? Is she the pathologi-
cally jealous type who doesn't want her man working alongside
another woman? Is Shelley getting the bum's rush from Waltzing
Matilda too?"

Bill threw himself into his chair and sighed. "Sheila knows
I was dreading this conversation, and she said what she did to
force me into having it," he explained. "Kate, this is it. Sheila's
the one I want."

"Let's face it, Bill, you've run enough consumer tests to
make an informed decision," I said bitterly. I wanted to be happy

for him. I would have been happy for him if it hadn't been for the stab of fear that Sheila's words had triggered in me.

He looked me in the eye and smiled. "True. Which means that now I've found her, I don't want to let her go. Marriage seems like the sensible option." He looked away. "And that means either Sheila moves over here or I move to Australia."

Silence. I knew what was coming but I didn't see why I should let him off the hook. I leaned back against the wall and folded my arms across my chest. Bill the Bear was turning from teddy to grizzly before my eyes, and I didn't like the transformation. Finally, a few sighs later, Bill said, "Me moving is the logical step. My work's more portable than hers. The jobs I've already been doing in Australia have given me some good contacts, while she has none in the rag trade over here. Besides, the weather's nicer. And the wine." He tried a pleading, little-boy-lost smile on me.

It didn't play. "So what happens to Mortensen and Brannigan?" I demanded, my voice surprising even me with its harshness.

Bill picked up the curly Sherlock Holmes pipe he occasionally smokes when he's stuck on a problem, and started fiddling with it. "I'm sorry, Kate, but I'm going to have to sell my share of the partnership. The problem I've got is that I need to realize the capital I've got tied up in the business so I can start again in Sydney."

"I don't believe I'm hearing this," I said. "You think you can just *sell* us to the highest bidder? Your parents own half the farmland in Cheshire. Can't you get them to stake you?"

Bill scowled. "Of course I bloody can't," he growled. "You didn't go cap in hand to your father when you wanted to become a partner. You funded it yourself. Besides, life's not exactly a bed of roses in cattle farming right now. I doubt they've got the cash to throw around."

"Fine," I said angrily. "So who have you sold out to?"

Bill looked shocked. "I haven't sold to anyone," he protested. "How could you think I'd go behind your back like that?"

I shrugged. "Everything else seems to have been cut and dried without consulting me. Why should that be any different?"

"Didn't you bother reading the partnership agreement when we drew it up? Paragraph sixteen. If either of us wants to sell our share of the business, we have to offer first refusal to the other partner. And if the remaining partner doesn't want to buy, they have the power of veto over the sale to any third party on any reasonable ground."

"'The final decision as to the reasonableness or otherwise of that ground to be taken by the partners in consultation with any employees of the firm,'" I quoted from memory. I'd written most of the agreement; it wasn't surprising I knew by heart what the key parts of it said. "It's academic, Bill. You know I can't afford to buy you out. And you also know damn well that I'm far too fond of you to stand in the way of what you want. So pick your buyer."

I jumped to my feet and wrenched the door open. "I'm out of here," I said, hoping the disgust and anger I felt was as vivid to him as it was to me. Sometimes, the only things that make you feel good are the same ones that worked when you were five. Yes, I slammed the door.

❧❖❧

I sat staring into the froth of a cappuccino in the Cigar Store café. The waitress was having an animated conversation with a couple of her friends drinking espressos in the corner, but apart from them, I had the place to myself. It wasn't hard to tune out their gossip and focus on the implications of what Bill had said. I couldn't believe what he planned to do to me. It undercut everything I thought I knew about Bill. It made me feel that my judgement wasn't worth a bag of used cat litter. The man had been my friend before he became my business partner. I'd started my career process-serving for him as a way of eking out my student grant because the hours and the cash were better than bar work. I'd toiled with him or for him ever since I'd jacked in my law degree after the second year, when I realized I could never spend my working days in the company of wolves and settled for the blond bear instead.

There was no way I could afford to buy him out. The deal we'd done when I'd become a partner had been simple enough. Bill had had the business valued, and I'd worked out I could afford to buy thirty-five per cent. I'd borrowed the money on a short-term loan from the bank and paid it back over four years. I'd managed that by paying the bank every penny I earned over and above my previous salary, including my annual profit shares. I'd only finished paying the loan off three months previously, thanks in part to a windfall that couldn't be explained either to another living soul or to the taxman without risking the knowledge getting back to the organized criminals who had inadvertently made me the gift. It had been a struggle to meet the payments on the loan, and I had no intention of standing under the kind of trees that deliver such dangerous windfalls ever again.

I had to face it. There was no way I could raise the cash to buy out Bill's sixty-five per cent at the prices of four years ago, never mind what the agency would now be worth, given the new clients we'd both brought in since then. I was going to be the victim of anyone who decided a two-thirds share in a profitable detective agency was a good investment.

A second cup clattered on to the table in front of me. Startled, I looked up and found myself staring into Shelley's amber eyes. "I thought I'd find you here," she said, tossing her mac over a chair and sitting down opposite me. Her face looked like one of those carved African ceremonial masks, all polished planes and immobility, especially now she'd abandoned the beads she used to wear plaited in her hair and moved on to neat cornrows. I couldn't tell from looking at her if she'd come to sympathize or to tell me off for my tantrum and plead Bill's case.

"And we thought Lincoln freed the slaves," I said bitterly. "How do you feel about being bought and sold?"

"It's not as bad for me as it is for you," Shelley said. "I don't like the new boss, I just walk out the door and get me another job. But you're tied to whoever Bill sells his share to, am I right?"

"As usual. Back on the chain gang, Shell, that's what I am. Like Chrissie Hynde says, circumstance beyond our control."

Shelley's eyebrows flickered. "Doesn't have to be that way, does it?"

"I'm not with you."

"This behaviour from Bill is not what we're used to."

"Of course it's bloody not," I interrupted petulantly. "It's this Sheila, isn't it? Like the man said, when you've got them by the balls, their hearts and minds will follow. And there's no doubting which part of Bill's anatomy Sheila's got a grip on."

"Doesn't matter who's behind it, the end result is the same," Shelley pointed out. "Bottom line is, Bill is not behaving like your friend, and in my book that absolves you from behaving like his friend."

"And?"

"You own thirty-five per cent of the business, don't you?" I nodded. "Free and clear."

"So you put your share on the market. Either as an independent entity, or as part of the whole package."

I frowned. "But that would devalue the business quite a lot. It's a different kettle of fish buying into an established agency where one of the partners is staying on to maintain the existing clients and another thing altogether to go for something that's nothing more really than a name and a bunch of office equipment."

"My point exactly," Shelley said.

"But I'd lose a lot of the money I've put in," I said.

"But Bill would stand to lose a hell of a lot more," Shelley said. "And he needs the cash a lot more than you do right now. What it would do is buy you a bit of time and a lot of say-so on the deal. It gives you a bargaining chip."

Slowly, I nodded. "Shelley, you are one mean mother," I said, admiration in my voice. "And I thought Bill was your blue-eyed boy."

Shelley's lips tightened. I noticed that between her nose and mouth, a couple of creases were graduating to lines. "Listen,

Kate, when I was growing up, I saw a lot of women doing the 'my kids, right or wrong' routine with teachers, with cops. And I see their kids now, running drugs, living behind bars. I've seen the funerals when another one gets shot in some stupid gang war. I don't like the end result of blind loyalty. Bill has been my friend and my boss a long time, but he's behaving like an arsehole to us both, and that's how he deserves to be treated."

I admired her cold determination to get the best result for both of us. I just didn't know if I could carry it through as ruthlessly as Shelley would doubtless demand. "You're right," I said. "I'll tell him I want to sell too."

Shelley smiled. "I bet you feel better already," she said shrewdly. She wasn't wrong. "So, haven't you got any work to do?"

I told her about the previous evening's adventures, and, predictably enough, she had a good laugh at my expense. "So now I need to see Dennis," I finished up. "Richard might know all there is to know about the music side of the rock business, but when it comes to the criminal side, he thinks seedy is something you listen to on your stereo. Whereas Dennis might not know his Ice-T from his Enya, but he could figure out where to make a bent earner in the 'Hallelujah Chorus,'" The only problem was, as I didn't have to remind Shelley, my friend and sometime mentor Dennis wasn't quite as accessible as normal, Her Majesty the Queen being unreasonably fussy about keeping her guests to herself.

When I met Dennis, like so many people in their late thirties, he'd just gone through a major career change. After a stretch in prison, he'd given up his previous job as a professional and highly successful burglar to the rich and famous and taken up the more demanding but less dangerous occupation of "a bit of ducking and diving" on the fringes of the law. Which included, on occasion, a bit of consultancy work for Mortensen and Brannigan. Thanks to Dennis, I'd learned how to pick locks, defeat alarm systems and ransack filing cabinets without leaving a trace.

Unfortunately, a little enterprise of Dennis's aimed at separating criminals from their cash flow had turned sour when
he'd inadvertently arranged one of his handovers in the middle
of a Drugs Squad surveillance. Instead of grabbing a couple of
major-league traffickers and one of those cocaine hauls that get
mentioned in the news, the cops ended up with a small-time
villain and the kind of nothing case that barely makes three
paragraphs in the local paper. Inevitably, Dennis paid the price of
their pique, seeing his scam blown sufficiently out of proportion
in court to land him with an eighteen-month sentence. Some
might say he got off lightly, given his CV and what else I happened to know he'd been up to lately, but speaking as someone
who would go quietly mad serving an eighteen-day sentence,
I wouldn't be one of them.

"When can you get in to see him?" Shelley asked.

Good question. I didn't have a Visiting Order nor any
immediate prospect of getting one. Once upon a time, I'd have
rung up and pretended to be a legal executive from his firm of
solicitors and asked for an appointment the next day. But security
had grown tighter recently. Too many prisoners had been going
walkabout from jails that weren't supposed to be open prisons.
Now, when you booked a brief's appointment at Strangeways,
they took the details then rang back the firm you allegedly
represented to confirm the name of the person attending and
to give them a code consisting of two letters and four numbers.
Without the code, you couldn't get in. "I thought about asking
Ruth to let me pose as one of her legal execs," I said.

Shelley snorted. "After the last time? I don't think so!"

The last time I'd pretended to be one of Ruth Hunter's
junior employees it had strained our friendship so severely it had
to wear a truss for months afterwards. Shelley was right. Ruth
wasn't going to play.

"I don't mean to teach you to suck eggs," Shelley said without a trace of humility or apology. "And I know this goes against
the grain. But had you thought about doing it the straight way?"

5

I pivoted on the ball of my right foot, bending the knee as I straightened my left leg, using the momentum to drive me forward and round in a quarter-circle. The well-muscled leg whistled past me, just grazing the hip that moments before had been right in its path. I grunted with effort as I sidestepped and jabbed a short kick at the knee of my assailant.

I was too slow. Next thing I knew, my right leg was swept from under me and I was lying on my back, lungs screaming for anything to replace the air that had been slammed out of them. Christie O'Brien stood above me, grinning. "You're slowing down," she observed with the casual cruelty of adolescence. Of course I was slow compared to her; she was, after all, a former British under-fourteen championship finalist. But Christie— Christine until she discovered fashion and lads—was above all her father's daughter. She'd learned at an early age that nothing succeeds like kicking them when they're down.

One of the other things I'd learned thanks to Dennis was Thai kick boxing, a sport he insisted every woman should know. The theory goes, a woman as small as I am is never going to beat a guy in a fair fight, so the key to personal safety is to land one good kick either in the shins or the gonads. Then it's "legs, don't let me down" time. Kick boxing teaches you how to land the kick and keeps you fit enough to leg it afterwards.

When he'd been sent down, Dennis had asked me to keep an eye on Christie. She'd inherited her mother's gleaming blonde hair and wide blue eyes, but her brains had come from a father who knew only too well the damage a teenage girl can wreak when the only adult around to keep an eye on things has a generous spirit and fewer brain cells than the average goldfish. Because she'd always been accustomed to seeing me around the gym, Christie had either failed to notice or decided not to resent the fact that I'd been spending a lot more time with her recently.

She filled me in on the latest school dramas of who was hanging out with whom and why as we showered next to each other—our club's strictly breeze block. You want cubicles, go somewhere else and pay four times as much to join. By the time we were towelling ourselves dry, I'd managed to swing the conversation round to Dennis. "You told your dad about this Jason, then," I asked her casually. She'd mentioned the lad's name once too often.

"You've got to be joking," she said. "Tell him about somebody he can't check out for himself and have the heavy mob kicking Jason's door in for a reference? No way. When he comes out'll be well soon enough."

"When you seeing him next?" I asked.

"Mum's got a VO for Thursday afternoon. I'm supposed to be going with her, but I've got cross-country trials and I don't want to miss them," she grumbled as she pulled a sweatshirt over her head. "Dad wouldn't mind. He'll be the one giving me a go-along if I miss getting on the team. But Mum gets really depressed going to Strangeways on her own, so I feel like I've got to go with her."

"I could go instead of you," I suggested.

Christie's face lit up. "Would you? You don't mind? I'm warning you, it's a three-hankie job coming home."

"I don't mind," I said. "I'd like to see your dad. I miss him."

Christie sighed and stared at her trainers. "Me too." She looked up at me, her eyes candid. "I'm really angry with him, you know? After he came out last time, he promised me he'd never do anything that would get him banged up again."

I leaned over and gave her a hug. "He knows he's let you down. It's hard, recognizing that your dad's not perfect, but he's just like the rest of us. He needs you to forgive him, Christie."

"Yeah, well," she said. "I'll tell Mum you'll pick her up dinner time Thursday, then." She got to her feet and stuffed her sweaty sports clothes into one of the counterfeit Head holdalls Dennis had been turning out the previous spring. "See ya, Kate," she said on her way out the door.

Knowing I was doing her a favour made me feel less like the exploitation queen of South Manchester. But not a lot less. So much for doing it the straight way.

⚜

When I emerged from the gym, I decided to swing round by Gizmo's to see if he'd got anywhere with my earlier request. If the old axiom, "If I was going there, I wouldn't start from here," didn't exist, they'd have to invent it for the journey from Sale to Levenshulme in mid-morning traffic. I knew before I started it was going to be hell on wheels, but for once, I didn't care. Me, reluctant to face Bill?

I crawled along in second while Cyndi Lauper reminded me that girls just wanna have fun. I growled at the cassette deck and swapped Cyndi for Tanita Tikaram's more gloomy take on the world. I knew exactly what she meant when she accused someone of making the whole world cry. I sat in the queue of traffic at the lights where Wilbraham Road meets Oxford Road in the heart of undergraduate city, watching them going about their student lives, backpacked and badly barbered. I couldn't believe it when the fashion world created a whole industry round grunge as if it was something that had just happened. The rest of us knew it wasn't anything new: students have been wearing layers against the cold, and workmen's heavy-duty checked shirts for cheapness, ever since I was a student a dozen years ago. Shaking my head, I glanced at the wall alongside the car. Plastered along it were posters for bands appearing at the local clubs. Some of the venues I recognized from razzing with Richard; others I knew nothing about. I hadn't realized quite how many live music venues there were in the city these days. I looked more closely at the posters, noticing one that had peeled away on the top right corner. Underneath, I could see, in large red letters, "UFF." It looked like Dan and Lice hadn't been making it up as they went along.

The impatient horn of the suit in the company car behind me dragged my attention away from the posters and back to the road. After the lights, the traffic eased up, and I actually managed to get into fourth gear before I reached Gizmo's. This time, I reckoned it would be cheaper to take my chances with the traffic wardens than the locals, so I left the car illegally parked on the main drag. Judging by the other drivers doing the same thing, the wardens were about as fond of hanging out in Levenshulme as I was. I hit the hole in the wall for some cash for Gizmo, then I crossed the road and rang his bell.

Gizmo frowned when he saw me. "Didn't you get the e-mail?" he asked.

"I've not been back to the office," I said, holding a tightly rolled wad of notes towards him. "Do I take it you've had some joy?"

"Yeah. You better come in," he said reluctantly, delicately removing the cash from my hand and slipping it into the watch pocket of a pair of grey flannels that looked as if they'd first drawn breath around the time of the Great War. "Somebody dressed as smart as you on the pavement around here looks well suspicious to the local plod. I mean, you're obviously not a native, are you?" he added as I followed him up the narrow stairs, the soles of my shoes sticking to the elderly cord carpet.

It was the first time he'd let me past his front door, and frankly, I wasn't surprised.

I followed Gizmo into the front room of the flat. It was a dislocating experience. Instead of the dingy grime and chipped paint of the stairway, I was in a spotlessly clean room. New woodblock flooring, matt grey walls, no curtains, double-glazed windows. A leather sofa. Two desks with computer monitors, one a Mac, one a PC. A long table with an assortment of old computers—an Atari, a Spectrum, an Amiga, an Amstrad PCW and an ancient Pet. A couple of modems, a flat-bed scanner, a hand-held scanner, a couple of printers and a shelf stacked with software boxes. There was no fabric anywhere in the room. Even the chair in front of the PC monitor was upholstered in leather. Gizmo might look like Pigpen, but the environment he'd created for his beloved computers was as near to the perfect dust-free room as he could get.

"Nice one," I said.

He thrust his hands into the pockets of a woollen waistcoat most bag ladies would be ashamed to own and said, "Got to look after them, haven't you? I've had that Pet since 1980, and it still runs like a dream."

"Strange dreams you have, Giz," I commented as he hit some keys on his PC and located the information I'd asked for. Within seconds, a sheet of paper was spitting out of one of the laser printers. I picked up the paper and read, "Sell Phones, 1 Beaumaris Road, Higher Crumpsall, Manchester." There was a phone number too. I raised an eyebrow. "That it?"

"All I could get," he said.

"No names?"

"No names. They're not listed at Companies House. They sound like they're into mobies. I suppose if you wanted to go to the trouble and *expense*"—stressing the last word heavily—"I could do a trawl through the mobile phone service providers and see if this lot are among their customers. But—"

"Thanks, but no thanks," I said. Breaking the law too many times on any given job is tempting fate. "Once is sufficient," I added. "Anything more would be vulgar."

"I'll be seeing you then," Gizmo said pointedly, staring past my shoulder at the door. I took the hint. Find what you're good at and stick to it, that's what I say.

⟿✦⟾

Beaumaris Road was a red-brick back street running parallel to the main drag of Cheetham Hill Road. Unsurprisingly, number one was on the corner. Sell Phones occupied what had obviously once been a corner shop, though it had been tarted up since it had last sold pints of milk at all hours and grossly inflated prices. I parked further down the street and pulled on a floppy green velvet cap and a pair of granny specs with clear glass to complete the transformation from desolate widow to total stranger. They didn't really go with my Levis and beige blazer, but fashion's so eclectic these days that you can mix anything if you don't mind looking like a borderline care-in-the-community case or a social worker.

I walked back to the corner, noting the heavy grilles over the window of Sell Phones. I paused and looked through to an interior that was all grey carpet, white walls and display cabinets of mobile phones. A good-looking black guy was leaning languidly against a display cabinet, head cocked, listening to a woman who was clearly telling the kind of lengthy tale that involves a lot of body language and lines like, "So she goes, 'You didn't!' and I go, 'I did. No messing.' And she looks at me gone out and she goes, 'You never!'" She was a couple of inches taller than me, but slimmer through the shoulders and hips. Her hair was a glossy black bob, her eyes dark, her skin pale, her cheekbones Slavic, scarlet lips reminding me irresistibly of Cruella De Vil. She looked like a Pole crossed with a racehorse. She was too engrossed in her tale to notice me, and the black guy was too busy looking exquisite in a suit that screamed, *"Ciao, bambino."*

I peered more closely through the glass and there, at the back of the shop, sitting behind a desk, head lowered as he took notes of the phone call he was engrossed in, was Will Allen in all his glory. I might not know his real name, but at least now I knew where he worked. I carried on round the corner and there, in the back alley behind the shop, was the Mazda I'd last seen parked outside my house the night before. At last something was working out today.

Now for the boring bit. I figured Will Allen wouldn't be going anywhere for the next hour or two, but that didn't mean I could wander off and amble back later in the hope he'd still be around. I reckoned it was probably safe to nip round the corner to the McDonald's on Cheetham Hill Road and stock up with some doughnuts and coffee to make me feel like an authentic private eye as I staked out Sell Phones, but that was as far away as I wanted to get.

I moved my Rover on to the street that ran at right angles to Beaumaris Road and the alley so that I had a good view of the end of Allen's car bonnet, though it meant losing sight of the front of the shop. I slid into the passenger seat to make it look like I was waiting for someone and took off the cap. I kept the glasses in place, though. I slouched in my seat and brooded on Bill's perfidy. I sipped my coffee very slowly, just enough to keep me alert, not enough to make me want to pee. By the time I saw some action, the coffee was cold and so was I.

The nose of the silver Mazda slipped out of the alleyway and turned left towards Cheetham Hill Road. Just on five, with traffic tight as haemoglobin in the bloodstream. Born lucky, that's me. I scrambled across the gear stick and started the engine, easing out into the road behind the car. As we waited to turn left at the busy main road, I had the chance to see who was in the car. Allen was driving, but there was also someone in the passenger seat. She conveniently reached over into the back seat for something, and I identified the woman who had been in Sell Phones talking to the Emporio Armani mannequin. I wondered if she was the other half of the scam, the woman who went out to chat up the widowers. They don't call me a detective for nothing.

The Mazda slid into a gap in the traffic heading into Manchester. I didn't. By the time I squeezed out into a space that wasn't really there, the Mazda was three cars ahead and I was the target of a car-horn voluntary. I gave the kind of cheery wave that makes me crazy when arseholes do it to me and smartly switched lanes in the hope that I'd be less visible to my target. The traffic was so slow down Cheetham Hill that I was able to stay in touch, as well as check out the furniture stores for bargains. But then, just as we hit the straight, he peeled off left down North Street. I was in the right-hand lane and I couldn't get across, but I figured he must be heading down Red Bank to cut through the back doubles down to Ancoats and on to South Manchester. If I didn't catch him before Red Bank swept under the railway viaduct, he'd be anywhere in a maze of back streets and gone forever.

I swung the nose of the Rover over to the left, which pissed off the driver of the Porsche I'd just cut up. At least now the day wasn't a complete waste. I squeezed round the corner of Derby Street and hammered it for the junction that would sweep me down Red Bank. I cornered on a prayer that nothing was coming up the hill and screamed down the steep incline.

There was no silver Mazda in sight. I sat fuming at the junction for a moment, then slowly swung the car round and back up the hill. There was always the chance that they'd stopped off at one of the dozens of small-time wholesalers and middlemen whose tatty warehouses and storefronts occupy the streets of Strangeways. Maybe they were buying some jewellery or a fur coat with their ill-gotten gains. I gave it ten minutes, cruising every street and alley between Red Bank and Cheetham Hill Road. Then I accepted they were gone. I'd lost them.

I'd had enough for one day. Come to that, I'd had enough for the whole week. So I switched off my mobile, wearily slotted myself back into the thick of the traffic and drove home. Plan A was to run a hot bath lavishly laced with essential oils, Cowboy Junkies on the stereo, the pile of computer magazines I'd been ignoring for the last month and the biggest Stoly and grapefruit juice in the world on the side. Plan B involved Richard, if he was around.

I walked through my front door and down the hall, shedding layers like some sixties starlet, then started running the bath. I wrapped myself in my bathrobe which had been hanging strategically over a radiator, and headed for the freezer. I'd just gripped the neck of the vodka bottle when the doorbell rang. I considered ignoring it, but curiosity won. Story of my life. So I dumped the bottle and headed for the door.

They say it's not over till the fat lady sings. Alexis is far from fat, and from her expression I guessed singing wasn't on the agenda. Seeing the stricken look on her face, I kissed Plan A goodbye and prepared for the worst.

6

"Chris?" I asked, stepping back to let Alexis in.

She looked dumbly back at me, frowning, as if trying to call to mind why I should be concerned about her partner.

"Has something happened to Chris?" I tried. "The baby?"

Alexis shook her head. "Chris is all right," she said impatiently, as if I'd asked the kind of stupid question TV reporters pose to disaster victims. She pushed past me and walked like an automaton into the living room, where she subsided onto a sofa with the slack-limbed collapse of a marionette.

I left her staring blankly at the floor and turned off the bath taps. By the time I came back with two stiff drinks, she was smoking with the desperate concentration of an addict on the edge of cold turkey. "What's happened, Alexis?" I said softly, sitting down beside her.

"She's dead," she said. I wasn't entirely surprised that somebody she knew was. I couldn't imagine anything else that would destroy the composure of a hard-bitten crime reporter like this.

"Who is?"

Alexis pulled a scrunched up copy of the *Yorkshire Post* out of her handbag. I knew it was one of the out-of-town papers that the *Chronicle* subscribed to. "I was going through the regionals, looking to see if anybody had any decent crime feature ideas,"

Alexis said bleakly as she spread the *YP* out on the table. DOCTOR DIES IN RAID, I read in the top right-hand section of the front page. Under the headline was a photograph of a dark-haired woman with strong features and a wide, smiling mouth. I read the first paragraph.

Consultant gynaecologist Sarah Blackstone was fatally stabbed last night when she disturbed an intruder in her Headingley home.

"You knew her?" I asked.

"That's the doctor who worked with us on Christine's pregnancy."

It was a strange way of expressing it, but I let it pass. Alexis clearly wasn't in command of herself, never mind the English language. "I'm so sorry, Alexis," I said inadequately.

"Never mind being sorry. I want you working," she said abruptly. She crushed out her cigarette, lit another and swallowed half her vodka and Diet Coke. "Kate, there's something going on here. That's definitely the woman we dealt with. But she wasn't a consultant in Leeds called Sarah Blackstone. She had consulting rooms here in Manchester and her name was Helen Maitland."

There are days when I'm overwhelmed with the conviction that somebody's stolen my perfectly nice life and left me with this pile of shit to deal with. Right then, I was inches away from calling the cops and demanding they track down the robber. After the day I'd had, I just wasn't in the mood for chapter one of an Agatha Christie mystery. "Are you sure?" I asked. "I mean, newspaper photographs . . ."

Alexis snorted. "Look at her. She's not got a face that blends into the background, has she? Of course it's Helen Maitland."

I shrugged. "So she uses an assumed name when she's treating lesbians. Maybe she just doesn't want the notoriety of being the dykes' baby doctor."

"It's more than that, KB," Alexis insisted, swallowing smoke as if her life depended on it. "She's got a prescription pad and she writes prescriptions in the name of Helen Maitland. We've not had any trouble getting them filled, and it's not like it was a one-off, believe me. There's been plenty. Which also makes me worried, because if the bizzies figure out that Sarah Blackstone and Helen Maitland are the same person, and they try and track down her patients, all they've got to do is start asking around the local chemists. And there we are, right in the middle of the frame."

All of which was true, but I couldn't see why Alexis was getting so wound up. I knew the rules on human fertility treatment were pretty strict, but as far as I was aware, it wasn't a crime yet to give lesbians artificial insemination, though if the Tories started to get really hysterical about losing the next election, I could see it might have its attractions as a possible vote winner. "Alexis," I said gently. "Why exactly is that a problem?"

She looked blankly at me. "Because they'll take the baby off us," she said in a tone of voice I recognized as the one I used to explain to Richard why you can't wash your jeans in the dishwasher.

"I think you might be overreacting," I said cautiously, aware that I wasn't wearing protective clothing. "This is a straightforward case, Alexis," I continued, skimming the story. "Burglar gets disturbed, struggle, burglar panics, pulls a blade and lashes out. Tragic waste of talented test-tube baby doctor." I looked up. "The cops aren't going to be interviewing her Leeds patients, never mind trying to trace people she treated in a different city under a different name."

"Maybe so, but maybe there's more to it than meets the eye," Alexis said stubbornly. "I've been doing the crime beat long enough to know that the Old Bill only tell you what they want you to know. It wouldn't be the first time there's been a whole other investigation going on beneath the surface." She finished her drink and her cigarette, for some reason avoiding my eye.

I had a strong feeling that I didn't know what the real story was here. I wasn't entirely sure that I wanted to know what it was that could disconcert my normally stable best buddy as much as this, but I knew I couldn't dodge the issue. "What's really going on here, Alexis?" I asked.

She ran both hands through her wild tangle of black hair and looked up at me, her face worried and frightened, her eyes as hollow as a politician's promises. "Any chance of another drink?"

I fetched her another Stoly and Diet Coke, this one more than a little weaker than the last. If she was going to swallow them like water, I didn't want her passing out before she'd explained why she was in such a state about the death of a woman with whom she'd had nothing more than a professional relationship. I slid the drink across the table to her, and when she reached out for it, I covered her hand with mine. "Tell me," I said.

Alexis tightened her lips and shook her head. "We haven't told another living soul," she said, reaching for another cigarette. I hoped she wasn't smoking like this around Chris or the baby was going to need nicotine patches to get through its first twenty-four hours.

"You said a minute ago you wanted me working on this. If I don't know what's going on, there's not a lot I can do," I reminded her.

Alexis lifted her eyes and gazed into mine. "This has got to stay between us," she said, her voice a plea I'd never heard from her before. "I mean it, KB. Nobody gets to hear this one. Not Della, not Ruth, not even Richard. Nobody."

"That serious, eh?" I said, trying to lighten the oppressiveness of the atmosphere.

"Yeah, that serious," Alexis said, not noticeably lightened.

"You know you can trust me."

"That's why I'm here," she admitted after a pause. The hand that wasn't hanging on to the cigarette swept through her hair again. "I didn't realize how hard it was going to be to tell you."

I leaned back against the sofa, trying to look as relaxed and unshockable as I could. "Alexis, I'm bombproof. Whatever it is, I've heard it before. Or something very like it."

Her mouth twisted in a strange, inward smile. "Not like this, KB, I promise you. This is one hundred per cent one-off." Alexis sat up straight, squaring her shoulders. I saw she'd made the decision to reveal what was eating her. "This baby that Chris is carrying—it's ours." She looked expectantly at me.

I didn't want to believe what I was afraid she was trying to tell me. So I smiled and said, "Hey, that's a really healthy attitude, acting like you've really got a stake in it."

"I'm not talking attitude, KB. I'm talking reality." She sighed. "I'm talking making a baby from two women."

The trouble with modern life is that there isn't any etiquette any more. Things change so much and so fast that even if Emily Post were still around, she wouldn't be able to devise a set of protocols that stay abreast of tortured human relationships. If Alexis had dropped her bombshell in my mother's day, I could have said, "That's nice, dear. Now, do you like your milk in first?" In my Granny Brannigan's day, I could have crossed myself vigorously and sent for the priest. But in the face of the encroaching millennium, all I could do was gape and say, "What?"

"I'm not making this up, you know," Alexis said defensively. "It's possible. It's not even very difficult. It's just very illegal."

"I'm having a bit of trouble with this," I stammered. "How do you mean, it's possible? Are we talking cloning here, or what?"

"Nothing so high tech. Look, all you need to make a baby are a womb, an egg and something to fertilize it with."

"Which traditionally has been sperm," I remarked drily.

"Which traditionally has been sperm," Alexis agreed. "But all you actually need is a collision of chromosomes. You get one from each side of the exchange. Women have two X chromosomes and men have an X and a Y. With me so far?"

"I might not have A level biology, but I do know the basics," I said.

"Right. So you'll know that if it's the man's Y chromosome that links up with the woman's X chromosome, you get a little baby boy. And if it's his X chromosome that does the business, you get a girl. So everybody knew that you could make babies out of two X chromosomes. Only they didn't shout too much about it, did they? Because if they did more than mention it in passing, like, it wouldn't take a lot of working out to understand that if all you need for baby girls is a pair of X chromosomes from two different sources, you wouldn't need men."

"You're telling me that after twenty-five years of feminist theory, scientists have only just noticed that?" I couldn't keep the irony out of my voice.

"No, they've always known it. But certain kinds of experiments are against the law. That includes almost anything involving human embryos. Unless, of course, it's aimed at letting men who produce crap sperm make babies. So although loads of people knew that theoretically it was possible to make babies from two women, nobody could officially do any research on it, so the technology that would make it possible science instead of fantasy just wasn't happening." The journalist was in control now, and Alexis paused for effect. She couldn't help herself.

"So what happened to change that?" I asked, responding to my cue.

"There was a load of research done which showed that men didn't react well to having their wives inseminated with donor sperm. Surprise, surprise, they didn't feel connected to the kids and more often than not, families were breaking up because the men didn't feel like they were proper families. Given that more men are having problems with their sperm production than ever before, the pressure was really on for doctors to find a way of helping inadequate sperm to make babies. A couple of years ago, they came up with a really thin needle that could be inserted right into the very nucleus of an egg so that they could deliver a single sperm right to the place where it would count."

I nodded, light dawning. "And somebody somewhere figured that if they could do it with a sperm, they could do it with another egg."

"Give the girl a coconut," Alexis said, incapable of being solemn and scared for long.

"And this doctor, whatever her real name is, has been doing this in *Manchester*?" I asked. I know they say that what Manchester does today, London does tomorrow, but this seemed to be taking things a bit far.

"Yeah."

"Totally illegally?"

"Yeah."

"With lesbian couples?"

"Yeah."

"Who are therefore technically also breaking the law?"

"I suppose so."

We looked at each other across the table. I didn't know about Alexis, but I couldn't help banner headlines flashing across my mind. The thought of what the tabloids would do with a story like this was enough in itself to bring me out fighting for the women who had gone underground to make their dreams come true, let alone my feelings for Alexis and Chris. "And the baby Chris is carrying belongs to both of you?" I asked.

"That's right. We both had to have a course of drugs to maximize our fertility, then Helen harvested our eggs and took them off to the lab to join them up and grow them on till she was sure they were OK. She did four altogether."

If I looked as aghast as I felt, Alexis's face didn't reflect it. "Chris is having *quads*?" I gasped.

"Don't be soft. 'Course she's not. There's a lousy success rate. You have to transplant at least three embryos to be in with a shout, and then it's only a seventy per cent chance that one of them's going to do the business. Helen transplanted three, and one of them survived. Believe me, in this game, that's a result."

"So what happened to the other one?" I asked. I had a horrible feeling I wasn't going to like the answer.

"It's in the freezer at home. In a flask of liquid nitrogen."

I'd been right. I felt slightly queasy at the thought and reminded myself never to go looking for a snack in Alexis's kitchen. I cleared my throat. "How do you know it works? How do you know the babies are . . . OK?"

Alexis frowned. "There was no way of proving it objectively. We had to take Helen's word for it. She introduced us to the first couple she had a success with. Their little girl's about eighteen months now. She's a really bright kid. And yes, I know they could have been bullshitting us, that it could have been a racket to rip us off, but I believed those two women. You had to be there, KB."

I thought I could probably make it through the night without the experience. "I see now why you thought they'd take the baby off you," was all I said.

"You've got to help us," Alexis said.

"What exactly did you have in mind?" I asked.

"Helen Maitland's files," Alexis said. "We've got to get rid of them before the police find them."

"Why would the police be looking for them in the first place?" I asked. "Like I said, it's a straightforward burglary gone wrong."

"OK, OK, I know you think I'm being paranoid. But this is our child's future that's at stake here. I'm entitled to go a bit over the top. But there's two reasons why I'm worried. One, suppose it didn't happen like the YP says? Suppose the person who killed Helen Maitland wasn't a burglar. Suppose it was some woman whose treatment hadn't worked and she'd gone off her box? Or suppose it was somebody who'd found out what was going on and was blackmailing Helen? Once the cops start digging, you know they won't stop. They might not be well bright, but you know as well as I do that when it comes to murder the bizzies don't ignore anything that looks like it might be a lead."

I sighed. She was right. Coppers on murder inquiries are never satisfied till they've got somebody firmly in the frame. And if the obvious paths don't come up with a viable suspect, they start unravelling every loose end they can find. "What's the second reason?" I asked.

"She had consulting rooms in Manchester. Sooner or later, somebody is going to notice she's not where she should be when she should be. And eventually, somebody's going to be emptying her filing cabinet. And if I know anything about people, whoever goes through those files isn't going to be dumping them straight in the bucket. It's only human nature to have a good root through. And then me and Chris are chopped liver, along with all the other dykes Helen Maitland has given babies to." Alexis finished her cigarette and washed it down with a couple of gulps of her drink. "We need you to find those files."

I crossed my legs at the ankles and hugged my knees. "You're asking a lot here. Interfering with a murder inquiry. Probably burglary, not to mention data theft."

"I'm not asking for a *favour* here, KB. We'll pay you."

I snorted with ironic laughter. "Alexis, is this how you really think my professional life works? People walk in and ask me to break the law for money? I thought you knew me! When punters walk into my office and ask me to do things that are illegal, they don't stay in the room long enough to notice the colour of the carpet. When I have to break the law, I go out of my way to make sure my clients are the last to know. If I do this for you, it won't be because you're offering to *pay* me for it, it'll be because I decide it needs to be done."

She had the grace to look abashed. "I'm sorry," she groaned. "My head's cabbaged with all this. I know you're not some mad maverick burglar for hire. It's just that you're the only person I know who's got the skills to get us out from under whatever's going to happen now Helen Maitland's dead. Will you do the business for us?" The look of desperation that had temporarily disappeared was back.

"And what if the things I find out point to a conclusion you won't like?" I asked, stalling.

"You mean, if you uncover evidence that makes it look like one of her lesbian patients killed her?"

"That's exactly what I mean."

Alexis covered her eyes and kneaded her temples. Then she looked up at me. "I can't believe that's what you'll find. But even if you do, is that any reason why the rest of us have to have our lives destroyed too?"

Just call me the girl who can't say no.

7

The pleasant, caring atmosphere of the Compton Clinic hit me as soon as I walked through the door. Air subtly perfumed and temperature controlled, decor more like a country house than a medical facility, bowls of fresh flowers on every surface. I could almost believe they employed the only gynaecologists in the world who warm the speculums before plunging them deep into a woman's most intimate orifice. I made a mental note to ask Alexis about it later.

The clinic was in St John Street, a little Georgian oasis off Deansgate that pretends very hard to be Harley Street. The doctors who have their private consulting rooms there obviously figure that one of the most convincing ways of doing that is to charge the most outrageous prices for their services. From what I'd heard, you could make the down payment on one of the purpose-built yuppie flats round the corner on what they'd charge you to remove an unsightly blackhead. If Helen Maitland demanded that kind of price for her treatments, I couldn't imagine there were enough dykes desperate for motherhood and sufficiently well-heeled to make it worth her while. But then, what do I know? I'm the only woman I'm aware of who's been using the pill *and* demanding a condom since she was sixteen.

The Compton Clinic was about halfway down on the right-hand side, a three-storey terraced house with a plague of plaques arrayed on either side of the door. Interestingly, Helen Maitland's name didn't appear on any of them. Neither did Sarah Blackstone's. I opened the heavy front door and found myself in a short hallway with a large sign directing me left to the reception area. I noted a closed-circuit TV camera mounted above the outside door, pointing down the hall towards the door I was being encouraged to use. It was a considerable incentive not to go walkabout, especially since I hadn't brought a tub of Vaseline to smear over the lens.

One of the many problems with my job is you do such a lot of different things in a day, you're seldom appropriately dressed. If I'd known what the carpet at the clinic was like, I'd have brought my snow shoes, but as it was, I just had to make do with wading through the deep pile in an ordinary pair of leather loafers. There were two other potential patients sitting a discreet distance from each other on deep, chintz-covered sofas, reading the sort of home-and-garden magazine the nouveaux riches need to copy to shore up their conviction that they've arrived and they belong.

A tip from the private-eye manual: magazines are one of the dead giveaways as to whether you're dealing with the NHS or the private sector. The NHS features year-old, dog-eared copies of slender weeklies that feature soap stars talking about their operations and TV personalities discussing their drink problems or their diets. The private sector provides this month's copies of doorstop glossies full of best-selling authors talking about their gardens and living with Prozac, and Hollywood stars discussing their drink problems, their diets and living with Prozac.

I managed to reach the reception desk without spraining my ankle. It was pure English country-house library repro, right down to the fake tooled-leather top and the cottage-garden prints on the wall behind it. The middle-aged woman sitting at the desk had a pleasant face, the lines on it carved by comfortable optimism rather than adversity, an impression supported by her Jaeger suit and the weight of the gold chains at neck and wrist. Her eyes betrayed her, however. They were quick, sharp and assessing as they flicked over my smartest suit, the lightweight wool in grey and moss green. It felt like she was instantly appraising the likely level of my bank balance and the concomitant degree of politeness required.

"How may I help you?" she asked, her voice the perfect match for the house-and-garden images of the decor.

"I'd like to make an appointment with Dr Maitland," I said, deliberately lowering my voice so she'd think I didn't want the other two women to overhear.

"One moment," she said, leaning to one side to stretch down and open one of the lower drawers in the desk. If Helen Maitland really was the murdered Dr Sarah Blackstone, the news hadn't made it to the Compton Clinic yet. The woman straightened up with a black A5 desk diary in her hand. She laid it on top of the larger diary that was already sitting open in front of her, and flicked through it to the following Sunday's date. Even I could see that every half-hour appointment was already filled up. If Alexis was right, there were going to be a lot of disappointed faces on Sunday.

I watched as the receptionist flicked forward a week. Same story. On the third attempt, I could see there were a couple of vacant slots. "The earliest I can offer you is 3.30 on the twenty-fourth," she said. There was no apology in her voice.

"Does it have to be a Sunday?" I asked. "Couldn't I see her before then if I come during the week?"

"I'm afraid not. Dr Maitland only consults here on a Sunday."

"It's just that Sundays are a little awkward for me," I said, trying the muscularly difficult but almost invariably successful combination of frown and smile. I should have known it was a waste of time. Every medical receptionist since Hippocrates has been inoculated against sympathy.

The receptionist's expression didn't alter a millimetre. "Sunday is the only day Dr Maitland consults here. She is not a member of the Compton partnership, she merely leases our facilities and employs our services in an administrative capacity."

"You mean, you just make appointments on her behalf?"

"Precisely. Now, would you like me to make this appointment for you, Ms . . . ?"

"Do you know where else she works? Maybe I could arrange to see her there?"

Ms Country House and Garden was too well trained to let her facade slip, but I was watching for any signs, so I spotted the slight tightening of the skin round her eyes. "I'm afraid we have no knowledge of Dr Maitland's other commitments," she said, her voice revealing no trace of the irritation I was sure she was starting to feel.

"I guess I'll just have to settle for the twenty-fourth, then," I said, pursing my lips.

"And your name is?"

"Blackstone," I said firmly. "Sarah Blackstone."

Not a flicker. The receptionist wrote the name in the half-past-three slot. "And a phone number? In case of any problems?"

I gave her my home number. Somehow, I don't think she had the same problems in mind as I did.

❦

I had time to kill before I headed over to South Manchester to pick up Debbie for our prison visit, but I didn't want to go back to the office. I hate violence and I don't like putting myself in situations where GBH seems to be the only available option. I cut down through Castlefield to the canal and walked along the bank as far as Metz, a bar and Mittel European bistro on the edges of the city's gay village. Metz is so trendy I knew the chances of being spotted by anyone I knew were nil. I bought a bottle of designer mineral water allegedly flavoured with wild

Scottish raspberries and settled down in a corner to review what little I knew so far.

I'd been taken aback when Alexis had revealed that she and Chris had been consulting Helen Maitland for six months. After all, we were best buddies. I had secrets from Richard, just as Alexis had from Chris. Show me a woman who doesn't keep things from her partner, and I'll show you a relationship on the point of self-destructing. But I was pretty certain I had no secrets from Alexis, and I'd thought that was mutual. Even though I understood her motives for not telling me about something so illegal, to discover she'd been hiding something this big made me wonder what else I'd been kidding myself about.

Alexis and Chris had been told about Dr Helen Maitland—in total confidence—by a close friend of theirs, a lesbian lawyer who'd been approached very cautiously by another couple who wanted to know the legal status of what they were planning to do. Because she knew about Alexis and Chris's desire to have a child, their lawyer friend introduced them to her clients. I sincerely hoped the Law Society wasn't going to hear about this—even two years of a law degree was enough for me to realize that what was going on here wasn't just illegal, it was unethical too. And let's face it, there aren't enough lawyers around who act out of compassion and concern for the prospect of losing one of them to be anything other than bleak.

Alexis had phoned the Compton Clinic and made an appointment for her and Chris to see Dr Maitland the following Sunday. Obviously, the word had spread since then, judging by the delay I'd faced. She'd been told, as I had been, to go to the back door of the clinic, as the main part of the building was closed on Sundays. Alexis had told me that the initial consultation made interviewing bereft parents look as easy as finding a non-smoking seat on a train. Dr Maitland had offered nothing, instigated nothing. It had been Alexis and Chris who had to navigate through the minefield, to explain what they wanted and what they hoped she could do for them. According to Alexis, Helen Maitland had been as stiff and unyielding as a steel shutter.

In fact, she'd nearly thrown them out when she was taking their details and Alexis admitted to being a journalist. "Why did you tell her?" I'd asked, amazed.

"Because I wanted her to work with us, soft girl," Alexis had replied scornfully. "She was obviously really paranoid about being caught doing what she was doing. That whole first consultation, it was like she was determined she wasn't going to say a word that would put her in the wrong if someone was taping the conversation. And then she was taking down all these details. Plus she insisted on leaving a three-week gap between the first and second appointments. I figured she must be checking people out. And I reckon that if what she found out didn't square with what she'd been told, you never got past that second appointment. So I had to tell her, didn't I?"

"How come she didn't throw you out then and there?"

The familiar crooked grin. "Like I always say, KB, they don't pay me my wages for working a forty-hour week. They pay me for that five minutes a day when I persuade somebody who isn't going to talk to a living soul to talk to me. I can be very convincing when I really want something. I just told her that being a journalist didn't automatically make me a scumbag, and that I was a dyke before I was a hack. And that the best way to make sure a story never got out was to involve a journo with a bit of clout."

I hadn't been able to argue with that, and I suspected that Helen Maitland hadn't either, especially since it would have been delivered with a hefty dollop of the Alexis Lee charm. So the doctor had agreed to work with them both to make Chris pregnant with their child. First, they each had to take courses of drugs that cost a small fortune and made both of them feel like death on legs. The drugs maximized their fertility and also controlled their ovulation so that on a particular Sunday, they'd both be at the optimum point for having their eggs harvested.

Helen Maitland herself had carried out this apparently straightforward procedure. According to Alexis, who never forgets she's
a journalist, the eggs were then transferred into a portable incubator which Helen Maitland could plug into the cigarette lighter
of her car and transport to her lab, wherever that was. Another
small detail I didn't have.

In the lab, one egg from Alexis would be stripped down
to its nucleus and loaded into a micropipette one tenth the
thickness of a human hair. Then one of Chris's eggs would be
injected with Alexis's nucleus and hopefully the chromosomes
would get it on and make a baby. This nuclear fusion was a lot
less immediately spectacular than nuclear fission, but its implications for the human race were probably bigger. It was obvious
why the doctor had chosen to use an alias.

I couldn't help wondering what would happen when men
found out what was going on. If there was one thing that was
certain, it was that sooner or later the world was going to know
about this. It didn't seem possible that Helen Maitland was the
only one who had worked out the practical means of making
men redundant. I had this niggling feeling that all over California, women were making babies with women and doctors with
fewer scruples than Helen Maitland were making a lot of money.

That was another thing that had become clear from Alexis's
story. In spite of their desperation, Helen Maitland wasn't bleeding her patients dry. The prescriptions were expensive, but there
was nothing she could do about that. However, her fees for the
rest of the treatment seemed remarkably cheap. She was charging less per hour than I do. If the medical establishment had
found out about that, she'd have been struck off a lot faster for
undercharging than she ever would have been for experimenting on humans.

There was no other word for it. What she had been doing
was an experiment, with all the attendant dangers. I didn't know
enough about embryology to know what could go wrong, but
I was damn sure that all the normal genetic risks a foetus faced

would be multiplied by such an unorthodox beginning. If I'd been the praying sort, I'd have been lighting enough candles to floodlight Old Trafford on the off chance it would give Chris a better chance of bearing a healthy, normal daughter. Being the practical sort, the best thing I could do would be to find Helen Maitland's killer before the investigation led to my friends. Or worse. I couldn't rule out the possibility that someone had killed Helen Maitland because they'd discovered what she was doing and decided she had to die. Anyone with so fundamental a set of beliefs wasn't going to stop at seeing off the doctor who had set these pregnancies in motion. There was a lot to do, and the trouble was, I didn't really know where to start. All I had was an alias and a consulting room that I hadn't been able to get near.

I finished my drink and stared moodily at the dirty grey water of the canal. The city has screwed so much inner-city renewal money out of Europe that the banks of our canals are smarter than Venice these days. The water doesn't stink either. In spite of that, I figured I'd be waiting a long time before I saw a gondola pass. Probably about as long as it would take me to raise the money to buy Bill out of the partnership.

I couldn't bear the idea of just throwing in the towel, though. I'd worked bloody hard for my share of the business, and I'd learned a few devious tricks along the way. Surely I could think of *something* to get myself off the hook? Even if I could persuade the bank to lend me the money, working solo I could never generate enough money to pay off the loan and employ Shelley, never mind the nonessentials like eating and keeping a roof over my head. The obvious answer was to find a way to generate more profit. I knew I couldn't work any harder, but maybe I could do what Bill had done and employ someone young, keen and cheap. The only problem was where and how to find a junior Brannigan. I could imagine the assorted maniacs and nerds who would answer a small ad in the *Chronicle*. Being a private eye is a bit like being a politician—wanting the job should be an automatic disqualification for getting it. I mean, what kind of person *admits* they want to spend their time spying on other people, lying about their identity, taking liberties with the law, risking life and limb in the pursuit of profit, and never getting enough sleep? I didn't have time to follow the path of my own apprenticeship—I'd met Bill when I was a penniless law student and he was having a fling with one of the women I shared a house with. He needed someone to serve injunctions and bankruptcy petitions, and I needed a flexible and profitable part-time job. It took me a year to realize that I liked the people I spent my time with when I was working for Bill a lot better than I liked lawyers.

I walked out of Metz and set off across town to where I'd parked my car. On my way through Chinatown, I popped into one of the supermarkets and picked up some dried mushrooms, five spice powder and a big bottle of soy sauce. There were prawns and char siu pork in the fridge already and I'd stop off to buy some fresh vegetables later. I couldn't think of a better way to deal with my frustrations than chopping and slicing the ingredients for hot and sour soup and sing chow vermicelli.

At the till, the elderly Chinese woman on the cash register gave me a fortune cookie to sample as part of a promotion they were running. Out on the street, I broke it open, throwing the shell into the gutter for the pigeons. I straightened out the slip of paper and read it. It was hard not to believe it was an omen. "Sometimes, beggars can be choosers," it said.

8

As my car rolled to a halt outside Debbie and Dennis's house on a modern suburban estate, the curtains started to twitch the length of the close. Before I could get out of the car and ring the bell, the front door was open and Debbie was coming down the drive of their detached home with gleaming blonde head held high for the benefit of the neighbours. She looked like a recently retired supermodel slumming it for the day. The dignified impression was only slightly diminished by the tiny stride imposed by the tightness of her skirt and the height of her heels. Debbie folded herself into the passenger seat of my car, her long legs gleaming with Lycra, and said, "Nosy so-and-sos. Did you see them nets? Up and down like a bride's nightie. Imagine having nothing better to do all day than spy on everybody else. That Neighbourhood Watch scheme is just a licence to poke your nose into other people's business, if you ask me. Sad bastards."

"How you doing, Debbie?" I asked in the first pause in the tirade.

She sighed. "You don't want to know, Kate."

She wasn't wrong. I'd had a brief taste of seeing the man I loved behind bars, and that had been enough for me to real-ize how hellish it must be to lose them to prison for months or years. "You know you can always talk to me, Debbie," I lied.

"I know, but it does my head in just thinking about it. Talking about it'd only make it worse." Debbie flicked open the cover of the car's ashtray with a manicured nail. Seeing it was clean and empty, she closed it again and breathed out heavily through her nose.

"It's OK to smoke if you don't mind having the window open," I told her.

She took a pack of Dunhills out of a handbag that I knew wasn't Chanel in spite of the distinctive gilt double C on the clasp. I knew it wasn't Chanel because I had an identical one in the same burgundy leather-look plastic. It had been a passing gift from Dennis about a year before, when he'd come by a vanload of counterfeit designer accessories. It had been good gear; Richard was still using the "Cerruti" wallet. She managed to light up without smudging her perfect lipstick, then said, "I flaming hate seeing him in there. I really appreciate you coming today. It'll do him good to see you. He always asks Christie if she's seen you and how you're doing."

From anyone other than Debbie, that would have been a deliberate crack, a sideswipe aimed at triggering a major guilt trip. But given that her IQ and her dress size are near neighbours, I knew she'd meant exactly what she said, no more and no less. It didn't make any difference to me; I still got the stab of guilt. In the seven weeks Dennis had been inside, I'd only got along to see him once so far, and that had been the week after he went down. Sure, I'd been stretched at work, with Bill clearing his desk before Australia. But that was only half the story. Like Debbie, I hated seeing Dennis inside Strangeways. Unlike her, nobody was going to give me a bad time for not visiting him every week. Nobody except me.

"I'm sorry I've not managed more often," I said lamely.

"Don't worry about it, love," Debbie said. "If I didn't have to go, you wouldn't catch me within a hundred miles of the place."

I refrained from pointing out she lived only half a dozen miles from the red-brick prison walls; I like Debbie too much. "How's he doing?"

"Not so bad now. You know how he is about drugs? Well, they've just opened this drug-free unit where you can get away from all the junkies and the dealers and he's got on it. The deal is if you stay away from drugs you get unlimited access to the gym. And if you work out daily, you get extra rations. So he's spending a lot of time on the weights. Plus the other blokes on this drug-free wing are mostly older like him, so it's not like being stuck on a wing with a load of drugged-up idiots." Debbie sighed. "He just hates being banged up. You know he can't be doing with anybody keeping tabs on him."

I knew only too well. It was one of the things that united the two of us, superficially so different, but underneath disturbingly similar. "And time passes a lot faster on the outside than it does behind those walls," I said, half to myself.

"Don't you believe it," Debbie said bitterly.

In silence, I navigated my way through the city centre, catching every red light on Deansgate before we passed the new Nynex arena. It's an impressive sight, towering over the substantial nineteenth-century edifice of Victoria Station. Unfortunately but predictably, it opened to a chorus of problems, the main one being that the seats are so steeply raked that people sitting in the top tiers have had to leave because they were suffering from vertigo.

I swung into the visitors' car park and stared up at another impressive sight—the new round-topped wall containing Her Majesty's Prison. The prisoners who destroyed half of Strangeways in a spectacular riot a few years ago ended up doing their successors a major favour. Instead of the horrors of the old Victorian prison—three men to a cramped cell without plumbing—they now have comfortable cells with latrines and basins. For once, the authorities listened to the people who have to run prisons, who explained that the hardest prisoners to deal with are the ones on relatively short sentences. A lifer knows he's in there for a long time, and he wants to make sure that one day he sees the outside again. A man who's got a ten-year sentence knows he'll only serve five years if he keeps his nose clean, so he's got a real incentive to stay out of trouble. But to some toerag who's been handed down eighteen months, it's not the end of the world to lose remission and serve the whole sentence. The short-term prisoners also tend to be the younger lads, who don't have the maturity to get their heads down and get through it. They're angry because they're inside, and they don't know how to control their anger. When cell blocks explode into anarchy and violence, nine times out of ten, it's the short-term men who are behind it.

So Strangeways has got a gym, satellite TV and a variety of other distractions. It's the kind of regime that has the rabid right-wingers foaming at the mouth about holiday camps for villains. Me, I've never been on a holiday where they lock you in your room at night, don't let you see your friends and family when-ever you want to and never let you go shopping. Whatever else Strangeways is, a holiday camp it ain't. Most of the loudmouths who complain would be screaming for their mothers within twenty-four hours of being banged up in there. Just visiting is more than enough for me, even though one of the benefits of the rebuilding programme is the Visitors' Centre. In the bad old days, visitors were treated so atrociously they felt like they were criminals too. It's no wonder that a lot of men told their wives not to bring the kids to visit. It was easier to deal with the pain of missing them than to put them through the experience.

Now, they actually treat visitors like members of the human race. Debbie and I arrived with ten minutes to spare, and there wasn't even a queue to check in. We found a couple of seats among the other visitors, mostly women and children. These days, a Visiting Order covers up to three adults, and small chil-dren don't count. With every prisoner entitled to a weekly visit, it doesn't take long for a crowd to build up. Nevertheless, we didn't have to hang around for long. Five minutes before our visit time, we were escorted into the prison proper, our bags were searched by a strapping blonde woman prison officer who looked like a Valkyrie on her day off from Wagner's Ring Cycle. Then we were led through anonymous corridors and upstairs to the Visitors' Hall, a large, clean room with views across the city from its long windows. With its off-white walls, vending machines, no-smoking rule, tables laid out across the room and tense atmosphere, it was like a church hall ready for a whist tournament.

We found Dennis sitting back in his chair, legs stretched in front of him. As we sat down, he smiled. "Great to see you both," he said. "Business must be slack for you to take the afternoon off, Kate."

"Christie's got a cross-country trial," Debbie said. "Kate didn't want me coming in here on my own." There was less bitterness in her voice than there would have been in mine in the same circumstances.

"I'm sorry, doll," Dennis said, shifting in his seat and leaning forward, elbows on the table, eyes fixed on Debbie with all the appeal of a puppy dog. But Debbie knew only too well what that cute pup had grown into, and she wasn't melting.

"Sorry doesn't make it to parents' night, does it?" Debbie said.

Dennis looked away. "No. But you're better off than most of this lot," he added, gesturing round the room with his thumb. "Look at them. Scruffy kids, market-stall wardrobes, you know they're living in shitholes. Half of them are on the game or on drugs. At least I leave you with money in the bank."

Debbie shook her head, more in sorrow than in anger. "Haven't you got it through your thick head yet that me and the kids wouldn't mind going without as long as we'd got you in the house?"

Time for me not to be here. I stood up and took the orders for the vending machines. There were enough kids milling around for it to take me a good ten minutes to collect coffees and chocolate bars, more than long enough for Dennis and Debbie to rehash their grievances and move on. By the time I got back, they were discussing what A levels Christie was planning on taking. "She should be sticking with her sciences," Dennis insisted forcefully. "She wants to get herself qualified as a doctor or a vet or a dentist. People and animals are always going to get sick, that's the only thing that's guaranteed."

"But she wants to keep up with her sport," Debbie said. "Three science A levels is a lot of homework. It doesn't leave her a lot of time for herself. She could be a PE teacher no bother."

Dennis snorted. "A teacher? You've got to be joking! Have you seen the way other people's kids are today? You only go into teaching these days if you can't get anybody else to give you a job!"

"What does Christie want to do?" I cut in mildly as I dumped the coffees in front of us.

Dennis grinned. "What's that got to do with it?" He was only half joking. "Anyway, never mind all this bollocks. No point us talking to each other when we've got entertainment on tap, is there, Debs? Tell us what you've been up to, Kate."

Debbie sighed. She'd been married to Dennis too long to be bothered arguing, but it was clear that Christie's future was occupying all of her spare synapses. As Dennis turned the headlamp glare of his sparkling eyes on me, I could sense her going off the air and retreating into herself. Suited me, heart-less bastard that I am. I didn't mind that Debbie was out of the conversation. That way I could get to the point without having to explain every second sentence. So I gave Dennis a blow-by-blow account of my aborted attempt to nail the gravestone scammers as a warm-up to asking for his help.

He loved the tale, I could tell. Especially the bit where Richard walked through the door with the takeaway and the Celtic cartoon characters. It was a short step from there to outlining Dan Druff's problems with the saboteurs. Dennis sat back again, linking his hands behind his chair with the expansive air of a man who knows his supplicant has come to the right place.

"Flyposting, isn't it?" he said as if delivering a profound pronouncement.

"Well, yeah, that's one of the problems they've been having," I said, wondering if his spell behind bars was blunting Dennis's edge. I had already explained that the Scabby Heided Bairns's posters had been covered up by other people's.

"No, that's what it's all about," he said impatiently. "This whole thing is about staking out territory in the flyposting game."

"You're going to have to give me a tutorial in this one, Dennis," I said. Ain't too proud to beg, and there are times when that's what it takes.

Happy that he'd established his superiority despite his temporary absence from the streets, Dennis filled me in. "Illegal flyposting is mega business in Manchester. Think about it. Everywhere you go in the city, you see fly posters for bands and events. The city council just don't bother prosecuting, so it's a serious business. The way it works is that people stake out their own territory and then they do exclusive deals with particular clubs and bands. The really clever ones set up their own printing businesses and do deals with ticket promoters as well. They'll do a deal with a club whereby they'll book bands for them, arrange the publicity and organize the ticket sales at other outlets. So for a band to get on and nail down a record deal, best thing they can do is get tied in with one of the boss operators. That way, they'll get gigs at the best venues, plenty of poster coverage on prime sites and their tickets get sold by all the key players."

"Which costs what?"

Dennis shrugged. "A big slice, obviously. But it's worth it to get noticed."

"And you think what's going on here is something to do with that?"

"Must be, stands to reason. Looks like your lads have picked the wrong punter to do business with. They'll have chosen him because he's cheap, silly bastards. He's probably some kid trying to break into the market and your band's getting his kicking."

I made the circular gesture with my hand that you do in charades when you're asking the audience to expand on their guesses. "Gimme more, Dennis, I'm not seeing daylight yet," I said.

"He'll have been papering somebody else's sites. If the person whose site he's been nicking doesn't know which chancer is behind the pirate flyposting, he'll go for the band or the venues the chancer's promoting. So your band are getting picked on as a way of warning off their cowboy promoter that he's treading on somebody else's ground."

I understood. "So if they want to get out from under, they need to get themselves a new promoter?"

He nodded. "And they want to do it fast, before somebody gets seriously hurt."

I gave a sardonic smile. "There's no need to go over the top, Dennis. We're talking a bit of illegal flyposting here, not the ice-cream wars."

His genial mask slipped and he was staring straight into my eyes in full chill mode, reminding me why his enemies call him Dennis the Menace. "You're not understanding, Kate," he said softly. "We're talking heavy-duty damage here. The live-music business in Manchester is worth a lot of dosh. If you've got a proper flyposting business up and running with a finger in the ticket-sales pie, then you're talking a couple of grand a week tax free for doing not a lot except keeping your foot soldiers in line. That kind of money makes for serious enforcement."

"And that's what my clients have been getting. Skinheads on super lager breaking up their gigs, their van being set on fire," I reminded him. "I'm not taking this lightly."

"You've still not got it, Kate. You remember Terry Spotto?"

I frowned. The name rang vague bells, but I couldn't put a face to it.

"Little runty guy, lived in one of the Hulme crescents? Strawberry mark down his right cheek?"

I shook my head. "I don't know who you mean."

"Sure you do. They found him lying on the bridge over the Medlock, just down from your office. Somebody had removed his strawberry mark with a sawn-off shotgun."

I remembered now. It had happened about a year ago. I'd arrived at work one Tuesday morning to see yellow police tapes shutting off part of the street. Alexis had chased the story for a couple of days, but hadn't got any further than the official line that Terry Spotto had been a small-time drug dealer. "That was about flyposting?" I asked.

"Terry was dealing crack but he decided he wanted a second profit centre," Dennis said, reminding me how expertly today's intelligent villains have assimilated the language of business. "He started flyposting, only he didn't have the nous to stay off other people's patches or the muscle to take territory off them. He got warned a couple of times, but he paid no never mind to it. Since he wouldn't take a telling, or a bit of a seeing to, somebody decided it was time to make an example. I don't think anybody's seriously tried to cut in since then. But it sounds like your lads have made the mistake of linking up with somebody who's too new on the block to remember Terry Spotto."

I took a deep breath. "Hell of a way of seeing off the competition. Dennis, I need to talk to somebody about this. Get the boys off the hook before this gets silly. Gimme a name."

"Denzel Williams," Dennis said. "Garibaldi's. Mention my name."

"Thanks." I hadn't been to Garibaldi's, but I'd heard plenty about it. If I'd had to guess where to find someone I could talk to about so dodgy a game, that's probably the place I'd have gone for.

"Anything else?"

I shook my head. "Not in the way of business. Not unless you know somebody with a wad of cash to invest in a private-eye business."

Dennis's eyebrows lowered. "What's Bill up to?"

I told him. Debbie tuned back in to the conversation and the subject kept us going for the remainder of the visit. By the time I'd dropped Debbie back at the house, I had a list of a dozen or so names that Dennis reckoned had the kind of money to hand that they could invest in the business. Somehow, I didn't think I'd be following any of them up. I'm unpopular enough with the Old Bill as it is without becoming a money laundry for the Manchester Mafia.

━━❖━━

Come five o'clock, I was parked down the street from Sell Phones. All I needed was a name and address on this pair of con merchants and I could hand the case over to the police as I'd already agreed with my clients. We had the names and addresses of nearly a dozen complainants, some of whom were bound to be capable of picking Will Allen or his female sidekick out of a line-up. I looked forward to handing the whole package over to Detective Chief Inspector Della Prentice, head honcho of the Regional Crime Squad's fraud task force. It wasn't exactly her bailiwick, but Della's one of the tightknit group of women I call friends, and I trusted her not to screw it up. There are coppers who hate private enterprise so much they'd let a villain walk rather than let a PI take an ounce of credit for a collar. Della isn't one of them. But before I could have the pleasure of nailing these cheap crooks, I had to attach names and addresses to them. And I was damned if they were going to defeat me two nights running.

This time I was ready for them. When Allen swung left down the hill, I was right behind him. I stayed in close touch as we threaded through back streets flanked by decaying mills half filled with struggling small businesses and vacant lots turned into car parks, across the Rochdale Road and the Oldham Road, emerging on Great Ancoats Street just south of the black glass facade of the old Daily Express Building. I slipped into the heavy traffic with just one car separating me from the silver Mazda, and stayed like that right across town, past the mail-order warehouses and through the council estates.

In Hathersage Road, the car pulled up outside a general store opposite the old Turkish Baths, closed down by the council on the grounds that it cost too much to maintain the only leisure facility within walking distance for the thousands of local inner-city residents. As one of those locals, it made me fizz with fury every time I paid an instalment of my council tax. So much for New Labour. I carried on past the parked car as the woman jumped out and headed into the shop. I pulled into a parking space further down the street, hastily adjusting my rear-view mirror so I could see what was going on. A few minutes later, she emerged carrying a copy of the *Chronicle* and a packet of cigarettes.

As the Mazda passed me and headed for the traffic lights, I hung back. The lights were on red, and I wasn't going to emerge till they changed. On green, the Mazda swung left into Anson Road, the overhanging trees turning daylight to dusk like a dimmer switch. They turned off almost immediately into a quiet street lined with large Victorian houses. About halfway down on the left, the red brick gave way to modern concrete. Filling a space equivalent to a couple of the sprawling Victorians was a four-storey block of flats in a squared-off U. The Mazda turned into the block's car park and stopped. I cruised past, then accelerated, swung the car round at the next junction and drove back in time to see Allen and the woman from Sell Phones disappear through the block's entrance door. Even from this distance, I could see the entry phone. There must have been close on fifty flats in the block.

A whole day had trickled through my fingers and I didn't seem to be much further forward with anything. Maybe I should follow Shelley's advice and put my share of the business on the market. And not just as a ploy.

9

It was too early in the evening for me to have anything better to do, so I decided to keep an eye on the gravestone grifters. I figured that since they'd both gone indoors, the chances were that they were going to have a bite to eat and a change of clothes before heading out to hit the heartbroken, so I took fifteen minutes to shoot back to my house, pick up my copy of that night's *Chronicle* from the mat and throw together a quick sandwich of Dolcelatte and rocket that was well past its launch-by date. It was the last of the bread too, I mentally noted as I binned the wrapper. So much for a night of chopping and slicing and home-made Chinese. I tossed a can of Aqua Libra into my bag along with the film-wrapped sandwich and drove back to my observation post.

Just after seven, the woman emerged alone with one of those expensive anorexic girlie briefcases that have a shoulder strap instead of a handle. She made straight for the car. I waited until she was behind the wheel, then I started my engine and swiftly reversed into the drive of the house behind me. That way I could get on her tail no matter which direction she chose. She turned left out of the car park, and I followed her back to Anson Road and down towards the bottom end of Kingsway, past rows of between-the-wars semis where the vast assortment

of what passes for family life in the nineties happened behind
closed doors, a world we were completely cut off from as we
drifted down the half-empty roads, sealed in our separate boxes.

Luckily we didn't have far to go, since I was acutely aware
that there wasn't enough traffic around to cover me adequately.
Shortly after we hit Kingsway, she hung a left at some lights
and headed deep into the heart of suburban Burnage. Again,
luck was on my side, a phenomenon I hadn't been experiencing
much of lately. Her destination was on one of the long, wide
avenues running parallel to Kingsway, rather than up one of
the narrow streets or cul-de-sacs built in an era when nobody
expected there would come a day when every household had at
least one car. In those choked chicanes, she couldn't have avoided
spotting me. When she did slow down, obviously checking out
house numbers, I overtook her and parked a few hundred yards
ahead, figuring she must be close to her target. I was right.
She actually stopped less than twenty yards in front of me and
walked straight up the path of a three-bedroomed semi with
a set of flower beds so neat it was hard to imagine a dandelion
with enough bottle to sprout there.

I watched her ring the bell. The door opened, but I couldn't
see the person behind it. Three sentences and she was in. I flicked
through my copy of that evening's *Chronicle* till I got to the
death announcements and read down the column. There it was.

*Sheridan. Angela Mary, of Burnage, suddenly on Tuesday at Man-
chester Royal Infirmary after a short illness. Beloved wife of Tony,
mother of Becky and Richard. Service to be held at Our Lady of
the Sorrows, Monday, 2 p.m., followed by committal at Stockport
Crematorium at 3 p.m.*

With that information and the phone book, it wouldn't
be hard to identify the right address. And you could usually tell
from the names roughly what age group you were looking at.
I'd have guessed that Tony and Angela were probably in their

middle to late forties, their kids late teens to early twenties. Perfect targets for the con merchants. Bereft husband young enough to notice an attractive woman, whether consciously or not. Probably enough money in the pot to be able to afford a decent headstone. The thought of it made me sick.

What was worse was the knowledge that even as I was working all this out, Will Allen's accomplice was giving the shattered widower a sales pitch designed to separate him from a large chunk of his cash. I couldn't just sit there and let it happen. On the other hand, I couldn't march up the path and unmask her unless I wanted her and her sleazy sidekick to cover their tracks and leave town fast. I couldn't call the cops; I knew Della was out of town at a conference, and trying to convince some strange officer that I wasn't a nutter fast enough to get them out here in time to stop it was way beyond my capabilities. I racked my brains. There had to be a way of blowing her out without blowing my cover.

There was only one thing I could come up with. And that depended on how well the Sheridans got along with their neighbours. If they'd had years of attrition over parking, teenage stereos and footballs over fences, I'd had it. Squaring my shoulders, I walked up the path of the other half of the Sheridans' semi. The woman who answered the door looked to be in her mid-thirties, thick dark hair pulled back into a ponytail, a face all nose, teeth and chin. She wore a pair of faded jeans, supermarket trainers and a Body Shop T-shirt demanding that some part of the planet should be saved. When she registered that it was a stranger on the doorstep, her cheery grin faded to a faint frown. Clearly, I was less interesting than whoever she'd been expecting. I handed her a business card. "I'm sorry to bother you," I started apologetically.

"Private investigator?" she interrupted. "You mean, like on the telly? I didn't know women did that."

Some days, you'd kill for an original response. Still, I was just grateful not to have the door slammed in my face. I smiled, nodded and ploughed on. "I need you help," I said. "How well do you know Mr Sheridan next door?"

The woman gasped. "He's never murdered her, has he? I know it were sudden, like, and God knows they've had their ups and downs, but I can't believe he killed her!"

I closed my eyes momentarily. "It's nothing like that. As far as I'm aware, there's nothing at all suspicious about Mrs Sheridan's death. Look, can I come in for a minute? This is a bit difficult to explain."

She looked dubious. "How do I know you're who you say you are?"

I spread my hands in a shrug. "Do I look the dangerous type? Believe me, I'm trying to prevent a crime, not take part in one. Mr Sheridan is about to be robbed unless you can help me here."

She gasped again, her hand flying to her mouth this time. "It's just like the telly," she said, ushering me into a narrow hallway where there was barely room for both of us and the mountain bike that hung on one wall. "What's going on?" she demanded avidly.

"A particularly nasty team of crooks are conning bereaved families out of hundreds of pounds," I said, dressing it up in the tabloid style she clearly relished. "They catch them at a weak moment and persuade them to part with cash for cut-price gravestones. Now, I'm very close to completing a watertight case against them, so I don't want to alert them to the fact that their cover's blown. But I can't just sit idly by while poor Mr Sheridan gets ripped off."

"So you want me to go and tell him there's a crook in his living room?" she asked eagerly.

"Not exactly, no. I want you to pop round in a neigh-bourly sort of way, just to see he's all right, and do what you can to prevent him parting with any money. Say things like, 'If this is a respectable firm, they won't mind you sleeping on this and talking it over with your funeral director.' Don't let on you're at all suspicious, just that you're a cautious sort of person. And that Angela wouldn't have wanted him to rush into anything without consulting other members of the family. You get the idea?"

She nodded. "I've got you. You can count on me." I didn't have a lot of choice, so I just smiled. "I'll get round there right away. I was going to pop round anyway to see how Tony was doing. We got on really well, me and Angela. She was older than me, of course, but we played tenpin bowls in the same team every Wednesday. I couldn't get over it when I heard. Burst appendix. You never know the hour or the day, do you? You leave this to me, Kate," she added, glancing at my card again.

We walked down the path together, me heading back to my car and her next door. As we parted, she promised to call me on my mobile to let me know what happened. I was on pins as I sat watching the Sheridans' house. My new sidekick was definitely a bit of a loose cannon, but I couldn't think of anything else I could have done that would have been effective without warning off Allen's partner in crime, particularly since they'd be on their guard after the earlier debacle at Richard's house. About half an hour passed, then the front door opened and my target emerged. Judging by the way she threw her briefcase into the car, she wasn't in the best of moods. I'd had my phone switched off all day to avoid communicating with the office, but I turned it back on as I pulled out behind the woman.

She was back inside the block of flats by the time my new confederate called. "Hiya," she greeted me. "I think it went off all right. I don't think she was suspicious, just brassed off because I was sitting there being dead neg about the whole thing. I just kept saying to Tony he shouldn't make any decision without the kids being there, and that was all the support he needed, really. She realized she wasn't getting anywhere and I wasn't shifting, so she just took herself off."

"You did really well. Do you know what she was calling herself?" I asked when I could get a word in.

"She had these business cards. Greenhalgh and Edwards. Tony showed me after she'd gone. Sarah Sargent, it says her name is. Will you need us to go to court?" she asked, the phone line crackling with excitement.

"Possibly," I hedged. "I really appreciate your help. If the police need your evidence to support a case, I'll let them know where to find you."

"Great! Hey, I think your job's dead exciting, you know. Any time you need a hand again, just call me, OK?"

"OK," I said. Anything to get out from under. But she insisted on giving me her name and phone number before I could finally disengage. I wondered how glamorous she'd find the job when she had to do a fifteen-hour surveillance in a freezing van in the dead of winter with a plastic bucket to pee in and no guarantee that she'd get the pictures she needed to avoid having to do the whole thing all over again the next day.

I started my engine. I didn't think the con merchants would be having another go tonight. But I still had miles to go before I could sleep. A little burglary, perhaps, and then a visit to clubland for a nightcap. Given that I wasn't dressed for either pursuit, it seemed like a good excuse to head for home. Maybe I could even squeeze in a couple of hours' kip before I had to go about my nocturnal business.

⚜

Never mind mice and men. Every time I make a plan these days it seems to go more off track than a blindfolded unicyclist. I hadn't taken more than a couple of steps towards my bungalow when I heard another car door open and I saw a figure move in my direction through the dusk. I automatically moved into position, ready for fight or flight, arms hanging at my side, shoulder bag clutched firmly, ready to swing it in a tight arc, all my weight on the balls of my feet, ready to kick, pivot or run. I waited for the figure to approach, tensed for battle.

It was just as well I'm the kind who looks before she leaps into action. I don't think Detective Constable Linda Shaw would have been too impressed with a flying kick to the abdomen. "DC Shaw?" I said, surprised and baffled as she stepped into a pool of sodium orange.

"Ms Brannigan," she acknowledged, looking more than a little sheepish. "I wonder if we might have a word?" Looming up in the gloom behind her, I noticed a burly bloke with more than a passing resemblance to Mike Tyson. I sincerely hoped we weren't going to get into the "nice cop, nasty cop" routine. I had a funny feeling I wouldn't come off best.

"Sure, come on in and have a brew," I said.

She cleared her throat. "Actually, we'd prefer it if you came down to the station," she said, her embarrassment growing by the sentence.

Now I was completely bewildered. The one and only time I'd met Linda Shaw, she'd been one of Detective Inspector Cliff Jackson's gophers on a murder case I'd been hired to investigate. There was a bit of history between me and Jackson that meant every time our paths crossed, we both ended up with sore heads, but Linda Shaw had acted as the perfect buffer zone, keeping the pair of us far enough apart to ensure that the job got done without another murder being added to the case's tally. I'd liked her, not least because she was her own woman, seemingly determined not to let Jackson's abrasive bull-headedness rub off on her. What I couldn't work out was why she was trying to drag me off to a police station for questioning. For once, I wasn't doing anything that involved tap-dancing over a policeman's toes. That might change once I got properly stuck in to the investigation of Alexis's murdered doctor, but even if it did, the detectives I'd be irritating were forty miles away on the other side of the Pennines. "Why?" I asked mildly.

"We've got some questions we'd like to ask you." By now, Linda wasn't even pretending to meet my eye. She was pointedly staring somewhere over my left shoulder.

"So come in, have a brew and we'll see if I can answer them," I repeated. I call it the irregular verb theory of life; I am firm, you are stubborn, he/she is a pig-headed, rigid, anally retentive stick-in-the mud.

"Like DC Shaw said, we'd like you to come down the station," her oppo rumbled. It was like listening to Vesuvius by stethoscope. Only with a Liverpudlian accent instead of an Italian one.

I sighed. "We can do this one of two ways. Either you can come into the house and ask me what you've got to ask me, or you can arrest me and we'll go down the station and I don't say a word until my brief arrives. You choose." I gave the pair of them my sweetest smile, somehow choking down the anger. I knew whose hand was behind this. It had Cliff Jackson's sadistic fingerprints all over it.

Linda breathed out hard through her nose and compressed her lips into a thin line. I imagined she was thinking about the rocket Cliff Jackson was going to fire at her when she got back to base without me meekly following at her heels. That wasn't my problem, and I wasn't going to be guilt-tripped into behaving as if it was. When I made no response, Linda shrugged and said, "We'd better have that brew, then."

The pair of them followed me down the path and into the house. I pointed at the living room, told them they were having coffee and brewed up in the kitchen, desperately trying to figure out why Jackson had sent a team round to hassle me. I dripped a pot of coffee while I thought about it, laying milk, sugar, mugs and spoons on a tray at the same time. By the time the coffee was done, I was no nearer an answer. I was going to have to opt for the obvious and ask Linda Shaw.

I walked through the living-room door, dumped the tray on the coffee table in front of the detectives and took the initiative. "This had better be good, Linda," I said. "I have had a bitch of a week, and it's only Tuesday. Tell me why I'm sitting here talking to you instead of running myself a long hot bath."

Linda flashed a quick look at her partner, who was enjoying himself far too much to help her out. He leaned forward and poured out three mugs of coffee. Looking like she'd bitten into a pickled lemon, Linda said, "We've received an allegation which my inspector felt merited investigation."

"From whom? About whom?" I demanded, best grammar on show.

She poured milk into her coffee and made a major production number out of stirring it. "Our informant alleges that you have engaged in a campaign of threats against the life of one Richard Barclay."

I was beyond speech. I was beyond movement. I sat with my mouth open, hand halfway towards a mug of coffee, like a Damien Hirst installation floating motionless in formaldehyde.

"The complainant alleges that this harassment has included placing false death announcements in the local press. We have verified that such an advert has appeared. And now Mr Barclay appears to have gone missing," the male detective asserted, sitting back in his seat, legs wide apart, arm along the back of the sofa, asserting himself all over my living room.

Anger kicked in. "And this informant. It wouldn't be an anonymous tip-off, would it?"

He looked at her, his face puzzled, hers resigned. "You know we can't disclose that," Linda said wearily. "But we have been trying without success to contact Mr Barclay since nine this morning, and as my colleague says, we have confirmed that a death announcement was placed in the *Chronicle* containing false information. It does appear that you have some explaining to do, Ms Brannigan." Any more apologetic and you could have used her voice as a doormat.

I'd had enough. "Bollocks," I said. "We both know what's really happening here. You get an anonymous tip-off and your boss rubs his hands with glee. Oh goody, a borderline legitimate excuse to nip round and make Brannigan's life a misery. You've got no evidence that any crime has taken place. Even if somebody did place a bullshit ad in the *Chronicle*, and *The Times* too for all I know or care, you've got nothing to indicate it's anything other than a practical joke or that it's anything at all to do with me." My voice rose in outrage. I knew I was on firm ground; I'd paid for the *Chronicle* announcement cash on the nail, making sure I popped in at lunch time when the classified ads department is at its busiest.

"It's our duty to investigate serious allegations," the Tyson lookalike rumbled. "And so far you haven't explained why anyone would want to accuse you of a serious crime like this. I mean, it's not the sort of thing most people do unless they've got a good reason for it. Like knowing about some crime you've committed, Ms Brannigan."

I stood up. I was inches away from really giving them something to arrest me for. "Right," I said, furious. "Out. Now. Never mind finishing your coffee. This is bollocks and you know it. You want to talk to Richard, sit outside on your arses and waste the taxpayers' money until he comes home. The reason you haven't been able to contact him, soft lad, is because he's a rock journalist. He doesn't answer his phone to the likes of you, and right now, he's probably sitting in some dive listening to a very bad band desperate to attract his attention. He'll be in the perfect mood to deal with this crap when he gets home. Now you," I added, leaning forward and pointing straight between his astonished eyes, "are new in my life, so you probably don't know there's a hidden agenda here."

I swung round to point at Linda, who was also on her feet and edging towards the door. "But you should know better, lady. Now walk, before I have to drag Ruth Hunter away from her favourite TV cop to slap you with a suit for harassment. Bugger off and bother some proper villains. Or don't you know any? Are you kicking your heels waiting for me to provide you with enough evidence to arrest some?"

Linda was halfway through the door by the time I'd finished my tirade. Her sidekick looked from me to her and back again before deciding that he'd better follow her and find out what the real story was here. I didn't bother seeing them out.

I couldn't believe Linda Shaw had let herself be sucked into Cliff Jackson's spiteful little game. But then, he was the boss, she had a career to think about, and women don't climb the career ladder in the police force by telling their bosses to shove their stupid vendettas where the perverts shove their gerbils. And as for their anonymous source—that cheeky, malicious little toad Will Allen was going to pay for ruining my evening. If he thought he could frighten me off with a bit of police harassment, he was in for the rudest shock of his life.

10

The front door closed on a silence so tremendous I could hear the blood beating in my brain. The last time I'd been this angry had nearly cost me my relationship with Richard, who had infuriated me to the point where violence seemed the most attractive option. This time it had been a police officer I'd nearly decked. The repercussions from that might have been less emotionally traumatic, but they would probably have cost me just as much in different ways. On the other hand, trying to sell a share in a business where the remaining partner is on bail for assault would present Bill with one or two problems . . . I nearly ran after Linda Shaw and begged her to wind me up again.

I rotated my head enthusiastically in a bid to loosen some of the knots the CID had put there and went through to the kitchen. I wasn't about to let Linda Shaw put me off the job I had planned for later that night, but I could allow myself the necessary indulgence of one stiff drink. I raked around in the freezer until I found the half-bottle of Polish lemon pepper vodka I'd been saving for a rainy day and poured the last sluggish inch into a tall slim tumbler. There was no freshly squeezed grapefruit juice in the fridge, which tells you all you need to know about the week I was having. I had to settle for a mixer bottle lurking behind the cheese. It needed the kind of shaking I'd wanted to give Linda Shaw. I'd barely swallowed the first mouthful when the silence gave up the ghost under the onslaught of the patio doors opening from the conservatory.

"Brannigan?" I heard.

Stifling a groan, I reached back into the fridge and pulled out one of the bottles Richard periodically donates from his world beer collection so he doesn't have to walk all the way back to his kitchen when he's in my bed. Staropramen from Prague, I noted irrelevantly as I grasped the bottle opener, wishing I were there. "Kitchen," I called.

"Hullawrerrhen," said another voice behind me. At least, that's what I think it said. I turned to see Dan Druff grinning warily in the doorway. Silently, I handed him the Czech beer and reached for the next bottle in line. Radeberger Pilsner. I popped the top just as Richard appeared alongside Dan.

"What the hell were Pinky and Perky after?" Richard demanded after the first half of the bottle had cleared his oesophagus.

"They spoke to you?"

He nodded. "Weird as fuck. They were just getting into their motor when we pulled up. The brick shithouse got all excited and said, 'That's him,' to the Chris Cagney wannabe. She looked absolutely parrot and got out of the car."

Richard paused to swallow again and Dan took up the tale. "She comes across to us and says to your man, 'Are you Richard Barclay?' and he goes, 'Yeah, who's asking?' And she goes, 'Police. Have you been the victim of any death threats?' And he looks at her as if she's just dropped off the planet Demented and shakes his head."

"So she turns round and says, 'Satisfied?' to her partner. She sounds dead narked, he looks as bemused as I feel, and off the pair of them go, little trotters twinkling all the way back to their unmarked pigsty," Richard concluded. "Now, I might not be Mastermind, but I reckon there's a higher chance of me winning the Lottery than there is of that little encounter being completely unconnected to you."

"I cannot tell a lie," I said.

Richard snorted. To Dan, he said, "Do you know the story about the two Cretans? One could only tell lies, the other could only tell the truth. Guess which one is Brannigan?"

"Hey," I protested. "This man is my client."

"That's right," Dan said. "Gonnae no' take the mince out of her?"

At last, something Richard and I could share, even if it was only total incomprehension. "What?" we both chorused.

Dan looked like he was used to the reaction. "Doesnae matter," he sighed. "When it does, I'll keep it simple enough for youse English, OK?"

I shooed the pair of them through to the living room and ran through my brief encounter. "Obviously, that toerag who was here the other night decided to warn me off," I concluded.

Richard frowned. "But how did he know who you were? Presumably, you were just Mrs Barclay to him. How did he make the connection to Kate Brannigan? Isn't that a bit worrying?"

"It would be if you hadn't shouted 'Brannigan' after me the other night when he was three steps in front of me," I said drily.

"Which is not good news because if this guy knows your name, he's going to come after you. And then he'll be really sorry," Dan chipped in, making a sideways chopping gesture with his hand. His faith was touching.

"I'm glad you dropped by," I said. "I've been making one or two inquiries about your problem. What I'm hearing as the most likely scenario is that it all comes down to flyposting. The person you're using is almost certainly invading somebody else's territory. Either by accident or deliberately."

Dan pushed a hand through his long red fringe. He looked puzzled. "It's kind of hard to get my head round that," he said. "The guy we're using isn't some new kid on the block. He's been knocking around the Manchester promotions scene for years. He did everybody when they were nobody."

"You're sure about that?" I asked. "He's not telling you porkies?"

Dan shook his head. "No way. We checked him out before we came down here. Lice knows this guy that used to drive the van for the Inspiral Carpets when they were just starting out, and it was him that told us about Sean."

"Sean?"

"Sean Costigan," Dan said. "The guy that does our promotions."

"I need to talk to him. Can you give me his number?"

Dan pulled a face and looked to Richard for help. My lover was too busy building a spliff that would have spanned the Mersey to notice. "I'm not supposed to give his number out," Dan finally said. Embarrassment didn't sit well on his ferocious appearance.

I took a deep breath. "I need to talk to him, Dan. I'm sure that when he told you not to hand out his number, he didn't have people like me in mind."

"I don't know," Dan hedged. "I mean, he's not going to be very happy when he finds there's a private polis on the end of his mobile, is he?"

Give me strength. "Tell him I'm the people's pig," I said, exasperated. "Look, if you feel bad about giving me his number, you're going to have to set up a meet between us. I can't make any more progress until I talk to Sean Costigan myself. So if you don't want to waste the money you've clocked up on my meter so far, you'd better get something sorted." I smiled sweetly. "More beer, anyone?"

✦

Brannigan's second rule of burglary: when in doubt, go home. I was already breaking rule number three, which states that you never burgle offices outside working hours because some nosey parker is bound to spot a light. One look at the back of the Compton Clinic told me that if I went ahead, I was going to be breaking the second rule too. Although the ginnel the clinic backed on to was only a narrow back alley, it was well lit. Never mind the block of flats behind me; any late-night carousers walking along Deansgate who happened to glance down the lane would immediately notice anything out of the ordinary.

And whatever means I used to get inside the clinic, ordinary wasn't on the menu. I'd already seen the closed-circuit video surveillance in the hall, which ruled out going in through the rear entrance and getting to the second-floor consulting room via the main staircase. Alexis had told me that when they went for their Sunday consultations, she and Chris followed instructions to approach by climbing a fire escape which led up to a heavy door which in turn gave on to a landing between the first and second floors. The only problem with that approach was the security floodlight mounted on the back of the building, which would make me as visible as a bluebottle on a kitchen worktop. And even if I got past that, the chances were strong that I wouldn't be able to make it through the fire door, which wasn't going to be conveniently wedged open for me as it had been for Alexis and Chris.

There was nothing else for it. I was going to have to brazen it out and hope there were no police cars cruising the quiet midnight streets. I walked round the block till I was looking at the front door of the clinic. Like a lot of people who spend a few grand on state-of-the-art security, they had neglected to spend fifty quid on serious locks. There were two mortices and a Yale, and just glancing at them, I knew I was only looking at ten minutes max with my lock picks. I undid the middle button on Richard's baggy but lightweight indigo linen jacket that was covering the leather tradesman's apron which houses my going-equipped-to-burgle kit, and took out my set of picks. I shoved my black ski cap up a couple of inches and switched on the narrow-beamed lamp I had strapped round my head. I studied the top lock for a few seconds, then chose a slender strip of metal and started poking around. Even with the handicap of latex gloves, I had both mortices open in less than six minutes. The Yale was the work of a couple of minutes. Now for the difficult bit.

I turned the handle and pushed the door open. I heard the electronic beep of a burglar alarm about to have hysterics as I closed the door firmly behind me. I set the timing ring on the diver's watch I was wearing. Locking the mortices should be slightly easier now I knew exactly which picks to use, but I'd be lying if I didn't admit that the wailing klaxon of the burglar alarm put me off my stride. Five minutes later, I was locked in with an alarm that was louder than the front row at a heavy-metal gig. I switched off my lamp, opened the inside door but didn't step into the hall just yet. There was still the small matter of the video camera. In the darkness, I strained my eyes to see if there were any dull glimmers, indicating sensors that would flood the hall with light. Nothing. I was going to have to chance it, and hope that the camera wasn't loaded with infrared film. Somehow, I doubted it.

Cautiously, I moved forward in the pitch black. Nothing happened. No lights came on, no passive infrared sensors blossomed into red jewels recording the sequence of my journey. I was so intent on my surroundings, I misjudged the length of the hall and went sprawling over the bottom stair. Thank goodness the deep-pile carpet continued up the stairs otherwise I'd have been on the fast track to Casualty. I picked myself up and went up as fast as I could manage without breaking anything. I might be in a clinic but I didn't fancy my chances if the doctors arrived to find their burglar languishing on the stair carpet with a broken leg.

I made it round the turn of the stairs to the first floor and started to climb again. At the head of the stairs, I started groping down the hallway for door handles. The first one I came to opened and I stumbled inside. I took my heavy rubber torch out of my apron and risked a quick flash. I was in a consulting room. No hiding place. I backed out onto the landing and tried the next door. A bathroom. No hiding place apart from cubicles where any self-respecting security guard would check instantly. The third door was locked, as was the fourth, across the hall. Next came another consulting room, but this time the swift sweep of my torch revealed a kneehole desk with a solid side facing the door. I hurried round the desk and squeezed myself into the narrow space, wriggling until I was comfortable enough to stay still for a while. I checked my watch, which indicated that it had been twelve minutes since the alarm was triggered. That meant it should switch itself off automatically in eight minutes. With luck, I might still have some residual hearing left by then. I stuffed my thumbs in my ears and waited.

When the alarm stopped, it was like a physical blow, snapping my head back. Almost beyond belief, I unjammed my ears, struggling to accept that the ringing noise that remained was only inside my head. My watch said eighteen minutes had passed since the alarm had started its hideous cacophony. That meant a key holder had arrived. I felt myself sweat with nerves, clammy trickles in my armpits and down my spine. If I was caught now, there wasn't a lie in the world that was going to keep me out of a prison cell. Trying not to think about it, I started a mental replay of every note of the six minutes of Annie Lennox's "Downtown Lights." I was coming to the end when I heard a low murmur of voices that definitely wasn't part of my mental soundtrack. Then the door of my shelter swung open, casting a rectangle of light on the far wall opposite me.

"And this is the last one," a man's voice said, sounding anxious. I made out two distorted shadows, one with a familiar peaked cap, before the light snapped on.

I sensed rather than heard a body moving nearer. Then a second voice, speaking from what seemed to be a couple of feet above my head, said, "Your alarm must be on the blink, sir. No sign of forced entry, no one on the premises."

"It's never done this before," the first voice said, sounding irritated this time.

"Have it serviced regular, do you?"

"I don't know, it's not my area of responsibility," the first voice said. "So what do we do now?"

"I suggest we reset it, sir, and hope it's just a one-off." The light died and the door closed. I exhaled slowly and quietly. I gave it five minutes, then I stepped out cautiously onto the landing. Nothing happened. I waved my arms around in a bizarre parody of a Hollywood babe work-out video. Still nothing.

I couldn't believe it. They'd spent a small fortune on perimeter security and a video camera, but they didn't have any internal tremblers or passive infrared detectors. And there I'd been, planning to keep setting the alarm off at five-minute intervals until they finally abandoned the building with an unset alarm. I almost felt cheated.

From what Alexis had told me, the second locked door I'd tried had been Helen Maitland's consulting room. I kneeled down in front of the door and turned on my headlamp. Interestingly, the lock on her consulting room had cost twice the total of all three front-door locks. A seven-lever deadbolt mortice. Just out of curiosity, I took a quick look at the other locked door. A straightforward three-lever lock that a ten-year-old with a Swiss Army knife could have been through in less time than it takes an expert to complete the first level of Donkey Kong. Helen Maitland hadn't been taking any chances.

It took nearly fifteen minutes of total concentration for me to get past the lock. I closed the door softly behind me and shone the torch in a slow arc round the room, like a bad movie. More wall-to-wall heavy-duty carpet in the same shade of champagne. Their carpet-cleaning bill must have been phenomenal. Curtained screen folded against the wall. Examination couch. Sink. Grey metal filing cabinet. Shredder. Printer table with an ink jet on it. Tall cupboard with drawers underneath. A leather chair with a writing surface attached to the right arm, set at an angle to a two-seater sofa covered in cream canvas. No pictures on the walls. No rugs, just basic hard-wearing, pale green, industrial-weight carpet. No desk. No computer. At least I knew it wasn't going to take me long to search. And by the look of things, nobody had been here before me.

I started on the filing cabinet. I was glad to see it was one of the old-fashioned ones that can be unlocked by tipping them back and releasing the lock bar from below. Filing-cabinet locks are a pig to pick, and I'd had enough fiddling with small pieces of metal for one night. I was doubly glad I hadn't had to pick it when I finally got to examine the contents. The bottom drawer contained photostats of articles in medical journals and offprints of published papers. A couple of the articles had Sarah Blackstone's name among the contributors, and I tucked them into the waistband of my trousers.

The next drawer up contained a couple of gynaecological textbooks and a pile of literature about artificial insemination. The drawer above that was partly filled with sealed packets of A4 printer paper. The top drawer held a kettle, three mugs, an assortment of fruit teas and a jar of honey. The cupboard held medical supplies. Metal contraptions I didn't want to be able to put a name to. Boxes of surgical gloves. Those overgrown lollipop sticks that appear whenever it's cervical smear time. The drawers underneath were empty except for a near-empty box of regular tampons. I love it when I'm snowed under with clues.

I sat back on my heels and looked around. The only sign that anyone had ever used this room was the shredder, whose bin was half full. But I knew there was no point in trying to get anything from that. Life's too short to stuff a mushroom and to reassemble shredded print-outs. But I couldn't believe that Helen Maitland had left nothing at all in her consulting room. That was turning paranoia into a fine art.

I knew from Alexis that the doctor worked with a laptop rather than a pen and paper, keying everything in as she went along. Even so, I'd have expected to find something, even if it was only a letterhead. I decided to have another look in the less obvious places. Under the examination couch: nothing except dust. Under the sofa cushions: not even biscuit crumbs.

It was taped to the underside of one of the drawers below the cupboard. A card-backed envelope containing three computer disks. I slid them out of the envelope and into the inside pocket of Richard's jacket. I checked my watch. I'd been inside the room getting on for twenty minutes and I didn't think there was anything more to learn here.

Back on the landing, I locked the door behind me. No point in telegraphing my visit to the world. I started off down the stairs, but just before I reached the first-floor landing, I realized there was a glow of light from downstairs. Cautiously, I crouched down, edged forward and peered through the bannisters. Almost directly below me, sitting on the bottom stairs was the unmistakable foreshortened figure of a police officer.

11

To be accused of one summary offence is unfortunate; to be accused of two within a twenty-four-hour period looks remarkably like carelessness. And since a reputation for carelessness doesn't bring clients to the door, I decided this wasn't a good time to attract the attention of the officer on the stairs. I shrank back from the bannisters and crept towards the upper flight of stairs. In the gloom, I noticed what I hadn't before. There actually were passive infrared sensors high in the corners of the stairwell; they were the ultra-modern ones that don't actually show a light when they're triggered. The reason nothing had happened when I'd waved my arms around on the upper landing earlier was that the alarm hadn't been switched on. Thank God for the need to impress clients with the luxury carpeting.

As I crouched at the foot of the second flight, I heard the crackle of the policeman's personal radio. I sidled forward again, trying to hear what he was saying. ". . . still here in St John Street," I made out. ". . . burglar-alarm bloke arrives. The key holder's worried . . . Yeah, drugs, expensive equipment . . . should be here by now . . . OK, Sarge."

Now I knew what was going on. The key holder had been nervous of leaving the building with what seemed to be a faulty alarm. Presumably, they had a maintenance contract that provided for twenty-four-hour call-out, and he'd decided to take advantage of it. It probably hadn't been difficult to pitch the Dibble into hanging around until the burglar-alarm technician arrived. It was a cold night out there, and minding a warm clinic had to be an improvement on cruising the early-morning streets with nothing more uplifting to deal with than nightclub brawls or drunken domestics.

I tiptoed back up to the top floor and considered my options. No way could I get past the copper. Once the burglar-alarm technician arrived and reset the system, I wasn't going to be able to get out without setting off the alarm again, and this time they'd realize it couldn't be a fault. OK, I'd be long gone, but with a murder investigation going on that might just lead back here, I didn't want any suspicious circumstances muddying the waters.

For all of five seconds, I considered the fire door leading off the half-landing below me. Chances were the hinges would squeak, the security lights would be on a separate system from the burglar alarm and I'd be spotlit on a fire escape with an apron full of exotica that I couldn't pretend was my knitting bag. Not to mention a pocketful of computer disks that might well tie me right into an even bigger crime. I could see only one alternative.

With a soft sigh, I got down on my knees again and started to unlock the door of Helen Maitland's consulting room.

⚜

I've slept in a lot less comfortable places than a gynaecologist's sofa. It was a bit short, even for me, but it was cosy, especially after I'd annexed the cotton cellular blanket from the examination couch and peeled off my latex gloves. I'd locked the door behind me, so I figured I was safe if anyone decided further investigations were necessary. Looking on the bright side, I'd managed to postpone a thrill-packed evening in Garibaldi's with some spaced-out rock promoter. And I'd used up every last bit of adrenaline in my system. I was too tired now to be scared.

As I drifted off to sleep, I had the vague sense that I could hear electronic chirruping in the distance, but I was past caring.

I'd set my mental clock to waken me around nine. It was five to when my eyelids ungummed themselves. Six hours sleep wasn't enough, but it was as much as I usually squeezed in when I was chasing a handful of cases as packed with incident as my current load seemed to be. I unfolded my cramped body from the sofa and did some languid stretching to loosen my stiffened muscles. I peed in the sink, rinsed it out with paranoid care then splashed water over my face, dumping the used paper towels in the empty bin below. It looked like Helen Maitland had even taken her used bin liners home. Learning a lesson in caution from her, I used a paper towel to open cupboard and box and helped myself to a pair of her surgical gloves, then moved across to the door and listened. I couldn't hear a thing.

As quietly as possible, I unlocked the door. I opened it a crack and listened some more. Now I could hear the sort of noises that an occupied building gives off: distant murmurs of speech, feet moving on stairs and hallways, doors opening and closing. I didn't know how appointments were spaced at the Compton Clinic, but I reckoned that the best time to avoid coming into contact with too many other people was probably around twenty-five past the hour. I softly closed the door and checked myself over. I'd taken off the ski cap and headlamp, but I still looked a pretty unlikely private patient in my black hockey boots, leggings and polo-neck sweater. Even the fashionable bagginess of Richard's designer-label jacket didn't lift the outfit much. If anyone did see me, I'd have to hope they put me down as someone in one of those arty jobs never seen by the general public—radio producer, publisher's editor, novelist, literary critic.

I watched the second hand sweep round until it was time. Then I inched the door open. The landing was clear. I slipped out and pulled the door closed behind me, holding the handle so the catch wouldn't click into place. I carefully released it and stepped away smartly. The door was going to have to stay unlocked, but with luck, by the time it was discovered, the fault in the burglar alarm would be ancient history. I tripped down the stairs with the easy nonchalance of someone who's just been given some very good news by their gynae. I didn't see another soul. When I reached the foot of the stairs, I sketched a cheery wave at the video camera. Then I was out on the street, happily sucking in the traffic fumes of the city centre. Free and clear.

I walked up the street to the meter where I'd left the car the night before, expecting to pay the penalty for parking without payment for the first hour of the working day. This close to the traffic wardens' HQ just off Deansgate, it was practically inevitable. By some accidental miracle that the gods had obviously intended for some other mortal, I hadn't been wheel-clamped. I didn't even have a ticket.

The luck didn't last, of course. The phone was ringing as I got through the door and I made the mistake of answering it rather than letting the machine deal with the call. "Your mobile has been switched off since this time yesterday," Shelley stated without preamble.

"I know that," I retorted.

"Have you lost the instruction manual? To turn it on, you depress the button marked 'power.'"

"I know that too."

"Are you coming in today?"

"I doubt it," I said briskly. "Stuff to do. Clinkers to riddle, pots to side, cases to solve."

"You are still working, then?" For once, Shelley's voice wasn't dripping sarcasm. It almost sounded like she was concerned about me, but that may have been my overactive imagination.

"I'm working on the gravestone scam, plus I have two other cases that are currently occupying significant amounts of my time," I said, probably more abruptly than I intended.

"What other cases?" Shelley asked accusingly. Back to normal, thank God. Shelley as sergeant major I could cope with; Shelley as mother hen wasn't part of the deal.

"New cases. I'll let you have the paperwork just as soon as I get to it," I said. "Now I've got to go. There's a librarian out there waiting for me to make her day." I cut the connection before Shelley could say anything more. I knew I was being childish about avoiding Bill, but until I could get my head straight about my future, I couldn't even bear to be in the office where we'd worked together so successfully.

I dumped my stale clothes in the laundry basket, left Richard's jacket by the door so I'd remember to take it to be dry-cleaned, and dived into the shower. Needles of water stung my flesh on the borderline of pain, stripping away my world-weariness. By the time I'd finished with the coconut shampoo, the strawberry body wash and the grapefruit body lotion, I must have smelled like a fruit salad, but at least I'd stopped feeling like chopped liver.

While I was waiting for the coffee to brew, I booted up my trusty PC and took a look at the disks I'd raided from Helen Maitland's consulting room. Each disk contained about a dozen files, all with names like SMITGRIN.DAT, FOSTHILL.DAT and EDWAJACK.DAT. When I came to one called APPLELEE.DAT my initial guess that the file names corresponded to pairs of patients was confirmed. I didn't have to be much of a detective to realize that this contained the data relating to Chris Appleton and Alexis Lee. The only problem was accessing the information. I tried various word-processing packages but whatever software Helen Maitland had used, it wasn't one that I had on my machine. So I tried cheating my way into the file, renaming it so my software would think it was a different kind of file and read it. No joy. Either these files were password protected, or the software was too specialized to give up its secrets to my rather crude methods.

I finished my coffee, copied the disks and sent Gizmo a piece of e-mail to tell him that he was about to find an envelope with three disks on his doormat and that I'd appreciate a print-out of the files contained on them. Then I went on a wardrobe mission for something that would persuade a doctor that I was a fit and proper person to talk to. Failing combat fatigues and a Kalashnikov, I settled for navy linen trousers, a navy silk tweed jacket and a lightweight cream cotton turtleneck. At least I wouldn't look like a drug rep.

I raided the cash dispenser again and stuffed some cash in an envelope with the originals of the disks and pushed the whole lot through Gizmo's letter box. I wasn't in the mood for conver-sation, not even Gizmo's laconic variety. Next stop was Central Ref. It was chucking it down in stair rods by then, and of course I hadn't brought an umbrella. Which made it inevitable that the nearest available parking space was on the far side of Albert Square down on Jackson's Row. With my jacket pulled over my head so that I looked like a strange, deformed creature from a Hammer Horror film, I sprinted through the rain-darkened streets to the massive circular building that manages to domi-nate St Peter's Square in spite of the taller buildings around it.

Under the portico, I joined the other people shaking themselves like dogs before we filed into the grand foyer with its twin staircases. I ignored the information desk and the lift and walked up to the reference room. Modelled on the British Museum reading room, the tables radiate out from the hub of a central desk like the spokes from a vast, literary wheel. Light filters down from the dome of the high ceiling, and everything is hushed, like a library ought to be. All these modern buildings with their strip lighting, antistatic carpets and individual carrels never feel like proper libraries to me. I often used to come and work in Central Ref. when I was a student. The atmosphere was more calm than the university law library, and nobody ever tried to chat you up.

Today, though, I wasn't after Halsbury's *Statutes of England*, or Michael Zander's analysis of the Police and Criminal Evidence Act. The first thing I wanted was Black's *Medical Directory*, the list of doctors licensed to practise in the UK, complete with their qualifications and their professional history. I'd used it before, so I knew where to look. Black's told me that Sarah Blackstone had qualified twelve years before. She was a graduate of Edinburgh University, a fellow of the Royal College of Obstetricians and Gynaecologists, and she had worked in Obs & Gynae in Glasgow, then one of the London teaching hospitals before winding up as a consultant at St Hilda's Infirmary in Leeds, one of the key hospitals in the north. It was clear from the information here plus the articles I'd taken from the consulting room that Dr Blackstone was an expert on subfertility, out there at the leading edge of an increasingly controversial field, a woman with a reputation for solid achievement. That explained in part why she'd chosen to operate under an alias.

Since the book was there in front of me, I idly thumbed forward. There was no reason why she should have chosen to use another doctor's name as an alias, except that Alexis had told me that Sarah Blackstone had written prescriptions in the name of Helen Maitland. While it wasn't impossible that she'd used an entirely fictitious name to do this, it would have been easier and safer to steal another doctor's identity. If she'd done that, uncovering the real Helen Maitland might just take me a step or two further forward.

Impatiently I ran my finger down the twin columns, past the Madisons, the Maffertys and the Mahons, and there it was. Helen Maitland. Another Edinburgh graduate, though she'd qualified three years before Sarah Blackstone. Member of the Royal College of Physicians. She'd worked in Oxford, briefly in Belfast, as a medical registrar in Newcastle, and now, like Sarah Blackstone, she was also a consultant at St Hilda's in Leeds, with research responsibilities. According to Black's, and the indices of the medical journals I checked afterwards, Helen

Maitland had nothing to do with fertility treatment. She was a specialist in cystic fibrosis, and had published extensively on recent advances in gene replacement therapy. On the surface, it might seem that there was no point of contact between the two women professionally; but the embryologist who worked on Helen Maitland's patients' offspring in vitro might well be the same one who worked with Sarah Blackstone's subfertile couples. They'd certainly work in the same lab.

Even if I had all the files on the disks I'd recovered in the night, I still needed to make some more checks. The original computer files, of which I was sure these were only backup copies, had to be on a computer somewhere. And I needed to check out whether the real Helen Maitland was sufficiently involved in Sarah Blackstone's fertility project to be a potential threat to Alexis and Chris, or whether she was simply an innocent victim of her colleague's deception.

Before I made the inevitable trip across the Pennines, I thought I'd make the most of being in Central Ref. Replacing the medical directory, I wandered across to the shelves where the city's electoral rolls are kept. I looked up the main index and found the volume that contained the street where "Will Allen" and his partner "Sarah Sargent" lived. I pulled the appropriate box file from the shelf and thumbed through the wards until I got to the right one. I found them inside a minute.

It's one of the truisms of life that when people pick an alias, they go for something that is easy for them to remember, so they won't be readily caught out. They'll opt for the same initials, or a name that has some connection for them. There, in Flat 24, was living proof. Alan Williams and Sarah Constable.

If I played my cards right, maybe I could get them done for wasting police time as well as everything else. That would teach them to mess with me.

12

I used the old flower-delivery trick on the real Helen Maitland. A quick call to St Hilda's Infirmary had established that Dr Maitland was doing an outpatients clinic that afternoon. A slow scan of the phone book had revealed that her phone number was ex-directory. Given the protective layers of receptionists and nurses, I didn't rate my chances of getting anywhere near her at work unless I'd made an appointment three months in advance. That meant fronting up at her home. The only problem with that was that I didn't know where she lived.

I headed for the hospital florist and looked at the flowers on offer. There were the usual predictable, tired arrangements of chrysanthemums and spray carnations. Some of them wouldn't have looked out of place sitting on top of a coffin. I suppose it saved money if your nearest and dearest seemed to be near death's door: one lot of flowers would do for bedside and graveside. Gave a whole new meaning to saying it with flowers. The only exception was a basket of freesias mixed with irises. When I went to pay for it, I realized why they only bothered stocking the one. It was twice the price of the others. I got a receipt. My client would never believe flowers could cost that much otherwise. I've seen the tired garage bunches she brings home for Chris.

The price included a card, which I didn't write out until I was well clear of the florist. "Dear Doctor, thanks for everything, Sue." Every doctor has grateful patients; the law of averages says some of them must be called Sue. Then I toddled round to the outpatients clinic and thrust the arrangement at the receptionist. "Flowers for Dr Maitland," I mumbled.

The receptionist looked surprised. "Oh, that's nice. Who are they from?"

I shrugged. "I just deliver them. Can I leave them with you?"

"That's fine, I'll see she gets them."

A couple of hours later, a tall, rangy woman emerged from the outpatients department with a long loping stride. Given that she was in her mid-to-late forties and she'd presumably done a hard day's work, she moved with remarkable energy. She was wearing black straight-leg jeans and cowboy boots, a blue and white striped shirt under a black blazer, and a trench coat thrown casually over her shoulders to protect her from the soft Yorkshire drizzle. In one hand, she carried a pilot's case; in the other, as if it were something that might explode, the basket of flowers. If this was Dr Helen Maitland, I had no doubt she wasn't the woman Alexis and Chris had seen. There was no way anyone could have confused her with the photograph in the paper by accident. This woman had fine features in an oval face, nothing like the strong, definite square face Alexis had shown me. Her hair was totally different too. Where Sarah Blackstone had a heavy mop of dark hair in a jagged fringe, this woman had dark blonde curls rampaging over the top of her head, while the sides and back were cropped short. I started my engine. Lucky I'd been parking in a "consultants only" slot, really. Otherwise I might have missed her.

She stopped beside an old MGB roadster in British racing green and balanced the flowers on the roof while she unlocked the car. The case was tossed in, followed by the mac, then she carefully put the flowers in the passenger foot well. She folded her long legs under the wheel and the engine started with a throaty growl. The presumed Dr Maitland reversed out of her parking space and shot forward towards the exit with the aplomb of a woman who would know exactly what to do if her car started fishtailing on the greasy Tarmac. More cautiously, I followed. We wove through the narrow alleys between the tall Victorian brick buildings of the old part of the hospital and emerged on the main road just below the university. She turned up the hill into the early-evening traffic and together we slogged up the hill, through Hyde Park and out towards Headingley. Just as we approached the girls' grammar school, she indicated a right turn. From where I was, it was hard to see where she was going, but as she turned, I saw her destination was a narrow cobbled lane almost invisible from the main road.

I positioned myself to follow her, watching as she shot up the hill with a puff of exhaust. At the top, she turned right. Me, I was stuck on the main drag, the prisoner of traffic that wouldn't pause to let me through. A good thirty seconds passed before I could find a gap, long enough for her to have vanished without trace. Quoting extensively if repetitiously from the first few scenes of *Four Weddings and a Funeral*, I drove in her wake.

As I turned right at the top of the lane, I saw her put the key in the lock. She was standing in front of a tall, narrow Edwardian stone villa, the car tucked into a parking space that had been carved out of half of the front garden. I carried on past the house, turning the next available corner and squeezing into a parking space. A quick call to the local library to check their electoral register confirmed that Helen Maitland lived there. I always make sure these days after the time that the florist trick failed because the target was a hay-fever sufferer who passed the flowers on to her secretary.

I gave Dr Maitland ten minutes to feed the cat and put the kettle on, then I rang the bell set in stone to the right of a front door gleaming with gloss paint the same shade of green as the car. The eyes that looked questioningly into mine when the door opened were green too, though a softer shade, like autumn leaves on the turn. "Dr Maitland? I'm sorry to trouble you," I started.

"I'm sorry, I don't . . . ?" Her eyebrows twitched towards each other like caterpillars in a mating dance.

"My name is Brannigan, Kate Brannigan. I'm a private investigator. I wondered if you could spare me a few minutes."

That's the point where most people look wary. We've all got something to feel guilty about. Helen Maitland simply looked curious. "What on earth for?" she asked mildly.

"I'd like to ask you a few questions about Sarah Blackstone." This wasn't the time for bullshit.

"Sarah Blackstone?" She looked surprised. "What's that got to do with me?"

"You knew her," I said bluntly. I knew now she did; a stranger would have said something along the lines of, "Sarah Blackstone? The doctor who was murdered?"

"We worked in the same hospital," Dr Maitland replied swiftly. I couldn't read her at all. There was something closed off in her face. I suppose doctors have to learn how to hide what they're thinking and feeling otherwise the rest of us would run a mile every time the news was iffy.

I waited. Most people can't resist silence for long. "What business is it of yours?" she eventually added.

"My client was a patient of hers," I said.

"I still don't see why that should bring you to my door." Dr Maitland's voice was still friendly, but the hand gripping the doorjamb was tightening so that her knucklebones stood out in sharp relief. I hadn't been suspicious of her a moment before, but now I was definitely intrigued.

"My client was under the mistaken impression that she was being treated by one Dr Helen Maitland," I said. "Sarah Blackstone was using your name as an alias. I thought you might know why."

Her eyebrows rose, but it was surprise rather than shock I thought I read there. I had the distinct feeling I wasn't telling her anything she didn't already know. "How very strange," she said, and I suspected it was my knowing that was the strange thing. I'd have expected any doctor confronted with the information that a colleague had stolen their identity to be outraged and concerned. But Helen Maitland seemed to be taking it very calmly.

"You weren't aware of it?"

"It's not something we doctors generally allow," she said drily, her face giving nothing away.

I shrugged. "Well, if you don't know why Dr Blackstone helped herself to your name, I'll just have to keep digging until I find someone who does."

As I spoke, the rain turned from drizzle to downpour. "Oh Lord," she sighed. "Look, you'd better come in before you catch pneumonia."

I followed her into a surprisingly light hallway. She led me past the stairs and into a dining kitchen so cluttered Richard would have felt perfectly at home. Stacks of medical journals threatened to teeter over onto haphazard piles of cookery books; newspapers virtually covered a large table, themselves obscured by strata of opened mail. The worktops and open shelves spilled over with interesting jars and bottles. I spotted olive oil with chillis, with rosemary and garlic, with thyme, oregano, sage and rosemary, olives layered in oil with what looked like basil, bottled damsons and serried rows of jams, all with neat, hand-written labels. On one shelf, in an Art-Nouveau-style silver frame there was a ten-by-eight colour photograph of Helen Maitland with an arm draped casually over the shoulders of a pale Pre-Raphaelite maiden with a mane of wavy black hair and enough dark eye make-up to pass as an extra in *The Rocky Horror Show*. On one wall was a cork board covered with snapshots of cats and people. As far as I could see, there were no pictures of Sarah Blackstone.

"Move one of the team and sit down," Dr Maitland said, waving a hand at the pine chairs surrounding the table. I pulled one back and found a large tabby cat staring balefully up at me.

I decided not to tangle with it and tried the next chair along. A black cat looked up at me with startled yellow eyes, grumbled in its throat and leapt elegantly to the floor like a pint of Guinness pouring itself. I sat down hastily and looked up to find Helen Maitland watching me with a knowing smile. "Tea?"

"Please."

She opened a high cupboard that was stuffed with boxes. I remembered the filing-cabinet drawer in the consulting room. "I've got apple and cinnamon, licorice, elderflower, peach and orange blossom, alpine strawberry—"

"Just plain tea would be fine," I interrupted.

She shook her head. "Sorry. I'm caffeine free. I can do you a decaff coffee?"

"No thanks. Decaff's a bit like cutting the swearing out of a Tarantino film. There's no point bothering with what's left. I'll try the alpine strawberry."

She switched on the kettle and leaned against the worktop, looking at me over the rim of the cup she'd already made for herself. Closer, the youthful impression of her stride and her style was undercut by the tired lines around the eyes. There was not a trace of silver in her hair. Either her hairdresser was very good, or she was one of the lucky ones. "Dr Blackstone's death came as a shock to all her colleagues," she said.

"But you weren't really colleagues," I pointed out. "You worked in different departments. You're medical, she was surgical."

She shrugged. "Hilda's is a friendly hospital. Besides, there aren't so many women consultants that you can easily miss each other."

The kettle clicked off, and she busied herself with tea bag, mug and water. When she slid the mug across the table to me our hands didn't touch, and I had the sense that this was deliberate. "She must have known you reasonably well to feel comfortable about pretending to be you. She was even writing prescriptions in your name," I tried.

"What can I say?" she replied with a shrug. "I had no idea she was doing it, and I have no idea why she was doing it. I certainly don't know why she picked on me."

"Were there other doctors she was more friendly with? Ones who might be able to shed some light on her actions?" I cut in. It was the threat of going elsewhere that had got me across the threshold, not the rain. Maybe repeating it would shake something loose from Helen Maitland's tree.

"I don't think she was particularly friendly with any of her colleagues," Dr Maitland said quickly.

That was an interesting comment from someone who was acting as if she were on the same footing as all those other colleagues. "How can you be sure who she was and wasn't friendly with? Given that you work in different departments?"

She smiled wryly. "It's very simple. Sarah lived under my roof for a while when she first came to Leeds. She expected to sell her flat in London pretty quickly, so she didn't want to get into a formal lease on rented property. She was asking around if anyone had a spare room to rent. I remembered what that felt like, so I offered her a room here."

"And she was here long enough for you to know that she didn't have particular friends in the hospital?" I challenged.

"In the event, yes. She was here for almost a year. Her London flat proved harder to shift than she imagined. We seemed not to get on each other's nerves, so she stayed."

"So you must have known who her friends were?"

Dr Maitland shrugged again. "She didn't seem to need many. When you've got a research element in your job and you have to work as hard as we do, you don't get a lot of time to build a social life. She went away a lot at weekends, various places. Bristol, Bedford, London. I didn't interrogate her about who she was visiting. I regarded it as none of my business."

Her words might have been cool, but her voice remained warm. "You haven't asked what she was doing with your identity," I pointed out.

That wry smile again. "I presumed you'd get round to that."

There was something irritatingly provocative about Helen Maitland. It undid all my good intentions and made my interview techniques disappear. "Did you know she was a lesbian when you offered her your spare room?" I demanded.

A small snort of laughter. "I presumed she was. It didn't occur to me she might have changed her sexuality between arriving in Leeds and moving in here."

She was playing with me, and I didn't like it at all. "Did she have a lover when she was living here?" I asked bluntly. Games were over for today.

"She never brought anyone back here," Dr Maitland replied, still unruffled. "And as far as I know, she did not spend nights in anyone else's bed, either in Leeds or elsewhere. However, as I have said, I can't claim to have exhaustive knowledge of her acquaintance."

"Don't you mind that she was using your name to carry out medical procedures?" I demanded. "Doesn't it worry you that she might have put you at professional risk by what she was doing?"

"Why should it? If anyone ever claimed that I had carried out inappropriate medical treatment on them, they would realize as soon as we came face to face that I had not been the doctor involved. Besides, I can't imagine Sarah would involve herself, or me, in anything unethical. I never thought of her as a risk taker."

"Why else would she be using your identity?" I said forcefully. "If it was all above board, she wouldn't have needed to pretend to be someone else, would she?"

Dr Maitland suddenly looked tired. "I suppose not," she said. "So what exactly was she doing that was so heinous?"

"She was working with lesbian couples who wanted children," I said, picking my words with care. If I'd learned anything about Helen Maitland, it was that it would be impossible to tell where her loyalties lay. The last thing I wanted was to expose Alexis and Chris accidentally.

"Hardly the crime of the century," she commented, turning to put her cup in the sink. "Look, I'm sorry I can't help you," she continued, facing me and running her hands through her curls, giving them fresh life. "It's three years now since Sarah moved out of here. I don't know what she was doing or who she was seeing. I have no idea why she chose to fly under false colours in the first place, nor why she chose to impersonate me. And I really don't know what possible interest it could be to anyone. According to the newspapers, Sarah was murdered by a burglar whom she had the misfortune to interrupt trying to find something he could sell, no doubt to buy drugs. That had nothing to do with anything else in her life. I don't know what your client has hired you to do, but I suspect that he or she is wasting their money. Sarah's dead, and no amount of raking into her past is going to come up with the identity of the crackhead who killed her."

"As a doctor, you'll appreciate the burdens of confidentiality. Even if I wanted to tell you what I've been hired to do, I couldn't. So I'll have to be the judge of whether I'm wasting my time or not," I said, staking out the cool ground now I'd finally raised Helen Maitland's temperature a degree or two.

"Be that as it may, you're certainly wasting mine," she said sharply.

"When did you see Sarah last?" I asked, taking advantage of the fact that our conversation had become a subtlety-free zone.

She frowned. "Hard to say. Two, three weeks ago? We bumped into each other in the lab."

"You didn't see each other socially?"

"Not often," she said, biting the words off abruptly.

"What? She shared your house for the best part of a year because the two of you got along just fine, then she moves out and the only time you see each other is when you bump into each other in hospital corridors? What happened? You have a row or what?"

Helen Maitland glowered at me. "I never said we were friends," she said, enunciating each word carefully. "All I said was that we didn't get on each other's nerves. After she moved out, we didn't stay in close touch. But even if we had fallen out, it would still have nothing to do with the fact that Sarah Blackstone was murdered by some junkie burglar."

I smiled sweetly as I got to my feet. "You'll get no argument from me on that score," I said. "What it might explain, though, is why Sarah Blackstone was hiding behind your name to commit her crimes."

I started for the door. "What crimes?" I heard.

Half turning, I said, "Obviously nothing to do with you, Dr Maitland, since you had nothing to do with her. Thanks for the tea."

She didn't follow me down the hall. I opened the door and nearly walked into a key stabbing towards me at eye height. I jumped backwards and so did the woman wielding the key. She was the original of the photograph in the kitchen. With her cascade of dark hair, skin pale as marble and a long cape-shouldered coat, she looked as extreme as a character in an Angela Carter story. "God, I'm sorry," she gasped. "You look like you've seen a ghost!"

No, just an extra from Francis Ford Coppola's *Dracula*, I thought but didn't say. "You startled me," I said, putting a hand on my pounding heart.

"Me too!" she exclaimed.

From behind me, I heard Helen Maitland's voice. "Ms Brannigan was just leaving."

The other woman and I skirted round each other, swapping places. "Bye," I said brightly as the door closed behind me. Trotting down the stone steps leading to the garden, I told myself off for being childish enough to give away my secrets to Helen Maitland just to score a cheap point because she'd made her way under my skin. It was hard to resist the conclusion that she had learned more from our interview than I had.

I didn't think she had lied to me. Not in so many words. Over the years, I've developed a bullshit detector that usually picks up on outright porkies. But I was fairly sure she wasn't telling me anything like the whole story. Whether any of it was relevant to my inquiries, I had no idea. But I had an idea where I might find some of the facts lurking behind her smoke screen of half-truths. When I got back to the car, I switched on my mobile and left a message for Shelley on the office answering machine. An urgent letter needed to go off to the Land Registry first thing in the morning. The reply would take a few days, but when it came, I had a sneaky feeling I'd have some bigger guns in my armoury to go after Helen Maitland with.

13

In these days of political correctness, it's probably an indictable offence to say it, but Sean Costigan didn't have to open his mouth to reveal he was Irish. I only had to look at him, even in the sweaty laser-split gloom of the nightclub. He had dark hair with the sort of kink in it that guarantees a bad hair life, no matter how much he spent on expensive stylists. His eyes were dark blue, his complexion fair and smooth, his raw bones giving him a youthful, unformed look that his watchful expression and the deep lines from his nostrils to the corners of his mouth denied.

I'd got home around nine after fish and chips in Leeds's legendary Bryan's, making the mistake I always do of thinking I'm hungry enough for a jumbo haddock. Feeling more tightly stuffed than a Burns Night haggis, I'd driven back with the prospect of an early night all that was keeping me going. I should have known better, really. Among the several messages on my machine—Alexis, Bill, Gizmo and Richard, just for a kickoff—there was one I couldn't ignore. Dan Druff had called to say he'd set up a meet at midnight in Paradise. Why does nobody keep office hours any more?

I've never been able to catnap. I always wake up with a thick head and a mouth that feels like it's lined with sheep-skin. I don't mean the sanitized stuff they put in slippers—I mean the

stuff you find in the wild, still attached to its smelly owner. I
rang Alexis, but she didn't want to talk in front of Chris, whom
she was keeping in the dark about Sarah Blackstone's murder on
account of her delicate condition. Richard was out—his message had been to tell me he wouldn't be home until late. We'd
probably meet on the doorstep as we both staggered home in
the small hours. Bill I still wasn't talking to, and Gizmo doesn't
do conversation. So I booted up the computer and settled down
for a serious session with my football team. Not many people
know this, but I'm the most successful manager in the history
of the football league. In just five seasons, I've taken struggling
Halifax Town from the bottom of the Conference League up
through the divisions to the Premier League. In our first season
there, we even won the Cup. This game, Premier Manager 3, is
one of my darkest secrets. Even Richard doesn't know about my
hidden nights of passion with my first-team squad. He wouldn't
understand that it's just fantasy; he'd see it as an excuse to buy
me a Manchester United season ticket for my next birthday so I
could sit next to him in the stands every other week and perish
from cold and boredom. He'd never comprehend that while
watching football sends me catatonic, developing the strategies
it takes to run a successful team is my idea of a really good time.
So I always make sure he's out when I sit down with my squad.

Around half past eleven, I told the boys to take an early
bath and grabbed my leather jacket. When I stepped outside the
door, I discovered the rain had stopped, so I decided to leave
the car and walk to the Paradise. It's only fifteen minutes on
foot, and the streets of central Manchester are still fairly safe
to walk around late at night. Especially if you're a Thai boxer.
Besides, I figured it wouldn't do me any harm to limber up for
looking chilled out.

The Paradise Factory considers itself Manchester's coolest
nightclub. The brick building is on the corner of Princess Street
and Charles Street, near Chinatown and the casinos, slightly off
the beaten track of clubland. It used to house Factory Records,

the famous indie label that was home to Joy Division and lots of other bands less talented but definitely more joyful. When Factory failed, a casualty to the recession, an astute local businesswoman took over the building and turned it into a poser's heaven. Officially, it's supposed to be an eclectic mix of gay and hetero, camp and straight, but it's the only club where I've been asked on the door to verify that I'm not a gender tourist by listing other Manchester gay and lesbian venues where I've drunk and danced.

As soon as I went through the door, I was hit by a bass rhythm that pounded stronger in my body than my heart ever had. It was hard to move without keeping the beat. I found Dan and Lice propped against a wall near the first bar I came to as I walked into the three-storey building. The guy I knew without asking was Sean Costigan stood slightly to one side, his wiry body dwarfed by his fellow Celts. His eyes were restless, constantly checking out the room. He let me buy the drinks. Both rounds. That wasn't the only way he made it plain he was there on sufferance. The sneer was another dead giveaway. It stayed firmly in place long after the formal introductions were over and he'd given me the kind of appraising look that's more about the labels and the price tags on the clothes than the body inside them.

"I don't know what the boys have been saying to you, but I want to make one thing absolutely plain," he told me in a hard-edged Belfast whine. "We are the victims here, not the villains." He sounded like every self-justifying Northern Irish politician I'd ever heard. Only this one was leaning over me, bellowing in my ear, as opposed to on a TV screen I could silence with one blast of the remote control.

"So how do you see what's been happening?" I asked.

"I've been in this game a very long time," he shouted over the insistent techno beat. "I was the one put Morrissey on the map, you know. And the Mondays. All the big boys, I've had them all through my hands. You're talking to a very experienced operator here," he added, wetting his whistle with a swig of the large dark rum and Coke he'd asked for. Dan and Lice nodded sagely, backing up their man. Funny how quickly clients forget whose side you're on.

I waited, sipping my extremely average vodka and bottled grapefruit juice. Costigan lit a Marlboro Light and let me share the plume of smoke from his nostrils. Sometimes I wonder if being a lawyer would really have been such a bad choice. "And I have not been trespassing," he said, stabbing my right shoulder with the fingers that held the cigarette. "I am the one trespassed against."

"You're telling me that you haven't been sticking up posters on someone else's ground?" I asked sceptically.

"That's exactly what I'm telling you. Like I said, we're the victims here. It's my ground that's getting invaded. More times than I can count in the past few weeks, I've had my legitimate poster sites covered up by cowboys."

"So you've been taking revenge on the guilty men?"

"I have not," he yelled indignantly. "I don't even know who's behind it. This city's always been well regulated, you know what I mean? Everybody knows what's what and nobody gets hurt if they stick to their own patch. I've been doing this too long to fuck with the opposition. So if you're trying to lay the boys' trouble at my door, you can forget it, OK?"

"Is there any kind of pattern to the cowboy flyposting?" I asked.

"What do you mean, a pattern?"

"Is it always the same sites where they're taking liberties? Or is it random? Are you the only one who's being hit, or is it a general thing?"

He shrugged. "It's all over, as far as I can tell. It's not the sort of thing you talk about, d'you understand? Nobody wants the opposition to think they're weak, you know? But the word on the street is that I'm not the only one suffering."

"But none of the other bands are getting the kind of shit we're getting," Dan interjected. God knows how he managed to follow the conversation. He must have trained as a lip-reader. "I've been asking around. Plenty other people have had some of their posters covered up, but nobody's had the aggravation we've had."

"Yeah, well, it's nothing to do with me, OK?" Costigan retorted aggressively.

There didn't seem to be anything else to say. I told Dan and Lice I'd be in touch, drained my drink and walked home staring at every poster I passed, wondering what the hell was going on.

⚜

I dragged my feet up the stairs to the office just after quarter past nine the next morning. I felt like I was fourteen again, Monday morning before double Latin. I'd lain staring at the ceiling, trying to think of good excuses for not going in, but none of the ones that presented themselves convinced either me or Richard, which gave them no chance against Shelley or Bill.

I needn't have worried. There was news waiting that took Bill off the front page for a while. I walked in to find Josh Gilbert perched on the edge of Shelley's desk, one elegantly trousered leg crossed casually over the other. I could have paid my mortgage for a couple of months easily with what the suit had cost. Throw in the shirt, tie and shoes and we'd be looking at the utility bills too. Josh is a financial consultant who has managed to surf every wave and trough of the volatile economy and somehow come out so far ahead of the field that I keep expecting the Serious Fraud Office to feel his collar. Josh and I have a deal: he gives me information, I buy him expensive dinners. In these days of computerization, it would be cheaper to pay Gizmo for the same stuff, but a lot less entertaining. Computers don't gossip. Yet.

Shelley was looking up at Josh with that mixture of wariness and amusement she reserves for born womanizers. When he saw me, he broke off the tale he was in the middle of and jumped to his feet. "Kate!" he exclaimed, stepping forward and sweeping me into a chaste embrace.

I air-kissed each cheek and stepped clear. The older he got, the more his resemblance to Robert Redford seemed to grow. It was disconcerting, as if Hollywood had invaded reality. Even his eyes seemed bluer. You didn't have to be a private eye to suspect tinted contacts. "I don't mean to sound rude," I said, "but what are you doing here at this time of the morning? Shouldn't you be blinding some poor innocent with science about the latest fluctuations of the Nikkei? Or persuading some lucky Lottery winner that their money is safe in your hands?"

"Those days are behind me," he said.

"Meaning?"

"I am thirty-nine years and fifty weeks old today."

I wasn't sure whether to laugh or cry. Ever since I've known him Josh has boasted of his intention to retire to some tax haven when he was forty. Part of me had always taken this with a pinch of salt. I don't move in the sort of circles where people amass the kind of readies to make that a realistic possibility. I should have realized he meant it; Josh will bullshit till the end of time about women, but he's never less than one hundred per cent serious about money. "Ah," I said.

"Josh has come to invite us to his fortieth birthday and retirement party." Shelley confirmed my bleak fear with a sympathetic look.

"Selling up and selling out, eh?" I said.

"Not as such," Josh said languidly, returning to his perch on Shelley's desk. "I'm not actually selling the consultancy. Julia's learned enough from me to run the business, and I'm not abandoning her entirely. I might be going to live on Grand Cayman, but with fax machines and e-mail, she'll feel as though I've only moved a few miles away."

"Only if you don't have conversations about the weather," I said. "You'll get bored, Josh. Nothing to do all day but play."

The smile crinkled the skin round his eyes, and he gave me the look Redford reserves for Debra Winger in *Legal Eagles*.

"How could I be bored when there are still beautiful women on the planet I haven't met?"

I heard the door open behind me and Bill's voice said, "Are we using 'met' in the biblical sense here?"

Bill and Josh gave each other the usual once-over, a bit like dogs who have to sniff each other's bollocks before they decide a fight isn't worth the bother. They'd never been friends, probably because they'd thought they were competitors for women. Neither had ever realized how wrong they were; Bill could never have bedded a woman without brains, and Josh never bedded one with an IQ greater than her age except by accident. Shelley had her pet theories on their respective motivations, but life's too short to rerun that seminar.

"So it's all change then," Bill said once Josh had brought him up to speed on his reasons for visiting. "You off to Grand Cayman, me off to Australia."

"I thought you'd only just come back," Josh said.

"I'm planning to move out there permanently. I'm marrying an Australian businesswoman."

"Is she pregnant?" Josh blurted out without thinking. Seeing my face, he gave an apologetic smile and shrug.

"No. And she's not a rich widow either," Bill replied, not in the least put out. "I'm exercising free will here, Josh."

I swear Josh actually changed colour. The thought of a man as dedicated as he was to a turbo-charged love life finally settling down, and from choice, was like suddenly discovering his body was harbouring a secret cancer. "So because of this woman, you're going to get married and live in *Australia*? My God, Bill, that's worse than moving to Birmingham. And what about the business? You can keep a finger on the financial pulse from anywhere you can plug in a PC, but you can't run an investigation agency from the other side of the globe."

"The game plan is that I'll sell my share of the agency here and start up again in Australia."

Josh's eyebrows rose. "At your age? Bill, you're only a
couple of years younger than me. You're really planning to start
from ground zero in a foreign country where you don't even
speak the language? God, that sounds too much like hard work
to me. And what about Kate?"

I'd had enough. "Kate's gotta go," I said brusquely. "People
to be, places to see. Thanks for the invite, Josh. I wouldn't miss it
for the world." I wheeled round and headed back out of the door.
I wasn't sure where I was going, and I didn't care. I knew I was
behaving like a brat, but I didn't care about that either. I stood on
the corner outside the office, not even caring about the vicious
northeasterly wind that was exfoliating every bit of exposed skin.
A giggling flurry of young women in leg warmers and tights
accompanied by a couple of well-muscled men enveloped me,
waiting for the lights to change as they headed for rehearsals at
the new dance theatre up the street, one of the handful of tangible
benefits we got from being UK City of Drama for a year. Their
energy and sense of direction shamed me, so I followed briskly in
their wake and collected my car from the meter where I'd left it
less than twenty minutes before. Given that I'd planned to be in
the office for a couple of hours, somebody was going to get lucky.

One quick phone call and fifteen minutes later, I was walking round the big Regent Road Sainsbury's with Detective
Chief Inspector Della Prentice. When I'd called and asked her
if she could spare half an hour, she'd suggested the supermarket.
Her fridge was in the same dire straits as mine, and this way we
could both stock up on groceries while we did the business. We
took turns pushing the trolley, using our packs of toilet rolls as a
convenient Maginot line between our separate purchases. I filled
her in on the headstone scam in the fruit and veg. department,
handing over a list of victims who should be able to pick out
Williams and Constable in an identity parade. She promised to
pass it on to one of her bright young things.

The outrageous tale of Cliff Jackson's waste of police time
kept us going as far as the chill cabinets. By the time we hit the

breakfast cereals, I'd moved on to the problems at Mortensen and Brannigan, which lasted right up to hosiery and tampons. Della tried an emerald-green ruffle against her copper hair. I nodded agreement. "I can see why Shelley suggested you putting your share of the business on the market too," Della said. "But that could present you with a different set of problems."

"I know," I sighed. "But what else can I do?"

"You could talk to Josh," she said. Sometimes I forget the pair of them were at Cambridge together, they're such different types. It's true that they were both fascinated by money but while Josh wanted to make as much of it as possible, Della wanted to stop people like him doing it illegally. She was too bright for him to fancy, so he gave her his respect instead, and a few years ago he did me the biggest favour he's ever managed when he introduced us.

"What good would that do? Josh deals with multinational conglomerates, not backstreet detective agencies. I can't believe he knows anyone with investigative skills and enough money to buy Bill out that he hasn't already introduced me to. Besides, investigative skills never seem to go hand in hand with the acquisition of hard cash. You should know that."

Della reached for a tin of black olives then turned her direct green eyes on me. "You'd be surprised at what Josh knows about," she said, giving a deliberate stage wink.

"I'm not even going to ask if the fraud task force is about to lose its major inside source," I said. "Besides, Josh is too busy extricating himself from business right now. He's not about to get involved in setting up a whole new partnership for me. Did you know he's retiring in a couple of weeks?"

Della nodded, looking depressed. "He's been saying he was going to retire at forty since he was nineteen."

"I wouldn't worry about it, Della. He'll never retire. Not properly. He'll die of boredom in a week if he's not spreading fear and loathing in global financial institutions. He'll always have fingers in enough pies to keep you busy."

Whatever I'd said, it seemed to have deepened Della's gloom. Then I twigged. If Josh was about to hit the big four zero, it couldn't be far off for Della. And she wasn't a multimillionaire with the world her oyster. She was a hardworking, ferociously bright woman in what was still a man's world, a woman whose career commitment left her no space for relationships other than a few close friendships. I stopped the trolley by the spirits and liqueurs, put a hand on her arm and said, "He might have made the money, but you've made the difference."

"Yeah, and everything at the agency is going to work out for the best," she said grimly. We looked at each other, registering the self-pitying misery that was absorbing each of us. Then, suddenly and simultaneously, we burst out laughing. Nobody could get near the gin, but we didn't give a damn. Like the song says, girls just wanna have fun.

14

If you think it's embarrassing to get a hysterical fit of the giggles with one of your best friends in Sainsbury's wines and spirits department, try having your mobile phone ring in the middle of it. Now that's *really* excruciating. At least when it's someone as laconic as Gizmo, you don't have to destroy your street cred totally by having a conversation. A series of grunts signifying "yes" and "no" will do just fine. I gathered he'd got the stuff I wanted and he was about to stuff it through my letter box unless I had any serious objections. I didn't. Even if it was Police Harassment Week and Linda Shaw and her sidekick were back on my doorstep, they could hardly arrest Gizmo for impersonating a postman.

Being midweek and mid-morning, we were through the checkouts in less time than it takes to buy a newspaper in our local corner shop. Della and I hugged farewell in the car park and went our separate ways, each intent on making some criminal's life a misery. "Talk to Josh," were her final words.

Gizmo had done me proud. Not only had he translated the files into a format I could easily read on my computer, but he'd also printed out hard copies for me. As far as her patient notes were concerned, Sarah Blackstone's passion for secrecy had been superseded by a medical training that had instilled the principle of always leaving clear notes that another doctor could follow through should you be murdered by a burglar between treatments. I flicked through until I found the file relating to Alexis and Chris. Not only were their names correct on the print-out, but so also were their phone numbers at home and work, address and dates of birth. Which meant the chances were high that all the other patients' details were accurate. If ever I needed to interview any of them, I knew where to start looking.

At one level, the job Alexis had hired me to do was now complete. I had checked out the consulting rooms and removed any evidence that might lead back to Sarah Blackstone's patients. But what I had were only backup copies. The originals were still out there somewhere, presumably sitting on the hard drive of the laptop that the doctor had used throughout her consultations. If Gizmo had cracked their file protection, it was always possible that the police had someone who could do the same thing. It was also possible that whoever had killed Sarah Blackstone had stolen her computer and was sitting on the best blackmail source since Marilyn Monroe's address book. Women who could afford this treatment could afford payoffs too. The game was a long way from being over.

What I needed now was more information. I understood very little of the patient notes sitting in front of me and I understood even less of the fertility technology that I was dealing with here. I needed to know what technical backup Sarah Blackstone had needed, and just how difficult it was to achieve what she had done. I also needed to know if this was something she could do alone, or if she'd have had to involve someone else. Time to beg another favour from someone I already owed one to. Dr Beth Taylor is one of the legion of women who have been out with Bill Mortensen without managing to accomplish what an Australian boutique bimbo had pulled off. Beth works part time in an inner-city group practice where nobody's had to pay a prescription charge in living memory. The rest of the time she lectures on ethics to medical students who think that's a county in the south of England. If she feels like a bit of light relief, she does the odd bit of freelance work for us when we're investigating medical insurance claims.

I tracked Beth down at the surgery. I didn't tell her about Bill's planned move. It wasn't that I thought it would hurt her feelings; I just couldn't bear to run through it yet again. Once we'd got the social niceties out of the way, I said, "Test-tube babies."

She snorted. "You've been reading too many tabloids. IVF, that's what you call it when you want a bit of respect from the medical profession. Subfertility treatment, when you want to impress us with your state-of-the-art consciousness. What are you after? Treatment or information?"

"Behave," I said scathingly.

"I know someone at St Mary's. He used to be a research gynaecologist, now he works part time in the subfertility unit. I bring him in to do a seminar on my course on the ethics of interference with human fertility."

"Would he talk to me?" I asked.

"Probably. He likes to show off what a new man he is. Nothing he loves more than the chance to demonstrate to a woman how sensitive he is to our reproductive urges. What is it you want to know, and why?"

"I need the five-minute crash course in IVF for beginners and a quick rundown on where the leading edge is right now. What can and can't be done. I'm not asking for anything that isn't readily available in the literature, I just need it in bite-sized pieces that a lay person can understand."

"Gus is your man, then. You didn't mention why this sudden interest?"

"That's right, I didn't. Is he going to want a reason?"

Beth thought for a moment. "I think it might be as well if you were a journalist. Maybe looking for nonattributable background for a piece you're doing following women's experiences of being treated for subfertility?"

"Fine. How soon can you fix it?"

"How soon do you need it?"

"I'm free for lunch today," I said. The devil finds work for idle hands; if you can't manage any other exercise, you can always push your luck.

"So I'll lie. I'll tell him you're young, gorgeous and single. Gus Walters, that's his name. I'll get him to call you."

Ten minutes later, my phone rang. It was Gus Walters. Young, gorgeous and single must have worked. I hoped he wouldn't be too disappointed. Two out of three might not be bad, but none ain't good. "Thanks for getting back to me so quickly," I said.

"No problem. Besides, I owe Beth a favour."

"Are you free for lunch today? I know it's short notice . . ."

"If you can meet me at half past twelve at the front entrance, I can give you an hour and you can buy me a curry," he said.

"Deal. How will I know you?" I asked.

"Oh, I think I'll know you," he said, voice all dark brown smoothness. Definitely a doctor.

≈✧≈

It's a constant source of amazement to me that the staff at Manchester's major hospital complex don't all have serious weight problems. They're only five minutes' walk from the Rusholme curry parade, as serious a selection of Asian restaurants as you'll find anywhere in the world. If I worked that close to food that good, cheap and fast, I couldn't resist stuffing my face at least twice a day. Richard might be convinced that the Chinese are the only nation on earth with any claim to culinary excellence, but for me, it's a dead heat with the chefs of the subcontinent. Frankly, as soon as I had sat down at a window table with a menu in front of me, I was a lot more interested in the range of pakoras than in anything Gus Walters could possibly tell me.

He was one of the non-rugby-playing medics: medium height, slim build, shoulders obviously narrow inside the disguise of a heavy, well-cut tweed jacket. His hands were long and slender, so pale they looked as if they were already encased in latex. Facially, he had a disturbing resemblance to Brains, the *Thunderbirds* puppet. Given that he'd opted for the identical haircut and very similar large-framed glasses, I wondered if he had enough sense of irony to have adopted them deliberately. Then I remembered he was a doctor and dismissed the idea. He probably thought he looked like Elvis Costello.

On the short walk to the nearest curry house we'd done the social chitchat about how long we'd lived in Manchester and what we liked most and least about the city. Now I wanted to get the ordering done with so we could cut to the chase. I settled for chicken pakora followed by karahi gosht with a garlic nan. Gus opted for onion bhajis and chicken rogan josh. He grinned across the table at me and said, "The orifice I get closest to doesn't bother about garlic breath." It rolled out with the smoothness of a line that never gets the chance to go rusty.

I smiled politely. "So tell me about IVF," I said. "For a start, what kind of technology do you need to make it work?"

"It's all very low tech, I'm afraid," he replied, his mouth turning down at the corners. "No million-pound scanners or radioactive isotopes. The main thing you need is what's called a Class II containment lab, which you need to keep the bugs out. Clean ducted air, laminar flow, temperature stages that keep things at body temperature, an incubator, culture media. The only really specialized stuff is the glassware—micropipettes and micromanipulating equipment and of course a microscope. Also, when you're collecting the eggs, you need a transvaginal ultrasound scanner, which gives you a picture of the ovary."

He was off and running. All I needed to do was provide the odd prompt. I was glad I wasn't his partner; I could just imagine how erotic his bedroom conversation would be. "So what are the mechanics of carrying out an IVF procedure?" I asked.

"OK. Normally, women release one egg a month. But our patients are put on a course of drugs which gives us an optimum month when they'll produce five or six eggs. The eggs are in individual sacs we call follicles. You pass a very fine needle through the top of the vagina and puncture each follicle in turn and draw out the contents, which is about a teaspoonful of fluid. The egg is floating within that. You stick the fluid on the heated stage of the microscope, find the egg, and strip off some of the surrounding cells, which makes it easier to fertilize. Then you put it in an individual glass Petri dish with a squirt of sperm and culture medium made of salts and sugars and amino acids—the kind of soup that would normally be around in the body to nourish an embryo. Then you leave them overnight in a warm dark incubator and hope they'll do what opposite genders usually do in warm dark places at night." He grinned. "It's very straightforward."

The food arrived and we both attacked. "But it doesn't always work, does it?" I asked. "Sometimes they don't do what comes naturally, do they?"

"That's right. Some sperm are lazy. They don't swim well and they give up the ghost before they've made it through to the nucleus of the egg. For quite a few years, when we were dealing with men with lazy sperm, there wasn't a lot we could do and we mostly ended up having to use donor sperm. But that wasn't very satisfactory because most men couldn't get over the feeling that the baby was a cuckoo in the nest." He gave a smile that was meant to be self-deprecating but failed. Try as he might, you didn't have to go far below the surface before Old Man reasserted itself.

"So what do you do now?" I asked.

But he wasn't to be diverted. He'd started so he was going to finish. "First they developed a technique where they made a slit in the 'shell' of the harvested egg," he said, waggling his fingers either side of his head to indicate he was using inverted commas because he was unable to use technical terms to a mere mortal. "That made it easier. Twenty-five per cent success rate. But it wasn't enough for some real dead-leg sperm. So they came up with SUZI." He paused expectantly. I raised my eyebrows in a question. It wasn't enough. Clearly I was supposed to ask who Suzie was.

Disappointed, he carried on regardless as the impassive waiter delivered our main courses. "That involves passing a very fine microneedle through the 'shell' and depositing two or three sperm inside, in what you could call the egg white if you were comparing it to a bird's egg. And still some sperm just won't make the trip to the nucleus of the egg. Twenty-two per cent success rate is the best we've managed so far. So now, clinics like ours out on the leading edge have started to use a procedure called ICSI."

"ICSI?" I thought I'd better play this time. Even puppies need a bit of encouragement.

"Intracytoplasmic Sperm Injection," he said portentously. "One step beyond."

I wished I hadn't bothered. "Translation?"

"You take a single sperm and strip away its tail and all the surrounding gunge until you're left with the nucleus. Then the embryologist takes a needle about a tenth the thickness of a human hair and pushes that through the 'shell,' through the equivalent of the egg white right into the very nucleus of the egg itself, the 'yolk.' Then the nucleus of the sperm is injected into the heart of the egg."

"Wow," I said. It seemed to be what was expected. "So is it you, the doctor, who does all this fiddling around?"

He smiled indulgently. "No, no, the micro-manipulation is done by the embryologist. My job is to harvest the eggs and then to transfer the resulting embryo into the waiting mother. Of course, we keep a close eye on what the embryologist does, but they're essentially glorified lab technicians. I've no doubt I could do what they do in a pinch. God knows, I've watched them often enough. See one, do one, teach one." It's hard to preen yourself while you're scoffing curry, but he managed.

"So, does the lab have to be on twenty-four-hour stand-by so you're ready to roll the minute a woman ovulates?" I'd been presuming that Sarah Blackstone did her fiddling with eggs and microscopes in the watches of the night when the place was deserted, but I needed to check that hypothesis.

"We don't just leave it to chance," Gus protested. "We control the very hour of ovulation with drugs. But big labs like ours do offer seven-days-a-week, round-the-clock service so we can fit in with the lives of our patients. There's always a full team on call: embryologist, doctor and nurse."

"But not constantly in the lab?"

"No, in the hospital. With their pagers."

"So anybody could walk into the lab in the middle of the night and wreak havoc?" I asked.

He frowned. "What kind of article are you researching here? Are you trying to terrify people?"

Furious with myself for forgetting I wasn't supposed to be a hard-nosed detective, I gave him a high-watt smile. "I'm sorry, I get carried away. I read too much detective fiction. I'm sure people's embryos are as safe as houses." And we all know how safe that is in 1990s Britain.

"You're right. The lab's always locked, even when we're working inside. No one gets in without the right combination." His smile was the smug one of those who never consider the enemy within.

"I suppose you have to be careful because you've got to account to the Human Fertilisation and Embryology Authority," I said.

"You're not kidding. Every treatment cycle we do has to be documented and reported to the HFEA. Screw up your paperwork and you can lose your licence. This whole area of IVF and embryo experimentation is such a hot potato with the God squad and the politically paranoid that we all have to be squeaky clean. Even the faintest suggestion that we were doing any research that was outside the scope of our licence could have us shut down temporarily while our lords and masters investigated. And it's not just losing the clinic licence that's the only danger. If you did mess around doing unauthorized stuff with the embryos that we don't transfer, you'd be looking at being struck off and never practising medicine again. Not to mention facing criminal charges."

I tore off another lump of nan bread and scooped up a tender lump of lamb, desperately trying not to react to his words. "That must put quite a bit of pressure on your team, if you're always having to look over your shoulder at what the others are doing," I said.

Gus gave me a patronizing smile. "Not really. The kind of people employed in units like ours aren't mad scientists, you know. They're responsible medical professionals who care about helping people fulfil their destiny. No Dr Frankensteins in our labs."

I don't know how I kept my curry down. Probably the thought of being tended by the responsible medical professional opposite me. Either that or the fact that I wasn't paying much attention because I was still getting my head round what he'd said just before. If I was short of a motive for terminating Dr Sarah Blackstone, Gus Walters had just handed me one on a plate.

15

A few days before, I'd have reckoned that as motives for murder go, the prospect of losing your livelihood was a pretty thin one. That had been before Bill's bombshell. Since then, I'd been harbouring plenty of murderous thoughts, not just against a business partner who'd been one of my best friends for years, but also against a blameless Australian woman I'd barely met. For all I knew, Sheila could be Sydney's answer to Mother Teresa. Somehow, I doubted it, but I'd been more than ready to include her in the homicidal fantasies that kept slipping into my mind. Like unwanted junk mail, I always intended to throw them straight in the bin, but every time I found myself attracted by some little detail that sucked me in. If a well-adjusted crime fighter like me felt the desire to kill the people I saw as stealing my dream, how easy it would be for someone who was borderline psychotic to be pushed over the edge by the prospect of losing their professional life. What Gus Walters told me handed motive on a plate to everyone Sarah Blackstone had worked with at St Hilda's, from the professor who supervised the department to the secretary who maintained the files.

There was nothing I could do now about pursuing that line of inquiry. By the time I'd got home and driven to Leeds, it would be the end of the medical working day. I made a mental note to follow it up, which freed my brain to gnaw away at the problem which had been uppermost there since Bill's return. Never mind murderers, never mind rock saboteurs, what I wanted the answer to was what to do about Mortensen and Brannigan. The one thing I was sure about was that I didn't intend to roll over and die, waiting for Bill to find the buyer of his choice. As I walked back through the red-brick streets dotted with grass-filled vacant sites that lie between Rusholme and my home, I was plagued by the question of whether I could find a way to generate enough income to pay off a loan big enough to buy Bill out while managing to remain personally solvent.

The key to that was to find a way to make the agency work more profitably. There was one obvious avenue that might prove lucrative, but I'd need an extra pair of hands. Back when I'd started working for Bill, I'd done bread-and-butter process-serving. Every week, I'd abandon the law library and turn up at the office, where Shelley would hand me a bundle of court papers that had to be served a.s.a.p.: Domestic-violence injunctions, writs and a whole range of documents relating to debt. My job was to track down the individuals concerned and make sure they were legally served with the court documents. Sometimes that was as straightforward as cycling to the address on the papers, ringing the doorbell and handing over the relevant bumf. Mostly, it wasn't. Mostly, it involved a lot of nosing about, asking questions of former colleagues, neighbours, drinking cronies and lovers. Sometimes it got heavy, especially when I was trying to serve injunctions on men who had been persistently violent to wives who took out injunctions one week and were terrorized, bullied, sweet-talked or guilt-tripped into taking their battering men back the next. The sort of men who see women as sexually available punchbags don't usually take kindly to being served papers by a teenager who barely comes up to their elbow.

In spite of the aggravation, I'd really got into the work. I'd loved the challenge of tracking down people who didn't want to be found. I'd enjoyed outwitting men who thought that because they were bigger and stronger than me, they weren't going to accept service. I can't say I took any pleasure slapping some of the debtors with bankruptcy papers when all they were guilty of was believing the propaganda of the Thatcher years, but even that was instructive. It gave me a far sharper awareness of real life than any of my fellow law students. So I'd quit to work for Bill full time as soon as the opportunity arose.

But I hadn't joined the agency to be a process-server. In the medium to long term, Bill wanted a partner and he was prepared to train me to do everything he could do. I learned about surveillance, working undercover, doing things with computers that I didn't know were possible, security systems, white-collar crime, industrial sabotage and espionage, and subterfuge. I learned how to use a video camera and how to bug, how to uncover bugs and how to take photographs in extreme conditions. I'd also picked up a few things that weren't on the syllabus, like kick boxing and lock picking.

Of course, as my skills grew, the range of jobs Bill was prepared to let me loose on expanded too. The end result of that was that we'd been content to let most of the process-serving fall into the laps of other agencies in the city. Maybe the time had come to snatch back that work for ourselves.

What I needed was a strategy and a body to serve the papers.

✧

Shelley sipped her glass of white wine suspiciously, as if she were checking it for drugs, and glanced around her with the concentration of a bailiff taking an inventory. She had only been in my house a couple of times before, since we tended to do our socializing on the neutral ground of bars and restaurants. That way, when Richard reached screaming point we could make our excuses and leave. It's not that he doesn't like Shelley's partner Ted, a former client who opted for a date with her instead of a discount for cash and ended up moving in. It's just that Ted has the conversational repertoire of a three-toed sloth and is about as quick on the uptake. Nice bloke, but . . .

"You can't stay out of the office forever," she said. A woman who's never been afraid to state the obvious, is Shelley.

"Call it preventative medicine. I'm trying to get a plan in place before I have to confront Bill," I said. "At the moment, every time I'm within three yards of him, I feel an overwhelming desire to cave his head in, and I don't fancy spending the next twenty years in prison. Besides, I do have some cases that I'm working on." I picked up the microcassette recorder on the table and flipped the cassette out of it. "I dictated some reports this afternoon. That brings me up to date. I've included the new client details."

Shelley leaned across and picked up the tape. "So why am I here? I don't guess it's because you couldn't go without my company for a whole day."

I explained my idea about generating more income by reclaiming process-serving work. Shelley listened, a frown pulling her eyebrows closer together. "How are you going to get the business? All the solicitors who used to put the work our way have switched to somebody else, and presumably they're satisfied with the service they're getting."

This was the bit I was slightly embarrassed about. I leaned back and looked at the ceiling. "I thought I could do a Charlie's Angel and try some personal visits."

I risked a look. Shelley had a face like thunder. Jasper Charles runs one of the city's biggest firms of criminal solicitors. The primary qualification for employment as a clerk or legal executive there is having terrific tits and long legs. The key role of these women, known in legal circles as Charlie's Angels, is to generate more business for the firm. Every day, one or more of the Angels will visit remand clients in prison, often for the slenderest of reasons. They'll get the business out of the way then sit and chat to the prisoner for another half-hour or so. All the other prisoners who are having visits from their briefs see these gorgeous women fawning all over their mates, and a significant proportion of them sack their current lawyers and shift their business to Jasper Charles. Every woman brief in Manchester hates them. "You've done some cheesy things in your time, Kate, but this is about as low as it gets," she eventually said.

"I know. But it'll work. That's the depressing thing."

"So you go out and prostitute yourself and you snatch back all this business. How you going to find the time to do it?"

"I'm not."

Shelley's head tipped to one side. Unconsciously, she drew herself in and away from me. "Oh no," she said, shaking her head vigorously. "Oh no."

"Why not? You'd be great. You're the biggest no-shit I know."

"Absolutely not. There isn't enough money printed yet to make me want to do that. Know what you're good at and stick to it, that's my motto, and what I'm good at is running that office and keeping you in line." She slammed her drink down on the table so hard that the wine lurched in the glass like the contents of a drunk's stomach.

So far, it was going just like I'd expected it to. "OK," I said with a small sigh. "I just thought I'd give you first refusal. So you won't mind me hiring someone else to do it?"

"Can we afford it?" was her only concern.

"We can if we do it on piecework, same as Bill did with me."

Shelley nodded slowly and picked up her glass again. "Plenty of students out there hungry for a bit extra."

"Tell me about it," I said. "Actually, I've got someone provisionally lined up."

"You never did hang about," Shelley said drily. "How did you find somebody so fast? How d'you know they're going to be able to cut it?"

I couldn't keep the grin from my face. Any minute now, there was going to be the kind of explosion that Saddam could have used to win the Gulf War if there had been a way of harnessing it. "I think he'll fit in just fine," I told her. "You know how wary I am of involving strangers in the business, but this guy is almost like one of the family." I got up and opened the door into the hall. "You can come through now," I called in the direction of the spare room that doubles as my home office.

He had to stoop slightly to clear the lintel. Six feet and three inches of lithe muscle, the kind you get not from pumping iron but from actually exercising. Lycra cycling trousers that revealed a lunchbox like Linford's and quads to match, topped with a baggy plaid shirt. He moved lightly down the hall, his Air Nikes barely making a sound. I stepped back to let him precede me into the living room and put my fingers in my ears.

"Donovan? What you doing here?" Shelley's thunderous roar penetrated my defences, no messing. The volume she can produce from her slight frame is a direct contradiction of the laws of physics. Don half turned towards me, his face pleading for help.

"I've hired him to do our process-serving, as and when we need him. We pay him a flat fee of—"

"No way," Shelley yelled. "This boy has a career in front of him. He is going to be an engineer. Not a private eye. No child of mine. No way."

"I quite agree, Shelley. He's not going to be a private eye—"

"You're damn right he's not," she interrupted.

"He's not going to be a private eye, any more than students who work in Burger King three nights a week are going to be stuffing Whoppers for the rest of their working lives. All he's doing is a bit of work on the side to relieve the financial pressures on his hardworking single mother. Because that's the kind of lad he is," I said quietly.

"She's right, Mam," Don rumbled. "I don't wanna do what she does. I just wanna make some readies, right? I don't wanna ponce off you all the time, OK?" He looked as if he was going to burst into tears. So much for muscle man. Forget valets; no man is a hero to his mother.

"He's not a kid any more," I said gently. For a long moment, mother and son stared at each other. Hardest thing in the world, letting kids go. This was worse than the first day at school, though. There was nothing familiar or safe about the world she was releasing him into.

Shelley pursed her lips. "About time you started acting like a man and took some of the responsibility for putting food on the table," she said, trying to disguise the pain of loss with sternness. "And if it stops you wasting your time with that band of no-good losers that call themselves musicians, so much the better. But all you do is serve papers, you hear me, Donovan?"

Don nodded. "I hear you, Mam. Like I said, I don't want to do what she does, right?"

"And you don't neglect your studies either, you hear?"

"I won't. I *want* to be an engineer, OK?"

"Why don't you two discuss the details on the way home?" I inserted tactfully. I had the feeling it was going to take a while for the pair of them to be reconciled at any level beyond the purely superficial, and I had a life to get on with.

≈❖≈

When I said "life," I'd been using the term loosely, I decided as I tagged on to the tail end of a bunch of girl Goths and scowled my way past the door security. If this was life, it only had a marginal edge on the alternative. Garibaldi's was currently the boss night spot in Manchester. According to the *Evening Chronicle*'s yoof correspondent, it had just edged past the Hacienda in the trendiness stakes with the acquisition of Shabba Pilot, the hottest DJ in the north. In keeping with its status, the door crew were all wearing headsets with radio mikes. They're supposed to make them look high tech and in control; I can never see them without remembering all those old black-and-white movies where little old dears ran old-fashioned telephone exchanges and eavesdropped on all the calls.

I'd dressed for the occasion. I couldn't manage the paper white, hollow-eyed *Interview with the Vampire* look adopted by the serious fashion victims, not without a minor concussion. So I'd opted for the hard-case pretentious-philosopher image. Timberland boots, blue jeans, unbleached cotton T-shirt that told the world that Manchester was the Ur-city, and a leather jacket with the collar turned up. Plus, of course, a pair of fake Ray-Bans, courtesy of Dennis's brother Nick. The look got me past the door no bother and didn't earn me a second glance as I walked into the main part of the club.

Garibaldi's belongs to a guy called Devlin. I've never met anybody who knows what his other name is. Just Devlin. He materialized in Manchester in the late seventies with a Cumbrian accent and more money than even the resident gangsters dared question. He started small, buying a couple of clubs that had less life in them than the average geriatric ward. He spent enough on the interior, the music and the celebs who could be bought for a case of champagne to turn the clubs into money machines. Since then Devlin has bought up every ailing joint that's come on the market. Now he owns half a dozen pubs, a couple of restaurants known more for their clientele than their cuisine, and four city-centre clubs.

Garibaldi's was the latest. The building used to be a warehouse. It sat right on the canal, directly opposite the railway arches that raise Deansgate Station high above street level. When Devlin bought it, the interior was pretty bare. Devlin hired a designer who took Beaubourg as his inspiration. An inside-out Beaubourg. Big, multi-coloured drainage pipes curved and wove throughout the building, iron stairs like fire escapes led to iron galleries and walkways suspended above the dancers and drinkers. The joys of postmodernism.

I climbed up steps that vibrated to the beat of unidentifiable, repetitive dance music. At the second level, I made my way along a gallery that seemed to sway under my feet like a suspension footbridge. It was still early, so there weren't too many people around swigging designer beers from the bottle and dabbing whizz on their tongues. At the far end of the gallery, a rectangular structure jutted out thirty feet above the dance floor. It looked like a Portakabin on cantilevers. According to Dennis, this was the "office" of Denzel Williams, music promoter and, nominally, assistant manager of Garibaldi's.

I couldn't see much point in knocking, so I simply stuck my head round the door. I was looking at an anteroom that contained a pair of battered scarlet leather sofas and a scarred black ash dining table pushed against the wall with a couple of metal mesh chairs set at obviously accidental angles to it. The walls were papered with gig posters. In the far wall, there was another door. I let the door close behind me and instantly the noise level dropped enough for me to decide to knock on the inner door.

"Who is it?" I heard.

I pushed the door open. The noise of the music dropped further, and so did the temperature, thanks to an air-conditioning unit that grunted in the side wall. The man behind the cheap wood-grain desk stared at me with no great interest. "Who are you?" he demanded, the strong Welsh vowels immediately obvious. Call me a racist, but when it comes to the Welsh, I immediately summon my irregular verb theory of life. In this instance, it goes, "I have considered opinions; you are prejudiced; he/she is a raging bigot." And in my considered opinion, the Welsh are a humourless, clannish bunch whose contribution to the sum total of human happiness is on the negative side of the ledger. The last time I said that to a Welshman, he replied, "But what about Max Boyce?" QED.

I had the feeling just by looking at him that Denzel Williams wasn't going to redeem my opinion of his fellow countrymen. He was in his middle thirties, and none of the deep lines that scored his narrow face had been put there by laughter. His curly brown hair was fast losing the battle with his forehead and the moustache he'd carefully spread across as much of his face

as possible couldn't hide a narrow-lipped mouth that clamped
meanly shut between sentences. "Do I know you?" he said when
I failed to reply before sitting in one of the creaky wicker chairs
that faced his desk.

"I'm a friend of Dennis O'Brien's," I said. "He suggested
I talk to you."

He snorted. "Anybody could say that right now."

"You mean because he's inside and it's not easy to check
me out? You're right. So either I am a genuine friend of Dennis's or else I'm a fake who knows enough to mention the right
name. You choose."

He looked at me uncertainly, slate-grey eyes narrowing
as he weighed up the odds. If I was telling the truth and he
booted me out, then when Dennis came out, Williams might
be eating through a straw for a few weeks. Hedging his bets,
he finally said, "So what is it you want? I may as well tell you
now, if you're fronting a band, you're about ten years too old."

I'd already had a very bad week. And if there's one thing
that really winds me up, it's bad manners. I looked around the
shabby room. The money he'd spent on that mandarin-collared
linen suit would probably have bought the office furnishings
three times over. The only thing that looked remotely valuable
in any sense was the big tank of tropical fish facing Williams. I
stood up and felt in my pocket for my Swiss Army knife. As I
turned away from him and appeared to be making for the door,
I flipped the big blade open, sidestepped and picked up the loose
loop of flex that fed power to the tank. Without a heater and
oxygenation, the fish wouldn't last too long. Tipped on to the
floor, they'd have an even shorter life span.

I turned and gave him my nastiest grin. "One wrong move
and the fish get it," I snarled, loving every terrible B-movie
moment of it. I saw his hand twitch towards the underside of
his desk and grinned even wider. "Go on, punk," I said, all
banzai Clint Eastwood. "Hit the panic button. Make my day."

16

I wouldn't have hurt the fish. I knew that, but Denzel Williams didn't. "For fuck's sake!" he yelled, starting up from his seat.

"Sit down and chill out," I growled. "I only wanted to ask you a couple of questions, but you had to get smart, didn't you?"

He subsided into his chair and scowled at me. "Who the fuck are you? Who sent you here?"

"Nobody sent me. Nobody *ever* sends me anywhere," I said. I was beginning to enjoy playing the bastard. I couldn't remember the last time I'd had so much fun. No point in lying, though. He could find out who I was easily enough if he cared enough to make trouble later. "The name's Brannigan. Kate Brannigan. I'm a private eye."

He looked shaken but not stirred. "And what do you think you're going to see here?" he sneered.

I shook my head wonderingly. "I can't believe Dennis said you were worth talking to. I've met coppers with better manners."

The reminder of who had recommended Williams to me worked wonders. He swallowed his surliness and said, "OK, OK, ask your questions, but don't piss about. I've got some people coming shortly, see?"

I saw only too well. Threatening the fish might hold Williams at bay, but it would cut no ice with his sidekicks. He'd

also be very unhappy at anybody else witnessing his humiliation. Held to ransom by a midget with a Swiss Army knife.
Regretfully I waved my posturing farewell and cut to the chase.
"Flyposting," I said. "My client's been having some problems.
Obviously nobody likes admitting they're being had over, but
somebody is definitely taking liberties. All I'm trying to do is
to check out whether this is a personal vendetta or if everybody
in the business is feeling the same pain."

"Who's your client, then?"

"Dream on, Denzel. Just a simple yes or no. Has anybody
been papering over your fly posters? Has anybody been fucking with your venues? Has anybody been screwing up gigs for
your bands?"

"What if they have?" he demanded.

"If they have, Denzel, you just got lucky, because you will
reap the benefit of the work I'm doing without having to part
with a single shilling. All I'm concerned about is finding out
who is pouring sugar in the petrol tank of my client's business,
and getting them to stop. Now, level with me before I decide
to have sushi for dinner. Have you been getting agg?"

"There's been one or two incidents," he grudgingly
admitted.

"Like?"

He shrugged. "Yeah, some of my posters have been papered
over." He took a deep breath. He'd obviously decided that since
he'd started talking, he might as well spill the lot. Funny how
the ones that seem the hardest often turn out the gobbiest. "The
fresh paperwork has always been promoting out-of-town bands,
so I'm pretty sure it's a stranger who doesn't know the way things
work here. We've had one or two problems with tickets too.
Some of the agents that sell tickets for our gigs have had phone
calls saying the gig's a sellout, not to sell any more tickets. We've
even had some scumbag pretending to be me ringing up and
saying the gig was cancelled. It's got to be somebody from out
of town. Nobody else would dare to mess with me." His tone

of voice left me in no doubt that when he got his hands on the new kid in town, the guy would be sorry he'd been born.

"Where specifically?"

He rattled of a list of names and venues. I hoped I'd be able to remember them later, because I didn't have a spare hand for note taking. "Any ideas who's behind it?" I asked.

He gave me the look I suspected he normally reserved for traffic wardens who thought that giving him a ticket would discourage him from parking on double yellow lines. "If I had any ideas, do you think he'd still be out there walking around?"

Ignoring the sarcasm, I persisted. "Anybody else been hit that you know of?"

"Nobody's boasting about it. But I know Sean Costigan's taken worse shit than I have. The Crumpsall firm's been hit, so has Parrot Finnegan. And Joey di Salvo."

"Collar di Salvo's lad?" I asked, surprised. I hadn't known the family of the local godfather were involved in flyposting. Whoever was muscling in on the patch was treading on the kind of toes that hand out a proper kicking.

"That's right."

"That's serious."

"We're talking war," Williams said. He wasn't exaggerating. People who deprive the di Salvos of what they regard as their legitimate sources of income have an unfortunate habit of winding up silenced with extreme prejudice.

"So are you all supposed to take your bats and balls and go home? Does the new team expect everybody to back down so they can pick up the business?"

Williams shrugged. "Who knows? But some of the boys that put the nod-and-a-wink record-company business our way are starting to get a bit cheesed off, see? They pay us to do a job and they're not too happy when their fancy posters get covered up the night after they've appeared. And one or two of the bigger managers are starting to mutter too. You're not the only one wanting to put a stop to this."

Before I could ask more, I heard the telltale sequence of sounds that revealed the outer door to the anteroom opening and closing. I dropped the electric cable and opened the office door. As I walked swiftly past a trio of sharp-suited youths who looked like flyweight boxers, I heard Williams shouting, "Fucking stop her."

By the time they got their brains to connect with their legs, I was out the door and sprinting down the gallery, head down, tanking past the bodies leaning over the railings and surveying the dancers down below. I could feel the rhythmic thud of the pursuing feet cutting across the beat as I swung onto the stairs and hurtled down as fast as I could go.

I had the advantage. I was small enough to weave through the bodies on the stairs and landings. My pursuers had to shove curious people out of the way. By ground level, I was hidden from my followers by the turn of the stair. I slid into the press of bodies on the dance floor, pulling off my shades and my jacket. I squirmed through the dancers till I was at the heart of the movement, imitating their blank-eyed stares and twitching movements. I couldn't even glimpse the three toughs who had come after me. That meant they probably couldn't see me either. That was just the way I wanted to keep it.

☙❧

There was one salt-and-pepper chicken wing left. My heart said yes, my head said no. It would be a lot easier to enlist Richard's help if he wasn't harbouring a grudge. "There you go," I said, shoving the foil container towards him. There was none of that false politesse about Richard. No, "Oh no, I couldn't possibly." I filled my bowl with spicy vermicelli and added a crab cake wrapped in sesame seeds and a couple of Szechuan king prawns. "I was at Garibaldi's earlier on," I said casually.

Richard's teeth stopped their efficient stripping job. "For fun?" he asked incredulously.

"What do you think?"

"Not," he said with a grin.

"You'd be right. You know Denzel Williams?"

He went back to his chicken wing, sucking it noisily as he nodded. "I know the Weasel," he said eventually. "So called because of his ability to worm his way out of any deal going. Doesn't matter how tight you think you've got him tied up. Doesn't even matter if you've got your lawyer to draw up the paperwork. If Weasel Williams wants out, he'll get out."

"Does he do the business for his bands?"

Richard shrugged noncommittally, filling his bowl again. "I've not heard many complaints. He seems to have a deal going with Devlin—he does the flyposting for all of the man's venues, and he has a ticket agency going on the side as well. He bought a jobbing printer's last year, so now he prints all his own posters and a lot of the band merchandising as well. T-shirts, posters, programmes, flyers. And, of course, he manages bands as well. He's one of the serious players."

"He's been having a taste of the same agg as Dan and the boys."

Richard looked surprised. "Weasel has? You must be looking at some operator, then. With Devlin's muscle to call on, I can't see the Weasel taking it from some street punk."

"That's what I figured. I need to find out who is behind it, and I don't think Denzel Williams knows. But somebody must." There was a short silence while we ate and digested what we'd been saying. "I need your help, Richard," I said.

He stopped eating. He actually stopped eating to look at me and consider what I'd just said. When Richard and I first got together, we'd both been wary, like experimental mice who have learned that certain activities result in pain and damage. Somehow, we'd managed to build a relationship that felt equal. We gave each other space, neither preventing the other from doing the things we felt were important. It had taken real strength from both of us not to interfere with the other's life when we felt we knew better, but mostly we'd managed it. Then a year

before, I'd had to call in every favour anybody ever owed me
to get him out of jail. He'd been stripped of power, reliant on
me, my skills and my contacts. Since then, our relationship had
been off balance. His last attempt to square things between us
had nearly cost us the relationship and driven me into someone
else's arms. Maybe I finally had a real opportunity to let him
take the first step towards evening the scores. "What is it you
think I can do for you?" he asked, his voice giving nothing away.

"You know every body in the rock business in this town.
Half of them must owe you. I need you to call in a couple of
favours and get me some kind of a lead into who's pulling the
strings here."

He shrugged and started eating again. "If the Weasel doesn't
know, I don't know who will. He's got the best grapevine in
town."

"I can't believe it's better than yours," I said, meaning it.
"Besides, there must be people who wouldn't lose any sleep at
the thought of Devlin and the Weasel getting a hard time. They
might be keeping their mouths shut out of pure *Schadenfreude*."

"Or fear," Richard pointed out.

"Or fear. But they're not necessarily going to be afraid of
talking to you off the record, are they? If they trust you as much
as you seem to think, they'll have slipped you unattributable
stuff before without any comebacks. So they know in advance
that you're not going to drop them in the shit with the Weasel
or with Devlin himself."

Richard ran a hand along his jaw and I heard the faint
rasp of the day's stubble. Normally, it's a sound I find irresistibly
erotic, but for once it had no effect. There was too much going
on under the surface of this conversation.

"Sure, I've covered their backs before. But I've never asked
questions like this before. It's a bit different from getting the
latest goss on who's signing deals with whom. Nosing into stuff
like this is your business, not mine. If I put the word around that
I'm looking for info on the cowboy fly posters, I'm the one the

finger will point at when you clear up the shit. I need to keep people's confidence or I don't get the exclusive stories and if I don't get the stories, I don't eat."

"You think I don't understand about keeping contacts cultivated? Look, based on what I've dug up so far, I've drawn up a list of places and people who have been hit. You must know somebody on the list who trusts you enough to tell you what they know about who's behind this business." I took the paper out of my pocket, unfolded it and proffered it across the table. It was so tense between us that if a car had backfired outside, we'd both have hit the deck.

Without taking it from me, Richard read the list. He tapped one name with a chopstick. "Manassas. I've known the manager there for years. We were muckers in London together before we both came up here. Yeah, I could talk to him. He knows I won't drop him in it." He took a deep breath and let it out in a slow sigh. "OK, Brannigan, I'll talk to him tomorrow."

"I'll come along."

He scowled. "Don't you trust me? He's not going to open up if I've got company, you know."

"Of course I trust you. But I need to hear what he's got to say for myself. Like you said, these are my kind of questions, not yours. Treat me like a bimbo all you want, but you have to take me with you."

Richard looked at me for a long minute, then he nodded gravely. "OK. I'll be happy to help." He grinned and the tension dissipated so suddenly it was hard to believe how wound up we'd both been moments earlier.

"I appreciate it." I put down my bowl and chopsticks and leaned forward to kiss him deeply, running my hands up the insides of his thighs. For an unheard of second time in the same Chinese meal, Richard lost interest in food. This time, for rather longer.

Later, we lay, too comfortable to move from the sofa. I reached over and pulled the throw over our sweaty bodies so we wouldn't get chilled too soon. My head in the crook between Richard's strong shoulder and his jaw, I told him about my decision to hire Don and claw back enough process-serving business to keep him busy. I didn't mention the Charlie's Angels ploy; the moment was too sweet for that, and besides, one lecture a day is more than enough for me.

"Will that be enough?" Richard asked dubiously.

"No," I said. Sometimes I wish I didn't have such a strong streak of realism. There are times when it would be a blessing to be afflicted with blind optimism.

"So what are you going to do?" he asked, gently stroking my back to show there was nothing aggressive in the question.

"I'm not entirely sure yet," I admitted. "Hiring Don is just a starting point. What I'm really worried about is if Bill goes we're going to lose a lot of the computer-security business. He's spent a lot of time and energy playing games with the big boys to establish his credentials in the field of computer security. Now, when it comes to making your system secure in the first place, or tracking down the creeps who are trying to steal your secrets or your money via your computer, Mortensen and Brannigan is right up there alongside some of the really big companies," I said proudly.

"And that's all tied in to Bill's name, right?" Richard chipped in, shoving me back on track.

"Give the boy a coconut," I said. "Most of the people Bill deals with don't even know who Brannigan is. They're fully paid up members of the laddish tendency. Not the sort of men who are going to be convinced that a woman knows her RAM from her ROM."

"Least of all a cute redhead with the best legs in Manchester," Richard said, reaching round me to check the accuracy of his comment with the hand that wasn't holding me.

"So the problem is twofold," I continued, trying to ignore the sensations his touch was triggering off. "First, I don't have the credibility. Secondly, if I'm being brutally honest—"

"Be brutal, be brutal," Richard interrupted with a mock moan.

"—I don't have the expertise either," I said firmly, wriggling away from his wandering fingers.

"You could learn," he murmured, refusing to be evaded. "You're a very quick learner."

"Only when I'm motivated," I said sternly, squirming down and away. "I can't get excited enough to put in the hours it takes to develop the skills. And I haven't got the patience to devote days to finding a leak and plugging it."

"So don't. Do what you've done with Don. GSI."

"GSI?"

"Get somebody in."

"Like who?" I asked sarcastically. "People with those kind of skills don't grow on trees. If they're straight, they're already earning far more than I could afford to pay them. And if they're dark-side hackers, they don't want to do anything as straight as work for me."

"Set a thief to catch a thief, isn't that what they say? Didn't you mention that Telecom had just given Gizmo the 'Dear John' note?"

I could have kissed him. But frankly, he didn't need the encouragement.

17

Private eyes should have the same motto as boy scouts: "Be Prepared." If I had to pass on one secret to any aspiring PI, that's what it would be. With that in mind, I settled down in my half of the conservatory with breakfast and the printed version of Sarah Blackstone's case notes. I needed to look more closely at the idea of her former colleagues having a motive for murder. If I was going to grip them by the lapels of their lab coats, thrust them against the wall and apply the red-hot pincers to treasured parts of their anatomy, I wanted to be sure I was asking the right questions.

Armed with the background information I'd picked up from the boy wonder of St Mary's, this time I was able to make a lot more sense of what I was reading. And it was the kind of sense that made the hairs on the back of my neck stand up. I flicked back through the pages to check that I wasn't misunderstanding what I saw in front of me. But there was no mistake. If I'd been short of motives for Sarah Blackstone's murder before, I was awash with them now.

Women tend to assume that it's only male doctors who are sufficiently arrogant, overbearing and insensitive to ride roughshod over their patients' lives. Wrong. Overexposure to these charming traits during training obviously rubs off on a lot of the women who go the distance too. However pleasant, supportive and discreet Dr Blackstone might have appeared to the women who consulted her, it seemed they hadn't so much been patients as the subjects of her experiments. That was the message that came through loud and clear from her notes.

It wasn't enough for her that she'd been breaking new ground by performing miracles that women had never had the chance to experience before; she wanted a different kind of immortality. What her notes told me was that she'd been playing a kind of Russian roulette to achieve it. She had been harvesting her own eggs for as long as she'd been treating other women. The notes were there. She'd persuaded one of her colleagues to do the egg collection, on the basis that Sarah was going to donate the eggs to women who couldn't produce fertile ones of their own. I knew now from my own research that because of the courses of fertility drugs involved in producing half a dozen eggs at once, she'd only have been able to harvest her own eggs two or three times a year. But that had been enough. Although she couldn't use her own eggs exclusively in the mix, she had been including one of her own eggs with each couple's batch. She'd have been growing on four or five embryos for each couple, and returning three of them to the womb. For every woman she'd successfully impregnated, there was a one-in-four or -five chance that the baby was not the child of the mother and her partner. Instead, it would be the result of a genetic mixture from the mother and Sarah Blackstone. And Chris was pregnant.

It was a nightmare, and one that I absolutely couldn't share with my client. And if I couldn't tell my best friend, there was nobody else I could dump on either. Certainly not Richard. After the recent rockiness of our road, the last thing he needed to hear about was a testosterone-free tomorrow. But it wasn't just the implications for Chris's pregnancy that bothered me. It was the long-term dangers within the gene pool. Judging by what I knew from Alexis, a lot of lesbian mothers in Manchester formed a close-knit social group, for obvious reasons. Their kids played together, visited each other's houses, grew up together. Chances were by the time they were adults, two women making babies together would be accepted medical practice, not some hole-in-the-corner criminal activity. What would happen if a couple of those girls fell in love, decided they wanted to make babies and they were half-sisters because they'd both come from Sarah Blackstone's eggs? Either they'd find out in preliminary genetic tests or, even worse, they'd start a cycle of inbreeding whose consequences could poison the future for children not yet imagined, never mind conceived. It was a terrifying thought. But it didn't surprise me that it was a possibility on the horizon. When society sets things up so that the only way people can achieve their dreams is to go outside the law, it automatically loses any opportunity to control the chain reaction.

It was also an experiment that wasn't hard to unravel. Any of the couples who were looking at a child who didn't look a bit like either of them but had a striking resemblance to their doctor wasn't likely to be handing out the benefit of the doubt. It's not hard to have private DNA testing done these days, and at around five hundred pounds, not particularly expensive either, compared to the cost of IVF treatment and the expense of actually having a child. A few weeks and the couple would have their answer. And if the mother's partner wasn't the biological co-parent, you wouldn't have to be a contender on *Mastermind* to work out that the chances were that the other egg had come from the person most concerned with the procedure.

The more I found out, the more the idea of a random burglar sounded as likely as Barry Manilow duetting with Snoop Doggy Dog. Forget her colleagues in Leeds. They'd still be there tomorrow. Right now, I needed to check whether there was a murderer on my own doorstep.

⚜

Lesley Hilton was Sarah Blackstone's first experimental mother. According to the files, she lived with her partner on the edge of the Saddleworth Moor, where the red-brick terraced slopes of Oldham yield to the Yorkshire stone villas built by those of the Victorians who managed to get rich on the backs of the ones toiling in the humid spinning mills. It was far from the nearest address to me, but Lesley's daughter Coriander must be around eighteen months old by now, and if she was Blackstone's baby, it might be obvious. It was as good a place to start as any, and better than most.

The house was one of a group of three cottages set at the foot of a steep field where sheep did the job I'd have cheerfully paid a gardener to do. Anything's preferable to having a herd of wild animals at the back door. The original tawny colour of the stone was smudged with more than a century's worth of grime. So much for the clean country air. I yanked an old-fashioned bell pull and heard a disproportionately small tinkle.

The woman who opened the door looked like a social worker in her fisherman's smock, loose cotton trousers and the kind of sensible leather sandals that make Clarks Startrite look positively dashing. She was short and squarely built, with dark blonde hair cut spiky on top. She peered at me through granny glasses, her chubby face smiling tentatively. "Yes?" she said.

I'd been working on a decent cover story all the way out along the Oldham Road. What I had was pitifully thin, but it was going to have to do. "I wonder if you could spare me a few minutes?" I started. "This isn't easy to talk about on the doorstep, but it concerns a Dr Sarah Blackstone."

Either Lesley Hilton had never heard the name before, or she had more acting skills than a family outing of Redgraves. She looked blank and frowned. "Are you sure you've got the right house?"

"You are Lesley Hilton?"

She nodded, her head cocked in what I recognized as the classic pose of a mother listening for a toddler who is probably dismantling the TV set as we speak.

"I think you probably knew Dr Blackstone as Dr Helen Maitland," I said.

This time the name got a reaction. Her cheekbones bloomed scarlet and she stepped back involuntarily, the door starting to close. "I think you'd better go," she said.

"I'm no threat to you and Coriander. I'm not from the authorities, I swear," I pleaded, fishing out a card that simply said "Kate Brannigan, Confidential Consultant," with the office address and phone number. I gave her the card. "Look, it's important that we talk. Dr Blackstone or Dr Maitland, whatever you prefer to call her, is dead and I'm trying to—"

The door closed, shutting off the expression of panic that had gripped Lesley Hilton's features. Cursing myself for my clumsiness, I walked back to my car. At least I hadn't blown it with someone who knew that Dr Helen Maitland was really Sarah Blackstone. I'd have put money on that. And if she wasn't aware of that, chances were she hadn't killed her.

❧

I fared better with Jude Webster, another of the early births. According to the files, she'd been a self-employed PR copywriter when she became pregnant. Judging by the word processor whose screen glowed on the table next to the pack of disposable nappies, she was still trying to earn some money that way. She had glossy chestnut hair which, considering the depth of the lines round her eyes, owed more to the bottle than to nature. Even though little Leonie was at the child minder, the buttons on Jude's cardigan had been done up in a hurry and didn't match the appropriate buttonholes, but I didn't feel it would help our rapport if I pointed that out.

The news of Sarah Blackstone's real identity and her death had got me across the threshold. I hadn't even needed a business card. Maybe she assumed I was another of the lesbian mothers come to bring the bad news. "I'm sorry," she now said, settling me down with the best cup of tea I'd had in weeks. "I didn't catch your connection to Dr Maitland . . . Dr Blackstone, I mean."

Time for the likeliest story since Mary told Joseph it was God's. "As you know," I started, "Sarah was a real pioneer in her field. I'm representing women who are concerned that her death doesn't mean the end of her work. What we're trying to do is to put together a sort of case book that those who follow in her footsteps will be able to refer to. But we want it to be more than just her case notes. It's an important piece of lesbian history. The experience of the women who led the way mustn't be lost."

Jude was nodding sympathetically. She was going for it, all the way. Pity she had acted totally blankly when I'd first mentioned the name Sarah Blackstone. "You're so right," she said earnestly. "So much of women's achievements and contributions just get buried because the books are written by men. It's vital that we reclaim our history. But—"

"I know, you're concerned about confidentiality," I cut in. "And let me tell you, I can fully appreciate why. Obviously, the last thing my clients want is for people's privacy to be compromised, especially in circumstances like these. It wouldn't serve anyone's interests for that to happen. But I can assure you that there will be nothing in the finished material to identify any of the mothers or the children."

We danced around the issue of confidentiality for a bit, then she capitulated. My Granny Brannigan always remarked that I had an honest face. She said it made up for my devious soul. Within an hour, Jude had told me everything there was to tell about the consultations that she and her partner Sue had had with Dr Blackstone. And it was all a complete waste of time. The first two minutes with the photograph album revealed a child that was the image of Sue, right down to an irrepressible cowlick above the right eye that wouldn't lie down and die. This time, Sarah Blackstone had missed.

By late afternoon, I knew the laws of probability had been on the doctor's side. But then, aren't they always? Ask anybody who's ever tried to sue a surgeon. At least two of the kids I'd seen bore more than a passing resemblance to the dead doctor. I was astonished the parents didn't seem to notice. I suppose people have always looked at their children and seen what they wanted to see. Otherwise there would be even more divorces than there are already.

At ten to five, I decided to hit one more and then call it a day. Jan Parrish and Mary Delaney lived less than a mile away from me in a red-brick semi on what had once been one of the city's smarter council housing estates. When the Tories had introduced a right-to-buy scheme so loaded with inducements that anyone in employment would have had to be crazy to say no, this estate had fallen like a line of dominoes. Now finding a resident who still paid rent to the council was harder than finding food in Richard's fridge.

Porches, car ports and new front doors had sprouted rampantly with no regard to any of their neighbours, each excrescence an indicator of private ownership, like a dog pissing on its own gatepost. Jan and Mary were among the more restrained; their porch was a simple red-brick and glass affair that actually looked as if it were part of the house rather than bolted on as a sad afterthought. I rang the bell and waited.

The woman who answered the door had an unruly mop of flaming red hair. It matched perfectly the small girl wrestling for freedom on her hip. I went through the familiar routine. When I got to the part where I revealed the doctor's real identity, Jan Parrish looked appalled. "Oh my God," she breathed. "Oh my God."

It was the first time I'd struck anything other than cracked plastic with that line. And that was even before I'd told her Sarah Blackstone was dead. "It doesn't get any better," I said, not sure quite how to capitalize on her state. "I'm afraid she's dead. Murdered, in fact."

I thought she was going to drop the baby. The child took the opportunity to abseil down her mother's body and stumble uncertainly towards me. I moved in front of her, legs together and bent at the knees like a hockey goalkeeper, and blocked her escape route. Jan picked her up without seeming to be aware of it and stepped back. "You'd better come in," she said.

The living room was chaos. If I'd ever considered motherhood for more than the duration of a movie, that living room would have put me off for life. It made Richard's mess look structured. And this woman was a qualified librarian, according to her medical record. Worrying. I shoved a pile of unironed washing to one end of a sofa and perched gingerly, carefully avoiding a damp patch that I didn't want to think too closely about. Jan deposited the child on the carpet and sat down heavily on a dining chair with a towel thrown over it. I was confused; I couldn't work out what Jan Parrish's excessive reaction to my exposure of her doctor's real identity meant. It didn't fit my expectation of how a killer would react. I couldn't see Jan Parrish as a killer, either. She didn't seem nearly organized enough. But she had been horrified and panicked by what I'd said and I needed to find out why. Playing for time, I gave her the rigmarole about lesbian history. She was too distracted to pay much attention. "I'm sorry it's been such a shock," I said finally, trying to get the conversation back on track.

"What? Oh yes, her being murdered. Yes, that's a shock, but it's the other thing that's thrown me. Her not being who she said she was. Oh my God, what have I done?"

That's exactly what I was wondering too. It wasn't that I was too polite to say so, only too cautious. "Whatever it was, I'm sure it had nothing to do with her death," I said soothingly.

Jan looked at me as if I was from the planet Out to Lunch. "Of course it didn't," she said, frowning in puzzlement. "I'm talking about blowing her cover with the letter."

I knew the meaning of every word, but the sentence failed to send messages from my ears to my brain. "I'm sorry . . . ?"

Jan Parrish shook her head as if it had just dawned on her that she had done something so stupid that even a drunken child of two and a half would have held fire. "We were all paranoid about security, for obvious reasons. Dr Maitland always impressed on us the importance of that. She told us never to write to her at the clinic, because she was afraid someone might open the letter by mistake. She said if we needed to contact her again, we should make an appointment through the clinic. But we were so thrilled about Siobhan. When she had her first birthday, we both decided we wanted Dr Maitland to know how successful she'd been. I'm a librarian, I'm back at work part time, so I looked her up in Black's. The *Medical Directory*, you know? And it said she was a consultant at St Hilda's in Leeds, so we sent her a letter with a photograph of Siobhan with the two of us and a lock of her hair, just as a sort of keepsake. But now you're telling me she wasn't Dr Maitland at all? That means I've exposed us all to a terrible risk!" Her voice rose in a wail and I thought she was going to burst into tears.

"When was this?" I asked.

"About three months ago," she said, momentarily distracted by Siobhan's sudden desire to commune with the mains electricity supply via a plug socket. She leapt to her feet and scooped up her daughter, returning her to the carpet but facing in the opposite direction. Showing all the stubbornness of toddlers everywhere, Siobhan immediately did a five-point turn and crawled back towards the skirting board. This time, I took a better look at her face. The hair might be Jan Parrish's but the shape of her face was unmistakable. I wondered whether Helen Maitland had also noticed.

"Well, if you haven't heard anything by now, I'd think you're all safe," I reassured her. "What did the letter actually say?"

She frowned. "I can't remember the exact wording, but something like, 'We'll never be able to thank you enough for Siobhan. You made a dream come true for us, that we could really share our own child.' Something along those lines."

"I wouldn't worry about it," I said. "That could mean anything. It certainly wouldn't make anyone jump to the conclusion that something so revolutionary was going on. And it doesn't give any clue as to who was actually treating you, does it? Unless the real Helen Maitland knew Sarah Blackstone was using her name, she's got no way of guessing. And if she did know, then presumably she was in on the secret too. I really don't think you should worry about it, honestly," I lied. I wanted to grab her by the shoulders and shake her for her stupidity. With a secret that held so much threat for her and her daughter, she should never have taken such an outrageous risk. Given that her mother faced a lifetime of discretion, I didn't like little Siobhan's chances of making it to adulthood without being taken into care and treated like an experimental animal in a lab. Instead, I made my excuses and left.

I hadn't found a serious suspect yet among the women who had been Sarah Blackstone's patients. I hoped I'd still be able to say that when I'd finished interviewing them. I cared far too much for Alexis and Chris to want to take responsibility for the hurricane of official and media attention that would sweep through their lives if I had to open that particular corner of Sarah Blackstone's life to public scrutiny.

Sometimes I think Alexis is psychic. I'd driven home thinking about her, and there she was on my doorstep. But it only took one glimpse of her face to realize she hadn't popped round to say how gratified she was at my concern for her. If looks could kill, I'd have been hanging in some psychopath's dungeon praying for the merciful end that death would bring.

18

Ask people what they think of when they hear the name "Liverpool" and they'll tell you first about the Scouse sense of humour, then about the city's violent image. Tonight, Alexis definitely wasn't seeing the funny side. I'd barely got out of my car before she was in my face, the three inches she has on me suddenly seeming a lot more. Her tempestuous bush of black hair rose round her head like Medusa on a bad hair day and her dark eyes stared angrily at me from under the lowering ledges of her brows. "What in the name of God are you playing at?" she demanded.

"Alexis, please stop shouting at me," I said quietly but firmly. "You know how it winds me up."

"Winds you up? Winds *you* up? You put me and Chris in jeopardy and you expect me to care about winding you up?" She was so close now I could feel the warmth of her breath on my mouth.

"We'll talk about it inside," I said. "And I mean talk, not shout." I ducked under the hand that was moving towards my shoulder, swivelled on the balls of my feet and walked smartly up the path. It was follow me or lose me.

Alexis was right behind me as I opened the inside door and marched into the kitchen. Mercifully, she was silent. Without asking, I headed for the fridge freezer and made us both stiff drinks. I pushed hers down the worktop towards her and after a long moment, she picked it up and took a deep swallow. "Can we start again?" I asked.

"I hired you to make some discreet inquiries and cover our backs, not stir up a hornet's nest," Alexis said, normal volume resumed.

"My professional opinion is that talking to other women in the same position as you is not exposing you to any danger, particularly since I have not identified you as my client to any of the women I have spoken to," I said formally, trying to take the heat out of the situation. I knew it was fear not fury that really lay behind her display. In her stressed-out place, I'd probably have behaved in exactly the same way, best friend or not. "I had a perfectly credible cover story."

"Yeah, I heard that load of toffee about lesbian history," Alexis said derisively, lighting a cigarette. She knows I hate smoking in my kitchen, but she clearly reckoned this was one time she was going to get away with it. "No flaming wonder you set off more alarm bells than all the burglars in Greater Manchester. It's not on, girl. I asked you to make sure we weren't going to be exposed because of Sarah Blackstone's murder. I didn't expect you to go round putting the fear of God into half the lesbian mothers in Manchester. What the hell did you think you were playing at?"

It was a good question, and one I didn't have an answer for yet. The one thing I knew for sure was that this wasn't the right time to tell Alexis that Sarah Blackstone had added her mystery ingredient to the primordial soup. I was far from certain there was ever going to be a right time, but I know a wrong one when I see it. "Who told you anyway?" I stalled.

"Jude Webster rang me. She assumed that because you had the names and addresses of all the women involved that you were kosher. But she thought she'd better warn me in case I didn't want Chris bothered in her condition. So what's the game?"

Inspiration had provided me with an attempt at an answer. "I wanted to make sure none of them knew Blackstone's real identity," I said. "If they had, they might have contacted her at her home under her real name, and there could be a record of that. A letter, an entry in an address book. I need to be certain that there isn't a chink in the armour that could lead the police back to this group of women if they get suspicious about the burglar theory and start routine background inquiries." I spread my hands in front of me and tried for wide-eyed innocence.

Alexis looked doubtful. "But they're not going to, are they? I've been keeping an eye on the local papers, and there's no sign the police are even thinking it might have been anything more than a burglary that went wrong. What makes you think it was?"

I shrugged. "If anybody she worked with had found out what she was up to, they had a great motive for getting rid of her. A scandal like this associated with the IVF unit at St Hilda's would have the place closed down overnight." This was thinner than Kate Moss, but given what I couldn't tell Alexis, it was the best I could do.

"Hey, I know it's hard getting a decent job these days, but I can't get my head round the idea of somebody knocking off a doctor just to avoid signing on," Alexis protested. Her anger had evaporated now I had anaesthetized her fears and her sense of humour had kicked in.

"Heat of the moment? She's arguing with somebody? They grab a knife?"

"I suppose," Alexis conceded. "OK, I accept you did what you did with the best of motives. Only it stops here, all right? No more terrorizing poor innocent women, all right?"

That's the trouble when friends become clients. You lose the power to ignore them.

⚜

Midnight, and we were arranged tastefully round the outer office of Mortensen and Brannigan. As soon as Richard had mentioned

the f-word to Tony Tambo, the manager of Manassas had insisted
that we meet somewhere nobody from clubland could possibly
see him talking to a woman who'd already been publicly asking
questions on the subject. Otherwise, flyposting was definitely off
the agenda. He'd vetoed a rendezvous in a Chinese restaurant,
a casino, an all-night caff in the industrial zone over in Trafford
Park and the motorway services area. Richard's house was off
limits because it was next door to mine. But the office was OK.
I couldn't work out the logic in that until Richard explained.

"Now they've converted the neighbouring building into
a student hall of residence, if anybody sees Tony coming out of
your building, they'll assume he's been having a leg-over with
some teenage raver," he said.

"And I bet he wouldn't mind that," I said drily.

"Show me a man over thirty who'd object to people making that assumption and I'll show you a liar," Richard replied
wistfully.

So we were sitting with the blinds drawn, the only light
coming from the standard lamp in the corner and Shelley's desk
lamp. Tony Tambo was hunched into one corner of the sofa,
somehow managing to make his six feet of muscles look half
their usual size. Although it was cold enough in the office for
me to have kept my jacket on, the slanting light revealed a sheen
of sweat on skin the colour of a cooked chestnut that covered
Tony's shaved skull. He was wearing immaculate taupe chinos,
black Wannabes, a black silk T-shirt that seemed moulded to his
pectorals and a beige jacket whose soft folds revealed it was made
of some mixture of natural materials like silk and cashmere.

It's a mystery to me, silk. For centuries it was a rare, exotic
fabric, worn only by the seriously rich. Then, almost overnight,
somewhere around 1992, it was everywhere. From Marks and
Spencer to market stalls, you couldn't get away from the stuff.
Kids on council estates living on benefits were suddenly wearing silk shirts. What I want to know is where it all came from.
Were the Chinese giving silkworms fertility drugs? Had they

been stockpiling it since the Boxer Rebellion? Or is there some deeper, darker secret lurking behind the silk explosion? And why does nobody know the answer? One of these days, I'm going to drive over to Macclesfield, grip the curator of the Silk Museum by the throat and demand an answer.

I was sitting in an armchair at right angles to the opposite end of the sofa from Tony. Richard was in Shelley's chair, his feet on the desk. The pool of light illuminated him to somewhere around mid-thigh, then he disappeared into darkness. The whole scenario looked like a straight lift from a bad French cop movie. I decided pretty quickly that there weren't going to be any subtitles to help me out. The questions were down to me.

"I really appreciate you talking to me, Tony," I said.

"Yeah, well," he mumbled. "I ain't said nothing yet. It's edgy out there right now, you know? Stability's gone, know what I mean? It's not a good time to stick your head above the parapet, people are too twitchy."

"Anything you tell me, nobody's going to know it came from you," I tried.

He snorted. "So you say. But if some bruiser's got you up against the wall, how do I know you ain't going to give him me?"

"You don't know for sure." I gestured round the office, which we've spent enough on to impress corporate clients. "But I didn't get a gaff like this by dropping people in the shit. Anyway, in my experience, if some bruiser's got you up against the wall, he's going to do what he's going to do. So there's not a lot of point in giving him any more bodies. It doesn't save you any grief."

He gave me a long, slow, head-to-toe look. "What's your interest?" he eventually said.

"I'm working for Dan Druff and the Scabby Heided Bairns." Sometimes you need to give a bit to get a lot.

"They got well unlucky," Tony observed.

"How do you mean? What have they done to deserve what they're getting?"

"Nothing. Like I said, they just got unlucky. Any war of attrition, somebody always has to be made an example of. To keep the rest in line. Dan and the Bairns just drew the short straw, that's all. Nothing personal. Least, I don't think it is. I haven't heard anything that says it is."

"So who's making the example of the boys?"

Tony took a packet of Camels out of his pocket and lit up without asking permission. I said nothing, but walked through into my office, took the saucer out from under a mother-in-law's tongue that wasn't ever going to dish out any more lip and pointedly slid it down the coffee table so it was in front of Tony. Richard took that as a sign and straightened up in the chair, using the desk top to roll a joint. Shelley was going to be well pleased in the morning to find tobacco shreds all over her paperwork. "So what's happening in the music business?" I asked, getting bored with all this mannered posturing we were playing at. "Who's making a bid for a piece of the action?"

"I don't think it's a piece of the action they want," Tony said in a sigh of smoke. "I think they want the lion's share."

"Tell me about it," I said.

"It started a couple of months ago. There was a wave of cowboy flyposting. Nobody seemed to know who was behind it. It wasn't the usual small-time gangsters trying to muscle in. So one or two of the major players decided to have a go at the bands and the venues who were having their posters put up by the cowboys. The intention was to find out who was behind it, but also to put the frighteners on the bands and the venues, so they'd come back to heel and abandon this new team."

Tony paused, staring into the middle distance. "So what happened?" I asked.

"They got a coating," he said simply.

"What happened?"

"They sent a team of enforcers along to one of the gigs. They found themselves staring down the barrels of half a dozen sawn-off shotguns. Not the kind of thing you argue with. So they went off to get tooled up themselves. By the time they came back, the Old Bill were waiting and the whole vanload got a nicking. And not a one of the door crew got lifted." Tony shook his head, as if he still couldn't quite comprehend it.

I was taken aback. I couldn't remember a time when Manchester villains had ever called the police in to sort out an internal matter. Whoever was trying for a takeover bid was so far outside the rules it must be impossible for the resident villains to know what the hell was coming round the next corner. "So what happened?" I asked.

"There were a lot of unhappy people around. I don't have to draw pictures, do I? So they decided they'd go down one of the venues mob-handed. Out of working hours, so the door crew wouldn't be around. They figured a good wrecking job would sort things out. They'd hardly got the door broken down when the Old Bill arrived even more mob-handed and nicked the fucking lot of them. They couldn't believe it. I mean, you're talking people who've got coppers on their teams. Where do you think they get the extra door muscle on Friday and Saturday nights? But there they were being faced down by a fucking busload of coppers in riot gear. You can't get that kind of a turnout when it all goes off in the Moss on a hot summer's night!" Tony crushed out his cigarette and pulled another one out of the pack.

"So, whoever is behind all of this has got a bit of pull?" It was more of a statement than a question.

"You could say that."

"Who is it, Tony?" I asked.

A drift of smoke from Richard's joint hid Tony's face for a moment. When it passed, his dark eyes met mine. I could see worry, but also a kind of calculation. I felt like I was being weighed in the balance. I'd wondered why Tony had agreed to talk to me. It hadn't seemed enough that he was an old mate of Richard's. Now I realized what the hidden agenda was. Like his buddies, Tony had been comfortable with the way things were run in the city. Like a lot of other people, he wasn't comfortable

with what was happening now. They'd tried to sort it out themselves in the conventional ways, and that hadn't worked. Now
Tony was wondering if he'd found a cleaner way of getting the
new team off the patch. "Somebody came to see me a couple
of weeks ago," he said obliquely. "A pair of somebodies, to be
precise. Very heavy-duty somebodies. They told me that if I
wanted Manassas to carry on being a successful club, I should
hand my promotions over to them. I told them I didn't negotiate
with messengers and that if they wanted my business, the boss
man had better get off his butt and talk face to face."

I nodded. I liked his style. It was a gamble, but he was on his
own turf, so it wasn't likely to have been too expensive. "And?"

"They went away. Two nights later, I was walking from
my car to my front door when three guys jumped me. They put
a sack over my head and threw me in the back of a van. They
drove me around for a while. Felt like we were going in circles.
Then they tipped me out in a warehouse. And I met the boss."

"Who is it, Tony?" I asked softly. He wasn't talking to me
any more. He was talking to himself.

"Peter Lovell. Detective Inspector Peter Lovell. Of the Vice
Squad. He's due to retire next year. So he's setting himself up
in business now to make sure he can replace all his backhanders
with a nice little earner."

There was a long pause. Then eventually I said, "What's
he like, this Lovell?"

"You ask the plod, they'll probably tell you he's a model
copper. He's got commendations, the lot. The top brass don't
want to know the truth, do they? Long as their cleanup rate looks
OK to the police committee, everything's hunky-dory. But this
Lovell, he's a real bastard. He's on the pad with all the serious
teams that really run the vice in this city. The faces behind the
class-act brothels, the boss porn men, the mucky-movie boys,
they're all paying Lovell's wages. But he makes it look good by
picking up plenty of the small fry. Street girls, rent boys, any
small-time operators that think they can live off the crumbs

from the top lads' tables. Whenever Lovell needs a good body, they're his for the taking, there to make him look like a hero in the *Chronicle*. But he never touches anybody serious." Tony's voice was bitter with contempt.

"What about his private life? He married?"

"Divorced. No kids."

"Girlfriend?"

Tony shook his head, his mouth twisting in a grimace. "Word is, he likes fresh meat. And his paymasters know it. Soon as they get some nice new recruit who's managed to avoid being raped, they give her to Lovell to break her in. Not too young, though. Not below about fourteen. He wouldn't like people to think he was a pervert." He spat out the word as if it tasted as unpleasant as Lovell himself.

I took a deep breath. It was going to be a real pleasure to nail this bastard. "How many people know he's the face behind the flyposting invasion?"

"Not many," Tony said. "It's not common knowledge, take it from me. One or two of the big players on the music scene, not more than that. That's the only reason there's not a war on the streets right now. They're keeping the lid on it, because as long as Lovell's still on the force, he can screw us all one way or another. But somebody's got to put a stop to him. Or else there's going to be blood and teeth on the floor."

I stood up. "I'm going to have to think about this, Tony," was all I said. We all knew what I meant.

He lit his cigarette and jammed it into the corner of his mouth. "Yeah," he muttered, unfolding his body from the sofa and making for the door.

"I'll be in touch," I said.

He jerked to a stop and half turned. "No way," he said. "You want to talk, get Richard to call me and we'll set something up. I don't want you anywhere near Manassas, you hear?"

I heard. He walked out the door and I moved over to the window, snapping the standard lamp off as I went. I pulled the blind back a couple of inches and gazed down three storeys to the shiny wet street below. A taxi sat at the traffic lights, its diesel ticking noisily above the background hum of the city. The lights changed and the taxi juddered off.

"I've never worked for gangsters before," I remarked as I watched Tony dodge out of the front door and double back past the student residence.

"It can't be that different. Some of your other clients have been just as dodgy, only they were wearing suits."

"There's one crucial difference," I said. "With straight clients, if you succeed, they pay. With gangsters, unless you succeed, *you* pay. I'm not sure I can afford the price."

Richard put an arm round my shoulders. "Better not fail then, Brannigan."

19

Even I don't know many people whose doors I can knock on just after one in the morning in the absolute certainty I won't be waking them up. But I didn't have any qualms about this particular door. I pressed the bell and waited, leaning up against the doorjamb to shelter from the persistent night rain.

After Tony had sloped off into the groovy world of nightclub Manchester, I'd felt too wired to go home to bed. Richard had tried to talk me into a Chinese followed by cool jazz in some Whalley Range cellar known only to a handful of the true faith. It hadn't been hard to say no. I've always thought jazz was for anoraks who think they're too intellectual for train spotting, and my stomach already felt like it had been stir-fried. Besides, I knew exactly how I could profitably fill the time till sleep ambushed me.

The door opened suddenly and, caught unawares, I tipped forward. I almost fell into Gizmo's arms. I don't know which of us was more appalled by the prospect, but we both jumped back like a pair of fifties teenagers doing the Bunny Hop. "You don't believe in office hours, do you?" Gizmo demanded belligerently.

"No more than you do. You going to let me in? It's pissing it down out here," I complained.

I followed him back upstairs to the computer room, where screens glowed softly in the dim interior and R.E.M. reminded me that nightswimming deserves a quiet night. "Tell me about it," I muttered, shaking the raindrops from my head well out of range of any hardware.

"Gimme a minute," he said. There were only two chairs in the room, both of them leather desk chairs. I sat in the one Gizmo wasn't occupying and waited patiently while he finished whatever he'd been in the middle of doing. After ten minutes, I began to wish I'd brought my own games software with me. I cleared my throat. "Be right there," he said. "This is crucial."

A few more minutes passed and I watched the headlights on Stockport Road sneak round the edge of the blinds and send slender beams across the ceiling, an activity that could give counting sheep a run for its money. Then Gizmo hit a bunch of keys, pushed his chair away from the desk and swivelled round to face me. He was wearing an elderly plaid dressing gown over jeans that were ripped from age not fashion and an unironed granddad shirt. Eat your heart out, corporate man. "Got some work for me, then?" he asked.

"Depends. You found another job yet?"

He snorted. "Come round to take the piss, have you? Like I said, Kate, I'm too old to be a wunderkind any more. Nobody believes in you if you're old enough to vote and shave unless your name's Bill Gates. No, I haven't got another job yet."

I took a deep breath. "You make a bit of money on the side, don't you? Doing bits and pieces for people like me?"

"Yeah, but not enough to support a habit like this," he said wryly, waving a hand round at the computers and their associated software and peripherals.

"But you're good at finding the weak points in systems and worming your way in, aren't you?"

He nodded. "You know I'm the best."

"How do you fancy working the other side of the street?"

He frowned suspiciously. "Meaning what, exactly?"

"Meaning going straight. At least in normal working hours. Meaning, coming to work for me."

"Thought you had a partner who did all the legit security stuff?" he demanded. "I don't want charity, you know. I either want a proper job or nothing."

"My partner is taking early retirement due to ill health," I said grimly.

"What's the matter with him?"

"Delusional psychosis. He thinks he's in love and wants to live in Australia."

Gizmo grinned. "Sounds like an accurate diagnosis to me. So what's the job description?"

"We do a lot of corporate computer security work, liaising with their software engineers and consultants to make their systems as unbeatable as we can get them. We also work with people whose systems have been breached, both plugging the holes and trying to track what's been raided and where it's gone. We've done a little bit of work with banks and insurance companies tracking money that's been stolen by breaching Electronic Fund Transfers. I know enough about it to pitch for the business, but not enough to do the work. That's where I'm going to need to replace Bill. Interested?"

He spun round on his chair a couple of times. "I think I might be," he said. "Are you talking a full-time job or ad hoc consultancy?"

"I'll be honest, Giz. Right now, I can't afford to take you on full time. Initially, it would have to be as and when I can bring the work in. But if you're as good as you say you are, we'll generate a lot of word-of-mouth business."

He nodded noncommittally. "When would you want me to start?"

"Mutually agreed date in the not-too-distant?"

"Dosh?"

"Fifty per cent of the net? Per job?"

"Gross."

I shook my head. "Net. I'm not a charity. Shelley has to put the pitch document together and she has to do all the admin. Her time comes off the fee. Plus phone expenses, faxes, photocopying. Most jobs, it's not big bucks. But sometimes it starts to run into money. Net or nothing."

"I can live with it. Net it is. Six-month trial, see how we both go on?"

"Suits me. There is one thing though, Giz . . . ?" His red-rimmed eyes narrowed in suspicion. "Well, two things," I continued. "A haircut and a smart suit." I held a hand up to stem the protest I knew was coming. "I know it breaks your heart to spend money on a suit that could be better spent on a new genlock adapter. And I know you think that anything more sophisticated than a number one all over once a year is for girlies, but these are deal breakers. If you like, I'll even come with you and make the process as painless as possible, but it's got to be done."

Gizmo breathed out heavily through his nose. "Fuck it, who do you think you are? I've managed to avoid that kind of shit working for Telecom, why should I do it for you?"

"Telecom have just fired you, Giz. Maybe corporate image had something to do with it, maybe not. Bottom line is, Telecom were a necessary evil for you. Working for me is going to be fun, and you know it. So get the haircut, get the suit."

He scowled like a small boy who's been told to wash behind his ears. "Yeah, well," he growled, scuffing his heels on the floor. "You drive a hard bargain."

I smiled sweetly. "You'll thank me for it one day. Let me know when you want to shop till you drop."

I walked downstairs alone, leaving Gizmo staring at a screen. I still didn't know where the money was going to come from to buy Bill out. But at least I was starting to feel like it might be possible for the agency to earn enough to pay it back.

Rasul and Lal's sandwich bar is one of Manchester's best kept secrets. Nestled under the railway arches at the trendy rather than the glossy end of Deansgate, it produces some of the finest butties in town. They like to name sandwiches after their regular customers, and I'm proud to reveal there's a Brannigan Butty up there on the board—tuna and spring onion in mayo with black olives and tomatoes in crusty French bread. Strictly speaking, it's a takeaway, but in the room behind the shop some of us get to perch and munch. I'm not sure of the criteria Rasul and Lal apply for admission to the back shop, but I've found myself sharing the privileged space with doctors, lawyers, Equal Opportunities Commission executives and TV technicians. The one thing we all have in common is that we're refugees, hiding from our lives for as long as it takes to scoff a sandwich and swallow a coffee.

When I arrived in the back shop the following morning, Della was already there. She'd opted for an egg mayonnaise sandwich. I was feeling less traditional, going for a paratha with a spicy omelette on top. There was no one else around apart from the brothers. There seldom is around ten, which was why I'd chosen it for our meeting. This was one time I absolutely didn't want to be seen publicly with Della.

We gave each other as much of a hug and kiss as our breakfasts would allow. She looked like she'd had more sleep than me, her skin glowing, her green eyes clear, copper hair pulled back into the kind of chignon that never stayed neat for more than five minutes on me when I had the hair for it. On Della, there wasn't a stray hair to be seen. I couldn't quite work out why, but Della was getting better looking with every passing year. Maybe it had something to do with cheekbones her whole body seemed to hang from. "Mysterious morning call," she remarked as we cosied up in the corner between the fridge and the back door.

"You'll understand why when I tell you what I've got for you."

"Goodies?" she inquired enthusiastically.

"Not so's you'd notice." I bit into my sandwich. Anything to postpone the moment when I delivered the bad news.

Realizing I needed to work up to this one, Della said, "We lifted your headstone con artists yesterday morning before their eyes were open. We'd fixed up an ID parade with some of the names you gave us, and we got enough positive identifications to persuade them that they might as well put their hands up and admit to the lot. Turns out they'd pulled the same routine in Birmingham and Plymouth before they turned up here. Nice work, Kate."

"Thanks. By the way, on the subject of those two, something occurred to me which you've probably thought of already."

"Mmm?"

"I was thinking about the business they're in. Mobile phones. I just wondered how straight the company is that they're working for. Given how many ways there are to make an illegal buck out of mobies, and given that this pair are cool as Ben and Jerry's in the way they operate, I wondered if it might be worth a poke about at Sell Phones."

"You know, that might not be such a bad idea. I was so busy with my own team this week, I never gave it a thought. But Allen and Sargent's arrest gives me the perfect excuse to get a search warrant on Sell Phones. Thanks for the thought," Della said, looking slightly embarrassed that she hadn't worked it out for herself. I knew just how she felt; I've been there too many times myself.

"No problem. However, I don't think you're going to be quite as thrilled about today's bulletin, somehow."

"Come on, get it over with. It can't be as bad as all that. The only news that deserves a face like yours is that Josh is a serial killer."

"What about a bent DI?" I said gloomily.

The smile vanished from Della's eyes. "I don't have to ask if you're sure, do I?"

"It's possible somebody's setting me up, but I don't think so. It fits the facts too well."

Della's mouth tightened into a grim line and she looked past me into the middle distance. "I absolutely hate corrupt police officers," she said bitterly. "They've always got some pathetic piece of self-justification, and it never ever justifies the damage they do. So, who are we talking about here? Just tell me it's not one of mine."

"It really isn't one of yours," I said, knowing it was pretty bleak as reassurances go. "It's a DI in Vice. Peter Lovell? Heard of him?"

Della's answer had to wait. Rasul came through to the fridge for another tray of sliced ham. "All right?" he asked cheerfully, far too polite to indicate that the expressions on our faces showed the exact opposite.

"Fine," we chorused.

When he'd left, Della said, "I know who you mean. I've never had anything to do with him directly, never met him socially, but I have heard the name. He's supposed to be a good copper. High body count, keeps his patch clean. What's the story?"

"I'm not too sure of the exact wording on the charge sheet, but it goes something like threatening behaviour, assault, illegal possession of firearms, conspiracy, incitement to cause an affray, obtaining money with menaces, improper use of police resources . . . Oh, and illegal billposting."

"If I didn't know you better, I'd say you were winding me up," Della said wearily. She looked at her half-eaten sandwich. "I just lost my appetite." She was about to bin it, but I stopped her. For some reason I was ravenous this morning. I had the last mouthful of my paratha and started on her leftovers. Ignoring every environmental health regulation from Brussels to Baltimore, Della pulled out her cigarettes and Zippo and sucked on a Silk Cut. "Details, then," she said.

Lal stuck his head round the door into the shop. "Can you crack the window if you're smoking, Del?" he asked. I was astonished. I'd never heard anyone contract Della's name and live. Not only did she ignore his liberty-taking, she even opened the window a couple of inches. Either Della was in a state of shock or there was something going on between her and Lal that I knew nothing about.

"It all started when Richard came home with Dan Druff and the Scabby Heided Bairns," I began. By the time I'd finished, Della looked like she was about to have a second close encounter with the half-sandwich she'd already eaten. "So right now, Lovell's winning," I finished up. "He's got the muscle to get what he wants, and the gangsters can't beat him the usual way because every time they make a move, their shock troops end up behind bars."

"I can't believe he'd be so stupid," she said. "He must be looking at having his thirty in when he retires. That's a good pension, and he's young enough to pull something decent in private security. And he's risking the lot."

I helped myself to a Kit Kat from an open box on a shelf behind me. "He's risking a hell of a lot more than that," I pointed out as I stripped the wrapper off. "He's risking his life. The people he's dealing with can't afford to lose that much face. If the normal ways of warning someone off aren't working with Lovell, somebody is going to shell out the requisite five grand."

"And then there *will* be a war. It doesn't matter how bent a bobby is, when he's dead, he's a hero. And when we lose one of our own, the police service doesn't stop till somebody has paid the price."

"I think they realize that," I said quietly. "They'll have to be desperate before they go for a hit. But every week that goes by where money goes into Lovell's pocket instead of theirs is a week when the ratchet gets screwed a notch tighter. I don't know how far away desperation is for the likes of Collar di Salvo's lad, but I know some of the other players are really hurting."

Della thumbed another cigarette out of the packet. "So Greater Manchester Police has to put a stop to Lovell on humanitarian grounds? Is that what you're saying?"

"Something like that. But I'm not talking GMP, I'm talking DCI Della Prentice and a small hand-picked team. If Lovell's been on the force this long, he must have a fair few in his corner, and I don't see how you can be sure who they all are. You need outsiders like you've got in the Regional Crime Squad."

Della did the time-wasting thing that smokers do to buy some space: fiddling with the cigarette, rolling the lighter round in her hand, examining the filter for holes. "So what do you suggest?" she asked.

"An undercover operation?"

"Nice of you to volunteer."

I shook my head. "No way. I'm not sticking my head above the trench on this one. Remember, I'm the one who doesn't believe in private health insurance, and the waiting list for key organ transplants is too long for my liking."

Della took another hit of nicotine then said, "Bottle gone?"

"Cheeky bastard," I growled. "My bottle's as sound as it's ever been."

"Really?" she drawled. God, I hate Oxbridge graduates. They learn that sarcastic drawl at their first tutorial and they never forget it. Those of us who grew up in the back streets shadowed by the dreaming spires never got past the snarl.

"Yeah, really," I snarled. "You're the police, it's your job to catch criminals, remember?"

"Problem is, you're not bringing me any hard evidence," Della said.

"So mount your own undercover operation. Leave me out of it."

"It's hard for us, Kate. We don't have any way into an undercover. We haven't got some tame club manager who's going to roll over and help us. And from what you've said, your contacts are not going to welcome Officer Dibble with open arms. They might well think it's better to deal with the devil they know. Whereas you . . ."

"Call yourself my friend, and you want me to go up against an animal like Lovell with his army of hard cases?"

Della shrugged. "You know you'll have all the backup you need. Besides, from what you tell me, there's been a lot of mouth but not a lot of serious action. Nobody's been killed, nobody's even had a serious going-over. Mr Lovell's merry men seem to specialize in violence against property. When it comes to sorting people out, he seems to go for remarkably law-abiding means. He calls the police. I think you'd be perfectly safe."

"Gee thanks," I said.

Della put a hand on my arm. Her eyes were serious. "I'm not asking you to do anything I wouldn't do myself. I'll hand-pick the backup team."

"You think that makes me feel any better? Everybody knows you're an even madder bastard than I am!" I pointed out bitterly, knowing I was beaten.

"So you'll do it?"

"I'll call you when I've got the setup sorted," I said resignedly. "I'm not a happy camper, I want you to know that."

"You won't regret this," Della said, pulling me into a hug.

"I better not."

Della paid for the Kit Kat on the way out.

＊＊＊

I thought it was about time I showed my face in the office lest Bill got to thinking he could start the revolution without me. With luck, he would still be busy showing Sheila the delights of the North West.

I don't know why I indulged myself with the notion that luck might be on my side. It had been out of my life so long I was beginning to think it had run off to sea. When I walked in Bill was sitting on Shelley's desk, going through a file with her. Given that I wasn't speaking to Bill and Shelley wasn't speaking to me, it looked like an interesting conversation might be on the cards. "Kate," Bill greeted me with a cheerful boom. "Great to see you." And I am Marie of Romania.

"Hi," I said to no one in particular. "Has anything come for me from the Land Registry?"

"If you checked your in-tray occasionally, you'd know, wouldn't you?" Shelley said acidly. It probably wasn't the time to tell her I'd gone through it at one that morning. Not if I wanted to keep my office manager.

"Have you thought any more about the implications of my move?" Bill asked anxiously.

I stopped midway to my office door, threw my hands up in mock amazement and said, "Oh dearie me, I *knew* there was something I was supposed to be thinking about. Silly me! It just slipped my mind." I cast my eyes up to the ceiling and marched into my office. "Of course I've bloody thought about it," I shouted as I closed the door firmly behind me. People who ask asinine questions should expect rude answers.

The letter from the Land Registry was sitting right on top of my in-tray. Their speed these days never ceases to amaze me. What I can't work out is why it still takes solicitors two months to convey a house from one owner to another. I flipped through the photocopied sheets of information that came with the covering letter. It confirmed the suspicion that had jumped up and down shouting, "See me, Mum, I'm dancing!" when I'd interviewed Helen Maitland.

I might have been warned off talking to Sarah Blackstone's former patients. But Alexis hadn't said anything about her former lover.

20

I'd gone into my first interview with the real Dr Helen Maitland without enough background information. I wasn't about to make the same mistake twice. After a late lunch in a Bradford curry café that cost less than a trip to McDonald's, I parked up in a street of back-to-back terraced houses that spilled down a hill on the fringe of the city centre. Half a dozen Asian lads and a couple of white ones were playing cricket on a scrap of waste ground where one of the houses had been demolished. When I didn't get out of the car at once, they stopped playing and stared curiously at me. I wasn't interesting enough to hold their attention for long, and they soon returned to their game.

I sat staring at a house halfway down the street. It looked well kempt, its garden free of weeds and its paintwork intact. It was a door I hadn't knocked on for a few years, and I had no idea what kind of welcome I'd get. Even so, it still felt like a more appealing prospect than quizzing Sarah Blackstone's medical colleagues. I'd first come here in search of a missing person. Not long after I'd found her, she ended up murdered, with her girlfriend the prime suspect. My inquiries had cleared the girlfriend, but in the process, I'd opened a lot of wounds. I hadn't spoken to Maggie Rossiter, the girlfriend, since the trial. But she was still on the office Christmas card list. Not because I ever expected her to put work our way, but because I'd liked her and hadn't been able to come up with a better way of saying so.

Maggie was a social worker and a volunteer worker at a local drug rehab unit, though you wouldn't suspect either role on first encounter. She could be prickly, sharp tongued and fierce. But I'd seen the other side. I'd seen her tenderness and her grief. Not everyone can forgive that sort of knowledge. I hoped Maggie was one who could.

I sat for the best part of an hour, listening to the rolling news programme on Radio Five Live to fight the boredom. Then an elderly blue Ford Escort with a red offside front wing drew up outside Maggie's house. As the car door opened, a small calico cat leapt from the garden to the wall to the pavement and wove itself round the legs of the woman who emerged. Maggie had had her curly salt-and-pepper hair cropped short at the back and sides, but otherwise she looked pretty much the same as when I'd seen her last, right down to the extra few pounds round the middle. She bent to scoop up the cat, draped it over her shoulder and took a briefcase and an armful of files out of the car. I watched her struggle into the house and gave it five more minutes.

One of my rules of private investigation is, always try to leave an interviewee happy enough that they'll talk to you a second time. I was about to find out how well I'd practised what I preached. When the door opened, hostility replaced interested curiosity so fast on Maggie's face that I wondered whether I'd imagined the first expression. "Well, well, well," she said. "If it isn't Kate Brannigan, girl detective. And whose life are you buggering up this week?"

"Hello, Maggie," I said. "I don't suppose you'd believe me if I said I was just passing?"

"Correct," she said sarcastically. "I'd also tell you that next time you're passing, just pass."

"I know you blame me for Moira's death . . ."

"Correct again. You going for three in a row?"

"If I hadn't brought her back, he'd just have hired somebody else. Probably somebody with even fewer scruples."

"It's hard to believe people with fewer scruples than you exist," Maggie said.

"Don't you ever listen to *Yesterday in Parliament?*"

In spite of herself, Maggie couldn't help cracking a smile. "Give me one good reason why I shouldn't close the door," she said.

"Lesbians will suffer?" I tried, a half-grin quirking my mouth.

"I don't think so," she sighed. The door started to close.

"I'm not joking, Maggie," I said desperately. "My client's a lesbian who could be facing worse than a murder charge if I don't get to the bottom of the case."

The door stopped moving. I'd hooked her, but she wasn't letting me reel her in too easily. "Worse than a murder charge?" she asked, her face suspicious.

"I'm talking about losing her child. And not for any of the conventional reasons."

Maggie shook her head and swung the door open. "This had better be good," she warned me.

I followed her indoors and aimed for a rocking chair that hadn't been there the last time I'd visited. The shelves of books, records and tapes looked the same. But she'd replaced the big Klimt with a blue-and-white print from Matisse's *Jazz* sequence. It made the room cooler and brighter. "I know I've got a cheek asking you for help, but I don't care how much I have to humiliate myself to do the business for my clients." I tried for the self-effacing look.

"Ain't too proud to beg, huh?" Maggie said sardonically.

"I'm hoping you won't make me. But I am going to have to ask you to promise me one thing."

"Which is?" she asked, sitting on the arm of the sofa, one foot on the seat, the other still on the floor.

"That you'll treat what I have to tell you with the same degree of confidence you'd offer to one of your own clients."

"If you want confidentiality, you can afford to pay a thera-pist for it. My clients don't have that option. But if that's the price for hearing this tale of yours, consider it paid. Nothing you tell me goes beyond these four walls, unless I think people are going to come to harm if I keep silence. Is that fair enough?"

"That'll do me. Did you know a doctor called Sarah Blackstone?"

The way her face closed down gave me the answer. "Tell me your tale. Then we'll see about questions," Maggie said, her voice harsh.

Time to rearrange the truth into a well-known phrase or saying. "My client and her partner were patients of Dr Blackstone. She was using them as human guinea pigs in an experiment to see if it's possible to make babies from two women. It is. And my client's partner is currently a couple of months pregnant." Maggie's attitude had melted like snow on a ceramic hob. She was staring at me with the amazement of a child who's just had Christmas explained to her. Then she remembered.

"But Sarah Blackstone's just been murdered," she breathed. "Oh my God."

"Exactly. Publicly, the police are saying she was killed by a burglar she disturbed. It's only a matter of time before the words 'drug-crazed' start showing up in their press briefings. My client is concerned that they have uncovered what Dr Blackstone was really doing, but they're keeping quiet about it while they carry out their investigations."

"So why are you here?"

Good question. This time, I'd had plenty of time to think about the interview so I had my lies ready. "I'm trying to get as much background on Sarah Blackstone as I possibly can. If there was more to her killing than meets the eye, I want to find out who was behind it. That way, I can hand the information to the police on a plate, which might stop any kind of investigation into what Sarah was really up to."

"Sounds plausible. But then, you always did," Maggie commented. She didn't appear to be overwhelmed with the desire to help me out.

"I don't have any contacts on the lesbian scene this side of the Pennines except you," I said. "Believe me, if there had been any other way of getting into this, I'd have gone for it. Being here under these circumstances probably thrills me about as much as it does you. But I need help, Maggie. If what Sarah Blackstone was doing gets into the public domain, there's going to be more than just an outcry. There's going to be a witch-hunt."

Maggie wasn't meeting my eyes. She looked like she was giving the matter serious thought and she didn't want to be distracted by any more passion from me. Eventually, she glanced across at me and said, "I might be able to help you with some aspects of your inquiry."

"Did you know Sarah Blackstone?"

Maggie shrugged. "Not well. We met through Women's Aid. I'm involved with the refuge in Leeds as well as the one here. Sarah used to run an informal clinic at the refuge in Leeds. She was also one of the doctors they call out to provide medical evidence when they get emergency admissions of women and children who have been badly beaten. We were both on the management committee up until a couple of years ago when Sarah resigned. She said she didn't have the time to give it the energy it demanded."

"What was she like?"

A smile ghosted on Maggie's face. "She was exhausting. One of those women who's always full of bounce, never doing anything by halves. Ambitious, clever, committed. She gave up a lot of her time for the causes she believed in. Passionate about the women she dealt with professionally. A great sense of humour. She could be a real clown sometimes."

"You make her sound like Mother Teresa."

Maggie gave a bark of laughter. "Sarah Blackstone? God, no. She had the faults to match her virtues. Like every doctor I've ever met, she was convinced she knew better than God.

She was stubborn, arrogant and sometimes flippant about things
that are never funny. And when she got a bee in her bonnet
about something, she wouldn't leave it alone until everybody
had agreed to go along with her ideas."

"Did you see much of her socially?"

"A bit. We'd end up at the same parties, barbecues, benefits,
you know the sort of thing."

Only by reputation, thank God. "Was she involved with
anyone when she died?" I asked. If Maggie was going to block
me, this was where it would start.

"I don't think so," Maggie said. She appeared to be sincere.
"The last relationship she was in ended round about the end
of last summer. The woman she was seeing, Diana, moved to
Exeter to start a new job, and there wasn't enough between them
for the relationship to survive. They'd been knocking around
together for the best part of a year, but not in a committed kind
of way. There was always something a bit aloof about Sarah, as
if she didn't want to let anyone too close."

"Did that include Helen Maitland?"

Maggie's eyebrows shot up. "That's been over for years.
How did you hear about Helen and Sarah?"

"Sarah used Helen's name as an alias. I wasn't sure whether
the connection between them went deeper than colleagues."
All perfectly truthful, as far as it went. There really wasn't any
need to tell Maggie that my suspicions had been confirmed by
the Land Registry. Before Helen Maitland's house had been
registered in her sole name, it had been jointly owned by Dr
Maitland and Dr Sarah Blackstone. I don't know many people
who buy houses with anyone other than their lover.

Maggie's mouth twisted into a rueful grimace. "And I just
told you it did, didn't I?"

"Well, I had my suspicions," I said. "What was the score
there?"

"Oh well, in for a penny . . . Let me see now . . . It must
be six or seven years ago that they first got together. Helen was

already in Leeds when Sarah arrived, and it was one of those thunderbolt things. I remember the night they met—it was at a Lesbian Line benefit. Somebody introduced them and they looked at each other like they both had concussion. They moved in together within a couple of weeks, and eventually bought a house together. Then it all fell apart."

"Why?"

Maggie squeezed the bridge of her nose between her thumb and forefinger, like a woman who's suddenly discovered she's got a sinus headache. "I had a lot on my mind," she said quietly. "It was around three years ago. Not a good time for me."

I stayed silent, remembering. It had been hard enough for me to accept Moira's death. For Maggie, it must have been a waking nightmare. I waited without impatience for her to fast forward from the worst days of her life. Some things even I'm sensitive to. After a few moments, she stopped massaging her forehead and tuned back in to the here and now. "I don't know if I ever knew the exact details, but I certainly don't remember them now. I've got a feeling it had something to do with Helen wanting kids and Sarah not. Whatever it was, it was serious. As far as I know, they never spoke again after the bust-up except through their lawyers. A mate of mine acted for Sarah and she said she'd never seen anything like it. It was as if they went from total love to total hatred overnight."

"That's interesting," I said, my brain working overtime. My first thought was that she'd got the bit about the kids the wrong way round. Then I thought about what it would mean if she hadn't.

Before I could pursue that line, Maggie shook her head wonderingly and said, "Oh, so that's what this is about, is it? Looking for a suitable dyke to replace your client on the suspect list?"

"You know I don't work like that. If I did, I'd have told the police about a certain incident three years ago . . ."

Her embarrassment was obvious even if it didn't stretch to an apology. "Yeah, well," she said. "Helen's not the type.

Believe me, I know her. She went out with my best mate for about a year not long after she came to Leeds. Anyway, Helen's had stuff to deal with in the last year that must have seemed a hell of a lot more significant to her than whatever Sarah Blackstone was up to."

"Like what?"

"Like cervical cancer. She had to have a complete hysterectomy. She's only been back at work for about three months."

I felt like a fruit machine with two lemons up and a fistful of nudges. "And has she been involved with anyone since Sarah?" I thought I knew the answer, but it's always worth checking.

"Oh yes," Maggie said. "She's got a girlfriend in York. Flora. A librarian at the university. Masses of black hair, like one of those Victorian maidens in distress."

"I think I've met her. Looks like she'd break if you spoke too loud?"

"You'd think so to see her doing that vulnerable innocent routine. But when you watch her in action, you soon see she's tough as old boots. If St George had rescued her from a dragon, he'd not have had her home long before he realized he'd spared the wrong one. And when it comes to Helen Maitland, that Flora's besotted. You could see from early on. Flora had Helen in her sights, and she was going to have her. A ruthless charm offensive, that's what it was. You never get the chance to get Helen on her own these days. Flora's never more than a heartbeat away."

"How long have they been together?"

Maggie frowned, trying to recall. "It's been a while now. Since before Helen was diagnosed. Mind, I get the impression that if it hadn't been for the cancer and the fact that she needed the emotional support, Helen would have dumped Flora a long time ago. You often see it in relationships—you get the one who worships and the one who's not much more than fond. Well, Helen's not the worshipper here. But she definitely wasn't hankering after Sarah, if that's what you're thinking. That relationship was dead and buried well before Sarah died," she added definitely.

Before I could say more, the front door opened and a tall woman in her twenties wearing an ambulance paramedic's uniform walked in. "Hi, hon," she said to Maggie, moving into the room and kissing the top of her head. She grinned at me. "Hi. We've not met."

"This is Amanda. She's the one who burns your Christmas cards," Maggie said drily.

The tall woman's face darkened in a scowl. "You're Kate Brannigan?" she demanded.

"That's me."

"My God," she said. "You've got a nerve. How dare you come round here hassling us! Haven't you done enough?" She took an involuntary step towards me.

I got to my feet. "It's probably time I was going," I said.

"You're not wrong," the paramedic snapped.

"It's all right, Mand," Maggie said, reaching out and touching her partner lightly on the hip. "I'll walk you to your car, Kate."

Amanda stood on the step watching us down the path. "She thinks you're the one who broke my heart," Maggie said as we walked up the hill towards my car. "I thought so too for a while. It took me about a year to realize I'd been idealizing Moira. She was a wonderful woman, but she wasn't really the fabulous creature I had constructed in my mind. If I'm brutally honest, I have to admit we'd never have gone the distance. There were too many things that separated us. But Amanda . . . With her, I do feel like I've got a future. So on the rare occasions when I remember you're on the planet, I don't think of you with anger. I think of you as the person who probably kept me out of prison so that I was free to meet Amanda."

We had reached my car. I held out a hand and we shook. "Thanks," I said.

"That's us quits now."

I watched her walk back down the pavement. She took the steps to her front door at a run and fell into the kind of hug that would have got her arrested twenty years before. I hoped I'd still be off her hate list by the end of this case.

⋰❖⋱

I walked up the wide path and stopped by the Egyptian temple, sitting down on a stone plinth between the paws of a sphinx. Over to one side, I could just see the columns of a Graeco-Roman temple, complete with enough angels for a barbershop quartet, if not a full heavenly choir. I leaned back and contemplated a Gothic spire like a scaled down version of Edinburgh's Scott Monument. The watery spring sunshine greened the grass up in sharp contrast to the granite and millstone grit. There's nothing quite like a Victorian cemetery for contemplation.

I didn't have to be back in Manchester until eight, and I needed a bit of space to think about the fragmented pieces of information I'd picked up about Sarah Blackstone's life and death. I'd persuaded myself without too much difficulty that I didn't really have enough time to nip over to Leeds and start interrogating the IVF-unit staff. Instead, Undercliffe Cemetery, out on the Otley Road, seemed the perfect answer, with its views across Bradford and its reminders of mortality. Surrounded by obelisks, crosses, giant urns, elaborately carved headstones and mock temples, thinking about death seemed the most natural thing in the world.

According to Alexis, the burglar who had allegedly been disturbed by Sarah Blackstone hadn't actually stolen anything. The only thing missing from the scene was the murder weapon, believed to be a kitchen knife. I found it hard to get my head around that. Even if he'd only just broken in when she walked in on him, there should have been some sign that a theft was in progress, even if it was only a gathering together of small, portable valuables. The other thing was the knife. If the murder weapon came from the kitchen, the reasonable burglar's response would be to drop it or even to leave it in the wound. That's because a burglar would be gloved up. A proper burglar wouldn't need to take the knife with him in case he'd left any forensic traces. Even the drug-crazed junkie burglar would have the sense to realize that taking the knife was a hell of a risk. It's harder to lose good-quality knives than most people think. They've got a way of getting themselves found sooner or later.

So if it wasn't a bona fide burglar, who was it? I shivered as a cold blast of moorland wind caught the back of my neck. I turned my collar up and hunched into the lee of the sphinx. Sarah Blackstone posed a risk to the future of her colleagues, there was no denying that. But the more I thought about it, the less likely it seemed that she'd been killed for that. Even if her secret had been discovered, presumably no one else was directly implicated. In spite of the truism that mud sticks, in my experience it dries pretty quickly and once it's been whitewashed over, nobody remembers it was ever there in the first place. So I could probably strike the angry/frightened colleagues.

There was no doubt in my mind that some of the babies Sarah Blackstone had made owed more to the doctor than the exercise of her skills. Her eggs had gone into the mix, and I had the evidence of my own eyes that she had cruelly duped some of her patients. Even though I'm a woman who'd rather breed ferrets than babies, I can imagine how devastating it would be to discover that a child you thought came equipped with half your genes was in fact the offspring of an egomaniac. I could imagine how Alexis would react if the child Chris was carrying was the result of so wicked a deception. It would be as well for Sarah Blackstone that she was already dead. So there was a group of women out there who, if they'd managed to put two and two together and unravel Sarah Blackstone's real identity, had an excellent motive for murder.

And then there was Helen Maitland.

21

The hardest part had been getting Tony Tambo to play. Briefing me was as far as he had wanted to go. Tony and his friends didn't mind pitting me against DI Lovell and his thugs, but they drew the line at taking too many risks themselves. I knew there was no point in simply phoning him and asking him to cooperate in a sting. What I needed was a pressure point. That's why I'd taken a trip to a certain Italian espresso bar before I'd gone to Bradford.

Every morning between eleven and twelve, Collar di Salvo sits in a booth at the rear of Carpaccio, just round the corner from the Crown Court building. Collar likes to think of himself as the Godfather of Manchester. In reality, the old man's probably got closer links to the media than the Mafia. Even though he was born in the old Tripe Colony in Miles Platting, Collar affects an Italian accent. He has legitimate businesses, but his real income comes from the wrong side of the law. Nothing heavy duty for Collar; a bit of what Manchester calls taxing and other, less subtle, cities call protection rackets; counterfeit leisurewear, mock auctions and ringing stolen cars are what keeps Mrs di Salvo in genuine Cartier jewellery and Marina Rinaldi clothes. And definitely no drugs.

The story goes that Collar got his nickname from his method of persuading rival taxation teams to find another way of earning a living. He'd put a dog collar round their neck, attach a leash to it and loop the leash over an overhead beam in his warehouse. Then a couple of his strong-arm boys would take the dog for a walk . . . History tells us that the competition took up alternative occupations in droves.

In recent years, with the rise of the drug lords, Collar's style of management and range of crimes has started to look like pretty small potatoes. But his is still a name that provokes second thoughts for anybody on the fringes of legality in Manchester. Given that young Joey, the heir apparent, was supposedly involved in the flyposting business, Collar seemed the obvious person to talk to. We'd never met and we owed each other no favours; but equally, I couldn't think of any reason why Collar wouldn't listen.

I walked confidently down the coffee bar and stopped opposite the old man's booth. "I'd like to buy you a coffee, Mr di Salvo," I said. He likes everyone around him to act like they're in a movie. It made me feel like an idiot, but that's not an unusual sensation in this job.

His large head was like the ruin of one of those Roman busts you see in museums, right down to the broken nose. Dark, liquid eyes like a spaniel with conjunctivitis looked me up and down. "Is-a my pleasure, Signorina Brannigan," he said with a stately nod. That he knew who I was simply confirmed everything I'd ever heard about him. The thug sitting opposite him slid out of the booth and moved to a table a few feet away.

I sat down. "Life treating you well?"

He shrugged like he was auditioning for Scorsese. "Apart from the tax man and the VAT man, I have no complaints."

"The family well?"

"Cosi, cosa."

Two double espressos arrived on the table, one in front of each of us. Never mind that I'd really wanted a cappuccino and a chunk of panettone. Fuelled by this much caffeine, I'd be flying to Bradford. "The matter I wanted to discuss with you concerns Joey," I said, reaching for the sugar bowl to compound the felony.

His head tilted to one side, revealing a fold of wrinkled chicken skin between his silk cravat and his shirt collar. "Go on," he said softly.

Joey was Collar's grandson and the apple of his beady eye. His father Marco had died in a high-speed car chase a dozen years ago. Now Joey was twenty, trying and failing to live up to the old man's expectations. The trouble with Joey was that temperamentally he took after his mother, a gentle Irish woman who had never quite recovered from the shock of discovering that the man she had agreed to marry was a gangster rather than a respectable second-hand car salesman. Joey had none of the di Salvo ruthlessness and all the Costello kindness. He was never going to make it as a villain, but his grandfather would have to be six feet under before Joey got the chance to find out what his real métier was. Until then, Collar was going to be faced with people like me bringing him the bad news.

"His flyposting business is suffering. I won't insult your intelligence by outlining the problem. I'm sure you know all about Detective Inspector Lovell. I'm sure you also know that conventional means of dealing with the problem are proving ineffective because of Lovell's access to law enforcement. Joey's difficulty happens to coincide with that of my client, and I'm offering to provide a solution that will make this whole thing go away." I stopped talking and took a sip of the lethal brew in my cup. My mouth felt sulphurous and dark, like the pits of hell.

"Very commendable," he said, one liver-spotted hand reaching inside his jacket and emerging with a cigar that could have done service as a pit prop, always supposing there were any pits left.

"I need your help to make it work," I continued as he chopped the end off his cigar and sucked indecently on it. "I need Tony Tambo's cooperation, and I don't have sufficient powers of persuasion to secure it."

"And you hope"—puff—"that in exchange"—puff—"for you getting Joey off the hook"—puff—"I will persuade Tony to help?"

"That's exactly right, Mr di Salvo."

"Why you want Tambo?"

"DI Lovell has been keeping a low profile. Not a lot of people know he's behind these attempts to take over the turf. But Tony's already had a face-to-face with him, so the man's got nothing to lose by coming in to a meeting. All Tony has to do is set it up. I'll do the rest. It's my head on the block, nobody else's."

Collar nodded. He closed his eyes momentarily. That didn't stop him abusing my air space with his cigar. His eyes opened and he stared into mine. Any more ham and he could have opened a deli counter. "You got it," he said. "Unless you hear otherwise, the meet will be at Tambo's club, half past eight, tonight. OK?"

"OK." I didn't want to ask how he was going to get it sorted that fast. To be honest, I didn't want to know. I stood up and was about to thank him when he said menacingly, "You don't like your coffee?"

I'd had enough of playing games. "It looks like sump oil and tastes worse," I said.

I thought he was going to bite the end off his cigar. Then he smiled, like a python who finds a dancing mouse too enter-taining to eat. I paid for both coffees on the way out, though. I'm not that daft.

⚜

Eight o'clock and Della Prentice had her hand down the front of my most audacious underwired bra. We were in an interview room at Bootle Street nick, and Della was making sure the radio mike was firmly anchored to the infrastructure of my cleavage. If Lovell paid the kind of attention to breasts that most Vice cops are prone to, I didn't want anything showing that shouldn't be. Nipples were one thing, radio mikes another altogether.

"Right," said Della. "He's not going to spot that unless things get rather more out of hand than we're anticipating." She stepped back and gave me the once-over. I'd gone for a shiny gun-metal Lycra leotard over black leggings and the black hockey boots I normally reserved for a bit of cat burglary. Draped over the leotard was an old denim jacket with slashed sleeves that revealed the temporary tattoos I'd got stencilled on both biceps. The make-up aimed for the recovering-junkie look; the hair was gelled into a glossy helmet. "Very tasteful," she commented.

"You can talk," I muttered. Della wore a white shirt with the collar turned up and the buttons undone almost as far as her navel. The shirt tucked into a black Lycra skirt a little wider than the average weightlifter's belt. Her legs were bare, her feet sensibly shod in flat-soled pumps. From her vantage point washing glasses behind the bar, no one would see more than the tarty top half and immediately dismiss her. With her hair loose and enough make-up to change the shape of eyes and mouth, Lovell was never going to recognize a woman DCI who might have been pointed out to him a couple of times across a crowded canteen. "Did you manage to pick up anything on the grapevine about Lovell?" I asked.

She pulled a face. "Not a lot. I didn't want word getting back to him that I was interested. I heard his wife divorced him because he was too handy with his fists, but that's hardly exceptional in the job. What I did find out, though, was that he claims to have a couple of weeks' time-share in a villa in Lanzarote. Very tasteful property up in the hills, swimming pool, terraced garden, half a dozen *en suite* bedrooms. A little bit of poking around and the calling in of a couple of favours reveals that the holding company that owns the villa is in turn wholly owned by Peter Lovell. Since the property's worth the thick end of quarter of a million, it does raise one or two questions about DI Lovell's finances."

"Nice one, Della," I said.

"That's not quite the end of it," she said as we walked up to the waiting car. "An old school friend of mine is married to a chap who manages one of the vineyards there, so I gave her a call. Her husband knows Lovell. Clothes by Versace, car by Ferrari, part owner of a restaurant, a bar and two discos in Puerto del Carmen," she said, her voice tight with anger.

"Obviously not the kind of life style one could sustain on a police pension."

"Quite. And about bloody time his gravy train hit the buffers. Let's go and make it happen."

The plan was simple enough. Della would be inside the club watching what was going down. Three of her most trusted lieutenants would be hidden within yards of the main bar where the meeting was scheduled for—two in the ladies' loo, one behind the DJ's setup. Another four hand-picked officers would be stationed outside the club, listening to the transmission from my radio mike. When they had enough on tape to hang Lovell out to dry, they would move in and relieve him of his liberty. A classic sting.

Considering Tony had only had eight hours to sort everything out, he'd come up with a credible cover story for me. I was the keyboard player in a new all-female band. We'd allegedly got together in Germany and we'd been touring in Europe, so successfully that we already had a recording contract with a small indie label in Hamburg. But we wanted more, so we'd come back to Britain to make a full-frontal assault on the music scene in a bid to get a major label contract. Because we were already fairly established, we didn't want to piss around. We wanted promotion, we wanted exposure. We wanted it fast and we wanted it top quality. And we'd told Tony Tambo we wanted to talk to the top man because we weren't going to waste time or money. Now I just had to pray that Lovell would give us enough to pull him on, or I was going to owe so many favours the only solution would be to leave town.

Thinking of favours reminded me of my grave robbers. "Did you turn over Sell Phones?" I asked.

Della nodded. "We sent a team in this morning. The shop was clean, but one of my bright boys noticed there was a trap door for a cellar. And lo and behold, there was a phone room down below."

"A phone room?"

Della raised her eyebrows. "You mean I've finally found a scam you haven't heard about?"

"Try me."

"OK. There's a little electronic box you can buy that allows you to eavesdrop on mobile phone calls. What it also tells you is the phone number of the mobile phone that's being used, and its electronic code number. With that information, you can reprogram the silicon chip in a stolen phone and turn it into a clone of a legitimate phone. You can then use that phone to call all over the world until the cellphone company cottons on and cuts you off. Normally, you can get a few hours' worth of calls, but if you're making international calls, sometimes they cut you off within the hour. So if you're cloning phones, you set aside a room with a dozen or so cloned phones in it, and hire the room out for, say, £20 per person per hour, and as soon as one phone gets cut off, the hirer just moves on to the next phone on the table. The hirer gets their calls dirt cheap and untraceable. And the crook's got virtually no outlay once they've got the original scanner and stolen phones."

"And you found one of these at Sell Phones?"

"We did."

"So I'm flavour of the month?"

"Let's see how tonight goes down."

At ten past eight, Della and I descended into the club via the fire escape, as I'd prearranged with Tony. He was waiting for us, nervously toking on his Camel. "Your friends got here," he said, his unease and resentment obvious.

"Where are we going to do this?" I asked.

Tony pointed to a small circular table in the far corner, surrounded on three sides by a banquette. "That's my table, everybody knows that. Anywhere else and he's going to be even more suspicious than he is already."

I followed him across the room while Della made for the bar and the dirty glasses stacked ready for her. The lights were up, stripping Manassas bare of any pretensions to glamour or cool. In the harsh light, the carpet looked stained and tacky, the furnishings cheap and chipped, the colours garish and grotesque. It was like seeing a torch singer in the harsh dressing-room lights before she's applied her stage make-up. The air smelled of stale sweat, smoke and spilled drink overlaid with a chemically floral fragrance that caught the throat like the rasp of cheap spirit.

Tony gestured for me to precede him into the booth. I shook my head. There was no way I was going to be sandwiched between him and Lovell. It wasn't beyond the bounds of possibility that I was about to become the victim of a classic double-cross, and if Tony Tambo had decided to hitch his wagon to the rising star rather than the comet starting to dip below the horizon, I wasn't about to make it any easier for him. "You go in first," I told him.

He scowled and muttered under his breath, but he did what he was told, slipping over upholstery cloth made smooth by hundreds of sliding buttocks. I perched right on the end of the seat, so Lovell wasn't going to be able to corner me without making a big issue of it. Tony pulled the heavy glass ashtray towards him. "I hope you know what you're doing," he said.

"So do I. Or we're all up shit creek."

"I fuckin' hate you women with the smart mouths, acting like you've got balls when all you've got is bullshit," he said bitterly, crushing out the remains of the cigarette with the sort of venom most people reserve for ex-lovers.

"You think I like hanging out with gangstas? Get real, Tony. It'll all be over soon, anyway."

He snorted. "So you say. Me, I think this'll be rumbling round for a long while yet." He leaned forward and shouted in Della's direction. "Hey, you!" Della looked up from the glass she was polishing. "Do something useful and bring me a fuckin' big Southern Comfort and lemonade."

Della's look would have shrivelled Priapus, but Tony was too tense to care. "You want the usual, Kate?" she asked me. I nodded.

The door at the far end of the club crashed open with the force that only a boot can produce. All three of us swung round, startled. In the doorway stood a tall, thin man dressed in the kind of warm-up suit top tennis players wear when arriving at Wimbledon. He was flanked by two men who could have played linebacker on an American football team without bothering with the body padding. Their shoulders were so wide they'd have had to enter my house sideways. They looked like they were built, not born, complete with suits cut so boxy they could have been constructed out of Lego.

The trio moved across the room at a measured pace and I had the chance to take a proper look at Peter Lovell. He had a narrow head with the regular features of a fifties matinée idol, an image nurtured by a head of thick brown hair swept straight back like Peter Firth's. It was an impression that crumbled at closer range, when skin wrecked by teenage acne became impossible to disguise or to deflect attention from. He stopped a few feet away from me, his minders closing ranks behind him. His eyes were like two granite pebbles, cold and grey as the North Sea in January. "Segue," he said contemptuously, his voice like hard soles on gravel. "What kind of a name is that?"

"It's Italian," I said. "It means 'it follows.' Which means my band is the next big thing, yeah?"

"That depends. And you're Cory?"

"That's right. Tony says you're the business when it comes to getting a band on the map."

Lovell slipped into the seat opposite me. "A brandy, Tony," he said. "Best you've got, there's a good lad."

"A large Hennessy over here, girl," Tony shouted. "What's keeping you?"

I didn't even glance at Della. "So what can you do for us, Mr . . . ?"

"My company's called Big Promo. You can call me Mr Big or Mr Promo, depending how friendly you want to be," he said without a hint of irony.

I acted like I was deeply unimpressed. "The question stands," I said. "We're really cooking in Europe, but this is where the serious deals get made. We want to be noticed, and we don't want to hang around. We don't want to be pissed about by somebody who doesn't really know what they're doing, who isn't up to playing with the big boys."

Something approaching a smile cracked his face. "Attitude, eh? Well, Cory, attitude is no bad thing in its place." Then he leaned forward and the smile died faster than a fly hitting a windscreen at ninety. "This is not the place. I'm not in the habit of dealing directly with people. It wastes time I could be using to make money. So the least, the very least, I demand from you is respect."

"Fine by me," I said. "So can we stop wasting your time? What can you do for us that makes you the one we should do business with?"

"Why don't you have a manager?" he demanded.

"We never found anybody we trusted enough. Believe it or not, I'm a qualified accountant. I can tell a good deal from a bad one."

"Then we're not going to have any problems. I'm offering the only good deal in town. This is my city. In exchange for forty per cent of your earnings, including any record deals you sign, I can place you in the key venues. I can make sure your tickets get sold, I can get you media coverage and I can paper the whole city with your tits." Lovell leaned back as Della approached with our drinks on a tray. Sensibly, she served Lovell first, then me, then Tony. As she walked away, Lovell said, "Since when did you start employing pensioners?"

"All she does is sort the glasses and stock the bar. She's out of here before the punters start coming in. The girlfriend's auntie," Tony said dismissively.

"I hear on the grapevine that there's been a bit of bother lately. Posters getting covered up, bands having their gigs wrecked, that kind of shit. What's to stop that happening to us?" I asked.

Lovell drummed his fingers on his brandy bowl. "Signing with us, that's what. You stupid cow, who do you think has been handing out the aggravation? I told you, this is my city. Anybody who thinks different has to take what's coming to them. You stick with me and nothing bad will happen to you. Ask Tony. He pays his taxes like a good 'un. You never have any bother, do you, Tone?"

"No," Tony said tonelessly, reaching for his cigarettes and lighting up. "No bother."

"Let me get this straight, then. You're saying if we pay you forty per cent of everything we make, you'll sort it for us. But if we choose somebody whose prices are more in line with the rest of the planet, we'll live to regret it? Is that what you're saying?"

Lovell picked up his glass and wasted the brandy in one swallow. "Sixty per cent of something's a lot better than a hundred per cent of fuck all. There's a lot of things can go wrong for a band trying to make a break in this town. Posters that never make it onto walls. Tickets that mysteriously don't sell. Riots at the few crappy gigs they manage to pick up. Vans full of gear burning up for no obvious reason."

"You saying that could happen to us if we don't sign up with you?"

He replaced the glass on the table with infinite care. "Not could. Will. It was you asked for this meeting," he reminded me, stabbing his finger towards the centre of my chest. "You need what I can do for you. Otherwise you might as well fuck off back to Germany."

I jerked back from his finger. I could relax now. Lovell had just nailed himself to the wall. "OK, OK," I said. "No reason why we can't do business. I was just checking."

Lovell got to his feet. "Well, you've done your checking and now you know what the score is. You don't ever get smart with me, bitch, you hear? I tell your poxy band where they play and when; you do no deals without consulting me first." He put a hand in his pocket and tossed a small mobile phone on the table. "Keep it on you. My number's programmed in at number one. That's the only number you call, you hear? I get any bills that say otherwise and you pay a service charge I guarantee you won't like. You can buy a charger unit anywhere that sells phones. I'll let you know when your first gig is."

Whatever he was going to say next was lost. The door to the club crashed open again and two men piled in, shouting, "Police. Don't move." The door to the ladies' toilet opened and the other two rushed into the room, heading for the minders. A fifth cop jumped over the DJ's turntables as Della ran out from behind the bar towards Lovell. Everybody was screaming, "Police. Don't move." The acoustics of the club had a strange effect on their voices, almost swallowing them in the vastness of the space.

Lovell's face went deep red from the neck up, like a glass filling with coloured liquid. "Fucking bitch," he yelled. "Let's get the fuck out of here."

But before he could go anywhere Della's sergeant, a rugby prop forward from Yorkshire, misjudged his run from the DJ's platform and cannoned into him. Seeing their boss floored and themselves outnumbered, the muscle decided that the game that had been keeping them in made-to-measure suits was over. Lovell was dead in the water. But that didn't mean Tweedledum and Tweedledee had to sink with him. In perfect sync, two right hands disappeared inside their jackets and emerged holding a matching pair of semiautomatic pistols.

Suddenly, everything went quiet.

22

It's not just the immediate prospect of being hanged that concentrates the mind wonderfully. Staring down the barrel of a gun does the trick just as well. For a long minute, nobody moved or said a word. Then Tweedledum gestured with his pistol towards Della. "You, bitch. Over here."

At first she didn't move. I knew what she was thinking. The more spread out we were, the harder it would be to keep us all covered. "I said, over here," the gunman screamed, dropping the nose of his pistol and firing. A chunk of wood from the dance floor leapt into the air inches from Della's feet and frisbeed away across the room. "Fucking do it," he shrieked. I've never understood why it is that the guys with the guns always sound more scared than those of us without them.

Slowly, cautiously, Della moved towards him. As soon as she came within reach, he pulled her to him by the hair, back against his chest, gun muzzle jammed into her neck. I knew then that these guys were the real thing. The neck is the professional's option. Much more sensible than holding it to the temple. The muzzle buries itself in the flesh of the neck rather than sliding on bone covered by sweating skin. Guns to temples are amateur city, a mark of someone who's watched more movies than they've committed crimes.

The man holding Della turned so that he and his companion were almost back to back. "Nobody fucking move," the other one screamed.

"Get this fucker off me," Lovell yelled.

"I said *nobody* fucking move, and that means you."

"You fucking *work* for me, shithead," Lovell screeched, his face purpling now with sheer rage.

"We just handed in our notice, OK?" the gunman shouted, his gun pointing at Lovell and the cop still sprawled on top of him. "OK, Let's go." He took a step backwards as his buddy moved forward. Awkwardly they made their way over to the fire exit. Given that only two cops had burst in the main door, I guessed that the remaining two men were outside the fire door. I sincerely hoped neither of them was the heroic type.

The gunmen had nearly made it to the fire door when Tony Tambo suddenly erupted into action. I don't know if he was playing at knights in shining armour or if it was just sheer rage at seeing his club abused like this, but he jumped up on the seat, ran straight across the table, leapt to the floor and went for the heavies. The one facing us didn't even pause for breath. He just let off two shots. The first caught Tony in the thigh, his leg bursting into shattered fragments of flesh and bone in a spray of blood. The second caught him in the abdomen as he fell, the exit wound bursting out of his back like someone had used a morphing program on his suit. His scream was like every nightmare you hope you'll never have. The groans that followed it weren't a whole lot better.

"I fucking warned you," the gunman shrieked, sounding like he was about to burst into tears. "Let's get the fuck out," he added.

His companion kicked the bar on the fire exit, which sprang open. I could just see the corner of the basement stairs that led up to the street. Then he shouted, "Get the fuck down here now, or the bitch gets it, you hear?" He stepped back, yanking Della with him. Nothing happened, so he sidestepped her, still holding her hair, leaned into the doorway and fired. I heard the singing whine of a ricochet against the stone walls of the stairway. Then he hauled Della in close again. "Get them down here," he snarled.

"Come down quietly," Della shouted. "That's an order."

By now, Tony had stopped groaning, so I was able to hear the sound of heavy feet on the steps. Two men edged through the door into the club. They followed the gestures of the man with Della and the gun and moved round the walls until they were almost parallel to Lovell and Della's sergeant. "OK. Nobody follow, you hear? Or the bitch dies," he screamed, rushing the door, followed by his companion.

As they disappeared, Lovell made a superhuman effort that caught the sergeant unawares. Suddenly he was wriggling free. I jumped onto the table and launched myself in a flying kick that would have got me suspended for life in any legitimate Thai boxing club. I hit Lovell in the side, and as we crashed to the ground together, I heard the satisfying crunch of snapping ribs and his simultaneous squeal of pain before the wind was completely knocked out of him. I rolled free and left him to Della's sergeant. I ran for the fire exit, along with one of the cops. The others were already out of the main door and heading for the street in a desperate bid to cut off the gunmen.

We reached the door at about the same moment the gunmen, slowed by an uncooperative Della, reached the street. With a roar that King Kong wouldn't have been ashamed of, the one trying to control her picked her up bodily and threw her down the flight of narrow stairs.

No amount of training in how to fall drills you for that sort of experience. Della tumbled down the steps in a loose ball, head defended by her forearms, bouncing off the walls. The cop and I stepped forward to break her fall. It was probably the worst thing we could have done. As she hit us, her leg shot out and snagged the wall. I heard the crack as bone snapped. Then we were a tumble of limbs. We settled with her face a couple of inches from mine.

"What a fuck-up," she breathed. Then she fainted. I managed to free one arm from under her in spite of the excruciating pain that ran like a flame up to my shoulder. When I saw the tattered sleeve of my jacket drenched in blood I fainted too.

～✦～

It had been a quiet night in Casualty until we hit the infirmary. Tony Tambo was on the critical list, having blood pumped into him and hanging on to life by sheer willpower, according to the nurse strapping up the wrist I'd merely sprained in the crush at the foot of the fire stairs. The blood had been Tony's. I'd landed in it when I'd rolled free of Lovell. Mr Big Promo was under arrest with four broken ribs and a collapsed lung, and I was half expecting one of Della's zealots to charge me with assault. Della herself had been sent down to the plaster room to have her ankle set and immobilized. The cop whom we'd both landed on was being kept in for observation with a double concussion, two unlovely black eyes and a missing front tooth. You couldn't get near the coffee machine in Reception for uniformed cops.

When the nurse had finished with the bandages, I walked down to the plaster room, taking it slowly to avoid jolting any part of my protesting body. I'd only just pushed the swing doors open when I heard a familiar Scouse accent. Alexis's cheerful raucousness was to my headache what Agent Orange is to house plants. Della's head swung round with all the belligerence of a punch-drunk boxer who's gone one round too many and we chorused, "Go *away*."

"Well, that's a charming way to greet your friends. Soon as the newsdesk hears there's a bit of a fracas involving DCI Prentice and a private eye called Brannigan, I say to them, 'I'll take care of this, the girls need to see a friendly face,'" Alexis said self-righteously.

"If you're here as a journalist, go away, Alexis," I said wearily. "If I said this has not been a good night, it would be the understatement of my life. Things have gone so wrong in the last hour that I'm desperate to hit somebody. Now, we might be in the right place for the aftermath of that sort of thing, but I really don't want it to happen to you."

"Me, I'd just settle for somebody to arrest," Della said, her voice sounding as emotionally exhausted as she had every right to feel. "So, as Kate said, Alexis the journalist can take a hike. Alexis the friend, however, is welcome to stay provided she has a set of wheels that can take us all home after this little fiasco has run its course."

"I'm sorry," I said.

Della shook her head. "It really wasn't your fault. I should have had the sense to realize he'd be walking around with armed minders. We should have let them all walk out of there then picked Lovell up in the middle of the night when he was on his own. I misjudged it."

That should have made me feel better. Instead, I felt infinitely worse. Della was on the point of being promoted to superintendent and an operation like this that could be painted as a screw-up wasn't going to help. Add to that the pariah status automatically granted to any police officer who puts other cops away, and it looked like my bright idea might have put Della's next promotion into cold storage. "You'd better come back and stay with me," I offered as the first stage in what was going to be a long apology. "You won't be able to manage the stairs at your place for a few days."

She nodded. "You're probably right. Won't Richard mind?"

"Only if you try to arrest him for possession."

Della managed a tired smile. "I think I can manage to restrain myself."

"So what actually happened?" Alexis chipped in, unable to restrain herself indefinitely.

"Gun battle in Manchester's clubland," I said. "Police officer held hostage. Man helping police with inquiries, two gunmen sought. Club owner seriously injured, two police officers with minor injuries. One private investigator who wasn't there."

Alexis grinned. "I hate it when you come home with half a tale."

⚜

Later, a lot later, when Della was asleep in my bed and Richard in his, I sat in the dark in the conservatory with a strong mixture of Smirnoff Black Label and freshly squeezed grapefruit juice and contemplated the capital D of the moon. Tony Tambo hadn't made it; one of Della's colleagues had rung to tell her not ten minutes after we got home. I sipped my drink and thought about how far reality had diverged from the simple little sting I'd envisaged. I'd gone in all gung ho and full of myself, and now a man was dead. He'd had a girlfriend and an ex-wife and a little daughter who was the apple of his eye, according to Richard. He wasn't supposed to behave like a hero, but then, I hadn't imagined there was going to be any need for heroics.

If my life was like the movies, my character would be planning vengeance, putting the word out in the underworld that she wanted those guys so bad she could taste it. And they would be delivered to her in such a way that she could decide their fate. But my life isn't like the movies. I knew I'd be doing nothing to discover the identities of the gunmen, where they hung out or who they ran with. That was the police's job, and I couldn't do it without placing more lives in danger. After what had happened to Tony Tambo, I was through with setting myself up against the major players.

I took a long cool swallow and tried not to think about Tony's daughter. Tried not to despise myself too much. Tried desperately to remember why I'd been working so hard to find a way to stay in this destructive game.

⚜

I woke around half past seven, just as the sun climbed over my back fence and hit the end of the wicker settee where I'd finally lost consciousness. I was still wearing the T-shirt and jogging

pants I'd put on after the shower I'd needed to get the last of
Tony Tambo's blood off me. If there's a female equivalent of
unshaven, I felt it. I rubbed the grit out of my eyes, wincing at
the arrow of pain in my left wrist, and stumbled through to the
kitchen. I was just filling the coffee maker with water when I
heard Della call me. "Be right there," I said, finishing the job.

Della was propped up on my pillows looking ten years older
than she had done the day before. According to my wardrobe
mirror, that still gave her a few on me. "How are you feeling?"
I asked.

"You see it all."

"That bad? Shit, I'd better take your shoelaces and belt
then."

Della reached out and limply patted my hand. "Do I smell
coffee?"

"You do. Life-support systems will be available shortly."

Ten minutes later, we were sharing the first pot of coffee of
the day. I even relaxed the house rules enough to let her smoke
in my bed. "What have you got on today?" she asked.

I shrugged. "I thought I might go down to the university
and see if I can sign up to finish my law degree this autumn."

Della was suddenly alert. "Part time?" she said suspiciously.

"Full time."

"Tony Tambo's death was not your fault," she said firmly.

"I know that. I just don't know if I want to do this job
any more. I didn't think it was going to be like this. Come to
that, it didn't use to be like this. I don't know if it's the world
that's turning nastier or if it's just that I've had a run of cheesy
luck, but some days I feel like there should be a task force of
counsellors, undertakers and paramedics in the car behind me."

Della shook her head, exasperated. "My God, you are feeling sorry for yourself this morning, aren't you? Listen, I'm the
one who screwed up royally last night. A man died, and other
people could have. The only way I could feel worse than I do
now is if it had been you lying there on the mortuary slab. I've

also probably kissed goodbye to my next promotion. But I'm not about to hand in my resignation. Even though I make mistakes, the police service needs people like me more than I need to gratify my guilt. I don't have to tell you about the dozens of sleazy, creepy exploitative PIs there are out there. Your business needs you, just like the police needs me. What about all the times when you've changed people's lives for the better? You got Richard out of jail, didn't you?"

"Yeah, but if it hadn't been for me, he wouldn't have been there in the first place," I reminded her.

"You've saved businesses from going down the tube because you've identified the people who were stealing their money and their ideas. You've done work that has helped to clear up major drug syndicates."

"Oh yeah? And that's really made a difference to the amount of drugs rattling around the streets of Manchester."

"What about that case you were working when I first met you? The land fraud? If it hadn't been for your work, Alexis and Chris would have been comprehensively ripped off and they wouldn't be living in their dream home now. You've made a real difference in their lives," Della insisted.

Her mention of Alexis and Chris reminded me forcibly of one job I still had to finish. Even if I was going to throw the towel in and sell my share of the business along with Bill, I couldn't walk away from Sarah Blackstone's murder.

When I failed to respond to Della, she gave my arm a gentle punch. "You see? It breaks my little police heart to say it, but this city needs people who don't carry a warrant card."

I swallowed my coffee. "You sound like Commissioner Gordon," I said acidly. "Della, I'm not Batman and this isn't Gotham City. Maybe I could make just as much difference as a lawyer. Maybe Ruth would take me on."

Della snorted. "Listen to yourself. You want to go from cutting the feet from under the villains to defending them? You couldn't be a criminal lawyer. It's not possible only to defend the innocent, and you know it."

"I sure as hell couldn't be a Crown Prosecutor either," I growled.

"I know you couldn't. It's just as impossible only to prosecute the guilty. The trouble with you, Kate, is you understand the moral ambiguity of real life. And you're lucky, because the job you do lets you exercise that. You decide who your clients will be. You decide to defend the innocent and nail the guilty. You're too moral to be a lawyer. You're a natural maverick. Exploit it, don't ignore it."

I sighed. Now I knew why Philip Marlowe didn't bother with buddies.

23

I'd got as far as Leeds before my determination ran out. It wasn't entirely my fault. Sherpa Tensing would have a job unravelling the roads in the centre of Leeds fast enough to take the right turning for the police admin building where I'd find the press officer I needed. Since I found myself inevitably heading for Skipton, I pulled off at Hyde Park Corner and killed some time with a decadent fruit shake in the radical chic Hepzi-bahz café while I reviewed where I was up to on the case that stood between me and a new life.

The more I looked at Sarah Blackstone, the more I grew convinced that this murder was about the personal, not the accidental or even the professional. Sure, one of her patients might have her suspicions about the biological co-parent of her daughter, but to confirm even that much wouldn't be easy for a lay person. And even if it were confirmed, it was still a long way from there to murder, given that her patients didn't even know her real name. Logically, if a patient had killed her, the body should have been in the Manchester clinic, not the Leeds house.

That thrust Helen Maitland into the position of front runner. I knew now that she had wanted a child but that Sarah Blackstone had refused her. God only knew why, given what she'd been doing for two of the three years since they split up. But since that separation, Helen had lost the capability to have children. If I'd learned one thing from Chris's relentless drive towards pregnancy, it was the overwhelming, obsessive power of a childless woman's desire for motherhood. Chris once described the feeling as possession. "It's there as soon as you wake up, and it's there until you go back to sleep," she'd explained. "Some nights, it even invades your dreams. Nothing matters except being pregnant. And it stops as soon as your body realizes it's pregnant. Like a weight lifting from your brain. Liberation."

If Helen Maitland had been feeling like that before her cancer was diagnosed, the arrival of a card from Jan Parrish with a photograph of a baby girl and a lock of silky hair must have seemed a grotesque gift, cruel and gratuitous and, at first glance, bewildering. But when she'd examined it more closely, she couldn't have failed to see the child's undoubted resemblance to Sarah Blackstone. Helen was nobody's fool. She must have known Sarah's work was at the leading edge of human fertility treatment. Seeing a photograph of a baby who looked so like Sarah must have set her wondering what her lover had done now, especially coming so soon after the final dashing of her own hopes.

For a doctor involved in research, tenacity is as necessary a virtue as it is in my job. Faced with a puzzle, Helen would not simply have shelved it any more than I would. Given her specialism in the area of cystic fibrosis, she would have routine access to DNA testing and to researchers working in the field. I knew it wasn't standard practice to obtain DNA from hair shafts—it's difficult, technically demanding and often a waste of time because the DNA it yields is too poor in quality to be meaningful. But I knew that it was possible. It was the sort of thing some eager-beaver researcher would doubtless be happy to do as a favour for a consultant. Having met Helen Maitland, I didn't doubt she could be both charming and terrifying enough to get it done.

Getting a comparison sample of Sarah's DNA wouldn't have been so difficult either—a couple of hairs from the collar of her lab coat would be enough, and probably easier than cut hair, since they would have the roots still attached. Checking the two DNA profiles against each other would tell Helen a truth that for her in particular was a stab to the heart.

Given her probably fragile state, who knew how she might react? She could easily have stormed round to Sarah's, determined to have it out with her ex-lover. It didn't take much to imagine a scenario ending in Sarah's heart pumping her blood out on to the kitchen floor instead of round her arterial system. Now I had two problems. The first was proving it.

The second was what I did with that proof.

≈❖≈

When the Yorkshire TV crowd started to pile in for lunch, the women in striped men's shirts and tailored jackets, the men in unstructured linen and silk, I decided it was time to go. I still had no idea how to deal with the second question, but it was academic if I couldn't answer the first.

This time, I decided to abandon the car in the Holiday Inn car park and make for the police station on foot. I hoped I wasn't going to be there long enough to be clamped. Just in case, I stuck my head into the restaurant, spotted a table where the half-dozen business lunchers included a couple of women. Then if I came back and the car was clamped, I could pitch the hotel into setting me free on the basis that I'd just had lunch, that table over there, no I didn't have the receipt because one of the others had paid for me. Usually works.

After I'd left Hepzi-bahz, I'd called ahead to warn the press officer I wanted to see not to go to lunch until I got there. At the front desk, I presented my official press card to the officer on duty, who gave it a cursory glance. It was, of course, a complete fake, based on a colour photocopy of Alexis's card plus a passport photograph of me, all shoved through the office laminating machine. Must have taken me all of ten minutes to cobble it together, and it would take close comparison with the real thing to tell the difference. I'd never try to get away with it in a police station in Manchester, where my face is too familiar to too many coppers, but over the Pennines it seemed a chance worth taking.

Ten minutes later, Jimmy Collier and I were nursing glasses in a busy pub which was a rarity in northern city centres in that it preferred customers to hear the sound of their voices rather than loud music. Jimmy was a dapper little man who could have been any age between thirty and fifty and dressed like he thought men's magazines had to have dirty pictures in them. He looked a bit like a penguin and walked like a duck, but there was nothing birdlike about the appetite with which he was attacking a cheese and onion barm that was approximately the size of a traditional Yorkshire flat cap. Along with his lunch, I fed him a story he swallowed as easily as the sandwich.

I told him I was working for one of the women's weekly magazines on a feature about burglary and home invasions. "What we want to do is give them a 'what you should do' guide, using real-life cases as an indicator of what you should and shouldn't do." I smiled brightly. "I thought the Sarah Blackstone murder was a perfect example of what you don't want the outcome to be," I added, letting the smile drop.

Collier nodded and mumbled something indecipherable. He swallowed, washed his mouthful down with a draught of Tetley, then said, "You're not kidding." It hardly seemed worth the wait.

"So . . . what can you tell me about this case?" I asked.

He wiped his mouth on the back of his hand. "Sarah Blackstone had been working late in the IVF laboratory at St Hilda's Infirmary. As far as we can ascertain, she left the hospital at around half past nine. At 10.27, we got a treble niner from a call box on the corner of her street. A woman who didn't give her name said she'd just been nearly knocked down by a black youth with what looked like a knife in his hand. He'd come running out of a house, leaving the door wide open. We took it seriously, because let's face it, between you and me, you don't get a lot of blacks living in a street like Pargeter Grove. We got there at 10.40, four minutes after the ambulance. Dr Blackstone was already dead. The knife had gone straight under her ribs and into her heart."

I took notes as he spoke. "And you reckon she disturbed a burglar?" I asked.

"That's right. A pane of glass in the back door was smashed. The key was in the lock. That's something to remind your readers about. Unbelievably stupid, but you'd be surprised how many people do that."

"I read that nothing appeared to have been stolen," I said.

"That's right. We reckon he'd just walked in the back door when she walked in the front. She were still wearing her mac. He didn't have time to do anything except strike out at her. I doubt he even had time to think about what he were doing, he just lunged at her. She was really unlucky. Not many stab wounds kill you as fast as that. When he saw what he'd done, he legged it empty-handed."

"Wasn't the house alarmed?"

"No, it was just a bit nervous!" He guffawed. I'd heard the riposte too many times to find it funny any more, but I smiled nevertheless. "She did have an alarm fitted," he continued. "But like a lot of people, I suppose she just left it switched off. People never think it's going to happen to them. You should stress that to your readers. If you've got an alarm fitted, never leave the house without setting it."

"Good point," I said appreciatively. He wasn't to know, after all, that Sarah Blackstone was so security conscious it bordered on the paranoid, and with good reason. Another argument against the random burglar. There was no way Sarah Blackstone would leave the alarm switched off. "This woman that phoned in—wasn't it a bit funny that she didn't give her name?" I asked.

He shook his head. "More often than not, they don't, around there," I deciphered through a mouthful of barm cake. "They don't want to get involved. Even when they're the only proper witness we've got. They don't want to have to miss work to come to court to give evidence, they're frightened that if they stick their necks out, it'll be their house the bad boys come to next. Far as they're concerned, their civic duty stops with the 999 call."

"That's your middle classes for you," I said.

"You're not wrong. Especially after the riots down Hyde Park. They're terrified of repercussions. We tell them they're safe to give evidence, but they don't believe us."

Neither did I. I'd heard too much about West Yorkshire Police. I know a woman whose house was being broken into by three teenagers with a sledgehammer in broad daylight. The next-door neighbour dialled 999 and the police arrived a full half-hour later, protesting that there wasn't a lot they could do since the burglars had already gone. I flicked back through my notes. "Fascinating case, this one. No forensic, I take it?"

"There are some indicators that the forensic team are working with," he said guardedly. "But they won't even tell me what they've got. All I know is that it's a bit of a struggle to make it look like one of the usual suspects." He winked.

"She took her time coming home from St Hilda's," I commented. "Can't be more than fifteen minutes' drive at that time of night."

"She'll have stopped off on her way home for a drink or fish and chips," he said confidently.

"Or popped round to see somebody who turned out not to be in," I suggested. "So you've no other eye witnesses except for the mystery caller?"

"That's right. It was chucking it down, so the usual dog walkers and drunks would have been head down and hurrying, that time of night. We were a bit surprised that no one saw him going over the back wall on his way in, since it's overlooked by the student residences, but we've not had a lot of luck all round with this one. Something else to tell your readers—set up a Neighbourhood Watch scheme if you want to cut down the risk of violent burglary in your street. It really works, according to our Community Security team."

"Community Security?"

He had the grace to look embarrassed. "What used to be called Crime Prevention," he admitted sheepishly.

Only it didn't. So in the same way that "closing hospital beds" became "care in the community," a quick name change had been necessary. I asked a few anodyne questions, bought Collier a second pint, then made my excuses and left before I had to watch him demolish a slice of Black Forest gateau about the same size as its namesake.

⚜

I sat on the top floor of the city art gallery under the huge Frank Brangwyn panels representing the horny-handed sons of toil of the industrial revolution, their bodies suspiciously like those of the desk-bound Stallone wannabes you see down every designer gym in the country. Today, though, I wasn't thinking about social change. I was staring at *The Rolling Mill* without seeing it. All I could see was the picture in my mind's eye of Helen Maitland's face, ugly with anger and pain as she lashed out at the woman she had once loved and who had deprived her of her dream of motherhood.

I had a pretty clear idea now what had happened. The results of DNA testing would have confirmed Helen's guess at what Sarah had been doing. This wasn't an experiment that had come out of nowhere; I could imagine the conversations as the lovers had snuggled together under the duvet, Sarah fantasizing about the day the technology would be there to make babies from two women, Helen dreaming of what it would mean to them, to her. But Sarah had refused, for whatever reason. And the refusal had driven a wedge so deeply between them that it was impossible to continue their relationship.

The scenario was as vivid as film to me. When she realized the truth, Helen must have gone round to confront Sarah. But Sarah hadn't been home. She'd been working late. I could picture Helen sitting in her car, impotent rage building like a bonfire. When Sarah had eventually arrived, Helen had probably been beyond rational conversation. She had insisted on being admitted and the two women had gone through to the kitchen. There, the argument had raged before Helen had snapped, seized a knife and thrust it deep into Sarah's body.

The act of murder must have sobered her. She'd had the sense to go to the back door and make it look like someone had broken in. If they'd had drinks, she had cleared glasses or cups. Then, making sure she was hidden by darkness, she'd slipped out of the house, back to her car, and driven to the phone box where she'd made the spurious 999 call.

It accounted for the awkward facts that spoke against it being a burglar. It covered the time gap between Sarah leaving the hospital and being found dead. It explained why the killer had taken the knife; she wouldn't have been wearing gloves and for her there was less risk in taking it home, sterilizing it and dumping it in her own cutlery drawer. She'd probably been bloodstained, but it had been raining that night and she'd likely been wearing a mac or raincoat that she could simply take off and dispose of later.

Helen Maitland had done a good job of covering her tracks. Lucky for her that West Yorkshire Police are crap. But if the police did start to take a serious interest in her rather than doggedly chasing their mystery burglar, there would be proof for the taking. A voice print of the 999 tape would match hers. A new mac would be another circumstantial nail in her coffin. And, of course, she'd have no alibi. They might be short on motive, but if they started to push Helen Maitland, the truth might pour out. If that happened, it was only a matter of time before they started knocking on Alexis and Chris's door. And that was what I'd been hired to prevent.

I sighed. It must have been louder than I thought, because the middle-aged attendant strolled casually into my line of vision, concern producing a pair of tram tracks between her eyebrows. "You all right, lovey?" she asked.

I nodded. "I'm fine. Just something I'm trying to work out."

She inclined her head. Now she understood. "We get a lot of that," she said. "Especially since Alan Bennett did that TV programme about the gallery."

Like a character in one of Bennett's screenplays, she walked on, nodding to herself, her shampoo-and-set hair as rigid as one of the Epstein busts next door. I roused myself and looked at my watch. Just gone four. Time to head for another confrontation. At least this time I could be fairly sure that I wouldn't end up staring down the barrel of a gun.

⋙❖⋘

I parked about fifty metres down the street from Helen Maitland's house and settled back to wait. By six o'clock, I knew the news headlines better than the newsreaders. Seven o'clock and I was expecting Godot along any minute. As the numbers on the clock headed towards 20.00 I decided I'd had enough. I needed to eat, and Bryan's was frying a haddock with my name on it not five minutes' drive away.

When I returned nearly an hour later, there were lights showing in Helen Maitland's house. When she opened the door to see me on her doorstep, she looked momentarily annoyed, then resigned. "The return of Sherlock Holmes," she said wryly.

"I have things to say you should listen to," I said.

Her eyebrows quirked. "And they say etiquette's dead. You'd better come in. Ms Branagh, wasn't it?"

"Brannigan," I corrected her as I followed her indoors. "Branagh's the actor. I do it for real." Sometimes I hear myself and think if I was a punter I'd laugh at me.

"Sorry, Ms *Brannigan*," Helen Maitland said. "Have a seat," she added as we arrived in the kitchen. I ignored her.

She leaned against the worktop, facing me, one hand absently stroking a tortoise-shell cat sprawled on the draining board. "Well, you have my undivided attention. I presume this is to do with Sarah?"

"I know you were lovers," I said bluntly. "I know you wanted children and she refused to go along with you. But after you split up, the technology was perfected that allowed Sarah to build babies from the eggs of two women rather than using sperm. But the immortality of being the first to do it wasn't enough for Sarah. She wanted her genes to carry on too. So she started mixing her own harvested eggs in with the patients'. And one of those patients was so grateful that she broke the injunction of secrecy and sent a photograph with a lock of hair to the doctor who'd helped her make her dream come true. To nice Dr Helen Maitland. How am I doing so far?"

Her face had remained impassive, but the hand stroking the cat had stopped, fur clenched between her fingers. She tried a smile that came out more like a snarl. "Badly. I don't have the faintest idea what you're talking about."

"Somewhere there will be a record of the DNA tests you ran on that lock of hair and on Sarah's DNA. You can't lose something like that. The police would have no trouble finding it. A lot of legwork, perhaps, but they'll get there in the end."

Her eyes were cautious now, watching me like a hawk's, hardly blinking. "I'm sorry, I must have missed a turning somewhere. How did we get to the police?"

"Don't, Dr Maitland. Neither of us is stupid, so stop acting like we both are. I can imagine how distressed you were when you discovered what Sarah was doing, especially after she had denied you the chance to be the first to try the treatment. Even more so since your own operation. You went round to see her, to confront her with the outrage she'd perpetrated against you. And she dismissed you, didn't she? She didn't take your emotions seriously, just like before when she'd dismissed your desires for motherhood."

Helen Maitland shook her head slowly from side to side. "I thought you said you were for real, Ms Brannigan. Sounds to me like you need treatment."

"I don't think so. I think you're the one with the problem, Dr Maitland. You might give the impression of being cool, smart and in control, and God knows, you're good at it. But then you'd have to be, to kill your ex-lover and get away with it."

She pushed off from the worktop and stood bristling at me, like one of her cats finding a strange tom on the front step. "You've gone too far. It's time you were leaving," she said, her voice low and thick with anger.

"I knew there was a temper lurking in there. It's the same temper that flared when you confronted Sarah and she dismissed your pain. It's the same temper that made you grab the nearest knife and thrust it under Sarah's ribs right into her heart."

"Get out," she said, anger and incredulity fighting in her. "I don't have to take this from you." She took a step towards me.

"You can't get away with it, Helen," I said, my hands coming up automatically, palms facing her. "Once the police start looking at you, they'll find the evidence. It's all there, once you accept that Sarah wasn't killed by a burglar. As soon as they match your voice against that 999 call, you're right there in the frame."

"That's not going to happen." The voice wasn't Helen Maitland's. It came from behind my right shoulder. I whirled round, straight into fighting stance, poised on the balls of my feet.

It was Flora. And in her hand was a shiny long-barrelled revolver.

24

Her small pale hands looked too fragile to wield a big cannon like that, but the barrel wasn't trembling. Whatever was driving Flora, it was powerful stuff. "Flora," Helen said calmly.

"It's all right, Helen," Flora said, not taking her eyes off me.

Not with me it wasn't. I'd had enough of people waving guns at me. And frankly, I didn't think Flora was in the same league as Peter Lovell's gunmen. I glanced over at Helen Maitland and let my jaw go slack.

"My God!" I exclaimed.

Out of the corner of my eye, I saw Flora's hand jerk as her eyes swivelled towards Helen. On the instant, I launched myself, right leg jabbing up and out at shoulder height, my own voice roaring in my ears like Bruce Willis on heat. Everything suddenly seemed to be in slo-mo: my foot connecting with her shoulder, Flora toppling towards the floor, her gun arm flying out to one side, her finger tightening on the trigger as I landed on top of her, my body tensing against the expected blast of the gunshot.

A tongue of flame spurted from the gun barrel, then died as Flora released her pressure on the trigger.

I'd been scared shitless by a cigarette lighter.

I'd been scared, no two ways about it. But now I was really, really cross. When I'd walked through the door, I'd been feeling sympathetic. My instincts had all been to find a way out of this situation that didn't mean Helen Maitland spending the rest of her useful life behind bars. Now I wasn't so sure that was what I wanted.

"That was really silly, Flo," Helen remarked in an offhand tone I'd never have been able to manage in the circumstances.

I disentangled myself from Flora's hair and limbs and pushed myself back to my feet. "It was a lot more than silly," I said. "For fuck's sake, I could have really hurt you, you pillock."

Flora threw the gun across the room. It clattered into the kitchen unit next to Helen. Then she curled up into a ball and burst into tears.

Helen picked up the lighter and laid it on the kitchen table, then moved to Flora's side. She crouched down and put her arms around her. It felt like Flora wept for a very long time, but it was less than five minutes by the kitchen clock. I didn't mind. It gave my heart time to return to its normal speed and rhythm.

Eventually Helen steered Flora into a kitchen chair and sat down beside her. "Even a real gun wouldn't stop the police running those voice comparisons," I said. "I'm not daft enough to embark on a confrontation like this without leaving a bit of insurance behind in case some idiot pulls some brainless stunt where I actually do get hurt."

"Then it's all over," Flora said dully.

"How can you say that?" Helen demanded, pulling away. "How can you think that I . . . That's crazy."

"It's not crazy, actually." Flora's voice was shaky. "You see, if the police did start to run comparisons on that 999 tape, they would find a match."

"Look, Flora, I don't know where you've got this idea from. I didn't kill Sarah," Helen protested. "I'm appalled you could think so."

"I *don't* think so. No one knows the truth better than me."

There was a silence as Helen and I digested the implications of Flora's words. Then the enormity of my second screw-up in two days hit me. I'd been right about the obsessive power of love being responsible for Sarah Blackstone's death. But I'd picked the wrong candidate for the killer. I'd been so convinced that Helen was the killer I hadn't even paid attention to Flora.

"Are you saying what I think you're saying?" Helen asked. There was an edge of horror in her voice.

"It was you, wasn't it?" I asked. Flora said nothing. She didn't have to. We both knew the truth now. "So tell me. Was I close? The scenario I painted? Was I on the right lines?"

Flora pushed her hair back with her free hand. "Why are you so keen to know the details? So you can run to the nearest police station and turn me in?"

I sighed. "The reason I became a private investigator was because I like to know the reasons why things happen. I understand the difference between the law and justice. I know that handing people over to the police isn't always the best way of ending things. If you want to prevent me going to the police, you've got more chance talking to me than you have trying to terrorize me. I have a client who has an interest in Sarah Blackstone's death. She has her own, very pressing, reasons for wanting to know the truth here."

While I had been speaking, Helen Maitland had been rummaging through a drawer in the kitchen table. As I got to the end of a speech that owed more to the British commanding officer in *The Great Escape* than any innate nobility of spirit, she pulled out a bashed packet of Silk Cut. "I knew there was a packet in here somewhere." She ripped the cellophane off, flipped the top up, tore out the silver paper, shoved a cigarette up with her thumb and drew it out with her lips. She picked up the gun and lit the cigarette. Pure bathos.

"I think we're in deep shit here, Flora," she said through a sigh of smoke, "but from what I've seen of Ms Brannigan, it seems to me she's the person who can best deal with that. I think you should tell us what happened."

Flora started crying again. I still wasn't impressed. "I didn't *mean* to kill her," she said through a veil of hair and tears.

"I know that," Helen soothed in her practical, no-nonsense way. There was going to be a reckoning between these two, I could see that in her eyes. But Helen Maitland had the sense to realize this wasn't the time or the place. "It's not your style, Flo."

Flora did a bit more weeping, and Helen just sat there smoking, her eyes never leaving her lover. It was impossible even to guess at what was going on behind that blank stare. Finally Flora sat back, pushed her hair away from her face and scrubbed her eyes with her small hands, like a child who's been crying from tiredness. She took a deep breath, gave Helen a pleading look, then turned to face me. "I really didn't mean to kill her," she said. "I didn't go there with that intention."

"Tell me about it," I said. Helen only crushed out one cigarette and lit a second.

Flora breathed out heavily through her nose. "This isn't easy," she complained.

"Easier than killing someone," I remarked.

"Not really," Flora said tremulously. "That happened in the heat of the moment. Before I even knew I had the knife in my hand, she was dead. Telling you is a lot harder, you have to believe that, Helen."

Helen nodded curtly. "So what happened, Flora? I want to know just as badly as Ms Brannigan does."

Flora pushed her hair back from her face and adopted a beseeching expression. I couldn't get a handle on this woman at all. The image she projected was of a fairly timid, vulnerable innocent. Then I'd get a flash from those dark eyes and I'd feel like an entire brigade of dark, supernatural nasties were dancing on my grave. I realized exactly what Maggie had meant about the dragon and the maiden. I could see that it might be a powerful erotic mixture, but it left me feeling pathetically grateful that the gun hadn't been for real. Flora was a woman who could easily have pulled the trigger then pulled the same "I didn't mean it" routine over me that she was giving us now over Sarah Blackstone.

"Can't it wait till we're alone?" Flora pleaded.

"Ms Brannigan already knows too much for us to throw her out now," Helen said. Somehow her words didn't scare me like Flora did. "I suspect that telling her the whole story is the best chance we've got of salvaging something from this mess." I couldn't have put it better myself.

Flora looked as if she was about to protest, then she registered the determination in her lover's face. "It all started when Helen was diagnosed with cervical cancer," she said.

"I know about that," I interrupted her, not wanting to let her get into a flow of pathos too early in her narrative. "It resulted in a complete hysterectomy What had that to do with the murder of Sarah Blackstone?"

Flora darted me a look of pure malice. It wasn't lost on Helen Maitland. This time, when she spoke, her voice was more brisk. "Helen was desperate to have a child, and as soon as she was diagnosed, she got a gynaecologist friend of hers, not Sarah, to harvest her eggs for the next three months."

"Why?" I asked.

Helen stared at the table and spoke rapidly. "Part of me hoped that a full hysterectomy wouldn't be necessary, that even if I couldn't produce fertile eggs any more, I might just be able to have a child by artificial insemination, or even surrogacy. You know, get someone else to carry my child. So we took what eggs we could harvest before my surgery and froze them. It's dodgy, freezing eggs; nobody really knows yet how successful it is. But I had this crazy idea that even if I couldn't have a child myself, at least my genes might continue. And if all else had failed, at least I could have made an egg donation to someone who needed it."

Not for the first time in the past few days, the desperate nature of the need to reproduce hit me between the eyes. I said

a small prayer to the goddess of infertility that it would continue to avoid taking up residence in my soul. "Right," I said,
determined to move this along and keep the emotional level as
low key as possible. "So Helen had her eggs frozen. How does
that get us to murder?"

"One morning a couple of months ago, Helen had a really
strange letter in the post. It was from Manchester—"

"I know about that too," I interrupted, partly to maintain
control over events, partly to impress both of them with how
much I'd already found out. "It contained a baby's photograph
and a lock of hair and a message of thanks."

Helen's composure showed a crack for the first time. "The
baby was the spitting image of Sarah at the same age. I couldn't
believe the similarity. I'd heard Sarah talking about the technical possibility of making babies from two women's eggs, and I
realized that's what she was probably doing. I work with cystics,
so I have access to DNA-testing facilities."

"They were able to get DNA from the cut hairs?" I asked.

"There are always researchers who love a challenge, and
one of the women at St Hilda's relished the chance to extract
viable DNA from the hair shafts. I bribed one of my students to
get a blood sample from Sarah. He told her it was for random
testing in some experiment he was doing into some obscure
aspect of blood chemistry, and she let him take it. The DNA
test was very clear. Sarah was one of the parents of the child."
She was smoking now like she'd made it her lifelong ambition
to be a forty-a-day woman.

This time, it was Flora who reached out, gripping Helen's
free hand tightly. Helen continued, almost talking to herself.
"It was all the more bitter because that was the issue that split
us up. I wanted a child desperately, but Sarah didn't. I knew
subfertility treatment was close to the stage where it would be
possible to make a child from two women. And she refused
point-blank to do it with us. She said she wasn't prepared to
experiment with my body. That if the experiment produced a

monster, or even a handicapped child, she wouldn't be able to live with herself. Me, I thought it probably had more to do with the fact that she absolutely didn't want to share her life with a child. I eventually came to the conclusion I'd rather have the possibility of a child than the certainty of life with her. You can imagine the kind of rows . . ." Her voice tailed off into a quiet exhalation of smoke.

"You must have been devastated to discover she was experimenting with other women," I said in the crass mode of television news reports.

Helen pulled a face. "I think if she had been in front of me when I got the DNA results through from the lab, I might have killed her. But the more I thought about it, the more I realized that I was actually glad that I hadn't had her child. That I didn't want a daughter of mine to consist of half Sarah's genes. Distance doesn't lend enchantment, you know. It allows you to put things in perspective. I hadn't stopped wanting a child, but I'd stopped caring about Sarah. I didn't even hate her any more. Despised her, yes, because there wasn't anything in her life she wouldn't betray. So I didn't actually want to kill her for very long."

"Long enough to tell Flora?" I asked softly.

Flora turned on me then, eyes wide and angry. "Don't try and blame Helen. She said nothing of the sort to me. It was my idea to go and see Sarah. Helen didn't even know I was going."

"So why did you go, if it wasn't to confront Sarah with her double-cross?"

"Yes," Helen said. "Why did you go to see her?"

Flora gave a weary smile. "I went to try to persuade her to do for us what she'd done for those other women. My eggs and yours. So we could share a child."

There was a long silence, Helen's eyes raking Flora's face as if she was trying to scour any falsehood from her words by reading her features. Then her head dropped into her hands. She didn't cry. After a few moments, she looked up, dry-eyed, and said, "That is an extraordinary thing to say."

"It's the truth," Flora said. "Why else would I have gone to see her?"

"I had no idea you felt like that."

"What? That I loved you that much, or that I wanted a child that much?" Flora challenged, chin up.

"Either or both," Helen said, her voice tired. "What did Sarah say?"

Flora looked away, her face clouding over. I was starting to feel seriously redundant here. "She laughed in my face. She said she wasn't going to give a baby to a brainless bimbo and a compulsive obsessive. So I told her that if she wouldn't cooperate, I'd go to the authorities and tell them exactly what she was doing."

"Not a clever move," Helen said, reaching for another cigarette. "Sarah and threats were never a comfortable mix." Her cool irony was starting to get to me. Sooner or later, an explosion was going to come. The longer she kept the lid on, the worse it was going to be. I hoped I'd be well out of the fallout zone when it did.

"How did she react to your threat?" I asked.

"She grabbed me by the lapels and shoved me up against the kitchen counter," Flora said, still incredulous that someone in her world would do such a thing. "She kept banging me against the counter, telling me I was a dirty blackmailing bitch and that she knew a lot of women who'd happily kill to keep the children she'd given them. I was terrified. She kept twisting her hand in my coat; it was so tight it was strangling me. I was desperate. I groped about on the worktop behind me and my hand touched a knife. I just grabbed it and thrust it up into her. I wasn't thinking, I just did it. And she sort of fell back onto the floor. I was standing there, holding the knife, watching her die. And I couldn't do a thing about it."

"You could have called an ambulance," Helen said, her voice cold.

"I did. I went straight to the phone box down the street and called an ambulance."

"Not then, you didn't," I said. "You did one or two other things first. You cleared up any signs of a struggle. You unlocked the back door, leaving the key in the lock, went outside and smashed a pane of glass to make it look like a burglary. You took off your bloodstained mac and checked nobody was about, then you walked calmly out of the front door and up to the phone box on the corner. And then you phoned 999 and told the operator you'd just seen a black man running out of an open door on that street with a bloodstained knife. By which time Sarah Blackstone was dead."

"It wouldn't have made any difference if I'd phoned straight-away," Flora said desperately. "She died so quickly. Honestly, Helen, she was dead in seconds."

"Not that quickly," I said coldly. "She can't have been dead for long otherwise the ambulance crew would have told the police there was a discrepancy between the time of death and the time of the call-out."

The way Flora looked at me, I was glad there wasn't a knife handy. "Let's face it, Flora, you couldn't really allow her to live, could you?" Helen said bleakly. "Not after what you'd done. No wonder you said to me the next day that you'd give me an alibi if the police came asking. You wanted to make sure you had one, didn't you? Just don't you dare ever say you did it for me."

Flora said nothing. Helen faced me. "I suspect there's a tape recorder whirring away in your handbag."

My jacket pocket, actually, but I wasn't about to tell them that in case either of them got any clever ideas. "Technology's got a bit smarter than that these days. I wouldn't still be alive if I didn't believe in insurance," I said.

"So now you go to the police, is that it?"

"Helen!" Flora wailed. "I can't go to jail!"

"I don't think that's necessary," I said. "The way Flora tells it, it sounds pretty much like self-defence that got out of hand. I don't think she's a risk to anyone else. I don't see a need for this to come out into the open."

A cynical smile curled Flora's lip. "You mean you don't want the world to know what that bitch Sarah was doing. I bet your client's one of those women she gave a baby to. She won't want that can of worms opened, will she?"

"Don't push your luck, Flora," Helen said. "Ms Brannigan holds your freedom in her hand. Or wherever she has her tape recorder stashed."

I nodded. "There are conditions to my silence," I said. "If anyone else is charged with Sarah's murder, I can't stand idly by. And if Sarah's secret work becomes public knowledge and I think it's anything to do with you, the tape goes to the police. Is that a deal?"

EPILOGUE

The cops picked up Peter Lovell's thugs a couple of weeks later in a routine raid on an after-hours shebeen in Bradford. They charged them with Tony's murder. The Crown Prosecution Service, who love bent coppers about as much as the police do, also added murder to Lovell's list of charges under the "joint enterprise" principle. According to Della, who was on the point of giving up the elbow crutches and moving back into her house, it looks like they're all going to go down for a very long time. Oh, and Dan Druff and the Scabby Heided Bairns signed a deal with an indie record company on the strength of their first Nazi-free gig. They've promised me the first pressing of the first single to roll off the production line. I can hardly wait. It'll look great framed on my office wall. Not.

The law on fraud being what it is, Alan Williams and Sarah Constable probably thought they were unlucky to do any time at all. But the police did a good job, tying them into ripping off the bereaved in Birmingham, Durham and Plymouth. They each got eighteen months, which they'll do easy time in an open prison. It probably won't stop them dreaming up another nasty little scam when they come out, but at least it's got them off the streets for a few months. Their boss at Sell Phones did a bit better; all they could get him on was obtaining phone calls by deception, on account of the laws in this country affecting telecommunications are so archaic it's hard to nail anybody on anything to do with cellular phones. And since nobody much likes phone companies, he only got a suspended sentence. He lost the business, though, which is a kind of rough justice.

I also got round to talking to Josh. He gave me a load of toffee about how he wanted to devote some of his capital to working with small businesses, and I told him to cut the crap and get to the horses. The deal we worked out meant he bought Bill's share of the business, but in recognition of my sole contribution to the profits, my stake in the partnership was upgraded to fifty-five per cent. So I got an extra twenty per cent for nothing except running the agency and doing all the hard graft . . . Josh also promised me that when I can afford it, I can buy him out for what he'd paid plus the rate of inflation. I know a good deal when I see it. I nearly bit his hand off. The best part about it was that overnight I stopped wanting to rip Bill's arm off and hit him with the wet end. That Sheila's a really good laugh when you get to know her.

Alexis was happy with the way I sorted things out with Helen and Flora. With the single-mindedness of all parents-to-be, she didn't much mind who'd killed Sarah as long as it wasn't going to bounce back and wreck her happy little idyll. I never did tell her about Sarah Blackstone's nasty little trick of dropping her own eggs into the mix. I couldn't bring myself to say anything that would poison Alexis's happiness.

It's just as well I didn't. When Chris gave birth six months later, there was no mistaking the genetic source of Jay Appleton Lee's shock of jet-black spikes. I swear the child cries with a Scouse accent.

⋟❖⋞

I wish I could close the account there. Everything in credit, almost a happy ending. It's never been that neat in my experience. About two months after the showdown in her kitchen, Helen

Maitland turned up at my office one afternoon around close of business. I left Shelley in charge and took her up to the café at the Cornerhouse for a herbal tea and a flapjack. Sometimes it's dead handy having an art cinema so close to the office.

Over a cup of wild strawberry she told me that Flora had just got a job in a university library in Wyoming. "I didn't know they had universities in Wyoming," I said. Cheap, I know, but I never claimed to be otherwise.

"Me neither," Helen said, smiling with the half of her mouth that wasn't clamped around a cigarette.

"You looking for jobs, then?"

"You mean am I going with her?"

I nodded. "I wondered if this was goodbye, don't worry, we're out of your life."

"I suppose it is, in a way. Flora won't be back, and the one thing I'd pray for if I had any religion left is to be allowed to forget the whole sorry mess. So you can rest assured you won't be hearing any more of this from me. And Flora . . . well, she has too much to lose. The police never arrested anyone, never even seriously questioned them. The case is going to die now, just like Sarah did."

"Better that way," I said.

"Better all round," she agreed. Her green eyes looked distantly over my shoulder. "I'm not going to join Flora, though. Ever since she told us what had happened, I've scarcely been able to tolerate being in the same room as her. I may have stopped loving or hating Sarah, but I never wanted her to die, not even in our most terrible fights. And I hate the thought that I was the instrument of her death."

"Don't be daft," I protested. "It was Flora who knifed her, not you. You didn't even know she was going to see her. You certainly didn't suggest it—that much was obvious from your reaction to Flora's confession."

"Maybe not overtly. But she'd never have dreamed up the idea if my obsession hadn't planted it. If I hadn't told her the meaning of the photograph and the lock of hair, she'd never have gone near Sarah. I may not have held the knife, but I carry the guilt."

I could tell there was no point in trying to get her to change her mind about that. We finished our drinks, talking about anything except Sarah and Flora. Then she excused herself, saying she had someone to meet. I sat by the first-floor window and watched her stepping out across Oxford Road, dodging cars and buses. I watched her long stride as far as the corner of Princess Street, where she turned left and disappeared.

The story was in the next night's *Chronicle*. DOCTOR DIES IN HOTEL PLUNGE. She'd taken a room on the top floor of the Piccadilly Hotel. She'd even brought a club hammer in her overnight bag in case the window didn't open far enough. At the inquest, they read out a note where she'd quoted that bit from Keats about ceasing on the midnight with no pain.

Some nights, I dream of Helen Maitland falling through the air, morphing into a bird and suddenly soaring just before she hits the ground. I hope someone somewhere is making babies with her eggs.

STAR STRUCK

For Tessa and Peps, the Scylebert Twins
(aka Margaret & Nicky).
Thanks for all the laughter—we'll
never feel the same about Isa.

ACKNOWLEDGEMENTS

I was a journalist for many years on a newspaper that became increasingly obsessed with the world of soaps. As a result, I have forgotten more than any respectable person would want to know about the private lives of many household names. Nevertheless, the fictional soap *Northerners* and its cast are entirely creatures of my imagination. Any resemblances to the real or fictional characters of any actual regular drama series are entirely coincidental and purely accidental. Besides, I'm not worth suing.

The legal advice came from Brigid Baillie, Jai Penna and Paula Tyler; any errors are either deliberate mistakes for dramatic effect, or just plain stupidity. Jennifer Paul also provided crucial information, in exchange for which I promise never to tell the story about the golden retriever.

Thanks too to my agents Jane Gregory and Lisanne Radice and my editors Julia Wisdom and Karen Godfrey, who, because of the wonders of e-mail, were able to shower me with queries the length and breadth of three continents.

PROLOGUE

Extract from the computer database of
Dorothea Dawson, Seer to the Stars

Written in the Stars for Kate Brannigan,
private investigator.

Born Oxford, UK, 4th September 1966.

★ Sun in Virgo in the Fifth House
★ Moon in Taurus in the Twelfth House
★ Mercury in Virgo in the Fifth House
★ Venus in Leo in the Fourth House
★ Mars in Leo in the Fourth House
★ Jupiter in Cancer in the Third House
★ Saturn retrograde in Pisces in the Eleventh House
★ Uranus in Virgo in the Fifth House
★ Neptune in Scorpio in the Sixth House
★ Pluto in Virgo in the Fifth House
★ Chiron in Pisces in the Eleventh House
★ Ascendant Sign: Gemini

1

SUN IN VIRGO IN THE 5TH HOUSE

On the positive side, can be ingenious, verbally skilled, diplomatic, tidy, methodical, discerning and dutiful. The negatives are fussiness, a critical manner, an obsessive attention to detail and a lack of self-confidence that can disguise itself as arrogance. In the 5th House, it indicates a player of games.

From *Written in the Stars*, by Dorothea Dawson

My client was about to get a resounding smack in the mouth. I watched helplessly from the other side of the street. My adrenaline was pumping, but there was no way I could have made it to her side in time. That's the trouble with bodyguarding jobs. Even if you surround the client with a phalanx of Rutger Hauer clones and Jean-Claude Van Damme wannabes in bulletproof vests, the moment always comes when they're vulnerable. And guess who always gets the blame? That's why, when people come looking for a minder, the house rule at Brannigan & Co: Investigations & Security states, "We don't do that."

But Christmas was coming and the goose was anorexic. Business had been as slow as a Post Office queue and even staff as unorthodox as mine expect to be paid on time. Besides, I deserved a festive bonus myself. Eating, for example. So I'd sent my better judgement on an early Yuletide break and agreed to take on a client who'd turned out to be more accident prone than Coco the Clown.

For once, it wasn't my fault that the client was in the front line. I'd had no say in what was happening out there on the street. If I'd wanted to stop it, I couldn't have. So, absolved from action for once, I stood with my hands in my pockets and watched Carla Hardcastle's arm swing round in a fearsome arc to deliver a cracking wallop that wiped the complacent smirk off Brenda Barrowclough's self-satisfied face. I sucked my breath in sharply.

"And cut," the director said. "Very nice, girls, but I'd like it one more time. Gloria, loved that smug little smile, but can you lose it at the point where you realize she's actually going to thump you? And let us see some outrage?"

My client gave a forbearing smile that was about as sincere as a beggar asking for tea money. "Whatever you say, Helen, chuck," she rasped in the voice that thrilled the nation three times a week as we shovelled down our microwave dinners in front of Manchester's principal contribution to the world of soap. Then she turned to me with an exaggerated wink and called, "You're all right, chuck, it's only make believe."

Everyone turned to stare at me. I managed to grin while clenching my teeth. It's a talent that comes in very handy in the private-eye business. It's having to deal with unscrupulous idiots that does it. And that's just the clients.

"That's my bodyguard," Gloria Kendal—alias Brenda Barrowclough—announced to the entire cast and crew of *Northerners*.

"We'd all worked out it wasn't your body double," the actress playing Carla said, apparently as sour in life as the character she played in the human drama that had wowed British audiences for the best part of twenty years.

"Let's hope you only get attacked by midgets," Teddy Edwards added. He'd once been a stand-up comedian on the working men's club circuit, but he'd clearly been playing Gloria's screen husband for so long that he'd lost any comic talent he'd ever possessed. I might only be five feet three in my socks, but I wouldn't have needed to use too many of my Thai-boxing skills to bring a lump of lard like him to his knees. I gave him the hard stare and I'm petty enough to admit I enjoyed it when he cleared his throat and looked away.

"All right, settle down," the director called. "Places, please, and let's take it again from the top of the scene."

"Can we have a bit of hush back there?" someone else added. I wondered what his job title was and how long I'd have to hang around the TV studios before I worked out who did what in a hierarchy that included best boys, gaffers and too many gofers to count. I figured I'd probably have long enough, the way things were going. There was a lot of time for idle reflection in this job. When Gloria was filming, silence was the rule. I couldn't ask questions, eavesdrop or burgle in pursuit of the information I needed to close the case. All there was for me to do was lean against the wall and watch. There was nothing remotely glamorous about witnessing the seventh take of a scene that was a long way from Shakespeare to start with. As jobs went, minding the queen of the nation's soaps was about as exotic as watching rain slide down a window.

It hadn't started out that way. When Gloria had swanned into our office, I'd known straight off it wasn't going to be a routine case. At Brannigan & Co, the private investigation firm that I run, we cover a wide spectrum of work. Previously, when I'd been in partnership with Bill Mortensen, we'd mostly investigated white-collar fraud, computer security, industrial espionage and sabotage, with a bit of miscellaneous meddling that friends occasionally dropped in our laps. Now Bill had moved to Australia, I'd had to cast my net wider to survive. I'd clawed back some process-serving from a handful of law firms, added "surveillance" to the letterheading and canvassed insurance companies for work exposing fraudulent claims. Even so, Gloria Kendal's arrival in our front office signalled something well out of the ordinary.

Not that I'd recognized her straight away. Neither had Shelley, the office administrator, and she's got the X-ray vision of every mother of teenagers. My first thought when Gloria had swept through the door on a wave of Estée Lauder's White Linen was that she was a domestic violence victim. I couldn't think of another reason for the wide-brimmed hat and the wraparound sunglasses on a wet December afternoon in Manchester.

I'd been looking over Shelley's shoulder at some information she'd downloaded from Companies House when the woman had pushed open the door and paused, dramatically framed against the hallway. She waited long enough for us to look up and register the expensive swagger of her mac and the quality of the kelly-green silk suit underneath, then she took three measured steps into the room on low-heeled pumps that precisely matched the suit. I don't know about Shelley, but I suspect my astonishment showed.

There was an air of expectancy in the woman's pose. Shelley's "Can I help you?" did nothing to diminish it.

The woman smiled, parting perfectly painted lips the colour of tinned black cherries. "I hope you can, chuck," she said, and her secret was out.

"Gloria Kendal," I said.

"Brenda Barrowclough," Shelley said simultaneously.

Gloria chuckled. "You're both right, girls. But we'll just let that be our little secret, eh?" I nodded blankly. The only way her identity was ever going to stay secret was if she kept her mouth shut. It was clear from three short sentences that the voice that had made Brenda Barrowclough the darling of impressionists the length and breadth of the comedy circuit wasn't something Gloria took on and cast off as readily as her character's trademark bottle-blonde beehive wig. Gloria really did talk in broad North Manchester with the gravelly growl of a bulldozer in low gear.

"How can I help you, Ms Kendal?" I asked, remembering my manners and stepping out from behind the reception desk.

She might not be a CEO in a grey suit, but she clearly had enough
in the bank to make sure we all had a very happy Christmas.

"Call me Gloria, chuck. In fact, call me anything except
Brenda." After twenty years of TV viewing, the raucous laugh
was as familiar as my best friend's. "I'm looking for Brannigan,"
she said.

"You found her," I said, holding out my hand.

Gloria dropped a limp bunch of fingers into mine and
withdrew before I could squeeze them—the professional sign of
someone who had to shake too many hands in a year. "I thought
you'd be a bloke," she said. For once, it wasn't a complaint,
merely an observation. "Well, that makes things a lot easier. I
were wondering what we'd do if Brannigan and Co didn't have
women detectives. Is there some place we can go and talk?"

"My office?" I gestured towards the open door.

"Grand," Gloria said, sweeping past me and fluttering her
fingers in farewell to Shelley.

We exchanged a look. "Rather you than me," Shelley
muttered.

By the time I closed the door behind me, Gloria was settled
into one corner of the sofa I use for informal client meetings.
She'd taken off her hat and tossed it casually on the low table
in front of her. Her own hair was a subtle ash-blonde cut in a
gamine Audrey Hepburn style. Somehow it managed not to
look ridiculous on a woman who had to be nudging sixty. She
had the clear skin of a much younger woman, but none of the
Barbie-doll tightness that goes with the overenthusiastic face-
lift. As I sat down opposite her, she took off the sunglasses and
familiar grey eyes crinkled in a smile. "I know it's ridiculous,
but even though people stare at the bins, they don't recognize
Brenda behind them. They just think it's some daft rich bitch
with delusions of grandeur."

"Living a normal life must be tough," I said.

"You're not kidding, chuck. They see you three times a
week in their living room, and they think you're a member of

the family. You let on who you are and next thing you know they're telling you all about their hernia operation and the state of their veins. It's a nightmare." She shrugged out of her coat, opened her handbag and took out a packet of those long skinny brown cigarettes that look like cinnamon sticks, and a gold Dunhill lighter. She looked around, eyebrows raised.

Stifling a sigh, I got up and removed the saucer from under the Christmas cactus. I'd only bought it two days before but already the buds that had promised pretty cascades of flowers were predictably starting to litter the windowsill. Me and plants go together like North and South Korea. I tipped the water from the saucer into the bin and placed it on the table in front of Gloria. "Sorry," I said. "It's the best I can do."

She smiled. "I used to work in a cat food factory. I've put my fags out in a lot worse, believe me."

I preferred not to think about it. "Well, Gloria, how can I help you?"

"I need a bodyguard."

My eyebrows rose. "We don't normally—"

"These aren't normal circumstances," she said sharply. "I don't want some thick as pigshit bodybuilder trailing round after me. I want somebody with a brain, somebody that can figure out what the heck's going on. Somebody that won't attract attention. Half my life I spend with the bloody press snapping round my ankles and the last thing I need is stories that I've splashed out on a hired gun. That's why I wanted a woman."

"You said, 'somebody that can figure out what the heck's going on,'" I said, focusing on the need I probably could do something useful about. "What seems to be the problem?"

"I've been getting threatening letters," she said. "Now, that's nothing new. Brenda Barrowclough is not a woman who minces her words, and there are a lot of folk out there as can't tell the difference between *Northerners* and the real world. You'd be too young to remember, but when I was first widowed in the series, back about fifteen years ago, I was snowed under with letters of condolence. People actually sent wreaths for the funeral, addressed to fifteen, Sebastopol Grove. The Post Office is used to it now, they just deliver direct to the studios, but back then the poor florists didn't know what to do. We had letters from cancer charities saying donations had been made to their funds in memory of Harry—that was my screen husband's name. Whenever characters move out, we get letters from punters wondering what the asking price is for the house. So whenever Brenda does owt controversial, I get hate mail."

I dredged my memory for recent tabloid headlines. "Hasn't there been some storyline about abortion? Sorry, I don't get the chance to watch much TV."

"You're all right, chuck. Me neither. You know Brenda's granddaughter, Debbie?"

"The one who's lived with Brenda since she was about ten? After her mum got shot in the Post Office raid?"

"You used to be a fan, then?"

"I still watch when I can. Which was a lot more back when Debbie was ten than it is now."

"Well, what's happened is that Brenda's found out that Debbie's had an abortion. Now, Brenda had a real down on Debbie's boyfriend because he was black, so the audience would have expected her to support Debbie rather than have a mixed-race grandson. But Brenda's only gone mental about the right to life and thrown Debbie out on her ear, hasn't she? So me and Sarah Anne Kelly who plays Debbie were expecting a right slagging off."

"And that's what's happened?"

Gloria shook her head, leaving a ribbon of smoke drifting level with her mouth. "Sort of," she said, confusing me. "What happens is the studio goes through our post, weeding out the really nasty letters so we don't get upset. Only, of course, you ask, don't you? I mean, you want to know if there's any real nutters out there looking for you."

"And the studio told you there was?"

"No, chuck. It weren't the studio. The letters I'm worried about are the ones coming to the house."

Now I was really confused. "You mean, your real house? Where you actually live?"

"Exactly. Now, I mean, it's not a state secret, where I live. But unless you're actually a neighbour or one of the reptiles of the press, you'd have to go to a bit of trouble to find out. The phone's ex-directory, of course. And all the official stuff like electricity bills and the voters' roll don't come under Gloria Kendal. They come under my real name."

"Which is?"

"Doreen Satterthwaite." She narrowed her eyes. I didn't think it was because the smoke was getting into them. I struggled to keep my face straight. Then Gloria grinned. "Bloody awful, isn't it? Do you wonder I chose Gloria Kendal?"

"In your shoes, I'd have done exactly the same thing," I told her. I wasn't lying. "So these threatening letters are coming directly to the house?"

"Not just to my house. My daughter's had one too. And they're different to the usual." She opened her handbag again. I wondered at a life where it mattered to have suit, shoes and handbag in identical shades. I couldn't help my mind slithering into speculation about her underwear. Did her coordination extend that far?

Gloria produced a sheet of paper. She started to pass it to me, then paused. I could have taken it from her, but it was an awkward reach, so I waited. "Usually, letters like this, they're semi-literate. They're ignorant. I mean, I might have left school when I were fifteen, but I know the difference between a dot and a comma. Most of the nutters that write me letters wouldn't know a paragraph if they woke up next to one. They can't spell, and they've got a tendency to write in green ink or felt-tip pens. Some of them, I don't think they're allowed sharp objects where they live," she added. I've noticed how actors and audiences often hold each other in mutual contempt. It looked like Gloria didn't have a whole lot of respect for the people who paid for the roof over her head.

Now she passed the letter across. It was plain A4 bond, the text printed unidentifiably on a laser printer. *"Doreen Satterthwaite, it's time you paid for what you've done. You deserve to endure the same suffering you've been responsible for. I know where you live. I know where your daughter Sandra and her husband Keith live. I know your granddaughter Joanna goes to Gorse Mill School. I know they worship at St Andrew's Church and have a caravan on Anglesey. I know you drive a scarlet Saab convertible. I know you, you bitch. And soon you're going to be dead. But there'll be no quick getaway for you. First, you're going to suffer."* She was right. The letter sounded disturbingly in control.

"Any idea what the letter writer is referring to?" I asked, not really expecting an honest answer.

Gloria shrugged. "Who the heck knows? I'm no plaster saint, but I can't think of anybody I've done a really bad turn to. Apart from my ex, and I doubt he could manage a letter to me that didn't include the words, 'you effing bitch.' He certainly can't manage a conversation without it. And besides, he wouldn't threaten our Sandra or Joanna. No way." I took her response for genuine perplexity, then reminded myself how she made her living.

"Have there been many of them?"

"This is the third. Plus the one that went to Sandra. That were about the sins of the mother. To be honest, the first couple I just binned. I thought they were somebody at the wind-up." Suddenly, Gloria looked away. She fumbled another cigarette from the packet and this time, the hand that lit it shook.

"Something happened to change your mind?"

"My car tyres were slashed. All four of them. Inside the NPTV compound. And there was a note stuck under the windscreen wipers. 'Next time your wardrobe? Or you?' And before you ask, I haven't got the note. It'd been raining. It just fell to bits in my hand."

"That's serious business," I said. "Are you sure you shouldn't be talking to the police?" I hated to lose a potential client, but it would have verged on criminal negligence not to point out that this might be one for Officer Dibble.

Gloria fiddled with her cigarette. "I told the management about it. And John Turpin, he's the Administration and Production Coordinator, he persuaded me not to go to the cops."

"Why not? I'd have thought the management would have been desperate to make sure nothing happened to their stars."

Gloria's lip curled in a cynical sneer. "It were nowt to do with my safety and everything to do with bad publicity. Plus, who'd want to come and work at NPTV if they found out the security was so crap that somebody could walk into the company compound and get away with that? Anyway, Turpin promised me an internal inquiry, so I decided to go along with him."

"But now you're here." It's observational skills like this that got me where I am today.

She flashed a quick up-and-under glance at me, an appraisal that contained more than a hint of fear held under tight control. "You're going to think I'm daft."

I shook my head. "I don't see you as the daft type, Gloria." Well, it was only a white lie. Daft enough to spend the equivalent of a week's payroll for Brannigan & Co on a matching outfit, but probably not daft when it came to a realistic assessment of personal danger. Mind you, neither was Ronald Reagan and look what happened to him.

"You know Dorothea Dawson?" Gloria asked, eyeing me out of the corner of her eye.

"'The Seer to the Stars'?" I asked incredulously. "The one who does the horoscopes in *TV Viewer*? The one who's always on the telly? 'A horse born under the sign of Aries will win the Derby'?" I intoned in a cheap impersonation of Dorothea Dawson's sepulchral groan.

"Don't mock," she cautioned me, wagging a finger. "She's a brilliant clairvoyant, you know. Dorothea comes into the studios once a week. She's the personal astrologer to half the cast. She really has a gift."

I bet she had. Gifts from all the stars of *Northerners*. "And Dorothea said something about these letters?"

"I took this letter in with me to my last consultation with her. I asked her what she could sense from it. She does that as well as the straight clairvoyance. She's done it for me before now, and she's never been wrong." In spite of her acting skills, anxiety was surfacing in Gloria's voice.

"And what did she say?"

Gloria drew so hard on her cigarette that I could hear the burning tobacco crackle. As she exhaled she said, "She held the envelope and shivered. She said the letter meant death. Dorothea said death was in the room with us."

2

SUN TRINE MOON

Creative thinking resolves difficult circumstances; she will tackle difficulties with bold resolution. The subject feels at home wherever she is, but can be blind to the real extent of problems. She will not always notice if her marriage is falling apart; she doesn't always nip problems in the bud.

From *Written in the Stars*, by Dorothea Dawson

Anybody gullible enough to fall for the doom and gloom dished out by professional con merchants like astrologers certainly wasn't going to have a problem with my expense sheets. Money for old rope, I reckoned. By Gloria's own admission, hate mail was as much part of the routine in her line of work as travelling everywhere with stacks of postcard-sized photographs to autograph for the punters. OK, the tyre slashing was definitely more serious, but that might be unconnected to the letters, an isolated act of vindictiveness. It was only because the Seer to the Stars had thrown a wobbler that this poison pen outbreak had been blown up to life-threatening proportions. "Does she often sense impending death when she does predictions for people?" I asked, trying not to snigger.

Gloria shook her head vigorously. "I've never heard of anybody else getting a prediction like that."

"And have you told other people in the cast about it?"

"Nobody," she said. "It's not the sort of thing you go on about."

Not unless you liked being laughed at, I reckoned. On the other hand, it might mean that the death prediction was one of Dorothea Dawson's regular routines for putting the frighteners on her clients and making them more dependent on her. Especially the older ones. Let's face it, there can't be that many public figures Gloria's age who go through more than a couple of months without knowing somebody who's died or dying. Gloria might have been catapulted into panic by her astrologer, but I couldn't imagine it being anything more than a stunt by Dorothea Dawson. Minding Gloria sounded like a major earner with no risk attached. Just what the bank manager ordered. I said a small prayer of thanks to Dorothea Dawson and told Gloria that for her, I'd be happy to make an exception to company policy. In fact, I would take personal responsibility for her safety.

The news seemed to cheer her up. "Right then, we'd better be off," she said, stubbing out her cigarette and gathering her mac around her shoulders.

"We'd better be off?" I echoed.

She glanced at her watch, a chunky gold item with chips of diamond that glittered like a broken windscreen in a street-light. "Depends where you live, I suppose. Only, if I'm opening a theme pub in Blackburn at eight and we've both got to get changed and grab a bite to eat, we'll be cutting it a bit fine if we don't get a move on."

"A theme pub in Blackburn," I said faintly.

"That's right, chuck. I'm under contract to the brewery. It's straightforward enough. I turn up, tell a few jokes, sing a couple of songs to backing tapes, sign a couple of hundred autographs and off." As she spoke, she was setting her hat at a rakish angle and replacing her sunglasses. As she made for the door, I dived behind the desk and swept my palmtop computer and my moby into my shoulder bag. I only caught up with her because she'd stopped to sign a glossy colour photograph of herself disguised as Brenda Barrowclough for Shelley.

Something terrible had happened to the toughest office manager in Manchester. Imagine Cruella De Vil transformed into one of those cuddly Dalmatian puppies, only more so. It was like watching Ben Nevis grovel. "And could you sign one, 'For Ted'?" she begged. I wished I had closed-circuit TV cameras covering the office. A video of this would keep Shelley off my back for months.

"No problem, there you go," Gloria said, signing the card with a flourish. "You right, Kate?"

I grabbed my coat and shrugged into it as I followed Gloria into the hall. She glanced both ways and down the stairwell before she set off. "The last thing I need is somebody clocking me coming out of your office," she said, trotting down the stairs at a fair pace. At the front door I turned right automatically, heading for my car. Gloria followed me into the private car park.

"This sign says, 'Employees of DVS Systems only. Unauthorized users will be clamped,'" she pointed out.

"It's all right," I said in a tone that I hoped would end the conversation. I didn't want to explain to Gloria that I'd got so fed up with the desperate state of car parking in my part of town that I'd checked out which office car parks were seldom full. I'd used the macro lens on the camera to take a photograph of a DVS Systems parking pass through somebody else's windscreen and made myself a passable forgery. I'd been parking on their lot for six months with no trouble, but it wasn't something I was exactly proud of. Besides, it never does to let the clients know about the little sins. It only makes them nervous.

Gloria stopped expectantly next to a very large black saloon with tinted windows. I shook my head and she pulled a rueful

smile. I pointed the remote at my dark-blue Rover and it cheeped
its usual greeting at me. "Sorry it's not a limo," I said to Gloria
as we piled in. "I need to be invisible most of the time." I didn't
feel the need to mention that the engine under the bonnet was
very different from the unit the manufacturer had installed. I
had enough horsepower under my bonnet to stage my own
rodeo. If anybody was stalking Gloria, I could blow them off
inside the first five miles.

I drove home, which took less than five minutes even in
early rush-hour traffic. I love living so close to the city centre, but
the area's become more dodgy in the last year. I'd have moved
if I hadn't had to commit every spare penny to the business. I'd
been the junior partner in Mortensen & Brannigan, and when
Bill Mortensen had decided to sell up and move to Australia, I'd
thought my career prospects were in the toilet. I couldn't afford
to buy him out but I was damned if some stranger was going to
end up with the lion's share of a business I'd worked so hard to
build. It had taken a lot of creative thinking and a shedload of
debt to get Brannigan & Co off the ground. Now I had a sleeping
partner in the Cayman Islands and a deal to buy out his share of
the business piecemeal as and when I could afford it, so it would
be a long time before I could consider heading for the southern
suburbs where all my sensible friends had moved.

Besides, the domestic arrangements were perfect. My lover
Richard, a freelance rock journalist, owned the bungalow next
door to mine, linked by a long conservatory that ran along the
back of both properties. We had all the advantages of living
together and none of the disadvantages. I didn't have to put up
with his mess or his music-business cronies; he didn't have to
deal with my girls' nights in or my addiction to very long baths.

Richard's car, a hot-pink Volkswagen Beetle convertible,
was in its slot, which, at this time of day, probably meant he was
home. There might be other showbiz journos with him, so I
played safe and asked Gloria to wait in the car. I was back inside
ten minutes, wearing a bottle-green crushed-velvet cocktail

dress under a dark-navy dupion-silk matador jacket. OTT for Blackburn, I know, but there hadn't been a lot of choice. If I didn't get to the dry cleaner soon, I'd be going to work in my dressing gown.

Gloria lived in Saddleworth, the expensively rural cluster of villages that hugs the edges of the Yorkshire moors on the eastern fringe of Greater Manchester. The hills are still green and rolling there, but on the skyline the dark humps of the moors lower unpleasantly, even on the sunniest of days. This is the wilderness that ate up the bodies of the child victims of Myra Hindley and Ian Brady. I can never drive through this brooding landscape without remembering the Moors Murders. Living on the doorstep would give me nightmares. It didn't seem to bother Gloria. But why would it? It didn't impinge either on her or on Brenda Barrowclough, and the half-hour drive out to Saddleworth was long enough for me to realize these were the only criteria that mattered to her. I'd heard it said that actors are like children in their unconscious self-absorption. Now I was seeing the proof.

In the December dark, Saddleworth looked like a Christmas card, early fairy lights twinkling against a light dusting of snow. I wished I'd listened to the weather forecast; the roads out here can be closed by drifts when there hasn't been so much as a flake on my roof. Yet another argument against country living. Gloria directed me down the valley in a gentle spiral to Greenfield. We turned off the main street into a narrow passage between two high walls. I hoped I wouldn't meet something coming the other way in a hurry. About a hundred yards in, the passage ended in two tall wrought-iron gates. Gloria fumbled with something in her handbag and the gates swung open.

I edged forward slowly, completely gobsmacked. I appeared to have driven into the set of a BBC period drama. I was in a large cobbled courtyard, surrounded on three sides by handsome two-storey buildings in weatherworn gritstone. Even my untrained eye can spot early Industrial Revolution, and this was a prime example. "Wow," I said.

"It were built as offices for the mill," Gloria said, pointing me towards a pair of double doors in the long left-hand side of the square. "Leave the car in front of my garage for now. Then the mill became a cat food factory. Sound familiar?"

"The factory where you used to work?"

"Got it in one." She opened the car door and I followed her across the courtyard. The door she stopped at was solid oak, the lock a sensible mortise. As we went in, a burglar alarm klaxoned its warning. While Gloria turned it off, I walked across the wide room that ran the whole depth of the building. Through the tall window, I could see light glinting off water. The house backed on to the canal. Suddenly life looked better. This house was about as impregnable as they come. Unless Gloria's letter writer had the Venetian skill of climbing a ladder from a boat, I was going to be able to sleep in my own bed at night rather than across the threshold of Gloria's bedroom.

"It's beautiful," I said.

"Especially when your living room used to be the cashier's office where you picked up your wages every week smelling of offal," Gloria said ironically.

I turned back to look round the room. Wall uplighters gave a soft glow to burnished beams and the exposed stone of the three outer walls. The furnishings looked like a job lot from John Lewis, all pastel-figured damask and mahogany. The pictures on the wall were big watercolour landscapes of the Yorkshire moorland and the expanse of stripped floorboards was broken up by thick pile Chinese rugs. There was nothing to quarrel with, but nothing that spoke of individual taste, unlike Gloria's clothes. "You live here alone?" I asked.

"Thank God," she said with feeling, opening a walk-in cupboard and hanging up her coat.

"Anyone else have keys?"

"Only my daughter." Gloria emerged and pointed to a door in the far wall. "The kitchen's through there. There's a freezer full of ready meals. Do you want to grab a couple and stick them in the microwave while I'm getting changed?" Without waiting for an answer, she started up the open-plan staircase that climbed to the upper floor.

The kitchen was almost as big as the living room. One end was laid out as a dining area, with a long refectory table and a collection of unmatched antique farm kitchen chairs complete with patchwork cushions. The other end was an efficiently arranged working kitchen, dominated by an enormous free-standing fridge-freezer. The freezer was stacked from top to bottom with meals from Marks and Spencer. Maybe country living could be tolerable after all, I thought. All you needed to get through the winter was a big enough freezer and an endless supply of computer games. I chose a couple of pasta dishes and followed the instructions on the pack. By the time they were thawed and reheated, Gloria was back, dressed for action in a shocking-pink swirl of sequins. All it needed was the Brenda Barrowclough beehive to define camp kitsch better than any drag queen could have.

"Amazing," I said faintly, scooping chicken and pasta into bowls.

"Bloody awful, you mean," Gloria said, sitting down in a flounce of candyfloss. "But the punters are paying for Brenda, not me." She attacked her pasta like an extra from *Oliver Twist*. She finished while I was barely halfway through. "Right," she said, wiping her mouth with the back of her hand. "I'll be five minutes putting on me slap and the wig. The dishwasher's under the sink."

With anyone else, I'd have started to resent being ordered around. But I was beginning to get the hang of Gloria. She wasn't bossy as such. She was just supremely organized and blissfully convinced that her way was the best way. Life would inevitably

be smoother for those around her who recognized this and went
along with it unquestioningly. For now, I was prepared to settle
for the quiet life. Later, it might be different, but I'd deal with
that when later rolled round. Meanwhile, I loaded the dishwasher
then went outside and started the car.

The drive to Blackburn was the last sane part of the evening. Gloria handed me a faxed set of directions then demanded
that I didn't mither her with problems so she could get her head
straight. I loaded an appropriate CD into the car stereo and drove
to the ambient chill of Dreamfish while she reclined her seat
and closed her eyes. I pulled up outside the pub three-quarters
of an hour later, ten minutes before she was due to sparkle. She
opened her eyes, groaned softly and said, "It's a bit repetitive, that
music. Have you got no Frank Sinatra?" I tried to disguise my
sense of impending doom. I failed. Gloria roared with raucous
laughter and said, "I were only winding you up. I can't bloody
stand Sinatra. Typical man, I did it my own bloody-minded way.
This modern stuff's much better."

I left Gloria in the car while I did a brief reconnaissance of
the venue. I had this vague notion of trying to spot any suspicious characters. I had more chance of hitting the Sahara on a
wet Wednesday. Inside the pub, it was mayhem on a leash. Lads
with bad haircuts and football shirts jostled giggling groups of
girls dressed in what the high-street chain stores had persuaded
them was fashion. Mostly they looked like they'd had a collision
with their mothers' cast-offs from the seventies. I couldn't think
of another reason for wearing Crimplene. The Lightning Seeds
were revealing that football was coming home at a volume that
made my fillings hurt. Provincial didn't begin to describe it. It
was so different from the city-centre scene I began to wonder
if we could have slipped through a black hole and ended up in
the Andromeda galaxy. What a waste of a good frock.

The special opening night offer of two drinks for the price
of one had already scored a clutch of casualties and the rest of

the partygoers looked like they were hellbent on the same fate. I ducked back out and collected Gloria. "I'll try to stay as close to you as I can," I told her. "It's a madhouse in there."

She paused on the threshold, took a swift look round the room and said, "You've obviously led a very sheltered life." As she spoke, someone spotted her. The cry rippled across the room and within seconds the youth of Blackburn were cheering and bellowing a ragged chorus of the theme song from *Northerners*. And then we were plunged into the throbbing embrace of the crowd.

I gave up trying to keep Gloria from the assassin's knife after about twenty seconds when I realized that if I came between her and her public, I was the more likely candidate for a stiletto in the ribs. I wriggled backwards through the crowd and found a vantage point on the raised dais where the DJ was looking as cool as any man can who works for the local building society during the day. I was scanning the crowd automatically, looking for behaviour that didn't fit in. Easier said than done, given the level of drunken revelry around me. But from what I could see of the people crammed into the Frog and Scrannage, the natives were definitely friendly, at least as far as Gloria/Brenda was concerned.

I watched my client, impressed with her energy and her professionalism. She crossed the room slower than a stoned three-toed sloth, with a word and an autograph for everyone who managed to squeeze alongside. She didn't even seem to be sweating, the only cool person in the biggest sauna in the North West. When she finally made it to the dais, there was no shortage of hands to help her up. She turned momentarily and swiftly handed the DJ a cassette tape. "Any time you like, chuck. Just let it run."

The lad slotted it into his music deck and the opening bars of the *Northerners* theme crashed out over the PA, the audience swaying along. The music faded down and Gloria went straight into what was clearly a well-polished routine. Half a dozen jokes with a local spin, a clutch of anecdotes about her fellow cast members then, right on cue, the music swelled up under her and she belted out a segued medley of "I Will Survive," "No More Tears," "Roll With It" and "No Regrets."

You had to be there.

The crowd was baying for more. They got it. "The Power of Love" blasted our eardrums into the middle of next week. Then we were out of there. The car park was so cold and quiet I'd have been tempted to linger if I hadn't had the client to consider. Instead I ran to the car and brought it round to the doorway, where she was signing the last few autographs. "Keep watching the show," she urged them as she climbed into the car.

As soon as we were out of the car park, she pulled off the wig with a noisy sigh. "What did you think?"

"Anybody who seriously wanted to damage you could easily get close enough. Getting away might be harder," I said, half my attention on negotiating a brutal one-way system that could commit us to Chorley or Preston or some other fate worse than death if I didn't keep my wits about me.

"No, not that," Gloria said impatiently. "Never mind that. How was I? Did they love it?"

⋘✦⋙

It was gone midnight by the time I'd deposited Gloria behind bolted doors and locked gates and driven back through the empty impoverished streets of the city's eastern fringes. Nothing much was moving except the litter in the wind. I felt a faint nagging throb in my sinuses, thanks to the assault of cigarette smoke, loud music and flashing lights I'd endured in the pub. I'd recently turned thirty; maybe some fundamental alteration had happened in my brain which meant my body could no longer tolerate all the things that spelled "a good night out" to the denizens of Blackburn's latest fun pub. Perhaps there were hidden benefits in aging after all.

I yawned as I turned out of the council estate into the enclave of private housing where I occasionally manage a full night's sleep. Tonight wouldn't be one; Gloria had to be at the studios by nine thirty, so she wanted me at her place by eight thirty. I'd gritted my teeth, thought about the hourly rate and smiled.

I staggered up the path, slithering slightly on the frosted cobbles, already imagining the sensuous bliss of slipping under a winter-weight feather-and-down duvet. As soon as I opened the door, the dream shattered. Even from the hallway I could see the glow of light from the conservatory. I could hear moody saxophone music and the mutter of voices. That they were in the conservatory rather than Richard's living room meant that whoever he was talking to was there for me.

My bag slid to the floor as my shoulders drooped. I walked through to the living room and took in the scene through the patio doors. Beer bottles, a plume of smoke from a joint, two male bodies sprawled across the wicker.

Just what I'd always wanted at the end of a working day. A pair of criminals in the conservatory.

3

VENUS SQUARES NEPTUNE

This is a tense aspect that produces strain in affairs of the heart because she has a higher expectation of love and comradeship than her world provides. She has a strong determination to beat the odds stacked against her.

From *Written in the Stars*, by Dorothea Dawson

It's not every night you feel like you need a Visiting Order to enter your own conservatory. That night I definitely wanted reinforcements before I could face the music or the men. A quick trip to the kitchen and I was equipped with a sweating tumbler of ice-cold pepper-flavoured Absolut topped up with pink grapefruit juice. I took a deep draught and headed for whatever Dennis and Richard had to throw at me.

When I say the conservatory was full of criminals, I was only slightly exaggerating. Although Richard's insistence on the need for marijuana before creativity can be achieved means he cheerfully breaks the law every day, he's got no criminal convictions. Being a journalist, he doesn't have any other kind either.

Dennis is a different animal. He's a career criminal but, paradoxically, I trust him more than almost anyone. I always know where I am with Dennis; his morality might not be constructed along traditional lines, but it's more rigid than the law of gravity, and a hell of a lot more forgiving. He used to be a professional burglar; not the sort who breaks into people's houses to steal the video and rummage through the lingerie, but the sort who relieves the very rich of some of their ill-gotten and well-insured gains. Some of his victims had so many expensive status symbols lying around that they didn't even realize they'd been burgled. These days, he's more or less given up robbing anyone except other villains who've got too much pride to complain to the law. That's because, after his last enforced spell of taking care of business from behind high walls with no office equipment except a phone card, his wife told him she'd divorce him if he ever did anything else that carried a custodial sentence.

I've known Dennis even longer than I've known Richard. He's my Thai-boxing coach, and he taught me the basic principle of self-defence for someone as little as I am—one crippling kick to the kneecap or the balls, then run like hell. It's saved my life more than once, which is another good reason why Dennis will always be welcome in my house. Well, almost always.

I leaned against the doorjamb and scowled. "I thought you didn't do drugs," I said mildly to Dennis.

"You know I don't," he said. "Who's been telling porkies about me?"

"Nobody. I was referring to the atmosphere in here," I said, wafting my hand in front of my face as I crossed the room to give Dennis a kiss on a cheek so smooth he must have shaved before he came out for the evening. "Breathe and you're stoned. Not to mention cutting your life expectancy by half."

"Nice to see you too, Brannigan," my beloved said as I pushed the evening paper to one side and dropped on to the sofa next to him.

"So what are you two boys plotting?"

Dennis grinned like Wile E. Coyote. My heart sank. I was well past a convincing impersonation of the Road Runner. "Wanted to pick your brains," he said.

"And it couldn't wait till morning?" I groaned.

"I was passing."

Richard gave the sort of soft giggle that comes after the fifth bottle and the fourth joint. I know my man. "He was passing and he heard a bottle of Pete's Wicked Bohemian Pilsner calling his name," he spluttered.

"Looking at the number of bottles, it looks more like a crate shouting its head off," I muttered. The boys looked like they were set to make a night of it. There was only one way I was going to come out of this alive and that was to sort out Dennis's problem. Then they might not notice if I answered the siren call of my duvet. "How can I help, Dennis?" I asked sweetly.

He gave me the wary look of a person who's drunk enough to notice their other half isn't giving them the hard time they deserve. "I could come back tomorrow," he said.

"I don't think that'll be necessary," I said repressively. "Like the song says, tonight will be fine."

Dennis gave me a quick sideways look and reached for his cigarettes. "You never finished your law degree, did you?"

I shook my head. It was a sore point with my mum and dad, who fancied being the parents of the first graduate in the family, but all it brought me was relief that business could never be so bad that I'd be tempted to set up shop as a lawyer. Two years of study had been enough to demonstrate there wasn't a single area of legal practice that wouldn't drive me barking within six months.

"So you couldn't charge me for legal advice," Dennis concluded triumphantly.

I raised my eyes to the heavens, where a few determined stars penetrated the sodium glow of the city sky. "No, Dennis, I couldn't." Then I gave him the hard stare. "But why would I want to? We've never sent each other bills before, have we? What exactly are you up to?"

"You know I'd never ask you to help me out with anything criminal, don't you?"

"'Course you wouldn't. You're far too tight to waste your breath," I said. Richard giggled again. I revised my estimate. Sixth bottle, fifth joint.

Dennis leaned across to pick up his jacket from the nearby chair, revealing splendid muscles in his forearm and a Ralph Lauren label. It didn't quite go with the jogging pants and the Manchester United away shirt. He pulled some papers out of the inside pocket then gave me a slightly apprehensive glance. Then he shrugged and said, "It's not illegal. Not as such."

"Not even a little bit?" I asked. I didn't bother trying to hide my incredulity. Dennis only takes offence when it's intended.

"This bit isn't illegal," he said firmly. "It's a lease."

"A lease?"

"For a shop."

"You're taking out a lease on a shop?" It was a bit like hearing Dracula had gone veggie.

He had the grace to look embarrassed. "Only technically."

I knew better than to ask more. Sometimes ignorance is not only bliss but also healthy. "And you want me to cast an eye over it to see that you're not being ripped off," I said, holding a hand out for the papers.

Curiously reluctant now, Dennis clutched the papers to his chest. "You do know about leases? I mean, it's not one of the bits you missed out, is it?"

It was, as it happened, but I wasn't about to tell him that. Besides, since I'd quit law school, I'd learned much more practical stuff about contracts and leases than I could ever have done if I'd stuck it out. "Gimme," I said.

"You don't want to argue with that tone of voice," Richard chipped in like the Dormouse at the Mad Hatter's tea party. Dennis screwed his face up like a man eating a piccalilli sandwich, but he handed over the papers.

It looked like a bog standard lease to me. It was for a shop in the Arndale Centre, the soulless shopping mall in the city centre that the IRA tried to remove from the map back in '96.

As usual, they got it wrong. The Arndale, probably the ugliest building in central Manchester, remained more or less intact. Unfortunately, almost every other building within a quarter-mile radius took a hell of a hammering, especially the ones that were actually worth looking at. As a result, the whole city centre ended up spending a couple of years looking like it had been wrapped by Christo in some bizarre pre-millennium celebration. Now it looked as if part of the mall that had been closed for structural repairs and renovation was opening up again and Dennis had got himself a piece of the action.

There was nothing controversial in the document, as far as I could see. If anything, it was skewed in favour of the lessee, one John Thompson, since it gave him the first three months at half rent as a supposed inducement. I wasn't surprised that it wasn't Dennis's name on the lease. He's a man who can barely bring himself to fill in his real name on the voters' roll. Besides, no self-respecting landlord would ever grant a lease to a man who, according to the credit-rating agencies, didn't even exist.

What I couldn't understand was what he was up to. Somehow, I couldn't get my head round the idea of Dennis as the natural heir of Marks and Spencer. Karl Marx, maybe, except that they'd have had radically different views of what constituted an appropriate redistribution of wealth. I folded the lease along its creases and said, "Looks fine to me."

Dennis virtually snatched it out of my hand and shoved it back in his pocket, looking far too shifty for a villain as experienced as him. "Thanks, love. I just wanted to be sure everything's there that should be. That it looks right."

I recognized the key word right away. Us detectives, we never sleep. "Looks right?" I demanded. "Why? Who else is going to be giving it the once-over?"

Dennis tried to look innocent. I've seen hunter-killer submarines give it a better shot. "Just the usual, you know? The leccy board, the water board. They need to see the lease before they'll connect you to the utilities."

"What's going on, Dennis? What's really going on?"

Richard pushed himself more or less upright and draped an arm over my shoulders. "You might as well tell her, Den. You know what they say—it's better having her inside the tent pissing out than outside pissing in."

I let him get away with the anatomical impossibility and settled for a savage grin. "He's not wrong," I said.

Dennis sighed and lit a cigarette. "All right. But I meant it when I said it's not criminal."

I cast my eyes upwards and shook my head. "Dennis O'Brien, you know and I know that 'not criminal' doesn't necessarily mean 'legal.'"

"Too deep for me," Richard complained, reaching for another bottle of beer.

"Let's hear it," I said firmly.

"You know how I hate waste," Dennis began. I nodded cautiously. "There's nothing more offensive to a man like me than premises standing empty because the landlords' agents are crap at their job. So I had this idea about making use of a resource that was just standing idle."

"Shop-squatting," I said flatly.

"What?" Richard asked vaguely. "You going to live in a shop, Den? What happened to the house? Debbie thrown you out, has she?"

"He's not going to be living in the shop, dope-head," I said sarcastically.

"You keep smoking that draw, you're going to have a mental age of three soon," Dennis added sententiously. "Of course I'm not going to be living in the shop. I'm going to be selling things in the shop."

"Take me through it," I said. Dennis's latest idea was only new to him; he was far from the first in Manchester to give it a try. I remembered reading something in the *Evening Chronicle* about shop-squatting, but as usual with newspaper articles, it had told me none of the things I really wanted to know.

"You want to know how it works?"

Silly question to ask a woman whose first watch lasted only as long as it took me to work out how to get the back off. "Was Georgie Best?"

"First off, you identify your premises. Find some empty shops and give the agents a ring. What you're looking for is one where the agent says they're not taking any offers because it's already let as from a couple of months ahead."

"What?" Richard mumbled.

Dennis and I shared the conspiratorial grin of those who are several drinks behind the mentally defective. "That way, you know it's going to stay empty for long enough for you to get in and out and do the business in between," he explained patiently.

"Next thing you do is you get somebody to draw you up a moody contract. One that looks like you've bought a short-term lease in good faith, cash on the nail. All you gotta do then is get into the shop and Bob's your uncle. Get the leccy and the water turned on, fill the place with crap, everything under a pound, which you can afford to do because you've got no overheads. And the Dibble can't touch you for it, on account of you've broken no laws."

"What about criminal damage?" I asked. "You have to bust the locks to get in."

Dennis winked. "If you pick the locks, you've not done any damage. And if you fit some new locks to give extra security, where's the damage in that?"

"Doesn't the landlord try to close you down?" Richard asked. It was an amazingly sensible question given his condition.

Dennis shrugged. "Some of them can't be bothered. They know we'll be out of there before their new tenant needs the premises, so they've got nothing to lose. Some of them have a go. I keep somebody on the premises all the time, just in case they try to get clever and repo the place in the night. You can get a homeless kid to play night watchman for a tenner a time. Give them a mobile phone and a butty and lock them in. Then if the landlord tries anything, I get the call and I get down there sharpish. He lays a finger on me or my lad, he's the criminal." Dennis smiled with all the warmth of a shark. "I'm told you get a very reasonable response when you explain the precise legal position."

"I can imagine," I said drily. "Do the explanations come complete with baseball bat?"

"Can people help it if they get the summons when they're on their way home from sports training?" He raised his eyebrows, trying for innocent and failing dismally.

"Profitable, is it?" I asked.

"It's got to be a very nice little earner, what with Christmas coming up."

"You know, Dennis, if you put half the effort into a straight business that you put into being bent, you'd be a multimillionaire by now," I sighed.

He shook his head, rueful. "Maybe so, but where would the fun be in that?"

He had a point. And who was I to talk? I'd turned my back on the straight version of my life a long time ago. If Dennis broke the law for profit, so did I. I'd committed burglary, fraud, assault, theft, deception and breaches of the Wireless Telegraphy Act too numerous to mention, and that was just in the past six months. I dressed it up with the excuse of doing it for the clients and my own version of justice. It had led me into some strange places, forced me into decisions that I didn't like to examine too closely in the harsh light of day. Once upon a time, I'd have had no doubt whether it was me or Dennis who could lay claim to the better view from the moral high ground.

These days, I wasn't quite so sure.

4

MOON SQUARES MARS

An accident-prone aspect, suggesting she can harm herself through lack of forethought. She is far too eager to make her presence felt and doesn't always practice self-control. Her feelings of insecurity can manifest themselves in an unfeminine belligerence. She has authoritarian tendencies.

From *Written in the Stars*, by Dorothea Dawson

Anyone can be a soap star. All you need is a scriptwriter who knows you well enough to write your character into their series, and you're laughing all the way to the BAFTA. I'd always thought you had to be an actor. But two hours on the set of *Northerners* made me realize that soap is different. About ten per cent of the cast could play Shakespeare or Stoppard. The rest just roll up to the studios every week and play themselves. The lovable rogues are just as roguish, the dizzy blondes are just as empty-headed, the salts of the earth make you thirst just as much for a long cold alcoholic drink and the ones the nation loves to hate are every bit as repulsive in the flesh. Actually, they're more repulsive, since anyone hanging round the green room is exposed to rather more of their flesh than a reasonable person could desire. There was more chance of me being struck by lightning than being star struck by that lot of has-beens and wannabes.

They didn't even have to learn their words. TV takes are so short that a gnat with Alzheimer's could retain the average speech with no trouble at all. Especially by the sixth or seventh take most of the *Northerners* cast seemed to need to capture the simplest sentiment on screen.

The main problem I had was how to do my job. Gloria had told everyone I was her bodyguard. Not because I couldn't come up with a decent cover story, but because I'd weighed up both sides of the argument and decided that if there was somebody in cast or crew who was out to get her it was time for them to understand they should back off and forget about it. Gloria had been all for the cloak and dagger approach, hoping I could catch the author of her threatening letters in the act of extracting vengeance, but I pointed out that if I was going to stay close enough to protect her, I'd be an obvious obstacle to nefarious doings anyway.

Besides, members of the public weren't allowed on the closed set of *Northerners*. The storylines were supposed to be top secret. NPTV, the company who made the soap, were so paranoid they made New Labour look relaxed. Everyone who worked on the programme had to sign an agreement that disclosure of any information relating to the cast characters or storylines was gross misconduct, a sacking offence and a strict liability tort. Even I had had to sign up to the tort clause before I was allowed into the compound that housed the interior and exterior sets, as well as the production suite and admin offices. Apart from location shooting to give the show that authentic Manchester ambience, the entire process from script conference to edited master tapes took place behind the high walls that surrounded NPTV's flagship complex.

A fat lot of good it did them. *Northerners* generated more column inches than any other TV programme in the country. The fuel for the flames had to come from somewhere, and tabloid

papers have always had deep pockets. There's not a tabloid journalist I've ever met who couldn't explain in words of one syllable
to a nervously dithering source that the NPTV legal threat of
suing for civil damages was about as solid as the plyboard walls
of Brenda Barrowclough's living room.

But NPTV insisted on their power trip, and I'd persuaded
Gloria it would be simpler all round if we were upfront. The
downside of being out in the open was that everyone was on
their guard. Nobody was going to let anything slip accidentally.
If my target was a member of the *Northerners* team, they'd be
very careful around me.

In order to be effective protection for my client, I had to
be visible, which meant that I couldn't even find a quiet corner
and catch up with my e-mail and my invoices. If Gloria was in
make-up, I was in make-up. If Gloria was on set, I was hovering
round the edges of the set, getting in everybody's way. If Gloria
was having a pee, I was leaning against the tampon dispenser.
I could have made one of those video diary programmes that
would have had any prospective private eye applying for a job
as a hospital auxiliary.

I was trying to balance that month's books in my head when
a hand on my shoulder lifted my feet off the floor. Spot the alert
bodyguard. I spun round and found my nose level with the top
button of a suit jacket. I took a step back and looked up. The
man must have been six-three, wide shouldered and heavy featured. The suit, whose tailoring owed more to Savile Row than
to Armani, was cut to disguise the effects of too many business
lunches and dinners, but this guy was still a long way off fat. On
the other hand, he looked as if he was still only in his early forties and in the kind of trim that betrays a commitment to regular
exercise. In a few years, when his joints started complaining and
his stamina wasn't what it had been, he'd swiftly slip into florid
flabbiness. I'd seen the type. Greed was always a killer.

The smile on his broad face softened the stern good looks
that come with a square jaw, a broad brow and deep-set eyes

under overhanging brows. "You must be Kate Brannigan," he said, extending a hand. "I didn't mean to startle you. I'm John Turpin."

For a man who'd gone out of his way to try to persuade Gloria to keep her problems in the family, he seemed amazingly cordial. "Pleased to meet you," I said.

"How are your investigations proceeding?" he asked, smiling down on me benevolently.

"I could ask you the same question." If the guy was trying to win me over with his affable helpfulness, the least I could do was take advantage and trawl for some information.

His smile curved up at one corner, suddenly turning his expression from magnanimous to predatory. "I'm afraid I'm more of a guardian of company confidentiality than Ms Kendal," he said, with a note of acid in his voice.

"But you expect me to share with you?" I asked innocently.

He chuckled. "Not really, but it never hurts to try. As you yourself so ably demonstrated. I had hoped we could keep Ms Kendal's little problem in-house, but if she insists on wasting her money on services we can provide more effectively and for free, I can't stop her."

"Can I tell her when to expect the results of your internal inquiry?" I wasn't playing the sweetness and light game any more. It hadn't got me anywhere so I figured I might as well turn into Ms Businesslike.

Turpin thrust one hand into his jacket pocket, thumb sticking out like Prince Charles always has. "Impossible to say. I have so many calls on my time, most of them rather more serious than the antics of some poison-pen writer."

"She had her car tyres slashed. All four of them. On NPTV premises," I reminded him.

"It's a bitchy business, soap," he said calmly. "I'm far from convinced there's any connection between the letters and the car tyres. I can't believe you find it hard to credit that Ms Kendal could annoy a colleague enough for them to lose their temper and behave so childishly."

"You're really not taking this seriously, are you?" I said, struggling to keep the incredulity out of my voice.

"That's what you're being paid for, Ms Brannigan. Me, I've got a television production company to run." He inclined his head and gave me the full charm offensive again. "It's been a pleasure."

I said nothing, just watched his retreating back with its double-vent tailoring that perfectly camouflaged the effects of too many hours sitting behind a desk. If our conversation was par for the course around here, the only surprise was that it had taken Gloria so long to get round to hiring me.

⋙◆⋘

In spite of Turpin's intervention, by lunchtime I was more bored than I'd been in the weeks before I finally managed to jettison A level Latin. If anyone had asked, I'd have admitted to being up for any distraction. I'd have been lying, as I discovered when my moby rang, right in the middle of the fifth run-through of a tense scene between my client and the putative father of her granddaughter's aborted foetus.

Mortified, I twisted my face into an apologetic grimace as the actor playing opposite Gloria glared at me and muttered, "For fuck's sake. What is this? Fucking amateur city?" The six months he'd once spent on remand awaiting trial for rape (according to the front page of the *Sun* a couple of months back) hadn't improved his word power, then.

I ducked behind a props skip and tucked my head down into my chest as I grunted, "Hello?"

"Kate? I've been arrested." The voice was familiar, the scenario definitely wasn't. Donovan Carmichael was a second-year engineering student at UMIST. He'd just started eking out his pathetic student grant by working part time for me as a process-server, doing the bread and butter work that pays his mother's wages. Did I mention Shelley the office tyrant was his mother? And that she hated the thought that her highly educated baby boy might be tempted to throw it all away to become a maverick of the mean streets like her boss? That probably explained why said boy was using his one phone call on me rather than on his doting mother.

"What for?"

"Being black, I think," he said angrily.

"What happened?"

"I was in Hale Barns." That explained a lot. They don't have a lot of six-feet-three-inch black lads in Hale Barns, especially not ones with shoulders wider than the flashy sports cars in their four-car garages. It would lower the property values too much.

"Doing what?"

"Working," he said. "You know? Trying to make that delivery that came in yesterday afternoon?" His way of telling me there were other ears on our conversation. I knew he was referring to a domestic violence injunction we'd been hired to serve. The husband had broken his wife's cheekbone the last time he'd had a bad day. If Donovan succeeded in serving the paper, there might not be a next time. But there were very good reasons why Donovan was reluctant to reveal his target or our client's name to the cops. Once you get outside the high-profile city-centre divisions that are constantly under scrutiny, you find that most policemen don't have a lot of sympathy for the victims of domestic violence. Especially when the guy who's been doing the battering is one of the city's biggest football stars. He'd given a whole new meaning to the word "striker," but that wouldn't stop him being a hero in the eyes of the boys in blue.

"Are they charging you with anything?"

"They've not interviewed me yet."

"Which nick are you in?"

"Altrincham."

I looked at my watch. I stuck my head round the side of the skip. They were about to go for a take. "I'll get someone there as soon as I can. Till then, say nothing. OK?" I said in a low voice.

I didn't wait for a reply, just ended the call and tiptoed back to the set. Gloria and the idiot boy she was acting opposite went through their interaction for the eighth time and the director announced she was satisfied. Gloria heaved a seismic sigh and walked off the set, dragging Brenda's beehive from her head as she approached me. "That's me for today, chuck," she said. "Drop me at home and you can have the rest of the day off."

"Are you staying in?" I asked, falling into step beside her as we walked to the dressing room she shared with Rita Hardwick, the actress who played Thelma Torrance, the good-time girl who'd never grown up.

"I am that. I've got to pick up next month's scripts from the office on the way out. I'll be lying in the Jacuzzi learning my lines till bedtime. It's not a pretty sight, and I don't need a spectator. Especially one that charges me for the privilege," she added with an earthy chuckle.

I tried not to look as pleased as I felt. I could have sent a lawyer out to rescue Donovan, but it didn't sound as if things had reached the point where I couldn't sort it out myself, and lawyers cost either money I couldn't afford or favours I didn't want to owe.

⚜

Two hours later, I was walking Donovan back to my car. The police don't like private eyes, but faced with me threatening a lawsuit for false imprisonment and racial harassment, they were only too happy to release Donovan from the interview room where he'd been pacing the floor for every one of the minutes it had taken me to get there.

"I didn't do anything, you know," Donovan complained. His anger seethed just below the surface. I couldn't blame him, but for all our sakes, I hoped the cycle ride back into town would get it out of his system.

"According to the copper I spoke to, one of the neighbours saw you sneaking round the back of the house and figured you for a burglar," I said drily.

"Yeah, right. All I was doing was checking if he was in the snooker room round the back, like his wife said he usually is if he's not training in the morning. I reckoned if he was there, and I walked right up to the French windows, he'd be bound to come over and open up, at least to give me a bollocking. When I saw the place was empty, I came back down the drive and went and sat on a wall down the road, where I could see him come home. It's not like I was hiding," he continued. "They only arrested me because I'm black. Anybody black on the street in Hale Barns has got to be a burglar, right?"

"Or a drug dealer. The rich have got to get their coke and heroin from somewhere," I pointed out reasonably. "Where's your bike?"

"Hale Barns. Chained to a lamppost, I hope."

"Let's go back out there and do it," I sighed.

The leafy lanes of Hale Barns were dripping a soft rain down our necks as we walked along the grass verge that led to our target's house. Wrought-iron gates stood open, revealing a long drive done in herringbone brick. There was enough of it there to build a semi. At the top of the drive, a matching pair of Mercedes sports cars were parallel parked. My heart sank. "I don't believe it," I muttered.

We walked up the drive towards a vast white hacienda-style ranch that would have been grandiose in California. In Cheshire, it just looked silly. I leaned on the doorbell. There was a long pause, then the door swung silently open without warning. I recognized his face from the back pages of the *Chronicle*. For once, I didn't have to check ID before I served the papers. "Yeah?" he said, frowning. "Who are you?"

I leaned forward and stuffed the papers down the front of the towelling robe that was all he was wearing. "I'm Kate Brannigan, and you are well and truly served," I said.

As I spoke, over his shoulder, I saw a woman in a matching robe emerge from an archway. Like him, she looked as if she'd been in bed, and not for an afternoon nap. I recognized her from the *Chronicle* too. From the diary pages. Former model Bo Robinson. Better known these days as the wife of the man I'd just served with the injunction her solicitor had sweated blood to get out of a district judge.

Now I remembered what I'd hated most about my own days as a process-server.

———✦———

The last thing Donovan had said before he'd pedalled off to the university library was, "Don't tell my mum I got arrested, OK? Not even as a joke. Not unless you want her to put the blocks on me working for you again."

I'd agreed. Jokes are supposed to be funny, after all. Unfortunately, the cops at Altrincham weren't in on the deal. What I didn't know was that while I'd been savouring the ambience of their lovely foyer (decor by the visually challenged, furnishings by a masochist, posters from a template unchanged since 1959) the desk sergeant had been calling the offices of Brannigan & Co to check that the auburn-haired midget and the giant in the sweat suit really were operatives of the agency and not a pair of smart-mouthed burglars on the make.

I'd barely put a foot inside the door when Shelley's voice hit me like a blast furnace. "Nineteen years old and never been inside a police station," came the opening salvo. "Five minutes working with you, and he might as well be some smackhead from Moss Side. That's it now, his name's on their computer. Another black bastard who's got away with it, that's how they'll have him down."

I raised my palms towards her, trying to fend off her fury. "It's all right, Shelley. He wasn't formally arrested. They won't be putting anything into the computer."

Shelley snorted. "You're so street smart when it comes to your business. How come you can be so naive about our lives? You don't have the faintest idea what it means for a boy like Donovan to get picked up by the police! They don't see a hardworking boy who's been brought up to respect his elders and stay away from drugs. They just see another black face where it doesn't belong. And you put him there."

I edged across reception, trying to make the safe haven of my own office without being permanently disabled by the crossfire. "Shelley, he's a grown man. He has to make his own decisions. I told him when I took him on that serving process wasn't as easy as it sounded. But he was adamant that he could handle it."

"Of course he can handle it," she yelled. "He's not the problem. It's the other assholes out there, that's the problem. I don't want him doing this any more."

I'd almost reached the safety of my door. "You'll have to take that up with Don," I told her, sounding more firm than I felt.

"I will, don't you worry about that," she vowed.

"OK. But don't forget the reason he's doing this."

Her eyes narrowed. "What are you getting at?"

"It's about independence. He's trying to earn his own money so he's not dipping his hand in your pocket all the time. He's trying to tell you he's a man now." I took a deep breath, trying not to feel intimidated by the scowl that was drawing Shelley's perfectly shaped eyebrows into a gnarled scribble. My hand on the doorknob, I delivered what was supposed to be the knockout punch. "You've got to let him make his own mistakes. You've got to let him go."

I opened the door and dived for safety. No such luck. Instead of silent sanctuary, I fell into nerd heaven. A pair of pink-rimmed eyes looked up accusingly at me. Under the pressure of Shelley's rage, I'd forgotten that my office wasn't mine any more. Now I was the sole active partner in Brannigan & Co, I occupied the larger of the two rooms that opened off reception. When I'd been junior partner in Mortensen & Brannigan it had doubled as Bill Mortensen's office and the main client interview room. Now, it was my sanctum.

These days, my former bolthole was the computer room, occupied as and when the occasion demanded by Gizmo, our information technology consultant. In our business, that's the polite word for hacker. And when it comes to prowling other people's systems with cat-like tread, Gizmo is king of the dark hill. The trade-off for his computer acumen is that on a scale of one to ten, his social skills come in somewhere around absolute zero. I'm convinced that was the principal reason he was made redundant from his job as systems wizard with Telecom. Now they've become a multinational leading-edge company, everybody who works there has to pass for human. Silicon-based life forms like Gizmo just had to be downsized out the door.

Their loss was my gain. There had had to be changes, of course. Plain brown envelopes stuffed with banknotes had been replaced with a system more appealing to the taxman, if not to the company accountant. Then there was the personal grooming. Gizmo had always favoured an appearance that would have served as perfect camouflage if he'd been living on a refuse tip.

The clothes weren't so hard. I managed to make him stop twitching long enough to get the key measurements, then hit a couple of designer factory outlets during the sales. I was planning to dock the cost from his first consultancy fees, but I didn't want it to terrify him too much. Now he had two decent suits, four shirts that didn't look disastrous unironed, a couple of inoffensive ties and a mac that any flasher would have been proud of. I could wheel him out as our computer security expert without frightening the clients, and he had a couple of outfits that wouldn't entirely destroy his street cred if another of the undead happened to be on the street in daylight hours to see him.

The haircut had been harder. I don't think he'd spent money on a haircut since 1987. I'd always thought he simply took a pair of scissors to any stray locks whose reflection in the monitor distracted him from what he was working on. Gizmo tried to make me believe he liked it that way. It cost me five beers to get him to the point where I could drag him across the threshold of the city-centre salon where I'd already had to cancel three times. The stylist had winced in pain, but had overcome his aesthetic suffering for long enough to do the business. Giz ended up with a seriously sharp haircut and I ended up gobsmacked that lurking underneath the shambolic dress sense and terrible haircut was a rather attractive man. Scary.

Three months down the line, he was still looking the business, his hollow cheeks and bloodshot eyes fitting the current image of heroin addict as male glamour. I'd even overheard one of Shelley's adolescent daughter's mates saying she thought Gizmo was "shaggable." That *Trainspotting* has a lot to answer for. "All right," he mumbled, already looking back at his screen. "You two want to keep the noise down?"

"Sorry, Giz. I didn't actually mean to come in here."

"Know what you mean," he said.

Before I could leave, the door burst open. "And another thing," Shelley said. "You've not done a new client file for Gloria Kendal."

Gizmo's head came up like it was on a string. "Gloria Kendal? *The* Gloria Kendal? Brenda Barrowclough off *Northerners*?"

I nodded.

"She's a client?"

"I can't believe you watch *Northerners*," I said.

"She was in here yesterday," Shelley said smugly. "She signed a photograph for me personally."

"Wow! Gloria Kendal. Cool! Anything I can do to help?" The last time I'd seen him this excited was over an advance release of Netscape Navigator 3.0.

"I'll let you know," I promised. "Now, if you'll both excuse me, I have some work to do." I smiled sweetly and sidled past Shelley. As I crossed the threshold, the outside door opened and a massive basket of flowers walked in. Lilies, roses, carnations and a dozen other things I didn't know the names of. For a wild moment, I thought Richard might be apologizing for the night before. He had cause, given what had gone on after Dennis had left. The thought shrivelled and died as hope was overtaken by experience.

"They'll be from Gloria Kendal," Shelley predicted.

I contradicted her. "It'll be Donovan mortgaging his first month's wages to apologize to you."

"Wrong address," Gizmo said gloomily. Given the way the day had been running, he was probably right.

"Is this Brannigan and Co?" the flowers asked. For such an exotic arrangement, they had a remarkably prosaic Manchester accent.

"That's right," I said. "I'm Brannigan." I stepped forward expectantly.

"They're not for you, love," the voice said, half a face appearing round the edge of the blooms. "You got someone here called Gizmo?"

5

JUPITER IN CANCER IN THE 3RD HOUSE

Jupiter is exalted in Cancer. She has a philosophical outlook, enjoying speculative thinking. She is good humoured and generous, with strong protective instincts. Her intuition and imagination are powerful tools that she could develop profitably. She has a good business sense and communicates well in that sphere. She probably writes very thorough reports.

From *Written in the Stars*, by Dorothea Dawson

It was hard to keep my mind on Gloria's monologue on the way in to the studios the next morning. The conundrum of Gizmo's mysterious bouquet was much more interesting than her analysis of the next month's storylines for *Northerners*. When the delivery man had announced who the flowers were for, Shelley and I had rounded on Gizmo. Scarlet and stammering, he'd refused to reveal anything. Shelley, who's always been quick on her feet, helped herself to the card attached to the bouquet and ripped open the envelope.

All it said was, "www gets real." I know. I was looking over her shoulder. The delivery man had placed the flowers on Shelley's desk and legged it. He'd clearly seen enough blood shed over bouquets to hang around. "So who have you been chatting up on the Internet?" I demanded. "Who's the cyberbabe?"

"Cyberbabe?" Shelley echoed.

I pointed to the card. "www. The worldwide web. The Internet. It's from someone he's met websurfing. Well, not actually met, as such. Exchanged e-mail with."

"Safer than body fluids," Shelley commented drily. "So who's the cyberbabe, Gizmo?"

Gizmo shook his head. "It's a joke," he said with the tentative air of a man who doesn't expect to be believed. "Just the guys trying to embarrass me at work."

I shook my head. "I don't think so. I've never met a techie yet who'd spend money on flowers while there was still software on the planet."

"Honest, Kate, it's a wind-up," he said desperately.

"Some expensive wind-up," Shelley commented. "Did one of your mates win the lottery, then?"

"There is no babe, OK? Leave it, eh?" he said, this time sounding genuinely upset.

So we'd left it, sensitive girls that we are. Gizmo retreated back to his hi-tech hermitage and Shelley shrugged. "No use looking at me, Kate. He's not going to fall for the 'You can talk to me, I'm a woman, I understand these things' routine. It's down to you."

"Men never cry on my shoulder," I protested.

"No, but you're the only one around here who knows enough about computers to find who he's been talking to."

I shook my head. "No chance. If Gizmo's got a cybersecret, it'll be locked away somewhere I won't be able to find it. We'll just have to do this the hard way. First thing tomorrow, you better get on to the florist."

Call me a sad bastard, but as I was driving Gloria to the studios, I was busy working out how we could discover Gizmo's secret admirer if she'd been clever enough to cover her tracks on the flower delivery. So I almost missed it when Gloria asked

me a question that needed more than a grunt in response. "So
you don't mind coming along tonight?"

"No, that's fine," I said, not quite certain what I'd agreed to.

"I'm really buggering up your social life, chuck," she continued. "If you've got a fella you want to bring along, you're
welcome, you know."

I must have shown how unlikely a prospect that was, since
Gloria chuckled. "He's a rock journalist," I said.

She roared with laughter. "Better not bring him anywhere
I'm singing, then," she spluttered. "I'm too old to be insulted."

By the time we reached the studios, the sky had clouded
over and large raindrops were plopping on the windscreen. "Oh
bugger," Gloria said.

"Problems?"

"We're supposed to be filming outside this morning. When
it's raining like this, they'll hang on to see if it clears up and fill the
time with the indoor scenes scheduled for this afternoon. I'm not
in any of them, so not only do I lose an afternoon off but I get a
morning hanging around waiting for the weather to change." She
rummaged in the bulging satchel that contained her scripts and
pulled out a crumpled schedule. "Let's see . . . Could be worse.
Teddy and Clive are in the same boat. D'you play bridge, Kate?"

"Badly. I haven't played against humans since I was a student, and these days the computer usually gives me a coating."

"You can't be worse than Rita Hardwick," she said firmly.
"That's settled then."

❧❀❧

"Two spades," I said tentatively. My partner, Clive Doran (Billy
Knowles, the crooked bookmaker with an eye for his female
employees), nodded approval.

"Pass," said Gloria.

"Three hearts."

"Doubled," announced Teddy Edwards, Gloria's screen
husband, the feckless Arthur Barrowclough, cowboy builder

and failed gambler. I hoped he had as much luck with cards in real life as he did on screen. What Gloria had omitted to mention in the car was that we were playing for 10p a point. I suppose she figured she was paying me so much she needed to win some of it back.

I looked at my hand. "Redoubled," I said boldly. Clive raised one eyebrow. My bid passed round the table, and we started playing. I soon realized that the other three were so used to each other's game that they only needed a small proportion of their brains to choose the next card. The bridge game was just an excuse to gossip in the relative privacy of Gloria's dressing room.

"Seen the *Sun* this morning?" Clive asked, casually tossing a card down.

"It'd be hard to miss it," Gloria pointed out. "I don't know about where you live, but every newsagent we passed on the way in had a board outside. Gay soap star exposed: Exclusive. I sometimes wonder if this is the end of the nineteenth century, not the twentieth. I mean, who gives a stuff if Gary Bond's a poof? None of us does, and we're the ones as have to work with the lad."

"They're bloody idle, them hacks," Teddy grumbled, sweeping a trick from the table that I'd thought my ace of diamonds was bound to win.

Clive sucked his breath in over his teeth. "How d'you mean?"

"It couldn't have taken much digging out. It's not like it's a state secret, Gary being a homo. He's always going on about lads he's pulled on a night out in the gay village." Teddy sighed. "I remember when it were just the red light district round Canal Street. Back in them days, if you fancied a bit, at least you could be sure it was a woman under the frock."

"And it's not as if he's messing about with kids," Gloria continued, taking the next trick. "Nice lead, Teddy. I mean, Gary always goes for fellas his own age."

"There's been a lot of heavy stories about *Northerners* lately," I said. I might be playing dummy in this hand, but that didn't mean I had to take the job literally.

"You're not kidding," Clive said with feeling, sweeping his thin hair back from his narrow forehead in a familiar gesture. "You get used to living in a goldfish bowl, but lately it's been ridiculous. We're all behaving like Sunday-school teachers."

"Aye, but you can be as good as gold for all the benefit you'll get if the skeletons are already in the cupboard," said Gloria. "Seventeen years since Tony Peverell got nicked for waving his willy at a couple of lasses. He must have thought that were dead and buried long since. Then up it pops on the front of the *News of the World*. And his wife a churchwarden." She shook her head. I remembered the story.

"He quit the programme, didn't he?" I asked, making a note of our winning score and gathering the cards to me so I could shuffle while Gloria dealt the next hand with the other pack.

"Did he fall or was he pushed?" Clive intoned. It would have sounded sinister from someone who didn't have a snub nose and a dimple in his chin and a manner only marginally less camp than Kenneth Williams. It was hard to believe he was happily married with three kids, but according to Gloria, the limp-wristed routine was nothing more than a backstage affectation. "And I should know," she'd winked. I didn't ask.

"What do you mean?" I asked now.

"John Turpin's what he means," Gloria said. "I told you about Turpin, didn't I? The management's hatchet man. Administration and Production Coordinator, they call him. Scumbag, we call him. Just a typical bloody TV executive who's never made a programme all his born days but thinks he knows better than everybody else what makes good telly."

"Turpin's in charge of cast contracts," Clive explained, sorting his cards. "So he's the one who's technically responsible when there's a leak to the press. He's been running around like all Four Horsemen of the Apocalypse rolled into one for the last six months. He threatens, he rants, he rages, but still the stories keep leaking out. One diamond."

"Pass. It drives him demented," Teddy said with a smug little smile that revealed rodent teeth.

"One heart?" I tried, wondering what message that was sending to my partner. When he'd asked what system of bidding I preferred, I'd had to smile weakly and say, "Psychic?" He hadn't looked impressed.

"It's not the scandals that really push his blood pressure through the ceiling. It's the storyline leaks." Gloria lit a cigarette, eyeing Teddy speculatively. "Two clubs. Remember when the *Sunday Mirror* got hold of that tale about Colette's charity?"

"Colette Darvall?" I asked.

"That's right."

"I must have missed that one," I said.

"Two diamonds," Clive said firmly. "Off the planet that month, were you? When her daughter was diagnosed with MS, Colette met up with all these other people who had kids in the same boat. So she let them use her as a sort of figurehead for a charity. She worked her socks off for them. She was always doing PAs for free, giving them stuff to raffle, donating interview fees and all sorts. Then it turns out one of the organizers has been ripping the charity off. He legged it to the West Indies with all the cash. Which would have been nothing more than a rather embarrassing tragedy for everyone concerned if it hadn't been for the unfortunate detail that he'd been shagging Colette's brains out for the previous three months."

"Oops," I said.

"By heck, you private eyes know how to swear, don't you?" Teddy said acidly. "I don't think 'oops' was quite what Colette was saying. But Turpin was all right about that. He stuck one of the press officers on her doorstep night and day for a week and told her not to worry about her job."

"That's because having a fling with somebody else's husband is sexy in PR terms, whereas flashing at schoolgirls is just sleazy," Clive said. "Have you taken a vow of silence, Teddy? Or are you going to bid?"

"Oh God," Teddy groaned. "Who dealt this dross? I'm going to have to pass. Sorry, Glo."

"Pass," I echoed.

"And I make it three in a row. It's all yours, Clive." Gloria leaned back in her chair and blew a plume of smoke towards the ceiling. "God, I love it when Rita's not here to whinge about me smoking."

"Better not let Turpin catch you," Clive said.

"He sounds a real prize, this Turpin," I said. "I met him yesterday and he was nice as ninepence to me. Told me nothing, mind you, but did it charmingly."

"Smooth-talking bastard. He did the square root of bugger-all about sorting out my security. Bloody chocolate teapot," Gloria said dismissively. "At least this latest furore about the future of the show has stopped him going on about finding out who's leaking the storylines to the press."

"The future of the show? They're surely not going to axe *Northerners*?" It was a more radical suggestion than abolishing the monarchy, and one that would have had a lot more people rioting in the streets. For some reason, the public forgave the sins of the cast of their favourite soap far more readily than those of the House of Windsor, even though they paid both lots of wages, one via their taxes, the other via the hidden tax of advertising.

"Don't be daft," Gloria said. "Of course they're not going to axe *Northerners*. That'd be like chocolate voting for Easter. No, what they're on about is moving us to a satellite or cable channel."

I stared blankly at her, the cards forgotten. "But that would mean losing all your viewers. There's only two people and a dog watch cable."

"And the dog's a guide dog," Teddy chipped in gloomily.

"The theory is that if *Northerners* defects to one of the pay-to-view channels, the viewers will follow," Clive said. "The men in suits think our following is so addicted that they'd rather shell out for a satellite dish than lose their three times weekly fix of an everyday story of northern folk."

"Hardly everyday," I muttered. "You show me anywhere in Manchester where nobody stays out of work for more than a fortnight and where the corner shop, the fast-food outlet and the local newsagent are still run by white Anglo-Saxons."

"We're not a bloody documentary," Teddy said. He'd clearly heard similar complaints before. His irritation didn't upset me unduly, since it resulted in him throwing away the rest of the hand with one hasty lead.

"No, we're a fantasy," Clive said cheerfully, sweeping up the next trick and laying down his cards. "I think the rest are ours. What we're providing, Kate, is contemporary nostalgia. We're harking back to a past that never existed, but we're translating it into contemporary terms. People feel alienated and lonely in the city and we create the illusion that they're part of a community. A community where all the girls are pretty, all the lads have lovely shoulders and any woman over thirty-five is veneered with a kind of folk wisdom."

I was beginning to understand why Clive hid behind the camp manner. Underneath it all there lay a sharper mind than most of his fellow cast members ever exhibited. He was just as self-absorbed as they were, but at least he'd given some thought to how he earned his considerable living. I bet that made him really popular in a green room populated by egos who were each convinced they were the sole reason for the show's success. "So you reckon the tug of fantasy is so strong that the millions who tune in three times a week will take out their satellite subscriptions like a bunch of little lambs?" I said, my scepticism obvious.

"*We* don't, chuck," Gloria said, lighting a fresh cigarette while Clive dealt the cards. "But the management do."

"That's hardly surprising," Teddy said. "They're the ones who are going to make a bomb whatever happens."

"How come?" I asked.

"The contract NPTV has with the ITV network is due for renegotiation. The network knows NPTV have been talking to satellite and cable companies with a view to them buying first rights in *Northerners* for the next three years. So the network knows that the price is going to have to go up. There's going to be a bidding war. And the only winners are going to be the management at NPTV, with their pocketfuls of share options. If they're wrong and the viewers don't follow the programme in droves, it doesn't matter to them, because they'll already have their hot sticky hands on the cash," Clive explained.

"So Turpin needs to plug the storyline leak," Gloria said, examining her cards.

"I'm not sure I follow you. Surely any publicity is good publicity?"

"Not when it involves letting the public know in advance what's going to happen," Teddy said, raising his eyes to the heavens as if I was stupid. I didn't react. After all, I wasn't the one who was currently fourteen quid out of pocket.

Clive took pity on my puzzlement. "If people know the big storylines in advance, a lot of them think it won't be the end of the world if they miss a few eps, because they know what they'll be missing. Once they get out of the habit of watching every ep religiously, their viewing habits drift."

"They find other programmes on at the same time that they get to like. They don't bother setting the video to watch us because they think they already know what's going to happen. Or they just go down the pub. Before you know it, they've lost touch with the programme," Gloria continued. "One heart."

"Especially now we're three times a week. You dip out for two, three weeks and when you come back, you don't know some of the faces. I'm going to pass this time."

Teddy tugged at his shirt collar, a mannerism either he'd borrowed from Arthur Barrowclough or the character had borrowed from him. "Two hearts. And every time the viewing figures drop, John Turpin sees his share of the profits going down."

"And we get to watch his blood pressure going up," Gloria said. "Three hearts," she added, noting my shake of the head.

"I'd have thought he'd be on to a loser, trying to find out who's behind it. It's too good an earner for the mole to give it up, and no journalist on the receiving end of a series of exclusives like that is going to expose a source," I said.

"It won't be for want of trying," Gloria said. "He's even got every script coded so that any photocopied pages can be traced back. I hope whoever it is really is making a killing, because they're not going to earn another shilling off NPTV if they're caught."

"You'll never work in this town again," Teddy drawled in a surprisingly convincing American accent. I was so accustomed to him behaving in character I'd almost forgotten he was an actor.

"And speaking of making a killing, Gloria, any more news from your stalker?"

Gloria scowled. "By heck, Clive, you know how to put a girl off her game. No, I've heard nowt since I took Kate on. I'm hoping we've frightened him off."

"How do you know it's a he?" Clive said.

"Believe me, Clive, I know."

We played out the hand in silence for a moment. In bridge as in life, I've always been better at defence than attack. Clive also seemed to relish the taste of blood and we left Gloria and Teddy three tricks short of their contract. My client raised her eyebrows and lit another cigarette. "She lied so beautifully, Teddy. I really believed her when she said she was crap at this."

"Don't tell Turpin," Teddy said sharply. "He'll hire her out from under you."

"My dears, for all we know, he's done that already," Clive said archly.

I should be so lucky, I thought as they all stared at me. I'm not proud about whose money I take. Maybe I should engineer another encounter with Turpin the hatchet man and kill two birds with one stone. Gloria's eyes narrowed, either from the smoke or because she could see the wheels going round in my head. "Don't even think about it," she warned me. "Chances are it's one of our brain-dead mates who's ratting to the vampires, and I don't want that on my conscience."

I nodded. "Fair enough. Whose deal is it?"

6

VENUS IN LEO IN THE 4TH HOUSE

She can show great extravagance, both practical and emotional, to those she cares for. She is loyal but likes to dominate situations of the heart. She has creative ability, which can sometimes lead to self-dramatization. Her domestic surroundings must be easy on the eye.

From *Written in the Stars*, by Dorothea Dawson

My second evening bodyguarding Gloria Kendal taught me that I really should pay more attention to the client. The evening engagement I'd so blithely agreed to turned out to be another of the nights from hell that seemed to be how Gloria spent her free time. That night, she was guest of honour at the annual dinner dance of the ladies' division of the North West branch of the Association of Beverage and Victuals Providers. I've never been in the same room as that much hairspray. If taste were IQ, there would only have been a handful of them escaping Special Needs education. I'd thought the Blackburn outfit would have blended in nicely at a women-only dinner, but I was as flash as a peahen at a peacock convention. I should have realized Gloria wasn't wearing those sequins and diamanté for a bet.

About ten minutes after we arrived in Ormskirk, I sussed this wasn't one of those dinners you go to for the food. I know

seventies food is coming back into fashion, but the Boar and
Truffle's menu of prawn cocktail, boeuf bourguignon and, to
crown it all, Black Forest gateau owed nothing to the Style
Police or the foodies. You could tell that every cooking fashion
in the intervening twenty years had passed them by. This was
a dinner my Granny Brannigan would have recognized and
approved of. It wasn't entirely surprising; nobody who had any
choice in the matter would spend a minute longer than they had
to in a town characterized by a one-way system that's twice the
size of the town centre itself. It's the only place I know where
they're so proud of their back streets they have to show them
to every unwary motorist who gets trapped there on the way
to Southport.

The landladies, most of whom almost certainly served better pub grub back home, didn't care. The only function of the
food they were interested in was its capacity to line the stomach
and absorb alcohol. It wasn't a night to be the designated driver,
never mind bodyguard.

Gloria was on fine form, though. She'd heeded what I'd
said about keeping her back to the wall and trying to make sure
there was a table between her and her admirers. It wasn't easy,
given how many of the female publicans of the North West
desperately needed to have their photographs taken in a clinch
with my client. But she smiled and smiled, and drank her gin
and made a blisteringly funny and scathing speech that would
have had a rugby club audience blushing.

"I'm sorry you've been landed with all this ferrying me
around," she said as I drove across the flat fields of the Fylde
towards the motorway and civilization.

"Who normally does it?" I asked.

"A pal of mine. He got the sack last year for being over fifty.
He's not going to get another job at his age. He enjoys the driving and it gives him a few quid in his back pocket." She yawned
and reached for her cigarettes. It was her car, so I didn't feel I
could complain. Instead, I opened the window. Gloria shivered

at the blast of cold air and snorted with laughter. "Point taken," she said, shoving the cigarettes back in her bag. "How much longer do you think we're going to have to be joined at the hip?"

"Depends on you," I said. "I don't think you've got a stalker. I've seen no signs of anybody following us, and I've had a good look around where you live. There's no obvious vantage point for anybody to stake out your home—"

"One of the reasons I bought it," Gloria interrupted. "Those bloody snappers with their long lenses make our lives a misery, you know. All those editors, they all made their holier-than-thou promises after they hounded Princess Di to her death, but nothing's changed, you know. They're still chasing us every chance they get. But they can't catch me there. Not that I'm likely to be doing anything more exciting than planting out my window boxes, but I'm buggered if the *Sun*'s readers have any right to know whether I'm having Busy Lizzies or lobelia this year."

"So that probably confirms that whoever has been sending the letters is connected to the show; they can keep tabs on you because they see you at work every day. And they can pick up background details quite easily, it seems to me. The cast members talk quite freely among themselves and you don't have to set out to eavesdrop to pick up all sorts of personal information. I've only been on the set for a couple of days and already I know Paul Naylor's seeing an acupuncturist in Chinatown for his eczema, Rita Hardwick's husband breeds pugs and Tiffany Joseph's bulimic. Another week and I'd have enough background information to write threatening letters to half the cast." What I didn't say was that another week among the terminally self-obsessed, and threatening letters would be the least of what I'd be up for.

"It's not a pretty thought, that. Somebody that knows me hates me enough to want me to be frightened. I don't like that idea one little bit."

"If the letters and the tyre slashing are connected, then it almost certainly has to be somebody at NPTV, you know. Of course, it is possible that the tyre slasher isn't the letter writer, just some sicko who took advantage of your concern over the letters to wind you up. I've asked you this before, but you've had time to think about it now: are you sure there isn't anybody you've pissed off that might just be one scene short of a script?"

Gloria shook her head. "Come on, chuck. You've spent time with me now. You've seen the way I am with the folk I work with. I'm a long way off perfect, but I don't wind them up like certain other people I could mention."

"I'd noticed," I said drily. "The thing is, now everybody at NPTV knows you're taking what Dorothea said seriously. The person who wrote you those letters is basking in a sense of power, which means that he or she probably won't feel the need to carry the threats through any further. Besides, they won't know whether I'm off the case altogether or I've taken the surveillance undercover. Much as I'd love to be on this hourly rate indefinitely, I'd be inclined to give it another couple of days and then I'll pull out."

"You're sure I'll be safe? I'm not a silly woman, in spite of how I come across, but what Dorothea said really scared me, coming on top of the business with the tyres. She's not given to coming the spooky witch, you know."

"When is she in next?"

"Day after tomorrow. Do you want to see her?"

"I want to interview her, not have a consultation," I said hastily.

"Oh, go on," Gloria urged. "Have it on me. You don't have to take it seriously." She opened her bag and took out a pen and one of the postcard-sized portraits of herself she carried everywhere for the fans who otherwise would have had her signing everything from their library books to any available part of their anatomies. "Give us your time, date and place of birth." She snapped on the interior light, making me blink hard against the darkness. "Come on, sooner you tell me, the sooner you get the light off again."

"Oxford," I said. "Fourth of September, 1966."

"Now why am I not surprised you're a Virgo?" Gloria said sarcastically as she turned off the light. "Caligula, Jimmy Young, Agatha Christie, Cecil Parkinson, Raine Spencer and you."

"Which proves it's a load of old socks," I said decisively. A couple of miles down the road, it hit me. "How come you can rattle off a list of famous Virgoans?"

"I married one. Well, not a famous one. And divorced him. I wish I'd known Dorothea then. Virgo and Leo? She'd never have let it happen. A recipe for disaster."

"Aren't you taking a bit of a chance, working with me?"

Gloria laughed, that great swooping chuckle that gets the nation grinning when things are going right for Brenda Barrowclough. "Working's fine. Nobody grafts harder than a Virgo. You see the detail while I only get the big picture. And you never give up. No, you'll do fine for me."

It's funny how often clients forget they've said that when a case doesn't work out the way they wanted it to. I only hoped Gloria wouldn't live to regret her words. I grunted noncommittally and concentrated on the road.

It was almost one when I walked through my own front door. Both my house and Richard's were illuminated only by the dirty orange of the sodium streetlights. I'd hoped he'd be home; I was suffering from what my best friend Alexis calls NSA— Non-Specific Anxiety—and my experience of self-medicating has told me the best cure is a cuddle. But it looked like he was doing whatever it is that rock journos do in live music venues in the middle of the night. It probably involved drugs, but Richard never touches anything stronger than joints and these days all the cops do with cannabis is confiscate it for their own use, so I wasn't worried on that score.

I turned on the kitchen light, figuring a mug of hot chocolate might prevent the vague feeling of unease from keeping me awake. I couldn't miss the sheet of paper stuck under a fridge magnet. "Babysitting for Alexis + Chris. Staying over. See you tomorrow. Big kisses." I didn't need to be a handwriting expert to know it was from my besotted lover. The only problem was, it wasn't me he was besotted with.

I'd know how to fight back if it was a beautiful blonde waving her perfectly rounded calves at him. But how exactly can a woman keep her dignity and compete with a nine-month-old baby girl?

※⋄※

The following day, we were let out to play. Because *Northerners* traded so heavily on its connection to Manchester, the city of cool, they had to reinforce the link with regular exterior and interior shots of identifiable landmarks. It had led to a profitable spin-off for NPTV, who now ran *Northerners* tours at weekends. The punters would stay in the very hotel where Pauline Pratt and Gordon Johnstone had consummated their adulterous affair, then they'd be whisked off on a walking tour that took in sites from key episodes. They'd see the tram line where Diane Grimshaw committed suicide, the alley where Brenda Barrowclough was mugged, the jewellery shop that was robbed while Maureen and Phil Pomeroy were choosing an engagement ring. They'd have lunch in the restaurant where Kamal Sayeed had worked as a waiter before his tragic death from streptococcal meningitis. In the afternoon, they visited the sets where the show was filmed, and a couple of cast members joined them for dinner, persuaded by veiled threats and large fees.

To keep that particular gravy train running, the show had to film on the streets of the city at least once a month. That day, they were filming a series of exterior shots at various points along the refurbished Rochdale Canal. According to Gloria, a new producer was determined to stamp his authority on the soap with a series of themed episodes. The linking theme of this particular week was the idea of the waterway providing a range of back-drops, from the sinister to the seriously hip. Gloria had drawn the short straw of an argument with Teddy outside Barca, Mick

Hucknall's chic Catalan bistro. On a summer afternoon, it might have been a pleasant diversion. On a bleak December morning, it was about as much fun as sunbathing in Siberia. It took forever to film because trains and trams would keep rattling across the high brick viaducts above our heads when the cameras were rolling.

I couldn't even take refuge in the cast or crew buses, since I needed to keep a close eye on Gloria. In spite of what I'd said the night before, I hadn't entirely ruled out the possibility of an obsessive fan who was stalking her. The fact that she spent so much of her time inaccessible might actually fuel his derangement. He could be planning to take action against her only when she was in a public place and in character.

I huddled under the awning of the catering truck, where a red-haired giant with a soft Highland accent supervised the pair of young women who were responsible for making sure there was a constant flow of bacon, sausage and/or egg butties for anyone who wanted them. They served me with a steaming carton of scalding coffee, which I held under my chin. Not for long, though. If my nose thawed out too quickly, there was always the possibility of it shearing off from the rest of my face.

I half listened to the conversation in the van behind me. It was a lot more interesting than the script Teddy and Gloria were working their way through. The caterers were discussing that day's lunch menu and the cast members in roughly equal proportions. I can't think why, but they seemed not to have a lot of respect for their customers. I was stifling a giggle at one particularly scurrilous comment about the randiness of one of the show's young studs being in inverse proportion to the size of his equipment when I was aware that I had company under the awning. The Rob Roy lookalike had abandoned his assistants and slipped out for a fag. The environmental health department would have been impressed.

He grinned. Close up, he was even more attractive than he was with a steaming array of food between us. His thick red-gold hair was swept back from a high, broad forehead. Eyes the blue of the Windows 95 intro screen sparkled above high cheekbones. He had one of those mouths romantic novelists always describe as cruel, which lets you know the heroine's probably going to end up in the guy's arms if not his bed. "Hiya," he said. "I'm Ross Grant. I own the location catering company."

The coffee had defrosted my lips enough for me to return his smile. "Kate Brannigan. I'm—"

"I know who you are," he interrupted, sounding amused. "You're Gloria's bodyguard. Dorothea Dawson, the Seer to the Stars, told her she was going to be murdered, and she hired you to protect her."

"You've been watching too much television," I said lightly. "People don't lash out the kind of money I cost without having good reason."

"I'm sorry," he said. "I didn't mean to insult your professionalism. Or to take the piss out of Dorothea. She's been really good to us."

"Predicting a sudden rush on bacon butties, you mean?"

He gave a sheepish grin. "Very funny. No, I mean it. You know how she's always on the telly? Well, she's recommended us to quite a few of the programmes she's been on. We've got a lot of work off the back of it. She's great, Dorothea. She really understands what it's like trying to make a living out of a business where you're constantly dependent on goodwill. So she goes out of her way for folk like us, know what I mean? Not like most of them round here, it's self, self, self. Working with people that are so full of themselves, we find it hard to take anything about them seriously."

This time it was my turn to smile. "They do lack a certain sense of proportion."

"But you're more than just a bodyguard, aren't you? Somebody said you're a proper private investigator."

"That's right. In fact, I almost never do this kind of work. But Gloria can be very persuasive."

"Don't I know it. This is the woman that had me up all
night making petits fours for her granddaughter's birthday party.
Is she really in danger, then?"

I shrugged. "Better safe than sorry."

"I'm sorry to hear that. She's the best of the bunch. I don't
like to think of her in fear of her life. I wasn't asking out of nosi-
ness," he added quickly. "I just wondered how long you were
going to be tied up working for Gloria."

"Why? Are you missing me already?"

He went that strange damson-purple that redheads go when
they blush. "Actually, I wanted to hire you."

"Hire me?" Suddenly this was a lot more interesting than
a mild flirtation to keep the cold out. "What for?"

"I don't know if you know, but *Northerners* has got a mole.
Somebody's been leaking stuff to the press. Not just the usual
sordid stuff about people's love lives and creepy things they did
twenty years ago, but storylines as well." All the humour had
left him now.

"I'd heard. John Turpin's supposed to be finding out where
the leak is."

"Yeah, well, Turpin's trying to pin it on me or my staff,"
Ross said bluntly.

"Why would he do that?"

He inhaled sharply. "Because we're convenient scapegoats.
Our contract's up for renewal at the end of January, and Turpin
seems to be determined to ditch me. Knowing that slimy bastard,
he's probably in bed with one of the other firms tendering for
the contract and he figures if he can blame me for the leaks he
can feather his own nest easier."

"But why would anybody believe him?" I asked.

Ross flicked his cigarette end on to a frozen puddle, where
it bounced once then sank through the hole it made. "We're the
outsiders, aren't we? We're not part of the team like the ones
who work inside the compound are."

"So how are you supposed to come by the advance story-lines?" I objected.

"We're involved in location filming for the show nearly every week. With them filming four weeks ahead of transmission, it's not hard to pick up the direction the stories are heading. The cast are always standing round the food wagon shooting their mouths off about storylines they don't like, or taking the piss out of each other about what their characters are up to. If me or my lassies had a mind to, we could be moles. It would be dead simple. But we're not."

"How can you be sure?"

"Well, I know it's not me. And I know it's not my wife." He gestured towards the open side of the van with his thumb. "She's the one with the red sweatshirt on. And I'd put money on it not being Mary, the other lassie, because she owns twenty per cent of the business and she's never been a woman who went for the short-term benefit."

I sighed. "I sympathize. But it's always impossible to prove a negative."

"I know that," he said. "That's not what I want to hire you for. I want you to find out who the real mole is and get me off the hook."

I shook my head. It nearly killed me, turning business down. "I'm already fully occupied taking care of Gloria. You'd be better off going to another firm." I gritted my teeth. "I could probably recommend somebody."

He shook his handsome head. "There would be no point. Turpin would never let them on to the location shoots, never mind inside the compound. I'm amazed Gloria's got away with having you on set. That's why you're the only one who can help me. I'll pay the going rate, I don't expect anything less."

I finished my coffee and tossed the cup in the nearby bin. "No can do," I said. "I can't take money under false pretences. I'd be lying if I said I could investigate the leaks at the same time as taking care of Gloria."

He looked as if he was going to burst into tears. His big shoulders slumped and his mouth turned down at the corners. I glanced back to the serving hatch in the side of the van and caught a murderous look from his wife. "Look," I sighed. "I tell you what I'll do. I'll keep my eyes and ears open, maybe make a couple of phone calls. If I come up with anything, you can pay me on results. How does that grab you?"

Laughing boy was back. He grinned and clapped a beefy arm round my shoulders. I thought my lungs had collapsed. "That's terrific. Fabulous. Thanks, I really appreciate it." He leaned over and smacked a sloppy kiss on my cheek.

"Ross?" his wife called sharply. "I need a hand in here."

"No problem," the big man said. "I'll be hearing from you then, Kate."

Somehow I doubted it. Before I could say anything more, I noticed Gloria rushing off the set and into the make-up caravan. Grateful for the chance to get out of the northerly wind that was exfoliating the few square centimetres of skin I had allowed to be exposed, I ran across and climbed aboard.

Gloria was sitting in front of a mirror, blowing on her hands as a make-up artist hovered around her. "Here she is," Gloria announced. "Me and my shadow," she sang in her throaty contralto. "Are you as cold as I am?"

"How many fingers have you got left?"

Gloria made a show of counting. "Looks like they're all still here."

"In that case, I'm colder," I said, waving a hand with one finger bent over.

"Freddie, meet Kate Brannigan, my bodyguard. Kate, this is Freddie Littlewood. It's his job to stop me looking like the raddled old bag I really am."

"Hi, Freddie."

He ducked his head in acknowledgement and gave me a quick once-over in the mirror. He had a narrow head and small, tight features framed by spiky black hair. With his black polo neck and black jeans like a second skin, he looked as if he'd escaped from one of those existential French films where you don't understand a bloody word even with subtitles. "Honestly, Gloria," he said. "I don't know why you listen to that Dorothea Dawson." His voice was surprising. There wasn't a trace of the high camp of his physical appearance. He could have read the radio news without a complaint.

"It's surprising how often she gets things right," Gloria said mildly as he expertly applied powder to her cheeks.

"And how often she causes trouble," he added drily. "All those sly little hints that people take a certain way and before you know it, old friends are at each other's throats. You watch, now she's got you all wound up and scared witless, I bet this week she'll tell you something that starts you looking out the corner of your eye at one of your best friends."

"I don't know why you've got it in for Dorothea," Gloria said. "She's harmless and we're all grownups."

"I just don't like to see you upset, Gloria," he said solicitously.

"Well, between me and you and the wall, Freddie, it wasn't what Dorothea said that upset me. I was already in a state. I'd been getting threatening letters. I'd had my tyres slashed to ribbons. All Dorothea did was make me realize I should be taking them seriously."

I could have clobbered her. I'd told her to carry on keeping quiet about the threatening letters and the vandalism, to let everyone think it was Dorothea's eerie warning that was behind my presence. And here she was, telling all to the man perfectly placed to be the distribution centre of the rumour factory. "Nice one, Gloria," I muttered.

It's not the people you go up against that make this job a bitch; it's the clients, every time.

7

SUN CONJUNCTION WITH MERCURY

She has a lively mind. Her opinions are important to her and she enjoys expressing them. Objectivity sometimes suffers from the strength of her views. Exchanging and acquiring information which she can subsequently analyse matters a lot.

From *Written in the Stars*, by Dorothea Dawson

When she finally finished filming her outdoor scene with Teddy, Gloria announced we were going shopping. I must have looked as dubious as I felt. "Don't worry, chuck," she laughed as I drove her into the NPTV compound. "We won't get mobbed. How do you think I manage when I've not got you running around after me?"

I was gobsmacked by the result. I'd seen her in plain clothes already, not least when she'd first come to the office. But this was something else again. I thought I was the mistress of disguise until I met Gloria. When she emerged from her dressing room after a mere ten minutes to slough off Brenda Barrowclough, I nearly let her walk past me. She'd cheated; this wasn't the outfit she'd worn when I'd driven her to work that morning. Wearing jeans and cowboy boots under a soft nubuck jacket that fell to mid-thigh, the image was entirely different. On her head perched a designer version of a cowboy hat, tilted to a jaunty angle. Instead of sunglasses, she'd gone for a pair of slightly tinted granny glasses that subtly changed the shape of her face. She looked twenty years younger. I wasn't going to be the only person who wouldn't instantly recognize Gloria now she'd ditched the wig and adopted a wardrobe that didn't include polyester.

Thankfully, she didn't have a major expedition in mind. Her granddaughter had been invited to a fancy dress party and she wanted to go as Esmeralda from *The Hunchback of Notre Dame*. "They've got outfits at the Disney Store, but they cost a fortune and I could make better myself," Gloria explained as I squeezed the car into a slot in the Arndale Centre car park. She never ceased to amaze me. This was a woman who could afford a hundred Esmeralda outfits without noticing the dent in her bank balance. But her pretence of meanness didn't fool me. Making the costume wasn't about saving money; it was about giving her granddaughter something of herself. It was also a way, I suspected, of reminding herself of the life she had come from.

We descended a claustrophobic concrete stairwell that reeked so strongly of piss it was a relief to step out into the traffic fumes of High Street. Gloria led me unerringly through the warren of Victorian warehouses that house the city's rag trade till we fetched up at a wholesaler who specialized in saris. Judging by the warmth of the welcome, she was no stranger. Merely because I was with her, I was offered tea too. While Gloria sipped from a thick pottery mug and browsed the dazzling fabrics, I hung around near the door, peering into the street with the avidity of the truly paranoid. The only people in sight were hurrying through the dank cold of the dying December day, coat collars turned up against the knife edge of the wind that howled through the narrow streets of the Northern Quarter. It wasn't a day for appreciating the renaissance of yet another part of the inner city. Nobody was going to be browsing the shop windows today. The craft workers must have been blessing their good fortune at having an enclosed market.

We emerged on the street just as darkness was falling, me staggering two steps behind Gloria toting a bale of fabric that felt heavy enough to clothe half of Lancashire. As we approached the Arndale from a slightly different angle, I realized we must be close to Dennis's latest venture. I couldn't help smiling at the thought of the double act Dennis and Gloria would be. It had been a long week, and I felt like some light relief, so I said, "A mate of mine has just opened a shop this end of the Arndale. Do you mind if we just drop in to say hello?"

"What kind of shop?"

"You remember what they used to say about how cheap it was to shop at the Co-op? On account of you could never find anything you wanted to buy?"

Gloria chuckled. "That good, eh? Oh well, why not? We've got nowt else on till tomorrow morning."

"I don't think it'll take that long."

It wasn't hard to spot Dennis's establishment. Sandwiched between a cut-price butcher and a heel bar in the subterranean section of the mall, it was notable for the dump bins of bargains virtually blocking the underpass and the muscle-bound minder keeping an eye on potential shoplifters. All he was wearing was a pair of jogging pants and a vest designed to show off his awesome upper body development. "High-class joint, then," Gloria remarked as we followed the chicane created by the dump bins, artfully placed to funnel us past whitewashed windows proclaiming, "Everything Under a Pound!" and into the shop.

By the door were three tills, all staffed by slack-jawed teenagers. The girls were the ones with the mascara. I think. Dennis was up near the back of the shop, stacking shelves with giant bottles of lurid green bath foam. We squeezed up a narrow aisle packed with weary shoppers who had the look and smell of poverty. My awkward parcel of material earned me a few hard words and a lot of harder looks.

Of course, I didn't get anywhere near Dennis before he noticed us. I swear that man has eyes in the back of his head.

"Kate," he said, his face creasing up in a delighted grin. "Fabulous!" He cleared a way through for us, telling his customers to kindly move their arses or take the consequences. "So, what do you think?" he asked almost before I was within bear-hug reach.

I gave the shelves the quick once-over. Exactly what I'd expected. Cheap and nasty, from the toys to the toiletries. "I think you're going to make a mint," I said sadly, depressed at the reminder of how many skint punters there are out there who needed to fill Christmas stockings on a weekly budget of the same amount that most MPs spend on lunch.

"Are you not going to introduce us, chuck?" Gloria said. I half turned to find her giving Dennis the appraising look of a farmer at a fatstock show. That was all I needed. Dennis has a habit of forgetting he's married, which is fine by me as long as I'm not personally involved with aiding and abetting it. I'm very fond of his wife Debbie, even if she doesn't have the brains God gave a lemming.

"I don't think so," I said. "This is just a flying visit."

I was too late. Dennis was already sliding round me and extending a hand to Gloria. "Dennis O'Brien at your service, darling," he said. Gloria slid her hand into his and he raised it to his lips, all the time fixing her with the irresistible sparkle of his intense blue eyes. I groaned.

"I'm Gloria Kendal."

His smile reminded me of crocodiles at feeding time. "I know," he said.

"It's the voice," I muttered. "Total giveaway."

"It's got nothing to do with the voice," he said. "It's because this lovely lady's with you. I can read, you know, Kate."

"What do you mean, it's because she's with me?"

Dennis cast his eyes heavenwards. "Tonight's *Chronicle*. You mean you've not seen it?"

"No. What about it?"

He jerked his head towards a door at the rear of the shop. "Through the back. It's in my ski-jacket pocket."

I looked at him. I looked at the door. I looked at Gloria. "On you go, chuck," she said. "I think I'm in safe hands here."

"That's all you know," I mumbled. But I dumped the fabric parcel on Dennis and left them to it while I went to chase whatever he'd seen in the evening paper. I didn't have to look hard. There wasn't much room in the bare concrete back shop to hide anything as big as Dennis's ski jacket, which was draped over one of two folding chairs by a cardboard computer carton doing a bad impersonation of a table. The paper was sticking out of a pocket and the story I was clearly supposed to be looking for was splashed across the front page. "**NORTHERNERS' STAR IN DEATH THREAT DRAMA**," I read.

"*Gloria Kendal, busybody Brenda Barrowclough in top soap* Northerners, *is at the heart of a real-life drama tonight. The award-winning actress has been warned that threatening letters sent to her home could mean death.*

"*The desperate warning was spelled out by her personal astrologer Dorothea Dawson, the TV Seer to the Stars. But following a savage act of vandalism on her Saab sports car, Ms Kendal has taken the danger to heart and has hired top local private investigator Kate Brannigan to act as bodyguard.*

"*The star of the Manchester-based soap has vowed not to be driven underground by the vicious poison-pen writer . . .*"

I skimmed to the end of the article, but there didn't seem to be any more meat on the bones. There were a couple of paragraphs mentioning previous cases where my name had unfortunately made it into the press, but nothing too damaging. What I couldn't figure out, apart from where the story had come from, was why nobody had called me all afternoon about it. Shelley should have been straight on to me the minute the paper landed, I thought. I was almost glad of the rare opportunity to put her in the wrong.

Then I took my moby out of my bag and realized I'd forgotten to switch it back on after I'd had it muted for the filming.

There were fourteen messages. I wasn't strong enough to deal with them yet. Besides, if the situation was out in the open, I needed to get my client away from the public eye as fast as possible. The last thing I needed was for some care-in-the-community case to hit on the idea of making a name for himself by metamorphosing into the secret stalker.

I hurried back to the shop, clutching the paper. I was too late. When I opened the door, it looked as if a small riot had enveloped the shop. At the eye of the storm was Dennis, standing on a counter with Gloria perched next to him. The massive bouncer had moved inside the store and was brandishing one of the red plastic under-a-pound fun cameras like King Kong with a fire engine. "Did you get that, Keith? Did you get that?" Dennis kept asking.

The shoppers had lost all interest in Dennis's wares, but for once he didn't care. "Melody, get on the blower to the *Sun* and tell them we've got exclusive pictures to sell of Gloria Kendal defying death threats and shopping in Manchester's best value-for-money store."

"Ah, shit," I muttered, lowering my head and thrusting through the crowd. Getting through to Gloria was a lot harder than Moses parting the Red Sea. Eventually I managed it, but only by elbowing a couple of elderly ladies in the ribs and stepping hard on the instep of a teenage girl who was still yelping in complaint minutes later. "Come on, Gloria, time to go home," I said grimly.

"I was just starting to enjoy myself," she complained good-naturedly, pushing herself to her feet.

"You're not whisking this wonderful woman off before we've had the chance to get to know each other?" Dennis demanded, sounding aggrieved.

"That's as good a reason as any," I grunted, trying to force a way through the clamouring crowd to the door.

Gloria turned to wiggle her fingers at him. "See you around, Dennis. I hope."

"Keith," I shouted. "Stop poncing around pretending to be David Bailey and give us a hand here. I need to get Gloria home."

The big bouncer looked to Dennis for guidance. He gave a rueful smile and nodded. "Sort it," he said.

Keith picked up the parcel of fabric and carved a path to the door in seconds flat. One look at biceps the size of cannonballs, and the obstructive punters just melted into the shelves. Gloria signed postcards as she walked, automatically passing them into the grasping hands of the fans. Out in the underpass, Keith thrust the bundle into my arms and I hustled Gloria towards a nearby bank of lifts that would take us back to the car park. "I like your friend," she said as we crammed in beside a pushchair and a harassed-looking woman who was too busy pacifying her toddler to care who was in the lift with her.

"He obviously likes you too. But then, his wife's a big fan of *Northerners*," I said drily.

"That's a pity," she said.

"I thought you needed all the viewers you could get just now."

Gloria raised her eyebrows, not entirely amused by my deliberate misunderstanding. "I meant, the existence of a wife. I was going to ask you for his number, but if he's a married man, I'm not interested."

"Worried about the press?"

She shook her head. "It's not fear of the *Sun* that stops me having affairs with married men. There are enough people out there ready to make women's lives a misery without me joining in."

The lift doors opened and Gloria stepped out, turning to give the young mother a hand with her pushchair. "You never cease to amaze me, Gloria," I said as we crossed the car park. "You must have *some* bad habits."

In response, she took out her cigarette packet and waved it at me. "One for the road," she said, climbing into the passenger seat of her Saab. "And I like a drink," she added as I started the engine. "And I have been known to play the odd game of bingo."

"You're too good for this world," I said wryly.

She plucked the *Chronicle* from the pocket where I'd stowed it and stared grim-faced at the front page. "I flaming hope not," she said.

⚜

After I dropped Gloria at home, where she planned a quiet night in with her sewing machine and a stack of Fred Astaire and Ginger Rogers movies, there was only one logical place to go. Even if it did involve one of those cross-country routes that looks sensible on the map but suddenly develops a mind of its own as soon as all human habitation falls out of sight.

My best friend Alexis and her partner Chris live in the wilds of the Derbyshire Peak District. Alexis claims she can be in her office in central Manchester twenty-three minutes after leaving home, but that's only because she's the crime correspondent of the *Chronicle* and so she starts work around half past six in the morning. I always feel like I need a Sherpa and a St Bernard with a barrel of brandy to make it to the dream home they built themselves. Chris is an architect, and she designed the small development in exchange for the skills of her neighbours, who did a lot of the heavy work as well as the plumbing and electrics. They ended up spending about eighty grand on a property that would sell for three times that on the open market.

Then they found the perfect way to spend all the money they'd saved. They had a baby. Chris actually did the bit that makes most people wince and cross their legs, but Alexis has just as much of a stake in Jay Appleton Lee. I'm about as fond of woodlice as I am of children, but even I have to admit—if only to myself—that I can see why Richard finds this particular baby as delightful as her parents do.

But that night I wasn't interested in admiring Jay's shock of black spiky hair or her latest tooth. It was Alexis I needed to see. I'd timed my arrival perfectly. Jay was en route from bath to bed, so all I had to do was make a few admiring noises before Chris whisked her away. Five minutes later, the three of us were installed in the comfortable living room, Chris and Alexis with dark smudges under their eyes that just about matched the glasses of Murphy's stout they were drinking.

"You having a night off, then, girl?" Alexis asked, her Scouse accent as rich as the creamy head on her glass. "Rather you than me, minding a soap star for a living."

"Just let me lie down for five minutes then I'll throw some pizza at the oven," Chris said, stifling a yawn and stretching out on the sofa, dumping her feet in Alexis's lap. "So what's she like, Gloria Kendal?"

"Brenda Barrowclough with a bit more insight, humour and style," I said. "At first, all I saw was that total self-absorption you get with actors. But the more I've got to know her, the more I've come to realize there's more to her than that. She's forthright, funny, generous. I'm amazed, but I actually like her." I told them about our adventures with Dennis. They both knew him well enough to fill in the gaps for themselves.

"I wish I'd been there. It sounds like one to cut out and keep," Alexis said, reaching for her cigarette packet. She took out a fag and began to go through the motions of smoking without actually lighting up. Another consequence of motherhood. She'd gone from fifty Silk Cut a day to smoking about a dozen and using a few others as the adult equivalent of a dummy. The only person who didn't see this as an improvement was Alexis herself.

"Thanks to the *Chronicle*." I scowled.

"The newsdesk were on to me about it," Alexis said. "I told them there wasn't any point in me ringing you for a quote. Or in them ringing you for a quote. I gave them this whole spiel about how you've got this Philip Marlowe code of conduct and you'd never grass up a client."

"Very noble of you," Chris said drily. "Respecting Kate's professional code. You really love pissing off the newsdesk, don't you?"

"Well," Alexis drawled. "They ask for it, don't they? So, is she really getting death threats?"

"I'll swap you," I said. "I'll give you some nonattributable background if you tell me where the story came from in the first place."

Alexis pulled a face and flicked the nonexistent ash from her cigarette. "You got me there, KB. You know I have as little to do with the brain-dead dickheads on the newsdesk as possible. And this didn't actually come as a tip directly to news. The story came through features, from Mack Morrissey, who does the showbiz beat. It'll have come from a contact."

"Any chance you could find out who?"

Alexis shrugged. "I don't know. Mack's a bit precious, you know. He wouldn't let any of us hairy-arsed hacks anywhere near his valuable artistic contacts."

"You could ask him," Chris chipped in.

"I could," Alexis admitted. "But there's a better way of finding out. I can't believe he got a tale like this for free. He'll have had to put a payment through the credits book."

"He won't have stumped up readies?" I asked.

Alexis shook her head. "Not this amount. It'll have been a few hundred. I'm surprised his contact gave the story to us, to be honest. It would have been worth a lot more to the nationals."

Another interesting piece of information to tuck away in the file marked, "Makes no sense." When the oddments of data reached critical mass, seemingly unrelated facts collided and rearranged themselves into logical sequences. It's a process normally called "woman's intuition."

"I'll check out the credits book in the morning," Alexis promised. "So what's the score with Gloria? Has she really had death threats? And does she really think you're going to throw yourself between her and the assassin's bullet?"

"How else will I catch it with my teeth?" I asked innocently. "People in Gloria's position are always getting hate mail. Recently, she's had a few letters that have seemed a bit more sinister than the usual run-of-the-mill stuff, and Dorothea Dawson threw some petrol on the flames. Bloody irresponsible, but what can you expect from a con merchant? None of these psychics and clairvoyants would earn a shilling if they had to stop preying on people's irrational fears. Take it from me, Alexis, nothing is going to happen to Gloria Kendal. All I'm there for is to put the frighteners on anybody who might be thinking about taking advantage of the situation."

Alexis's eyebrows rose and she ran a hand through thick dark hair recently shorn from a wiry thicket to a shrubby bush less accessible to tiny grasping fists. Another consequence of motherhood. "You've not met Dorothea yet, then?"

I frowned. "No, but what difference does that make?"

"I didn't think you'd be calling her a con artist if you'd met her."

I stared open-mouthed at Alexis. "You're not telling me you believe in that crap, are you?"

"Of course not, soft girl. But Dorothea Dawson's not a charlatan. She's sincere about what she does. I interviewed her a few years back, when I was still working for features. Before I actually met her, I was saying exactly the same as you're saying now. And I had to eat my words. It wasn't that she told me anything world shattering, like I was going to meet a tall dark handsome stranger and do a lot of foreign travel. She didn't make a big production number out of it, just said very calmly that I had already met the love of my life, that my career was going to make a sideways move that would make me a lot more satisfied and it probably wouldn't be the fags that killed me but they wouldn't help."

I shook my head. "And this revelation turned you into a believer?" I said sarcastically.

"Yeah. Because she didn't grandstand. She was dead matter-of-fact, even apologized for not having anything more exciting to tell me. She came across as a really nice woman, you know? And she's not just in it for the money. Sure, she charges rich bastards like the *Northerners* cast an arm and a leg, but she does a lot of freebies for charity."

"That's right," Chris added. "She donated a full personal horoscope to the Women's Aid charity auction last month. And you remember that mental health job I designed a couple of years ago?"

I nodded. It had been a major renovation project for Chris, turning an old mill in Rochdale into housing units for single homeless people with mental health problems. "I remember," I said.

"Well, I happen to know that Dorothea Dawson was the biggest single donor for that scheme. She gave them fifty grand."

"You never told me that," Alexis complained. "That would have made a good diary piece."

"That's precisely why I didn't tell you," Chris said drily. "It was supposed to be confidential. She didn't want a big song and dance about it."

"It's a lot of money," I said diplomatically.

"So she can't be a con artist, can she?" Alexis demanded. "They rip people off. They don't donate that sort of cash to charity. It's not like she'd need a tax loss, is it? I mean, a load of her earnings must be cash, so she could stash a bundle undeclared anyway."

I held my hands up in submission. "OK, I give in. Dorothea Dawson is a sweet little old lady, grossly misunderstood by cynical unbelievers like me. It must be written in my stars."

"Anyway, KB, you sure taking care of Gloria isn't just a front?" Alexis demanded, changing tack in an obvious bid to wrong-foot me.

"For what?" I asked, baffled.

"Working for the management at NPTV. They've got a major mole in there, which is the last thing you need when you're trying to finesse a major deal with the networks. I heard they've got a mole hunt going on. You sure they've not hired you to find out who's stirring the shit for them?"

I shook my head. "Sorry. You'll have to get your follow-up somewhere else."

"I thought they'd be happy about all the press stories about the show," Chris said. "I'd have thought it would increase the ratings. I had to go to London the other day on the train, and the two women opposite me talked about *Northerners* nonstop."

"I think the scandalous stories about the stars whet people's appetites," I said. "According to my sources, what the management don't like are the storyline leaks. They reckon that makes people turn off."

Before anyone could say more, my moby began to bleat insistently. "Goodbye, pizza," I said mournfully, grabbing my bag and reaching for the phone. "Brannigan," I grunted.

"It's me."

My heart sank. "Donovan, you've not been arrested again?"

8

MOON IN TAURUS IN THE 12TH HOUSE

The emotional swings of the moon are minimized in this placing, leading to balance between impulsiveness and determination. She is sociable, but needs to recharge her batteries in solitude which she seeks actively. Imaginative and intuitive, she has an instinctive rapport with creative artists though not herself artistic.

From *Written in the Stars*, by Dorothea Dawson

This time it was Alderley Edge, the village that buys more champagne per head of population than anywhere else in the UK. Donovan had been there to serve a subpoena on a company director who seemed to think the shareholders should fund the entire cost of his affair with a member of the chorus of Northern Opera. The detached house was in a quietly expensive street, behind tall hedges like most of its neighbours. Donovan had borrowed his mother's car and sat patiently parked a few doors down from the house for about an hour waiting for his target to return.

When the man came home, Donovan had caught him getting out of his car. He'd accepted service with ill grace and stormed into the house. Donovan had driven home via his girlfriend's student residence bedsit to pick up some tutorial handouts for the essay he was writing. He'd arrived home to find the police waiting. They hadn't been interested in an explanation. They'd just hauled him off in a police car to the local nick, where they'd informed him he was being arrested on suspicion of burglary.

By the time I arrived, tempers were fraying round the edges. It turned out that at some point during the day, a neighbour of the company director had been burgled. And another nosy neighbour had happened to jot down Shelley's car number because, well, you just don't get black people sitting around in parked cars in the leafy streets of Alderley Edge. The neighbour had arrived home a few minutes after Donovan had driven off, discovered the burglary and called the police. When the nosy neighbour saw the police arrive (within five minutes, because Alderley Edge is middle-class territory, not a council estate where you wait half an hour for a response to a treble-niner reporting a murder in progress) he nipped across to tell them about the suspicious black man.

The police computer spat out Shelley's address in response to the car registration number, and the bizzies were round there in no time flat. Things were complicated by the fact that the bloke Donovan had served the subpoena on decided to get his own back and denied all knowledge of a young black process-server with a legitimate reason for being in the street.

It took me the best part of an hour to persuade the police that Donovan was telling the truth and that I wasn't some gangster's moll trying to spring my toy boy. Thighs like his, I should be so lucky.

The one good thing about the whole pathetic business was that Shelley had been out when the police had turned up. With luck, she'd still be out. As I drove him home, I said, "Maybe this isn't such a good idea, you doing the process-serving."

"I'm serving the papers properly, what's the problem?" he said defensively.

"It's not good for your image or your mother's blood pressure if you keep getting arrested."

"I'm not letting those racists drive me out of a job," he protested. "You're saying I should just lie down and let them do it
to me? The only places I have a problem are the ones where rich
white people think that money can buy them a ghetto. People
don't call the cops when *you* go to serve paper in Alderley Edge,
or when I turn up on a doorstep in Hulme."

"You're right. I'm sorry. I wasn't thinking it through," I
said, ashamed of myself for only seeing the easy way out. "The
job's yours for as long as you want it. And first thing tomorrow,
I'll get your mother to have some proper business cards and ID
printed up for you."

"Fine by me. Besides, Kate, I need the money. I can't be
scrounging off my mother so I can have a beer with my mates,
or go to see a film with Miranda. The process-serving's something I can fit around studying and having fun. You can't do
that with most part-time jobs."

I grinned. "You could always get an anorak and work with
Gizmo on the computer security side of things."

Donovan snorted. "I don't think Gizmo'd let me. Have
you noticed he's got well weird lately?"

"How can you tell?" I signalled the right turn that would
bring me into the narrow street of terraced brick houses where
the Carmichael family lived.

"Yeah, right. He's always been well weird. But this last
few weeks, he's been totally paranoid android about his files."

"He's always been secretive about his work," I reminded
him. "And not unreasonably. A lot of what we do for clients on
computer security is commercially sensitive."

"There's secretive and there's mentally ill. Did you know
you even need a password to get out of his screen savers?"

"Now you are exaggerating," I said.

"You think so? You try it the next time he goes to the loo.
Touch a key when one of the screen savers is running and you'll
be asked for a password. You didn't know?" Donovan's eyebrows
rose in surprise. He opened the car door and unfolded his long

body into the street. Then he bent down and said anxiously, "Check it out. I'm not making it up. Whatever he's up to, he doesn't want anybody else to know. And it is your hardware he's doing it on."

"It'll be OK," I said, trying to reassure myself as much as Donovan. "Gizmo wouldn't take risks with my business." Which was true enough, I thought as I drove home. Except that what Gizmo thought was fair game didn't necessarily coincide with the law's view. And if he didn't think it was wrong, why would he imagine it might be risky?

The response to the *Chronicle*'s story sharply polarized the *Northerners* cast in a way I hadn't seen before. Up to that point, I'd been beginning to wonder whether I could possibly be right about this being an inside job. Ten minutes in the NPTV compound that morning showed me the truth. People who had been all smiles and friendship the day before now had pursed lips and suddenly found they had somewhere else to look when Gloria passed. I actually heard one minor cast member say to another, supposedly apropos of something else, "Too grand for the likes of us, of course."

"What happened to that lot?" I asked as soon as Gloria closed the dressing room door behind us.

Rita Hardwick, who shared the room and played rough and ready tart with a heart Thelma Torrance, paused in stitching the tapestry she passed the slack time with. "Got the cold shoulder, did she?" she said with grim good humour.

"Yeah," I said, not caring about showing my puzzlement. "Yesterday, everybody's everybody's pal and today, it's like we've got a communicable disease."

"It happens when you get a big show in the papers," Gloria said, putting her coat on a hanger and subsiding into a chair. "It's basically jealousy. The people below you in the pecking order resent the fact that you're important enough to make the front page of the *Chronicle* and have the story followed up by all the tabloids the next day."

I'd already seen the evidence of Gloria's importance to the tabloids. When I'd arrived to collect her that morning, we'd had to run the gauntlet of reporters and photographers clustered round the high gates that kept Gloria safe from their invasive tendencies.

"Aye," said Rita. "And the ones above you in the pecking order reckon you need cutting down to size before you start snapping too close at their heels. Not that there's many above you these days, Glo."

"Stuff like this shows you who your real friends are," Gloria added.

"Aye, and we've all got precious few round here," Rita said, thrusting her needle ferociously into the material. "There's plenty would stab you in the back soon as look at you if they thought they could get away with it."

If a bit of newspaper coverage was all it took to create a poisonous atmosphere like the one we'd just walked through, I hated to think how Gloria's colleagues would react if someone actually did them serious damage. "Have you had much personal publicity lately?" I asked, wondering if an excess of press attention had provoked one of her fellow cast members into sending her the original threatening letters.

Gloria shook her head. Rita disagreed. "There's been a lot of stories about the abortion issue, Glo. Brenda and Debbie have been all over the tabloids."

"But that's Brenda, not me. The punters don't know the difference, but the people who work here do."

"It doesn't make any odds to some of that lot," Rita said. "Eaten up with jealousy, they are." She glanced at her watch. "Bloody hell, is that the time? I've got an appointment with Dorothea in five minutes." She shoved her sewing into a tapestry bag.

"You're all right. I didn't see the van when we parked up." Gloria gave me a considering look. "You wanted a word with Dorothea, didn't you, chuck?"

Rita stared. "By heck, Kate, I'd not have put you down as a lass who wanted her horoscope reading."

I bristled. "The only stars I want to ask Dorothea Dawson about are the ones that work for *Northerners.*"

Rita giggled. "If that crystal ball could talk . . ."

"Aye, but going to Dorothea's like going to the doctor. You can say owt you like and know it'll go no further," Gloria said. "Rita, chuck, do you mind if I just pop in ahead of you for a quick word with Dorothea, to see when she can fit Kate in?"

"Be my guest. I'll walk across with you."

The three of us left the studio building and crossed the car park. Over at the far end, near the administration block, I noticed a camper van that hadn't been there when we'd arrived shortly before. It was painted midnight-blue, but as we drew closer, I could see there was a Milky Way of golden stars arcing across the cab door and the van's side. The door into the living section of the van had a zodiac painted on it in silver, the glyphs of the signs picked out in gold. Even I could recognize the maiden that symbolized my Virgo star sign. I also identified the familiar three-legged symbol of Mercedes-Benz. I didn't need my background information from Chris to realize there was obviously serious money in Dorothea Dawson's profession.

Rita knocked and a familiar husky voice told us to come in. I expected a full blast of the histrionic mystic, complete with joss sticks and Indian cotton, but when it came to her personal environment, Dorothea clearly preferred the opulent to the occult. Leather, velvet, shag-pile carpet and wood panelling lined the luxurious interior. In the galley, I could see a microwave and a fridge. On a pull-out shelf sat a laptop and a portable colour printer, an ensemble that must have cost the thick end of three grand. Instead of a bloody awful tape of rainforest noises backed by Pan pipes and whales singing, the background music sounded like one of those "not available in the shops" collections of Romantic Classics. The only concession to the mystic world of the zodiac was the dining table, surrounded on three sides by a bench seat. It was covered in a dark-blue chenille cloth and on it sat a massive crystal ball. If it had had a set of finger holes, we could have gone ten-pin bowling.

"Nice to see you all, ladies," Dorothea Dawson said as we piled through the door. She was smaller than I expected from TV. But then, they all were. Her hair was pure silver, cut in a chin-length bob that hid the fact that her jaw was too heavy for her small features. Her skin was criss-crossed with the fine wrinkles of an apple that's been left lying around too long. Either she was older than she sounded or she'd loved the sun too much when she was younger. "And you must be Kate Brannigan," she said, acknowledging me with a nod, assessing me with eyes like amethyst chips.

"Saw me in your crystal ball, did you?" I asked more pleasantly than I wanted to. I've never liked charlatans.

"No, I saw you in the *Manchester Evening Chronicle*," she said with wry amusement. I found myself liking her in spite of all my prejudices against people who prey on the gullible. "You want to talk to me about my last session with Gloria?"

"Good guess," I said.

"And I want you to cast her horoscope," Gloria butted in, as usual incapable of holding her tongue.

Dorothea cocked her head, a knowing smile on her lips. "Virgo, with . . . an air sign rising, at a guess. Probably Gemini, with such a smart mouth."

I tried not to look as surprised as I felt. A one-in-twelve chance of getting my sun sign right multiplied up to a one-in-a-gross chance of hitting the sun sign and the ascendant. Not that I believed any of that rubbish; I only knew my rising sign because I'd spent half an hour the night before on the computer with some astrological chart-casting shareware I'd pulled down from the Internet. But however she'd reached her conclusion, Dorothea was right. "I couldn't say," I lied, determined to show her my scepticism. "Gloria can give you my details."

"I have a very full diary today," Dorothea said, sounding far more like a businesswoman than she had any right to.

She looked businesslike too, in a high-necked Edwardian-style white blouse under a soft black wool crepe jacket. A silver and amethyst brooch the size of a credit card was pinned to the jacket, like an abstract representation of her hair and eyes. She flicked open a desk diary on the seat beside her while Gloria produced a piece of paper with a flourish. "That's Kate's time, date and place of birth."

Dorothea put it on the seat beside her without a glance. "I couldn't possibly take you through your chart *and* answer your questions, Kate."

"It's the answers to my questions I'm interested in."

Dorothea raised one eyebrow. I used to do that, but I grew out of it. "Pity. You should always seize opportunity when it presents itself. Who knows when you'll get a second chance to find out what really makes you tick?" She sounded amused.

"I'll manage somehow," I said.

"I'm sure you will, and that's without reading your chart. Gloria, you're my final appointment today. How would it be if I saw Kate then? Or are you in a hurry to get home?"

"That's fine, Dor," Gloria said. "We'll get out your road now and let Rita get her money's worth. See you at half past five."

She shooed me out ahead of her into the car park. "We'd better get a move on," she said. "I'm due in make-up and I'm not frocked up yet."

"Gloria, is Dorothea normally fully booked?" I asked, trailing in her wake.

"Oh aye. If you're not one of her regulars, you can wait a month or more for her to fit you in unless you're prepared to go to her consulting room."

"All half-hour appointments?"

"That's right. From nine till half past five," Gloria confirmed.

"Just as a matter of interest, how much does Dorothea charge?"

"For half an hour, she charges twice what you do for an hour, chuck."

It was one of those bits of information that stops you dead in your tracks. I'm not cheap. Well, only where Richard's concerned, but even he hasn't worked that out yet. Four times my hourly rate was serious money. Sometimes I wonder if I'm in the right business.

━━◆━━

The day passed. Wardrobe, make-up, rehearsal, film. No diverting phone calls, no murderous attacks on the client. No chance either of finding out who had written the poison-pen letters or the identity of the mole that Ross Grant wanted me to drag kicking and screaming into the daylight; thanks to the *Chronicle*, nobody was talking to me. I supposed the cast members had fallen out of love with me because for today I was more famous than them. The crew were just too busy and besides, the novelty of having a real live private eye about the place had worn off.

By the time five rolled around, I was beginning to think that I should start charging boredom money the way that some people charge danger money. I was convinced by now that whoever was writing threatening letters to Gloria was getting satisfaction from knowing they'd frightened her enough to hire me. Given the number of opportunities to cause her serious harm, even with me in tow, it was significant that we'd not even had so much as a near miss in the car. I'd accompany her on her weekend personal appearances, then I intended to call it a day.

Her face restored to street levels of make-up and Brenda's outfit back in wardrobe where it belonged, Gloria was ready for her session with Dorothea. "Walk me across to the van, chuck," she said. "I'll see Dorothea on my own, but if you come over about five to six, you can walk me back to my dressing room then pop back to ask her whatever it is you want to know."

An unrelenting sleet was falling as we joined the dozens of people scurrying across the car park, desperately seeking shelter. I'd helped myself to one of the umbrellas in an equipment skip by the entrance to the outdoor set, and I wrestled with the gusty wind to keep it over Gloria's head. At the caravan, I knocked. I heard Dorothea tell Gloria to come in. She disappeared inside and I closed the umbrella and sprinted for Gloria's car, parked only a few spaces away. Waiting for her there, I could at least listen to the radio.

I closed my eyes and leaned back in the seat, the day's news washing over me. The traffic reporter warned about drifting snow on trans-Pennine routes. "Great," I muttered, wondering how bad the road to Saddleworth would be. If the weather was going to close in, it might be worth suggesting to Gloria that she spend the night in my spare room to save myself the double journey over snowy moorland roads.

Almost before I knew it, the twenty-five minutes were up. I abandoned the condensation-fogged car and legged it for Dorothea's camper. I knocked on the door of the van and Gloria called, "Just coming, chuck." The door opened, the warm light from inside spilling on to the Tarmac and revealing the waterlogging that was creeping up the sides of my brown ankle boots. "I'll send her right back," Gloria said over her shoulder as she emerged, closing the door behind her.

I did my trick with the umbrella and escorted Gloria back to her dressing room. The production area already felt deserted. Nobody on *Northerners* loved their job so much they wanted to hang around after the end of filming on a Friday. I was slightly concerned about leaving Gloria vulnerable in her dressing room. Both Rita and Dorothea knew about my appointment with the astrologer, and either could have mentioned it unthinkingly to a third party. Given the speed rumour moved at in NPTV, the cleaners and secretaries all probably knew Gloria would be alone in a virtually empty building from six o'clock.

"I want you to lock the door behind me, OK?" I told her. "And don't let anybody in except me. It doesn't matter how much you think you can trust them. If anyone turns up, tell them they'll have to wait until I get back. Promise?"

Gloria grinned. "All right, boss. Whatever you say."

I waited outside the door until I heard the Yale lock snap into place behind me. Then I hurried out of the building and ran back across the car park to Dorothea's van. There was no answer to my knock, but I knew she was expecting me to return. Besides, it wasn't the kind of night where you hang around in freezing sleet waiting for someone else to stop playing power games. I opened the door and stepped into the dimly lit interior.

Dorothea Dawson lay sprawled across her chenille table-cloth, one side of her head strangely misshapen and dark with spilled blood. A few feet away, her crystal ball glowed in the lamplight at the end of a flecked trail of scarlet clotting the deep pile of the champagne-coloured carpet.

I backed away momentarily, dragging my eyes from the compelling horror before me. I stared wildly around, checking there was no one else in the confined space. Then the thought hit me with the force of a kick to the stomach that Dorothea might still be alive. For a long moment I didn't know if I could bring myself to touch her.

But I knew that if she died because I'd been squeamish that the guilt would far outweigh the revulsion I felt now. I tried to swallow whatever it was that was preventing me from breathing and inched forward, carefully avoiding the track the crystal ball had left. I stretched my hand towards Dorothea's outflung arm and grasped her wrist. Her skin was the same temperature as mine, which made it all the more horrible that I couldn't find a pulse.

I backed away, appalled. I'd been right to warn Gloria to take care. There was a killer out there.

I'd been catastrophically wrong about the target, though.

9

MARS OPPOSES THE MIDHEAVEN

She has a high opinion of herself and is not always diplomatic enough to hide it. She can be too bold and belligerent in pursuit of what she knows to be right. But this opposition provides great energy, allowing her to be enterprising and independent. Her speed and competitiveness often take the wind out of the sails of authority figures.

From *Written in the Stars*, by Dorothea Dawson

I didn't know what to do. I didn't think I could bear to stay in that confined space with Dorothea's corpse, but I couldn't just walk away leaving the camper van unsecured. Besides, I couldn't stand guard outside because I'd be soaked to the skin in minutes. It seemed important to me that I shouldn't face the police looking like a drowned rat.

The compromise I found was to move down to the cab. The passenger seat was designed so that it could either face out through the windscreen or swing round to act as an extra chair in the living section of the van. Luckily for my peace of mind, it was currently configured to face forward.

I scrambled through the gap between the seats, surprised to find myself gasping for air as if I'd been running. I gripped the armrests and forced myself to breathe evenly. I wanted to make sure I didn't sound like an emergency operator's idea of a murderer. I concentrated on the tracks of the melting sleet slithering down the windscreen that blurred the floodlights around the car park and tried to forget the image branded on my mind's eye. Only when my breathing had returned to normal did I take out my phone and dial 999. Once I was connected to the police control room, I said, "My name is Kate Brannigan and I am a private investigator. I want to report what appears to be a murder."

The woman on the end of the phone had obviously assimilated her training well. With no apparent indication that this was any more extraordinary an occurrence than a burglary in progress, she calmly said, "Where are you calling from?"

"My mobile. I'm in the car park of the *Northerners* compound. It's just off Alan Turing Way, near the velodrome."

"And can you tell me what appears to have happened?"

"I'm in a camper van. It belongs to Dorothea Dawson. The astrologer? I'd arranged a meeting with her. I walked in and found her lying dead. It looks like someone's caved her head in with her crystal ball. I tried to find a pulse, but there's nothing." I could hear my voice cracking and swallowed hard.

"Are you still there?"

"Yes. I'm in the camper van. You can't miss it. It's a big dark-blue Mercedes. Down the far end, away from the entrance. Most of the cars have gone now; there's just a few down this end of the car park." I was gabbling, I knew, but I couldn't stop myself.

"We'll have some officers with you very soon. Please don't touch anything. Can you give me your number, please?"

I rattled off the number automatically. "We will be with you very shortly," she concluded reassuringly. I wasn't comforted. This was an opportunist killing. Normally, there would be people in the car park, chatting and gossiping on their way to their cars, pausing and taking notice. But tonight, the weather meant everyone had their heads down, rushing for shelter and paying no attention to anything except the quickest route to their wheels.

Then there was the time element. There had only been a gap of ten minutes at the very outside between Gloria and me leaving the van and me returning. But someone had been bold or desperate enough to seize that tiny window of opportunity to invade Dorothea's camper van. They'd caught her unawares, obviously, and smashed the heavy crystal ball into her skull so swiftly she'd had no time to react.

Then they'd slipped back into the night. No time to search or steal. Time only to kill and to disappear again. Suddenly, I realized the killer might only have been feet away from me as I pounded across the car park through the sleet. Minutes—no, seconds—earlier and I could have come face to face with someone ruthless enough to have killed me too.

The thought hit me like a blow to the heart. My mouth went dry and a violent shiver ran through me from head to foot. My stomach started to heave and I barely got the door open in time. Second-hand lunch splattered on to the puddled car park. I retched and retched long past the point where my stomach was empty, hanging on grimly to the door with one hand.

That's how the police found me. I hadn't even been aware of the approaching sirens. I figured they must have turned them off when they reached the security gates at NPTV. Now, it was only the flashing blue lights that announced their arrival. I looked up blearily, my hair stuck to my head with sleet and sweat, and took in two liveried police cars and an ambulance. The occupants were out and running almost before the cars came to a standstill.

They headed towards me. I straightened up and pointed weakly to the door that led directly into the living section. "She's in there," I croaked. Three of them shifted their angle of approach. The fourth moved towards me, blocking any getaway I might have planned. He wasn't to know we were on the same side. Not surprising; it was a role I found pretty unfamiliar myself. After a quick scan of his colleagues' faces to check there was no opposition, the first policeman opened the door and cautiously stuck his head inside the van. I heard the hiss of indrawn breath and a muffled curse.

Now the paramedics were also at the door, trying to get past the knot of police officers. "Let us in," I heard one of them say impatiently.

"No way," the cop who'd seen the body said. "That's a crime scene."

"She could be alive," the paramedic protested, attempting to shove through the barrier of blue uniforms.

"No way," the policeman repeated. He looked about as good as I felt. "Take it from me, there's nothing you can do for her."

"She didn't have a pulse when I found the body," I said.

"When was that?" the officer keeping an eye on me asked.

"About two minutes before I made the treble-niner."

My unthinking use of a professional term won me a quizzical look. One of his colleagues was speaking into his radio, collar turned up against the wind-driven sleet. Grumbling, the paramedics headed back to the shelter of their ambulance. I inched back so that I was out of the worst of the weather, making sure I kept my hands in sight. I knew that right now I had to be their prime suspect. One being a prime number.

Another car splashed through the puddles, illuminating a couple of executives making for their cars, too worried about getting wet to care about the presence of police cars and ambulances. The new arrival skidded to a halt only feet away from the front of Dorothea's Mercedes. The doors swung open, switching on the interior light, and the impossible happened.

Things got worse.

～❈～

Twenty minutes later, I was sitting in the *Northerners* green room, instantly commandeered by the police as a temporary incident room until their own purpose-built caravan could be brought over. Opposite me sat Detective Sergeant Linda Shaw, her hands wrapped around a cardboard cup of instant coffee. I didn't mind Linda; she probably had more in common with me than she'd ever have with the hard-nosed bastard she worked for.

I suspected Detective Chief Inspector Cliff Jackson had an auburn-haired doll in his desk drawer. I was convinced he stuck pins into it at regular intervals. It was the only explanation I could think of for that stabbing pain I sometimes got in my left ankle. Jackson had been one of the senior murder detectives in the city for the last seven years or so. You'd think he'd be pleased that I've made a significant contribution to his clear-up rate. You'd be wrong. Now, whenever the planets really want to gang up on me, they send me an encounter with Jackson.

Linda Shaw stood between Jackson and me like a buffer zone between warring Balkan armies. As soon as he'd seen me pale-faced and shivering in the cab of Dorothea's van, the wheels had started going round in his head as he imagined the many ways he could use my presence at the murder scene to make my life hell. He'd sped across the intervening Tarmac without even pausing to put on his raincoat. "What the fuck are you doing here?" he greeted me.

"Working," I said. "How about you?"

He turned scarlet. "Don't push your luck, Brannigan," he stormed. "I'm here less than a minute and already you're looking at spending the night in the cells. You just don't know when to keep your smart mouth shut, do you?"

"If you want me to keep my mouth shut, that's fine by me. I'll make my one call to my solicitor and then you'll get 'no comment' from here to eternity," I snarled back. "And as soon as I get home, I'll be on the phone to Alexis Lee. The world should hear how a material witness in the murder of the nation's favourite astrologer gets treated by Manchester's finest."

"Sir." Linda's voice was quiet but urgent. "Sir, you're needed inside the van. The scene-of-crime lads are right behind us, and the rest of the team has just got here. Why don't I find a quiet corner and take a statement from Ms Brannigan? Then we'll have an idea where we're up to?"

"I don't want you sticking your nose in this, Brannigan," Jackson snapped, straightening an electric-blue tie that clashed disturbingly with his lilac shirt. "You give your statement to DS Shaw and then you bugger off out of it. That's not an invitation, it's an instruction. I'd love to arrest you for obstruction. But then, I shouldn't have to tell you that, should I? She's all yours, Detective Sergeant."

I had led Linda from the van to the production building, suggesting it would be a good idea to get someone to contact John Turpin to tell NPTV what was going on and find out where we could talk. She'd got it sorted, right down to discovering where the nearest coffee machine was. Finally we had a moment to give each other the once-over. I saw a woman hovering around the crucial cusp of thirty, the skin around her eyes starting to show the attrition of long hours and late nights, the slight downturn to her mouth revealing the emotional price of dealing with people who have been violently bereaved, and the ones responsible for smashing those lives to smithereens.

I didn't want to think about what she saw. I opened the batting. "Detective Sergeant, eh? Congratulations."

"Thanks. I hear you've come up in the world too. Brannigan and Co, not Mortensen and Brannigan any more."

"Cliff keeps tabs on me, does he? At least I get to be my own boss. But you're still stuck being Jackson's bag carrier."

"There are worse jobs in the police service," she said drily.

"Especially if you're a woman."

She inclined her head in agreement. "So, help me to keep my job and tell me what happened here tonight?"

"You know I don't have any problem with you, Linda. Ask what you want. As long as you don't expect me to breach my client's confidentiality, I'll tell you all I can."

She took me through the reason for my presence, then on to the precise circumstances of my discovery. We'd just got to the part where I described trying to find Dorothea's pulse when the door crashed open. Gloria staggered in dramatically, hair plastered to her head, eye make-up spreading like a bad Dusty Springfield impersonation. "Kate," she wailed. "Thank God you're all right! Oh Kate, I can't believe it. Not Dorothea," she continued, stumbling towards me. Think Vanessa Redgrave playing King Lear. I had no choice but to jump to my feet and support her. She'd have had no problem collapsing in a heap for effect. I had no doubt that she was sincerely upset, but being a thespian she couldn't help going over the top so much she made the Battle of the Somme look like a little skirmish.

I put an arm round her and steered her to the nearest sofa. Linda was staring at her with avid eyes. I didn't think it was Gloria's bedraggled appearance that had gobsmacked her. She was star struck. I've seen it happen. Normal, intelligent people faced with their heroes become open-mouthed, wittering wrecks. Back before she became crime correspondent, Alexis once got to interview Martina Navratilova for the features department. She claims the most intelligent question she managed to come out with was, "What did you have for breakfast, Martina?"

So now I had a star struck detective, an hysterical soap star and a cop who wanted to arrest me for daring to find a murder victim. This was turning into the worst night for a very long time.

"I can't believe it," Gloria was saying for the dozenth time. This time, however, she moved the narrative forward. "I keep thinking, I must have been the last person to see her alive."

The words brought Linda back to something approximating normality. "What do you mean, Ms Kendal?" she asked gently, crossing to the sofa and sitting next to Gloria.

"Gloria, this is Detective Sergeant Shaw. She's involved in the inquiry into Dorothea's death."

Gloria fixed Linda with eyes brimming with sooty tears. When this was all over, I'd have to speak to her about waterproof mascara. "What happened, chuck? All they'd say out in the car park was that there had been an accident, that Dorothea were dead. I'd gone out looking for you. You were gone so long, I was beginning to worry. I had this feeling . . ." Her voice tailed off into another whooping sob. "Oh God, I can't believe it," she wailed. I got up and silently fetched her a glass of water. She emptied it in a few swift gulps then clutched it histrionically to her bosom.

Linda patted her free hand. "It's hard to grasp, losing a friend," she said. "But the best thing you can do for Dorothea now is to help us find the person responsible for this."

"It wasn't an accident, then?" Gloria demanded. I saw an alertness spring into her eyes that hadn't been there a moment before.

Linda obviously hadn't. "You'll have to brace yourself for a shock, I'm afraid, Gloria. It looks like Dorothea has been murdered."

Gloria's face froze. The tears stopped as suddenly as they would when the director yelled, "Cut." "Murdered?" she said, her voice an octave lower. "I don't understand. Dorothea were fine when I left her. And Kate went right back to her. How could anybody have murdered her?"

"That's what we're here to find out," Linda said reassuringly. Much more of this and I was going to throw up. A couple of generations ago, it was the professional classes who got this kind of veneration from the police. Before that, you had to have a title. But in Britain in the 1990s, the prerequisite for deference from Officer Dibble was celebrity.

I cleared my throat. "Apart from the killer, it seems likely that Gloria was the last person to see Dorothea alive."

"Do you have any idea what time that might have been?" Linda asked Gloria.

"Just before six," I said. "I'd been sitting in Gloria's car in the car park, waiting for her to finish her half past five session with Dorothea. And before you ask, I didn't notice anyone hanging around suspiciously, just a lot of people rushing to their cars and a few others crossing from the production building to the admin block. At five to six, I left the car and went to the camper van. I knocked, and Gloria came out."

"Did you see Dorothea?" Linda asked me. I couldn't believe she was getting into this with Gloria present. It broke all the unwritten rules about interviewing witnesses separately.

"No, I didn't enter the van."

"Did you hear her voice?"

I shook my head. "The wind was blowing, there were cars driving past, she wouldn't have been shouting anyway."

I could see the implications registering with Linda. I could also see her dismissing the possibility that Gloria could have killed Dorothea for no more substantial reason than that Brenda Barrowclough could never have done such a thing. "She said cheerio to me and said she'd expect Kate along in a few minutes. But Kate's right. She wasn't shouting. There was no reason why she should, and she wasn't one for raising her voice at the best of times," Gloria said kindly, as if she was explaining something obvious to a child.

"Was the door on the latch, or did it automatically lock behind you?" Linda asked.

"Just on the latch. We'd all knock and walk in when it were time for our appointments," Gloria said. "She were strict about not overrunning, was Dorothea."

"And how long was it before you got back to the van?" Linda asked me.

I'd already given the timing a lot of thought. "Ten minutes, tops. Maybe three minutes to walk Gloria back to her dressing room, a few minutes to make sure she was going to lock the door behind me, then a couple of minutes back."

"It's not long," Linda observed.

Suddenly, Gloria burst into tears again. "It's terrible," she wailed. "It's a warning. It's a warning to me. All those letters, and Dorothea's premonition. There's a killer out there and he's after me!"

I couldn't quite see the logic, but Gloria's fear seemed real enough. She sobbed and hiccupped and wailed. Linda and I exchanged desperate looks, neither sure how to deal with this. Then as abruptly as her hysterics had begun, they ended and she took control of herself. "This is aimed at me," Gloria said, her voice shaky. "Everybody knew I relied on Dorothea. Everybody knew Dorothea had predicted there was death in the room that last time I saw her. She's been killed to put the fear of death into me."

"I don't think that's likely," Linda said soothingly. "It's a very extreme thing to do if all this letter writer wants to do is frighten you. It's more likely that it's all just a horrible coincidence."

"Oh aye?" Gloria sat upright, her shoulders straightening. It was a classic Brenda Barrowclough move that signalled to *Northerners* viewers that it was flak-jacket time. "And is it just a horrible coincidence that I was the last person to see Dorothea alive? If somebody had it in for Dorothea, there must have been plenty of other times they could have killed her without taking the risk that somebody would see them going in or out of the van. Or even walk in on them. The only reason anybody would have for killing her when they did was to make it look like I was the killer. You mark my words, whoever killed my friend has got it in for me an' all."

There was a moment's stunned silence. "She has a point," I said.

"So what are your lot going to do to protect me?" Gloria demanded.

Linda just stared.

"The short answer is, nothing," I told her. "Even if they had the bodies, you wouldn't be a priority, on account of your poison-pen letters don't actually threaten to kill you. That's right, isn't it, Linda?"

Linda made a strangled sort of noise. I figured she was agreeing with me.

"Right then," said Gloria. "I'll have to keep relying on Kate." She gathered herself together. I suddenly understood the expression "girding your loins." Gloria stood up and said, "Come on, chuck. I've had enough of this. I'm distraught and I need to go home and have a lie-down."

She was halfway to the door when she looked behind to check I was following. I gave Linda a hapless shrug. "We'll need formal statements," Linda tried plaintively.

"Call my lawyer in the morning," Gloria said imperiously. "Kate, who's my lawyer?"

I grinned. Jackson was going to love this. "Same as mine, of course. Ruth Hunter."

The last thing I heard as the door swung shut behind us was Linda groaning, "Ah, shit." In grim silence we marched out of the building. The sleet had stopped, which was the one good thing that had happened since lunchtime. Gloria swept straight through the mêlée of activity around Dorothea's van, looking neither to right nor left. I scuttled in her wake, trying to look invisible to anyone who might be tempted to alert Jackson. We made it to the car without a challenge.

Once we'd got past the two bobbies working with the NPTV security men on the main gate, all the fight went out of Gloria. Her shoulders slumped and she reached for her cigarettes. "This is an emergency," she said. "Don't you dare open that bloody window." She inhaled deeply. "You know I didn't kill Dorothea, don't you?"

I pulled a wry smile. "You're an actress, Gloria. Would I know if you had?"

She snorted. "I'm no Susan Sarandon. I play myself with knobs on. Come on, Kate, did I kill Dorothea?"

"I can't believe you did," I said slowly.

"That'll do me. So you'll try and find out who's done this? Before he decides it's my turn? Or my granddaughter's?"

"Cliff Jackson, the cop that's in charge of this? He's not a bad investigator. But he's been wrong before. I'll give it my best shot."

"I'll sleep easier knowing that," she said, toking on her cigarette as if it gave life instead of stealing it.

"Speaking of sleep . . . Do you want to stay over at my place tonight? I'm thinking partly of the weather and partly from the security point of view."

Gloria frowned. "It's nice of you to offer, but I could do with being in my own space. I need to feel grounded. And I don't want to be under your feet. You're going to have to get stuck into your inquiries tomorrow, and I don't want to get in the road."

"I don't want to leave you on your own. Even behind those high walls." I thought for a moment, then pulled over to the roadside and took out my phone. A couple of phone calls and I had it sorted. It meant an awkward detour via the students' union, but as soon as Gloria saw Donovan in all his hulking glory, she was perfectly happy for me to hoof it the mile across town to my house while she disappeared over the hills and far away with the best-looking bodyguard either side of the Pennines. The only question was whether she'd still respect him in the morning.

I stepped out briskly. The temperature was plummeting now the sleet had stopped, the pavements rapidly icing over. Twice the only thing that saved me from crashing to the pavement was a handy lamppost. All I wanted was to curl up in my dressing gown with a very large amount of Absolut Citron and a smudge of grapefruit juice. With luck, Richard might be home early, preferably armed with a substantial Chinese. He always says Friday night is amateurs' night out as far as live music is concerned. I could almost taste the salt and pepper king prawns. I should have known better. Nights like that just don't get better. The man I suppose I love was home all right. But not home alone. I found him fast asleep in his bed, his arms around someone else. When I walked into the room, her eyes snapped open. She took one look at me and screamed.

Sensible girl.

10

MERCURY IN VIRGO IN THE 5TH HOUSE

She can turn her hand to anything. She has a discriminating intellect but tends to be overcritical of herself and others in times of stress. She analyses problems with tenacity and is capable of painstaking research. She is logical, sceptical and can be obsessive.
From *Written in the Stars*, by Dorothea Dawson

Divorce may have deprived Richard of most of the last five years of his son Davy's life, but because a lot of his work is done at night, he did most of the daytime childcare for the first three. Thankfully the old skills hadn't deserted him. That meant I didn't have to take any responsibility for the most remarkable child on the planet (if you believed Alexis and Chris). I watched with a mixture of relief and astonishment as he spooned greyish-pink mush into the eager mouth of his nine-month-old girl-friend. He managed it almost without looking, and without ever breaking off in mid-sentence. He'd already changed a nappy without flinching, which was a long way away from my idea of getting the day off to a good start.

I remember when northern men would have died rather than admit they knew how Pampers worked. Now, they pin you to the wall in café bars and tell you it's possible for men to produce tiny amounts of breast milk. Certainly, Jay's arrival had already achieved the seemingly impossible task of ending the superficial hostilities between Alexis and Richard. Before Jay, Alexis maintained she was a real journo and Richard a sycophant; Richard that he was a real journo and Alexis a police lackey. Work never entered their conversations any more.

As he did about once a week, Richard had taken Jay for the night to give Chris a chance at a straight eight hours. Oddly, when Jay spent the night with him, she slept through till seven in the morning. When Chris was within earshot, Jay would invariably pierce the night with her cries at two, four and six o'clock. I could see she was going to grow up into the kind of clever manipulator I wouldn't mind having on the staff. Never mind putting her name down for Eton, I was putting her name down for Brannigan & Co.

"So what are your plans for today?" Richard asked as we sat in the conservatory watching wet snow cascading from the sky.

"I've got Donovan minding Gloria, so I probably don't need to go over there. I've told him she's to stay indoors, but looking at the weather, I don't think there'll be much temptation to leave the fireside. I'm going to do some background research in the *Chronicle* library so I can start asking sensible questions about Dorothea Dawson."

"Great," he said enthusiastically. "You can take Jay in with you. I was supposed to drop her at the *Chronicle* crèche so Alexis can pick her up, but if you're going in anyway, I can stay home and get on with some writing."

Time for the application of the Kate Brannigan irregular verb theory of life. In this case, "I am diplomatic, you are economical with the truth, s/he is a lying little gobshite." "No problem," I said. Why should I mind drumming my fingers on the table while Richard finished feeding her, changing her, swaddling her for the outside world, swapping the baby seat from his car to mine then strapping her in? It wasn't as if I had anything important like a murder to solve, after all.

I eventually tracked Alexis down in the office canteen. "Your daughter is in the crèche," I told her. "So's her car seat."

"That's great," she said. "I'll bob along in a minute and say hello. We really appreciate it, you know. It's the only time we get a decent night's sleep. She been OK?"

"As far as I know. She screamed her socks off when I got home last night, but that's just because she can't stand any competition for Richard's attention. So I left them to it. She probably had a better night's sleep than I did."

Alexis shook her head, smiling. "I know you love her really."

She knew more than I did. I smiled vacantly and said, "Dorothea Dawson."

"She didn't see that coming, did she?"

I love journalistic black humour. It always comforts me to know there are people more cynical than me around. "What's this morning's story?"

"What's your interest?" she asked, instantly on the alert. Her cigarettes came out and she lit one for real.

"I found the body."

Alexis ran her free hand through her hair so it stood up in a punk crest. "Shit," she said. "The bizzies never said anything about that at the press conference. They said the body had been discovered by a member of staff, the lying gets."

"You're surprised?"

"No. Cliff Jackson would superglue his gob shut before he let the name 'Brannigan' pass his lips. Unless the sentence also contained the words, 'has been charged with.' So give, KB. A first-person colour piece, that's just what I need for the city final." Her notebook had appeared on the table.

"What are they saying?"

"That she was killed in her camper van in the car park of the NPTV compound by a blow to the head around six last night. And that's about all. What can you give me?"

I sighed. "It isn't exactly something I want to dwell on. I needed to talk to Dorothea about the warning she'd given Gloria the last time she'd done a reading for her. I'd arranged to see her after her final client of the day. When I got there, I knocked but there was no reply. I knew she was expecting me, so I opened the door and walked in. She was lying face down on the table with her head caved in. It was obvious she was dead. Her crystal ball was lying on the carpet at the end of a track of blood. It looked to me as if that's what the killer used. It's much bigger than the usual crystal ball. It must be nine, ten inches across."

Alexis nodded as she took notes. "She was famous for it. Claimed it came from some mystical mountain mine. Me, I reckon it came from Pilkington Glass at St Helens." She gave me an apologetic grin. "Sorry about this but . . . How did you feel?"

"Sick. Can we talk about something else?"

"What, like Cliff Jackson's marital problems?"

"He's got marital problems?"

Alexis nodded, a grim little smile on her face. "In spades. His wife's run off with another bloke."

"What took her so long?"

"She probably couldn't find the key to the handcuffs. The best bit, though, is who she's run off with." Alexis paused for effect. I rotated my wrist in the classic "get on with it" gesture. "His oldest lad's in his second year at Liverpool University. His wife's only run off with the lad's best mate."

"You're kidding!"

"Would I lie to you?"

"How long have you been sitting on this?" I demanded.

"I only found out this morning. I was trying to get a comment from Jackson and he was going totally ballistic. I know one of his DCs from way back, so I cornered her and asked why Jackson was being even more of a pain than usual and she told me. So don't expect any favours."

"I'll bear that in mind." I grinned. "Couldn't happen to a nicer bloke, though. By the way, did you get anywhere in tracking down who was the source of your story about me minding Gloria?"

Alexis savoured her last mouthful of smoke and regretfully crushed the stub in the ashtray. "One of those things. Every Friday, the news credits book goes up to accounts so the payments can be processed. It doesn't come back till Monday morning. I was too late getting to it yesterday. Sorry."

"I'll just have to possess my soul in patience," I complained.

"So who was Dorothea's last appointment with? Which member of the *Northerners* cast was the last person to see her alive?"

"You'll have to ask Jackson that one." I didn't have much hope that I'd be able to keep Gloria's name out of the papers, but the longer I could, the better for her. "Any chance I can pillage the library? I could use some background on Dorothea."

"You digging into this, then?"

I shrugged. "If he's not made an arrest overnight, the chances are Jackson's stuck. Which means he'll be wasting time making my life hell. The best way to get him out of my face is to give him something else to think about. I figured if I took a trawl through the cuttings, something might occur to me that I could slip to Linda Shaw."

I could see from her eyes that Alexis didn't believe a word of it, but she knew better than to try to push me in a direction I didn't want to travel. "You'll tell me when you're ready," she said. "Come on, I'll sort you out."

Ten minutes later, I was beginning to wish I hadn't asked. A stack of manila files six inches deep contained the *Chronicle*'s archive on Dorothea Dawson, newly returned from the news reporters who had been writing the background feature for that day's paper. Another two ten-inch stacks contained the last year's cuttings about *Northerners*.

I tore a hole in the lid on the carton of coffee I'd brought up from the canteen, took the cap off my pen and began to explore Dorothea Dawson's past.

I'd got as far as her early TV appearances when Alexis burst in, a fresh cigarette clamped between her teeth. The librarian shouted, "Crush that ash, shit-for-brains!" Alexis ignored him and grabbed my arm, hustling me out into the corridor.

"Where's the fire? What the hell's going on, Alexis?"

"Your mate Dennis has just been arrested for murder."

I understood each of the words. But together they made no sense. "They think Dennis killed Dorothea Dawson?" I asked uncomprehendingly.

"Who said anything about Dorothea?"

"Alexis, just explain in words of one syllable. Please?"

"Some villain called Pit Bull Kelly was found dead early doors in one of the underground units in the Arndale. The place was empty, but apparently it had been squatted. According to my contact, they had a tip-off that it'd been Dennis who'd been using the place, and when they checked his fingerprints with records, they found them all over the place. So they've arrested him."

I still couldn't get my head round it. Dennis was a hard man, no stranger to violence. But for a long time, he'd not lifted a hand in anger to anyone. The crimes he'd committed had all been against property, not people. The notion of Dennis as a killer struck at the heart of everything I believed about him. Alexis's words were a blow that felled my confidence in my own judgement. "I need to speak to Ruth," I said, pushing past her and heading blindly down the corridor towards the lifts. I was halfway there when I had to turn back and collect my jacket and bag from the library.

"Calm down, KB," Alexis said pointlessly as I passed her.

"I don't want to be calm," I shouted over my shoulder. "Sometimes I get fed up with calm." I half ran along the corridor and, too wound up to wait for the lift, started down the stairs. I could hear Alexis's feet pounding away behind me. "He's not a killer, Alexis," I shouted up at her. "He loves his wife, he loves his daughter too much. He wouldn't do this to them."

Her footsteps stopped. I could hear her gasping for breath. "Phone me," she managed to get out.

I didn't bother to reply. I was too agitated. Alexis would forgive me, I knew that. Specifically, she'd forgive me when she got the inside story. At the bottom of the stairwell, I pushed open the door to the car park and got into my car. My breath was coming in deep gulps and my hands were shaking. I realized it was probably delayed shock from the night before kicking in as soon as my defences were down. I was close to Dennis, but not that close, I told myself.

When my pulse was back within the normal range, I took my phone out and dialled the number of Ruth Hunter's moby. If being hated by the police and the judiciary is a measure of success in criminal defence work, Ruth must be one of the best solicitors in the North West. Behind her back, they call her firm Hunter, Killer & Co. A big woman in every sense of the word, she sails into court in her bespoke tailoring like an outsize catwalk queen and rips the Crown Prosecution case to rags. If she didn't have clients, I suspect she'd do it anyway, just for the hell of it. She drives Officer Dibble wild by turning up to cop shops in the middle of the night in her millionaire husband's Bentley Mulsanne turbo. She can park that car in streets where my Rover would be stripped to the chassis in ten minutes and know it'll be there unscathed when she comes back. If she wasn't one of my closest friends, I'd string garlic round my neck just to walk past her office.

"Ruth Hunter," the voice said briskly.

"It's Kate. I heard about Dennis."

"What took you so long?" she asked drily. "It's at least three hours since they lifted him."

"Are they charging him?"

"I can't talk now as I'm sure you'll appreciate."

That meant she was in a police station, probably with a custody sergeant breathing down her neck. "When can we talk?"

"Your office, three o'clock."

"I'll be there. Should I go and see his wife?"

"I'd leave it for now. Maybe tomorrow. Things are a little . . . volatile at the moment. I'll see you later." The line went dead.

I could imagine. Most of the contents of the glass cupboard were probably in bits. Debbie's never had a problem expressing her emotions and Dennis was on his final warning following the twelve-month stretch he'd recently done. She'd told him then, one more serious nicking and she'd file for divorce. She'd probably started shredding his suits by now, unless she was saving that for when they charged him.

The clock said half past eleven. I couldn't face sitting in the *Chronicle* library for another three hours, and I didn't want to kick my heels at home. It's ironic. I spend half my life complaining that I never have time to do my washing or ironing, then when I get a couple of hours to myself, I'm too wound up to do anything constructive. I needed to find something that would make me feel like I was being effective. Then I remembered Cassandra Cliff. Cassie had once been one of the household names among the stars of *Northerners*. Then some creepy hack had left no stone unturned to find the slug who revealed that years before she'd been cast as Maggie Grimshaw, the bitch goddess gossip queen of *Northerners*, Cassie had been Kevin.

In the teeth of the hurricane of publicity, NPTV pointed out that they had an equal opportunities policy that protected transsexuals and that Cassie's job was safe with them. They were using "safe" with that particular meaning Margaret Thatcher inaugurated when she claimed the National Health Service was safe in her hands. Within months, Maggie Grimshaw had been killed off and Cassie was not only unemployed but unemployable.

She didn't run weeping into the wilderness. She sold the inside story of life on *Northerners* to the highest bidder, and there were no holds barred. Cassie never featured in any of the show's regular anniversary celebrations, but I suspected that didn't keep her awake at night. She'd chosen not to be bitter and instead of frittering away the money she made from her exposé, she set up a shop, magazine and social organization for transvestites and transsexuals.

Cassie had been a key source for Alexis for years, and we'd met following the death of a transvestite lawyer I'd been investigating. I'd met her a couple of times since then, most recently at Alexis and Chris's housewarming party. I knew she still kept in touch with a couple of people from *Northerners*. She might well know things Gloria didn't. More to the point, she might well tell me things Gloria wouldn't.

Energized by the thought of action, I started the car and headed for Oldham. Cassie's shop, Trances, was in one of those weary side streets just off the main town centre where some businesses survive against all the odds and the rest sink without trace, simply failing to raise the metal shutters one morning with no advance warning. There was little traffic and fewer pedestrians that afternoon; the wet snow that was melting away in Manchester was making half-hearted attempts at lying in Oldham, and ripples of slush were spreading across the pavements under the lash of a bitter wind. Anyone with any sense was sitting in front of the fire watching a black and white Bette Davis movie.

The interior of Trances never seemed to change. There were racks of dresses in large sizes, big hair on wig stands, open shelves of shoes so big I could have got both feet in one without a struggle, racks of garish magazines that no one was ever going to read on the tram. The key giveaway that this was the land of the truly different was the display case of foam and silicone prostheses—breasts, hips, buttocks. The assistant serving behind the counter took one look at me and I could see her contemptuously classifying me as a tourist. "Hi," I said. "Is Cassie about?"

"Have you an appointment?"

I shook my head. "I was passing."

"Are you a journalist? Because if you are, you're wasting your time. She's got nothing to say to anybody about *Northerners*," she said, her Adam's apple bobbing uncontrollably.

"I'm not a journalist," I said. "I know Cassie. Can you tell her Kate Brannigan's here?"

She looked doubtful, but picked up the phone anyway. "Cassandra? There's someone here called Kate Brannigan who wants to see you." There was a pause, then she said, "Fine. I'll send her up." The smile she gave me as she replaced the receiver was apologetic. "I'm sorry. The phone hasn't stopped ringing all day. It's always the same when there's some big *Northerners* story. If it's not that, it's Channel Four researchers doing documentaries about TSs and TVs."

I nodded and made for the door at the back of the shop that I knew led to Cassie's office and, beyond that, to her private domain. Cassie was waiting for me at the top of the stairs, immaculate as ever in a superbly tailored cream suit over a hyacinth-blue silk T-shirt. I'd never seen her in anything other than fabulous clothes. Her ash-blonde hair was cut in a spiky urchin style, her make-up subtle. From below, her jawline was so taut I had to suspect the surgeon's knife. If I earned my living from looking as convincing as Cassie, even I'd have submitted to plastic surgery. "Kate," she greeted me. "You've survived, then."

I followed her down the hallway and into her office, a symphony in limed wood and grey leather. She'd replaced the dusty-pink fabric of the curtains and cushions with midnight-blue and upgraded the computer systems since I'd last been there. She'd obviously tapped a significantly profitable niche in the market. "Survived?" I echoed.

Cassie sat on one of the low sofas and crossed legs that could still give any of her former colleagues a run for their money. "I saw the story in the *Chronicle*. My idea of hell would be running interference for Gloria Kendal," she said.

"Why do you say that?" I sat down opposite her.

"Unless she's changed dramatically, she's got a schedule that makes being Prime Minister look like a part-time job, she's about as docile as a Doberman and she thinks if she's hired you, she's bought you."

I grinned. "Sounds about right."

"At least you're not a bloke, so you're relatively safe," Cassie added archly.

I hoped Donovan was. "I expect you can guess why I'm here?"

"It's got to be Dorothea. Except that I can't think why you'd be investigating her murder when it's Gloria you've been working for."

I pulled a face. "It's possible that the person who killed Dorothea is the same one who is threatening Gloria. I'm just nosing around to see what I can dig up."

Cassie smiled, shaking her head slightly. "You'll never make an actress until you stop pulling your earlobe when you're stretching the truth."

My mouth fell open. I'd never realized what my giveaway body language was, but now Cassie had pointed that out, I became instantly self-conscious. "I can't believe you spotted that," I complained.

She shrugged. "My business depends on being able to spot deception. I've got good at it. It's all right, Kate, I don't need to know the real reason you're interested in who killed Dorothea. I'm happy to tell you whatever I know. I liked Dorothea. She was a worker, like me."

"How did the connection with *Northerners* begin?"

Cassie frowned in concentration. "I've got a feeling it was Edna Mercer who first discovered her. You remember Edna? Ma Pickersgill?"

"She's dead now, isn't she?"

Cassie's smile was sardonic. "Ma Pickersgill died of a heart attack when her house was burgled five years ago. Edna's still alive, though you'll never see her at an NPTV function."

"She left under a cloud?"

"Alzheimer's. Towards the end, it was touch and go whether she'd stay lucid long enough for them to get her made up and on set. As for learning lines, forget it. Anyway, I'm pretty sure it was Edna who brought Dorothea to the studios. She'd come across her in some dead-end seaside town and Dorothea had hit a couple of nails on the head. So Edna, who was a woman given to enthusiasms, persuaded enough of us to sign up for sessions with Dorothea to make it worth her while coming over for the day. I was impressed, in spite of myself."

"You surprise me," I said. "I'd have thought your feet were too firmly planted on the ground to care what's written in the stars."

Cassie smiled wryly. "Dorothea was very good. Whether you believed in it or not when you went in to see her, by the time you came out you were convinced she'd got something. After that first visit, we were all eating out of her hand. So it became a regular thing. The word spread through the cast, and soon she was coming more or less every week."

"What kind of stuff did she tell you?"

"She'd cast your horoscope, and she'd kick off every session by explaining some little thing in your chart. That was one of the clever things about the way she operated—you had to keep going to see her if you wanted her insight into every element of your personal horoscope. Then she'd talk about the current relationships between the planets and how they might affect you.

"She did phenomenal research, you know. She knew everything there was to know about everybody she had deal-ings with. Dorothea made a habit of gathering every snippet, no matter how insignificant it seemed. You know how these things go—Edna would say something in passing about Rita's son, then three months later Dorothea would say something to Rita about her son, knowing full well that Rita knows she's never mentioned the boy to Dorothea. It all contributed to the myth of omniscience."

"Making a virtue out of being a know-all. That is clever," I acknowledged. "So was that it?"

Cassie shook her head. "She'd finish off by asking if there was anything bothering you that you wanted guidance with.

You'd tell her and she'd gaze into her crystal ball and give you advice. She didn't go in for the riddle of the Sphinx stuff—she'd say things like, 'You're never going to have emotional support from your husband while you're married to an Aries with Capricorn rising. You either have to get out of the marriage or find what you're lacking in your friendships.'"

"More therapy than prediction, then?"

"A mixture of both. And actors are very gullible people." Her smile reminded me that she'd once been an actor, and not just on the screen.

"So why would anyone have it in for her?" I asked.

"I haven't a clue. I hadn't heard that anybody had fallen out with her. She could be irritating when she was trying to impress you with how mystical and spiritual she was, but that's no reason to kill somebody."

Changing tack, I said, "What about Gloria? Has anybody from *Northerners* got it in for her?"

Cassie chuckled, a warm, throaty sound. "How long have you got? The only surprising thing about Gloria is that she's still alive."

11

MOON SQUARES MIDHEAVEN

She can feel insecure socially because she tends to find herself in conflict with conventional norms. She will construct a world of her own where she can be herself, but will maintain the pretence of being tough and self-sufficient to the outside world. She does not express emotion readily, but nevertheless will often choose a caring or self-sacrificing role in life.

From *Written in the Stars*, by Dorothea Dawson

It was the first time anybody had even hinted that Gloria wasn't the most popular girl in the school. I leaned forward and said as calmly as I could manage, "And there was me thinking everybody loved Gloria."

"They do. That's why she provokes thoughts of murder on a regular basis. Or at least, she always used to. It drives you insane to be around somebody who's always kind, always generous, always doing charity work, always making time for the fans. There are people in the cast of *Northerners* who have a permanent inferiority complex thanks to Gloria." Cassie's voice was light, but there was an edge of something harder in her eyes.

"But like you just said, that's no reason to kill somebody."

Cassie raised her perfectly shaped eyebrows. "No? Well, you have more experience in these matters than I do. I tell you

what people would kill for, though, and that's their roles in
Northerners. Gloria's hot right now. The public adore her, and
the management knows it. Granted, nobody's bigger than the
show, but when actors are riding the crest of the wave, they do
get a certain amount of input into the storylines. If somebody in
the cast knew Gloria was suggesting a storyline that would see
them written out, that'd be a strong enough motive for some
of the idiots in the cast to put her out of the picture. But then,
it's not Gloria who's been murdered, is it?"

I sighed. "No. But one way or another, Dorothea's death
has rebounded quite nastily on Gloria's life. She was the one
who was in the room when Dorothea talked about the presence
of death. She never said anything similar to anyone else, as far
as I've been able to find out."

Cassie suddenly jumped to her feet. "Stay there a minute,"
she said, crossing to a door in the far wall. "I'll be right back."

The minute stretched into two, then five. The more I
thought about what she'd suggested, the more uneasy I became.
I pulled out my phone and rang Gloria's number. "Hiya, chuck,"
she greeted me.

"Everything OK?" I asked.

"Grand as owt. We're watching a Bette Davis video and
having a lovely time."

All right for some. "Can I speak to Donovan?" I waited
while she summoned him. He came on the line almost immediately. "Don? How's things?"

"Nothing except endless phone calls from the papers. Gloria just tells them she's too devastated to talk and puts the phone
down. It's a class act." He sounded both admiring and cautious.

"I've got something to do in town, but I'll be over in a
couple of hours to relieve you. Is that OK?"

"Great." I wasn't imagining the relief in his voice. Considering they've grown up in the inner city, Shelley's kids have
led remarkably sheltered lives. There was no way Donovan had
the sophistication to deal with a demanding woman like Gloria

indefinitely. If I didn't rescue him before nightfall, his mother almost certainly would, and then we'd have another corpse on our hands. And I'm still too young to die.

Cassie returned just as I finished the call, carrying a paperback. She held it up so I could see the cover, a misty head-and-shoulders shot of Dorothea looking significantly younger than when I'd met her. *If I'd Known Then, by Dorothea Dawson. The Life of a Stargazer,* was emblazoned top and bottom across the cover. "It was published about four years ago," Cassie said, handing it to me. "Bestseller list for four weeks, then the remainder pile, I suspect."

I opened it. The title page had an inscription. *To my darling Cassie. Fire and water make for a steamy combination! Where you are is better for you than where you were. Go in peace. Love, Dorothea Dawson.* "She seemed to know you well," I remarked.

"Not as well as she liked to think," Cassie said drily. "Like most people, she thought anyone whose sexuality or gender was expressed differently from the mainstream had to be obsessed with sex. Anyway, you're welcome to borrow it. It's life with all the edges smoothed down, but it does show you a bit of what the woman herself was like."

I pocketed the book and thanked her. It was clear from the way she was still standing that as far as Cassie was concerned, there was no more to be said. But before I left, I had to ask her one thing. "You know they've got a mole," I said. "Any ideas who it might be?"

An indefinable bitterness crept into Cassie's face. She knew all about the damage that moles could do to the foundations of a life. "John Turpin must be biting the carpet," she said. "There's nothing the management hates more than storyline leaks."

"This isn't just storyline leaks," I pointed out. "It's the kind of stuff that ruined your career."

She sighed. "I know. I try not to think about it because it reminds me of what was probably the worst point in my life. When I was splashed all over the tabloids, I think I was actually more depressed than I ever was when I was still trapped inside a male shape. So when I see other people's lives being trashed in the same way, I just try to tune out and remind myself that it turned into the best thing that could have happened to me. But I don't know who's ratting on the *Northerners* cast any more than I know who gave me up."

"You never found out?"

"I never found out. There were so few people who knew, you see, and I trusted them all with my life. I always thought someone from the Amsterdam clinic where I had my surgery must have been over here on holiday or on business or something and seen me on the TV."

I got to my feet. "Was Ross Grant doing the outside catering when you were on the show?"

"Ross? Big cuddly Scotsman? Wife with eyes like a hawk? Yeah, he took over the contract about a year before I was demolished. Wait a minute . . . You're not suggesting Ross is the mole?"

"I'm not, but Turpin seems determined to give it a whirl."

Cassie laughed scornfully. "Ross hasn't got the malice to do it or the brains to cover his tracks."

"What about his wife?"

"Why should she? Why risk the goose that lays the golden eggs?"

"Greed?"

Cassie looked sceptical. "I can't see her going in for that kind of short-term thinking."

"Not even if she thought they were going to lose the contract? That way she kills two birds with one stone. She gets her revenge on Turpin for dumping them and she earns a nice little nest egg to cushion the blow while they look for other work."

"They already have other work," Cassie objected. "Or they used to, at any rate. *Northerners* is their most regular source of income, but they do cater for other people's location shoots. So it wouldn't be the end of the world if they did lose the contract.

And if she was discovered, it would mean the end of their business altogether. I just don't see it."

As I walked back to my car, I pondered what Cassie had said. For it to be worth the mole's while, he or she had to be indifferent to the outcome of being found out. That meant it was either someone sufficiently skilled to overcome the stigma of being known in the TV business as the *Northerners* mole, or someone who was prepared to risk their career to vent their venom against the programme or its makers.

However I cut it, it didn't sound like a cast member to me.

❧❖❧

I was back in my office by three. I wasn't alone; Gizmo was in the computer room in weekend uniform of jeans, Converse baseball boots with holes in the toes, and three shirts. When I'd stuck my head round the door, he'd lifted his head long enough to tell me he was working on some new computer security subroutines for a local mail order company that had started direct selling via the Internet. Who was I to doubt him? Even if he had gone pink around the ears?

As soon as I had five minutes that I didn't need for sleeping, I was going to have to do some digging.

Ruth walked through the door with ten seconds to spare. She's the only person I know who's even more punctual than me. One of the mysteries of the universe for both of us is how we ended up hitched to men who think if you get to the cinema in time to see the British Board of Film Classification certificate, you're far too early. If I could change one thing about Richard, that's what it would be.

She pulled me into her arms and gave me the kind of hug that always makes me feel five years old. It was exaggerated today because she was swathed in a vast silver-grey fake fur that felt like the best fluffy toy a child ever held. "You look like the Snow Queen," I said, disentangling myself and giving her an admiring look from the perfectly pleated blonde hair to the soft leather boots that clung to her well-shaped calves.

"I was aiming for the scary-monster effect," she said, shrugging out of her fur and dropping into a chair.

"Did it work?"

She pulled a face. "Dennis is still in custody, so it rather looks as if I failed."

"What's the score?" I asked, switching on the cappuccino machine that was one of the few permanent reminders of my former business partner Bill Mortensen.

Ruth shook her head wearily. "It's really not looking good for him. Especially with a record that includes burglary, robbery and grievous bodily harm."

"Grievous bodily harm? I didn't know about that."

"He was twenty-two and he'd just come out of the Paras after a tour in Northern Ireland where his best friend was shot by a sniper in front of his eyes. Post-traumatic shock hadn't been invented then, otherwise a good brief would have walked him out of the door on that set of circumstances. He hasn't been convicted of a violent offence since, but it's still sitting there among his previous convictions like a great fat toad. Any battered body found in the vicinity of his fingerprints is always going to point to Dennis."

I passed her a cup of frothy coffee and perched with my own on the corner of the desk. "What exactly happened?"

Ruth filled me in succinctly. Patrick "Pit Bull" Kelly was one of a gang of eight brothers from the unappetizing redbrick terraces of Cheetham Hill in North Manchester. They were all small-time criminals, good only at getting caught. Pit Bull had been running a shop-squat scam like Dennis, but since he lacked Dennis's nerve or imagination, he'd steered clear of the city centre and worked his own familiar turf with its restricted numbers of punters, none of whom had much cash to spare. When he'd heard about Dennis's operation, he'd decided he wanted a slice so last night he'd told two of his brothers he was going into town to "take that scumbag O'Brien's shop off him."

The next anyone had seen of Pit Bull Kelly had been early that morning. The manager of the cut-price butcher's shop next door to Dennis's squat got more than he'd bargained for when he went to open up. He'd opened the door to the service corridor that ran behind the six-unit section. Facing him was a brindle-and-white pit bull terrier, the bulges of muscle making the hair on its shoulders and ribs stand out like a bristly halo. Its teeth were bared in a rictus that would have made Jaws look friendly, but instead of growling, it was whimpering. The poor bloke froze in his tracks, but the dog showed no signs of attacking him. Instead, it had backed up to Dennis's back door and started howling. According to Ruth, the witness claimed it sounded like the hound from hell.

He didn't know what to do, so he shut the door and called the mall security. Grateful for something more interesting than teenage troublemakers, two uniformed guards had arrived within minutes. They had the local beat bobby in tow, less than thrilled at having his illicit tea break with the security men broken up. When they opened the corridor, the same thing happened. The dog showed its teeth, backed off and started howling outside the door to Dennis's shop.

The bobby decided they should take a look inside. The door obviously wasn't locked, but there was something heavy behind it. A bit of brute force got the door far enough open for the copper to stick his head inside and check out the obstruction. Which happened to be the corpse of Pit Bull Kelly.

How he'd died was far from obvious. There was no blood, no visible wound. But the bobby was sensible enough to realize that somebody who looked as dodgy as Pit Bull Kelly probably hadn't dropped down dead with a heart attack. He'd radioed for back-up. By mid-morning, the fingerprint team had matched Dennis's prints with the ones all over the curiously empty shop. And the pathologist had given them the tentative information that he thought Pit Bull Kelly had died from a sub-arachnoid haemorrhage.

"What's a sub-arachnoid haemorrhage?" I asked, my first interruption. Ordinarily I'm not that restrained, but, unusually in lawyers, Ruth actually tells a story with all the pertinent details in place.

Ruth tilted her head sharply to one side and pressed her fingers under the angle of her jaw. "Just behind the jawbone here, there's a very vulnerable blood vessel. Rupture that and you're brain-dead in seconds. Normally it's protected by the jaw. And by the way we instinctively duck our heads when any threat approaches. It's almost impossible to hit accidentally, but it could be caused by, for example, a stiff-fingered karate blow to the neck."

"And Dennis was a Para," I said hollowly.

"Dennis was indeed a Para. He says he never learned any karate in the service, but we both know what a bugger it is to try proving a negative."

"So the police are saying that Dennis was there, Dennis had good reason to get into a ruck with Pit Bull Kelly, so Dennis must have murdered him then emptied his stock out of the shop to cover his tracks?"

Ruth nodded. "That's about the size of it. That, or Dennis caught Pit Bull Kelly in the act of stealing all his stock."

"What's Dennis's version?"

"Perfectly plausible, as you'd expect. According to him, the landlord turned up yesterday with a couple of heavies who were even bigger than Keith. He gave Dennis twenty-four hours to get out or suffer the consequences. Dennis thought this was a not unreasonable proposition, so he spent yesterday evening with Keith and a couple of the lads, loading the stock into a van. Keith and the others went off with the van around half past nine, and Dennis went home, where he spent the rest of the evening watching a video with Debbie. They then went to bed, together, and woke up, again together, at around eight this morning."

"That's his alibi? The blonde with no brain?"

"The blonde with no brain who has previously been caught out giving him false alibis," Ruth said drily.

"Wasn't Christie home?" I asked. Dennis's daughter obviously couldn't testify that he'd been in bed all night, but at least she'd have been a more credible witness to his TV viewing.

"She stayed overnight with a friend." Ruth carefully placed her empty cup on the side table. "I won't deny it's looking bad, Kate."

I nodded. "I'll do what I can."

Ruth stood up and enveloped herself in the fake fur. "I know Dennis will appreciate it. I think they'll probably charge him tomorrow and bring him before the Mags on Monday. Once he's remanded, you'll be able to visit him and see if there's anything he can tell you that he'd prefer me not to know. If you need anything, you know where to find me."

We hugged, the silken fur stroking my face. "Just leave the coat," I said. "I've got to go to Saddleworth."

Ruth groaned. "It's not the coat you'll need, it's a team of huskies and a sled. You're surely not going there for pleasure, are you?"

I laughed. "They do pleasure in Saddleworth? A place where their idea of a good time is brass bands, Morris dancing and the annual Ducking of the Greenfield Trollop? I don't think so."

"So, strictly business," Ruth said, adjusting her pelt so not a breath of chill air could penetrate. "No fun Saturday night with Richard, then."

"He's probably babysitting," I said, more of an edge in my voice than I'd intended.

Ruth's eyebrows rose. "The boy getting broody, is he?"

"If he is, he's wasting his energy," I told her firmly.

"I'd keep an eye on that, if I were you," Ruth said ominously as she swept out.

Where would we be if it wasn't for the love and support of our friends?

12

MERCURY SQUARES THE ASCENDANT

She is inclined to keep her own counsel, but can't resist poking her nose into everybody else's business. She's never quite got to grips with the idea that there are times when it's tactful to keep her advice to herself. She is a quick worker, energetic and inventive. She tends to be a chameleon, appearing all things to all people.

From *Written in the Stars*, by Dorothea Dawson

It's not often I feel sorry for journalists. But I had to admit my heart went out to the handful of hacks still staking out the entrance to Gloria's enclave. The temperature was already below zero, and the interiors of their cars were no match for a winter's night on the edge of Saddleworth Moor. They perked up momentarily when I swung into the narrow lane, a couple of them even getting out and trotting through the freezing slush in my wake.

But I was through the gate and gone long before they caught up. I hadn't had to use the intercom; I'd phoned Donovan just as I was approaching precisely so I wouldn't have to run the gutter-press gauntlet. As I got out of the car, Gloria appeared in her doorway. She was wearing a high-necked, sparkling, midnight-blue evening dress that hung straight down from her bosom in an elegant fall. On her feet were glittering gold strappy sandals. She looked ready for the Oscars on a balmy California evening, not a charity auction in a Manchester hotel on the coldest night of the year. My charcoal wool crepe suit that doubles up for evening wear and impressing the hell out of clients left me feeling seriously underdressed. Gloria clearly agreed.

"You do know this is a black-tie affair?" she asked.

"I'm a minder, not a model," I snapped, forcing her to step backwards as I hurried inside. Donovan was looming in the living room, a certain tension noticeable around his deep-set eyes. "Any problems, Don?"

"Everything under control," he reported, thrusting his big hands into the pockets of his jeans, which made his shoulders look even more like an American footballer's padding. "Are you going to drop me off in town, or what?"

Gloria swept past me and slipped her arm through one of Donovan's. His eyes widened like a startled Bambi. "Kate, don't you think it would be better if Donovan escorted me tonight? All I'm thinking is that you've been splashed all over the papers, and I don't want you to have to spend your evening fending off nosy parkers."

She didn't want anyone stealing her limelight, more like. Besides, women like Gloria like to impress people. What better fashion accessory than a drop-dead-gorgeous toy boy like Donovan? That would take everyone's mind off death threats and on to prurient scandal. "I thought you just said it was black tie," I said sourly.

Gloria gazed up at Donovan. "Have you not got a dinner jacket, chuck?"

"Sorry, no." Relief relaxed his features into a smile.

"Never mind," Gloria said. "Harry Gershon the tailor's on the committee for tonight's do. I'll give him a bell and you can tell him your measurements and he'll bring a suit along."

"Oh," Donovan croaked. "But . . ."

Gloria gave him the hundred-watt smile. I could see sweat on his upper lip and it was nothing to do with the central heating.

"We'll have a great time, Donovan. I promise you." Her throaty chuckle left almost nothing to the imagination.

"That might not be such a bad idea," I said slowly, an idea beginning to form.

"But Kate," Donovan protested, apprehension and betrayal in his voice.

"If I take Gloria's car and shove a Brenda wig over my hair, I can act as a decoy and pull the press off. Then you'll get a clear run into town. I've got some work to do digging into Dorothea's past, so I can get on with that while you two are out enjoying yourselves."

Donovan looked like I'd just given him life with a recommendation for twenty-five years. "You mean you want me to carry on bodyguarding Gloria?" he asked desperately.

"At least, chuck," Gloria purred, delighted to be getting her own way.

"And I'll pick Gloria up later at the hotel and bring her back here," I said sweetly, enjoying the irritation that flashed in her eyes as she watched her bubble burst.

Donovan grinned with relief. "That's great. I don't think I can do tomorrow, Kate, because I've got to finish an essay for Monday."

And I am Marie of Romania, I thought to myself. "No problem. I'll handle it. OK?" I asked Gloria.

"You're the boss," she pouted. "I'll get you my spare Brenda wig." She disentangled her arm from Donovan, gave him a little pat on his iron-hard gluteus maximus and sashayed out of the room.

Donovan moved to my side and stooped close to my ear. "I thought you were going to make me spend another night here," he whispered. I thought only the prospect of his mother's anger had the power to make him that twitchy.

"You survived last night intact, didn't you?" I asked sweetly.

He straightened up and scowled. "Only just," he muttered. "What's the polite way to tell somebody ten years older than your mum to take her hand off your thigh?"

"You obviously found one," I said drily.

"I went to the toilet a lot," he said bitterly. "And the spare bedroom's got a bloody big chest of drawers that fits nicely behind the door. It took me all my time to get it shifted, and it's just as well I did because I swear I woke up to the sound of the door handle turning."

I stifled a snort of laughter. "Sorry, Don," I giggled. "I know it's not funny. What happened?"

"I did snoring. Loudly. Eventually she went away. She must think I'm a pretty crap bodyguard if I can sleep through that."

I grinned. "Somehow I don't think it's the guarding capabilities of your body that she's interested in. Don't worry, I'll come and rescue you in good time tonight."

We shut up and moved apart as we heard Gloria's approach. She came in twirling a rigid platinum-blonde beehive on the end of her finger. "There you go, chuck. One Brenda Barrowclough barnet." She tossed it in my direction. Donovan stretched out a long arm and intercepted it, then handed it ceremoniously to me.

"Let's see what you look like," he said, a mischievous grin lighting up his eyes.

I pulled the wig over my head. It wasn't a bad fit, and in the poor light of the streetlamps I reckoned it would be good enough to fool anyone expecting Gloria. Five minutes later and I was proving myself right, always a feeling I enjoy. At the end of the narrow lane leading to Gloria's, I slowed to turn on to the main road. To either side, headlights snapped on and engines coughed into life. "Gotcha," I said under my breath as I led the cavalcade down the road towards Oldham. As far as I could see, they were all nailed to my tail. I was just grateful there were no tunnels between Saddleworth and Manchester. And that it was too cold for riding motorbikes.

I drove to the office, not particularly wanting to invite the rat pack back to my own doorstep. I managed to find a parking space that wasn't illegal enough to earn a ticket on a Saturday night, aware of the four press cars hovering nearby, trying to find nonexistent spaces where they could abandon ship and follow "Gloria." I got out of the car, pulled the wig off and ran my hand through my hair. I wiggled my fingers at the hacks and walked round the corner to my office. Nobody followed me. Like private eyes, journos always know when they've just been had over by an expert. One humiliation was enough for one evening.

The office was dark and empty, Gizmo having finally remembered he had a home to go to. I brewed myself a cappuccino and stretched out on the clients' sofa to skim the authorized version of Dorothea's life. The two hundred and fifty pages of largish print left a lot of scope for the imagination. The rosy glow of a happy Lancashire childhood in a poor but honest family, followed by an adolescence troubled only by the upheavals surrounding the discovery of her psychic powers and the difficulties of coming to terms with a "gift" that set her apart from her contemporaries.

She had married at twenty to a man eight years older than her, referred to only as Harry. The marriage lasted less than a chapter. If Dorothea's cursory dismissal was anything to go by, the real thing hadn't endured much longer. Because she'd needed to support herself, she'd started charging for astrological consultations. By the time Edna Mercer had stumbled across her, she'd graduated from her front room to her own booth on a seaside pier.

Northerners had changed everything. Within months of becoming the personal astrologer to a handful of cast members, she was the most sought-after stargazer in the country. A year after Edna Mercer had plucked her from relative obscurity, she had a monthly slot on daytime TV, syndicated weekly newspaper columns and pre-recorded local radio horoscopes. Now, a few years after her book had appeared, she had been edged from pole position among astrologers by the high-profile appearances of Mystic Meg on the national lottery broadcasts, but Dorothea Dawson was still Seer to the Stars in the public's mind. The amazing thing, the one fact that had kept her going through the tough times, was the certain knowledge that once she reached a particular point in her astrological cycle, she would be a star herself. And the moon is made of green cheese.

Bored by the book's relentless tabloid prose and frustrated by its deliberate superficiality, I gave up on it after an hour or so. I knew that compared to the police, my chances of uncovering Dorothea's killer were slim. They had forensic evidence and teams of trained officers who could question everybody who'd ever crossed the threshold of the NPTV compound. All I had going for me was the chance that my informal networks could produce information that was denied to the police. Cassie had been some help, but I needed a lot more.

There was one source that I suspected wouldn't occur to Cliff Jackson if he thought from now till next Christmas. Even if it did, a private operator like me was always going to get a far better response from the anarchic community of the Internet than a copper ever would. Even the straightest suit turns into a bit of a rebel when he—or she—ventures into cyberspace.

Reluctantly abandoning the comfort of the sofa, I slouched in front of my PC and got on-line. I went straight to one of the search engines that act as the nearest thing the ever-expanding web has to a road map. Within minutes, I had a list of addresses for websites and newsgroups that might be useful sources of information. I posted a message in a dozen places—the technological equivalent of the personal column of the newspaper, with considerably faster and better results. While I was on-line, I posted a couple of other inquiries, to see if something I'd half remembered was the truth or just wishful thinking. Finally, I checked my own e-mail and printed out a couple of requests for information from investigators abroad. They were after routine background checks that would take them days or weeks but which I could polish off in a matter of hours thanks to my local knowledge. It used to be a lot easier for people to disappear abroad. Now it's really true that you can run but you can't hide.

I switched off the computer and checked the time. Way too early to pick up Gloria. There was no chance of Richard being home on a Saturday night, at least not before *Match of the Day*. But I knew someone who would be.

As I parked outside the O'Briens' house, a couple of pairs of curtains in the deeply suburban close twitched open, shards of light sparking on their frosted lawns like glitter on Christmas cards. Even thick middle managers know that nobody as small as me gets into the police, so the pale stripes of curtain gaps soon disappeared. Debbie answered the door with a defiant glower that turned her beauty into a threat. "Oh, it's you," she said. "I thought it was the Old Bill come back for another run through the laundry basket. Bastards. Come on in."

It was hardly a gracious invitation, but I don't suppose I'd have been any better behaved in the circumstances. I followed her into the immaculate and characterless kitchen. I'd been right about the glasses. The cabinet was empty. I didn't think that was because Debbie was secretly having a party in the next room. "Want a drink?" she asked.

When I started working in Manchester, the first time someone had asked me that I'd said, "No thanks, I'm driving." He'd given me a very strange look. It took me about six months and a lot of thirsty encounters to realize that when you're offered a drink around here, they mean tea or coffee. "Coffee," I said. "White, no sugar."

The silence grew thick between us while Debbie brewed up, the hiss as boiling water exploded coffee granules perfectly audible. She's never quite sure what to make of me. Being a woman whose IQ is around the same as her continental shoe size, she can't quite make herself believe that any woman would prefer to go out to work to support herself from choice. She also finds it hard to get her head round the notion that any heterosexual woman could spend serious time with her husband without having designs on his body. Every now and again Dennis or I or their teenage daughter Christie convinces her that our relationship is purely platonic. Then she forgets what platonic means and we have to start all over again. Sometimes I think it would just be easier if I told her I was a lesbian.

On second thoughts, perhaps not.

"Ruth says you're going to help him," Debbie said flatly as she plonked the mug in front of me.

"I'll do what I can. But I'm not sure what I can usefully do. It's not like I can track down missing alibi witnesses or anything."

Debbie bristled. "That's because he was here with me all night."

"You're sure he didn't pop out for a packet of fags or anything?" I asked.

Debbie glared at me. "Whose side are you on? You sound like the bloody bizzies. Look, he didn't pop out for a packet of fags because I buy his fags at the supermarket, right?" She swung away from me and yanked open one of the tall kitchen units. The cupboard contained an unbroached carton of Dennis's brand and a half-full wrap of hers. "Even Dennis can't smoke two hundred fags a night."

"I'm just checking, Debbie," I said calmly. "I'm on Dennis's side. I only asked because if he did bob out for ten minutes, you can bet the Dibble are going to find out and use that to make you look like a liar."

She lit a cigarette, then gripped her right elbow with her left hand in a classic defensive gesture. "Look, I know I gave him a moody alibi one time. But you've got to when it's your man. And I'm not lying this time. He really was here all night. Him and Keith and the lads had been loading up the stock. He was too knackered even to go out for a pint."

I held my hands up in a placatory gesture. "I believe you. The problem I've got is that I'm not up to speed with who hates who among the Cheetham Hill villains. Until I can speak to Dennis, I haven't a clue whose doors I should be kicking in."

Debbie sighed a long ribbon of smoke. "No point in asking me. I've always kept my nose out. There is one thing, though," she added, frowning as she thought. The absence of permanent lines on her forehead demonstrated what a rare event I was witnessing.

"What's that?" I had little hope of a result, but my mother brought me up to be polite.

"The dog. I can't understand how come the dog was in the corridor and Pit Bull Kelly was in the shop."

"Pit Bull must have been attacked as he walked in the door."

"So how did whoever killed him get out past the dog? That's a killer dog, that. It wouldn't let Pit Bull's killer walk. It'd rip his throat out."

She had a point. I sipped my coffee and thought about it. "A bit of a puzzle, that," I said.

"Plus," she added with a triumphant air, "if Pit Bull went down the shop to front up Dennis, he'd never have moved an inch without the dog. If Dennis had been in the shop, it would have been the dog that went through the door first, not that gutless wonder Pit Bull. Plus, if Dennis had still been using the shop, his night watchman would have been inside."

"Of course," I breathed.

"So the dog being in the corridor proves Dennis wasn't there."

Somehow, I thought a jury might need a bit more convincing than the dog that didn't rip a throat out in the night. But at least it gave me somewhere to start.

⚜

Traditionally, the serious players in Manchester's drug wars have been the black gangs of Moss Side and the white gangs of Cheetham Hill. The Cheetham Hill lads have been around longer, their criminal roots deep in the cracks between the paving stones of the narrow terraced streets north of the wholesale district of Strangeways, their horizons bisected by the central tower of the Victorian prison and the slender black chimney of Boddingtons Brewery. Most of them are descended from long lines of gangsters and scam artists; it's a mark of status in Cheetham Hill to reveal your great-granddad did time for black marketeering during the war.

The Kellys were one of the oldest families, and most of them stuck to the old ways. Protection rackets and schneid sports gear, long firm frauds and small-time thieving, that was the Kellys' style. The team of brothers had always had contempt for the drug lords, which was about the only good thing you could say for them.

I had to endure three boozers where I drank beer straight from the bottle because I wasn't prepared to risk the glasses before I found a pair of grieving Kelly brothers. The Dog and Brewer was the kind of dump where your feet stick to the carpet and the fag ash forms a paste on the bottom of ashtrays that nobody has bothered to dry after rinsing them under the tap. Most of the punters had the blurred jawlines and bleary eyes of people who have smoked and drunk so much for so long change seems pointless. The women wore clothes that might have flattered them fifteen years before but now insulted them even more than the flabby men in ill-fitting casual clothes who were buying them drinks. Tom Jones was rejoicing loudly that again he'd touch the green, green grass of home.

I brazened out the eyes on me and bought a bottle of Carlsberg. "Any of the Kelly boys in?" I asked the barman, my fingers resting lightly on the fiver on the bar.

He looked at the money and gave me the once-over. I obviously didn't look like a cop, for he jerked his head towards two shaggy-haired men in padded flannel work shirts at the far end of the bar. Before I could turn back, the fiver was gone. One good thing about lowlife dives is that the information comes cheap.

I picked up my bottle and pushed through the crowd until I was standing next to the two men. Their blue eyes were blood-shot, their stubbled cheeks scarlet with the stout and whisky they were pouring down their throats. "I'm sorry for your loss, gentlemen," I said. "Will you let the *Evening Chronicle* buy you a drink?"

The taller of the two managed a half-hearted leer. "I'll let you buy me a drink any time, darling."

I signalled the barman and blew a tenner on drink. "Hell of a shock," I said, raising my bottle to clink against their glasses.

"I told him he was a dickhead, going up against Dennis O'Brien. Hard bastard, that one," the smaller brother slurred.

"I heard the dog was supposed to be good protection," I said. "Bit of a handful, I heard. They say he gave the Old Bill a hard time."

The taller one grinned. "Thank fuck for that. I'm Paul, by the way, and this is Little Joe."

I shook the outstretched paw. "I'm Kate. How come Patrick went to see O'Brien on his own? If the guy's so tough?"

Little Joe snorted. "Because he was a big girl's blouse. He was always trying to prove he was a hard man, our Patrick, but he was about as hard as Angel Delight. He was complaining that Dennis O'Brien had muscled in on his racket, and we all got so fucked off with listening we told him to go and sort O'Brien out if he was so pissed off."

"And he'd had enough to drink to think he was man enough to take on that South Manchester scumbag." Paul shook his head. "He was an eejit, Patrick."

"Especially when he had a drink in him." Little Joe shook his head too.

"And a draw," Paul concluded.

"So he'd been drinking and smoking dope before he went off to the Arndale to front up O'Brien?" I asked.

"That's right," Little Joe confirmed. "I mean, what kind of bastard has to top some drunken tosser just to make a point? O'Brien could just have broken a few bones and chucked Patrick out on his ear. He didn't have to go and kill him. Anybody could see Patrick was an eejit."

"What about the dog, though?" I persisted.

Paul gave a contemptuous bark of laughter. "Yeah, well, even a hard nut like O'Brien might have thought twice about taking on that mad bastard dog. I can't figure out how the dog didn't rip his throat out."

Suddenly, Little Joe's eyes were full of tears. "He didn't have to kill him, though, did he? The bastard didn't have to kill my baby brother." His hand snaked out and grabbed my lapel. "You tell them that in your paper. My baby brother was a big soft lump. Even with a drink and a draw in him, he wouldn't have done to O'Brien what that shit O'Brien done to him. You tell them, d'you hear? You tell them."

I promised I'd tell them. I promised several times. I listened to the Kelly boys telling me the same things a few more times, then made my excuses and left. I carried my own haze of stale smoke and spilled drink into the car and made for the city centre.

I virtually had to drag Gloria off Donovan in the end. She'd been taking advantage of having a driver to attack the champagne with the brio of an operatic tenor. As she slid from happy to drunk to absolutely arseholed, so her amorousness had grown, according to Donovan, who I found with a slew of red lipstick below one ear and one shirt-tail hanging down the front of his trousers. He was keeping Gloria upright by pure strength, lurking in a corner near the revolving doors.

"Why didn't you sit her down in a quiet corner of the bar?" I hissed as we steered her into the street. It was like manipulating one of those wooden articulated models artists use, only life-sized and heavy as waterlogged mahogany.

"Every time I sat down she climbed on my lap," he growled as we poured Gloria into the passenger seat of her car.

"Fair enough." I slammed the door and handed him my car keys. "Thanks, Don. You did a good job in very trying circumstances."

He scratched his head. "I expect it'll be reflected in my pay packet."

Like mother, like son. "It would be nice to find my car outside my house sometime tomorrow, keys through the letter-box. I'll talk to you soon." I patted his arm. It was like making friends with one of the Trafalgar Square lions.

Gloria was snoring gently when I got behind the wheel. The engine turning over woke her up. She rolled towards me, hand blindly groping for my knee. "I don't think so," I said firmly, returning it to her own lap.

Her eyes snapped open and she looked at me in astonish-ment. "Hiya, chuck," she said blearily. "Where did Donovan go?"

"Home to bed."

She gurgled. I hoped it was a chuckle and not the overture to a technicolour yawn. "Lucky girl," she slurred. "Poor old Glo. Whatchou been up to, then? Bit of nookie with the boyfriend?"

We turned into Albert Square, where the giant inflatable red and white figure of Santa Claus clutched the steeple that rises out of the middle of the town hall roof. It looked vaguely obscene in the garish glare of the Christmas lights. I jerked my thumb upwards. "He's seen more action than I have tonight. I've been trying to find out about Dorothea's past," I said, more to fill the space than in any hope of a sensible response.

"Bloody tragic, that's what it was. Tragic," Gloria mumbled.

"Murder always is."

"No, you daft get, not the murder, her life. It was tragic." Gloria gave me one of those punches to the shoulder that drunks think are affectionate. The car swerved across two lanes and nar-rowly missed a bus. Gloria giggled as I wrestled with the wheel.

"What was tragic?" I asked, my jaw clenched so tight the muscles hurt.

"She never got over losing him." She groped in her evening purse for a cigarette and lit up.

"Losing who? Her husband?"

"Flamin' Nora, Kate. When did a woman ever regret losing a no-good waste of space like her old man?" she reproached
me. "Her son, of course. She never got over losing her son."

"I didn't know she'd had a son."

"Not a lot of people know that," Gloria intoned in a very
bad impersonation of Michael Caine. "She had a son and then
she had post-natal depression."

"And the baby died?"

"'Course he didn't die," she said scornfully. "He got taken
off her. When she got put away."

This was beginning to feel like one of those terrible black
and white northern kitchen sink dramas scripted by men with
names like Arnold and Stanley. "When you say 'put away,' do you
mean sectioned, Gloria?" I asked as sweetly as I could manage.

"Tha's right," she said. "Put away in the loony bin. He
did that to her. Her old man had her put away because having
the baby had sent her a bit off her rocker. Christ, every woman
goes a bit off her rocker when she's had a littl'un. If they put us
all away just because we went a bit daft, there'd be a hell of a
lot of men changing nappies. Right bastard he must have been."

"So Dorothea's baby was adopted then, is that what you're
saying?"

"Aye. Taken off her and given to somebody else. And they
gave her electric shocks and cold showers and more drugs than
Boots the Chemist and wondered why it took her so bloody long
to get better. Bastards." She spat the last word vehemently, as
if it was personal, her eyes on the swirl of pinprick snowflakes
tumbling thinly in the cones of sulphur-yellow streetlights.

"Did Dorothea tell you about this?"

"Who else? It were when I asked her to do a horoscope
for my granddaughter. We'd gone out for a meal and we ended
up back at my place, pissed as farts. And she started on about
how she could be a grandmother half a dozen times over and
she'd never be any the wiser. When she sobered up, she made

me swear not to tell another living soul. And I haven't, not until now. Tragic, that's what it was. Tragic."

I came at the subject half a dozen different ways before we finally arrived back at the deserted alley leading to her fortification. Each time I got the same version. No details added, no details different. Dorothea might have been lying to Gloria, but Gloria was telling me the truth.

I helped her out of the car and across cobbles covered in feathery white powder to her front door. I wasn't in the mood to go any further. I wanted home and bed and the sleep that would make sense of the jumbled jigsaw pieces of information that were drifting through my head like the snow across the windscreen. And not a snow-plough in sight.

God, I hate the country.

13

SUN CONJUNCTION WITH PLUTO

Compromise is not in her vocabulary. She is not afraid of initiating confrontations and is a great strategist. She enjoys conflict with authority, she will not stand for personal or professional interference, but she is capable of transforming her own life and the world around her. People can be nervous of her, but this is a splendid aspect for a detective.

From *Written in the Stars*, by Dorothea Dawson

I woke up with that muffled feeling. It didn't go away when I stuck my head out from under the duvet. Richard only grunted when I slipped out of bed and pulled on my dressing gown before I died of hypothermia. The central heating had obviously been and gone while I was still sleeping, which made it sometime after nine. I lifted the curtain and looked out at a world gone white. "Bugger," I said.

Richard mumbled something. "Whazza?" it sounded like.

"It's been snowing. Properly."

He pushed himself upon one elbow and reached for his glasses. "Lessee," he slurred. I opened one side of the curtain. "Fabulous," he said. "We can make a snowman."

"And what about Gloria? I'm supposed to be minding her."

"Not even a mad axeman would be daft enough to go on a killing spree in Saddleworth in this weather," he pointed out, not unreasonably. "It'll be chaos on the roads out there. And if Gloria's got the hangover she deserves, she won't be thinking about going anywhere. Come back to bed, Brannigan. I need a cuddle."

I didn't need asking twice. "I obey, o master," I said ironically, slipping out of my dressing gown and into his arms.

The second time we woke, the phone was to blame. I noted the clock as I grabbed the handset. I couldn't believe it was nearly noon. I'd obviously needed the sleep. Or something. "Yes?" I said.

"It's me, chuck." It was the voice of a ghost. It sounded like Gloria had died and somehow missed the pearly gates.

"'Morning, Gloria," I said cheerfully, upping the volume in revenge for her attempt at groping my knee. "How are you today?"

"Don't," she said. "Just don't. For some reason, I seem to have a bit of a migraine this morning. I thought I'd just spend the day in bed with the phone turned off, so you don't have to worry about coming over."

"Are you sure? I could always send Donovan," I said sadistically.

I sensed the shudder. "I'll be fine," she said. "I'll see you tomorrow, usual time." Click. I didn't even get the chance to say goodbye.

Richard emerged, blinking at the snow-light. "Gloria?" he asked.

"I'm reprieved for the day. She sounds like the walking dead."

"Told you," he said triumphantly. "Shall we make a snowman, then?"

By the time we'd made the snowman, then had a bath to restore our circulation, then done some more vigorous horizontal exercises to raise our core body temperatures, it was late afternoon and neither of us could put off work any longer. He had some copy to write for an Australian magazine fascinated by Britpop. Personally, I'd rather have cleaned the U-bend, but I'm the woman who thinks the best place for Oasis is in the bottom of a flower arrangement. I settled down at my computer and trawled the Net for responses to last night's queries.

I downloaded everything, then started reading my way through. I immediately junked the tranche from people who thought it must be cool to be a private eye, would I give them a work-experience placement? I also quickly dumped the ones that were no more than a rehash of what had been in the papers and on the radio. That left me with half a dozen that revealed Dorothea had had a breakdown back in the 1950s. There were two that seemed to have some real credibility. The first came from someone who lived in the picturesque Lancashire town where Dorothea had grown up. It read:

Dear Kate Brannigan

I am a sixteen-year-old girl and I live in Halton-on-Lune where Dorothea Dawson came from. My grandmother was at school with Dorothea, so when I saw your query in the astrology newsgroup, I asked her what she remembered about her.

She said Dorothea was always a bit of a loner at school, she was an only child, but there was nothing weird or spooky about her when she was growing up, she was just like everybody else. My gran says Dorothea got married to this bloke Harry Thompson who worked in the bank. She says he was a real cold fish which I think means he didn't know how to have a good time, except I don't know what they did then to have a good time because they didn't have clubs or decent music or anything like that.

Anyway, Gran says Dorothea had this baby and then she went mad and had to go into the loony bin (Gran calls it that, but she really means a mental hospital). Anyway, her husband went away and was never seen again, and when Dorothea came

out of the hospital after a couple of years, she only came back
to pack her bags and get the next bus out.

I don't know what happened to the baby, Gran says it probably got put in a home, which is not a good place to be brought
up even if your mum is a bit barking.

I hope this helps.

Yours sincerely
Megan Hall

The other was better written. I didn't much care; literary
style wasn't what I was after.

Dear Ms Brannigan

It may come as a surprise that a man of my age knows how
to <surf the Internet>, but I am a contemporary of Dorothea
Dawson. I was a year younger than her, but my sister was in
the same class at school, and was the nearest Dorothea had to a
close friend. Dorothea used regularly to come to our house for
tea, and the two girls often played together.

That all changed when Dorothea met Harry Thompson.
He was a bank clerk, good-looking in a rather grim sort of way,
and he was drawn to girls inappropriately young. When they
met, Dorothea was, I think, a rather young 17, and he must have
been 25 or 26. He was what I think we would now call a control freak and Dorothea was always on pins lest she upset him.

Quite why she agreed to marry him none of us ever knew,
though it may well have been the only route she could see by
which she could escape the equally oppressive regime of her
stepmother. They were married and within eighteen months
Dorothea was confined to the cheerless Victorian world of the
local mental hospital following an appalling experience with
what we now term post-natal depression.

Harry resolutely refused to have anything to do with the
child, claiming that the baby was tainted with the same mad-
ness that had claimed the mother. An ignorant and cruel man,

he sought and gained a transfer to a branch of the bank in the Home Counties, handing the child over to an adoption agency. What became of the baby, I have no knowledge. This far on, I am ashamed to say that neither my sister nor I can remember if the child were a boy or girl; in my sister's defence, I would say that by that time, thanks to Harry, there was little contact between her and Dorothea.

When she finally was allowed to leave the mental hospital, Dorothea was very bitter and wanted to cast her past entirely from her. My sister was saddened by this, but not surprised. We were delighted to see her rise to celebrity, though both horrified by the news of her death.

I do hope this is of some assistance. Should you wish to talk to me, you will find me in the Wakefield telephone book under my parish of St Barnabas-next-the-Wall.

With best wishes
Rev. Tom Harvey

I wasn't surprised that Gloria had called the whole sorry business tragic. I couldn't help wondering where Harry Thompson was now and what he was doing. Not to mention the mysterious baby. I kept having visions of a swaddling-wrapped infant abandoned on the doorstep of the local orphanage. I think I saw too many BBC classic serials when I was a child.

It was time for some serious digging, the kind that is well beyond my limited capabilities with electronic systems. I copied the two key e-mails to Gizmo, with a covering note explaining that I needed him to use his less advertised skills to unearth all he could about Harry Thompson and the riddle of the adopted child. Then I started accessing what legitimate data sources were available on a Sunday evening to answer the queries that had come in from the two foreign agencies.

When the doorbell rang, I exited the database I'd been in and severed my connection. Those on-line services charge by the minute and I wasn't prepared to put myself in hock if it took me five minutes to dislodge a Jehovah's Witness or a local opportunist offering to dig my car out of snow that would probably be gone by morning. To my astonishment, it was Gizmo. "I just sent you an e-mail," I said.

"I know, I got it." He marched in without waiting to be asked, stamping slush into my hall carpet. On the way to the spare room that doubles as my home office, he shed a parka that looked like it had accompanied Scott to the Antarctic and had only just made it home again. By the time I'd hung it up, he was ensconced in front of my computer. "Gotta beer?"

I was shocked. I didn't think I'd ever seen Gizmo with any kind of liquid within three feet of a keyboard. Same with food. If it wasn't for thirst and hunger and bodily functions, I've often thought he would spend twenty-four hours a day in front of a screen. "I'll get one," I said faintly. I raided Richard's fridge and came back with some elderberry beer made to an old English recipe, a grand cru wheat beer and a smoked rye ale. I swear to God the beer drinkers are getting even more pretentious than the winos and foodies. I mean, how can you have a grand cru beer? It's like going into McDonald's and asking for one of their gourmet burgers.

Gizmo went for the elderberry beer. Judging by the look on his face as it hit his taste buds, he'd have preferred a can of supermarket own-brand lager. I sat on the edge of the bed and sipped the Stoly and grapefruit juice I'd sensibly sorted for myself. "You were about to tell me what was in my e-mail that made you rush round," I lied.

Gizmo shifted in his seat and wrapped his legs around each other. I'd seen it done in cartoons, but I'd always thought until then it was artistic licence. "I felt like some fresh air." Lie number one. I shook my head. "I was a bit worried about discussing hacking in e-mail that wasn't encrypted." Lie number two. I shook my head again. "I wanted to check what virus protection you've got running on this machine because I've not looked at it for a while and there's all sorts of clever new shit out there."

I shook my head sadly. "Strike three, Giz. Look, you're here now. You've made the effort. You might as well tell me what you came to tell me because we're both so busy it could be weeks before there's another window of opportunity." I felt like a detective inspector pushing for a confession. I hoped it wasn't going to be another murder.

Gizmo ran a finger up and down the side of the beer bottle, his eyes following its movement. "There's this . . ." He stopped. He looked up at me like dogs do when they're trying to tell you where it hurts. "I've met . . . well, not actually met . . ."

Light dawned. "The flowers," I said.

The blush climbed from the polo neck of his black sweater, rising unevenly like the level of poured champagne in a glass. He nodded.

"'www gets real.' The cyberbabe," I said, trying to sound sensitive and supportive. The effort nearly killed me.

"Don't call her that," Gizmo said, a plea on his face. "She's not some bimbo. And she's not a saddo Nethead who hasn't got a life. She's really interesting. I've never met a woman who can talk about computer code, politics, sociology, music, all of those things."

All of those things I never knew Gizmo knew anything about. Except computer code, of course. "You've never met this one," I said drily.

"That's kind of what I wanted to talk to you about."

"A meeting? Getting together for real?" I checked my voice for scepticism and thought I'd probably got away with it.

"What do you think?"

What did I think? What I really thought was that Gizmo was probably typical of the people who spent their nights chattering to strangers in Siberia and São Paulo and Salinas, weird computer geeks telling lies about themselves in a pathetic attempt to appear interesting. A blind date with Gizmo would probably have turned me celibate at sixteen. On the other hand, if I'd been a geek too—and there were one or two female nerds out there, most of them inevitably working for Microsoft—I might have been charmed, especially since my efforts at grooming had rendered Gizmo almost indistinguishable from the human species. "Does she work for Microsoft?" I asked.

He gave me a very peculiar look. "That's sick. That's like asking a member of CND if he fancies someone who works for MOD procurement."

"Has she got a name?"

His smile was curiously tender. "Jan," he said. "She has her own consultancy business. She does training packages for the computer industry."

"So how did you . . . meet?"

"Remember when Gianni Versace got shot? Well, there was a lot of discussion on the Net about it, how the FBI were using the on-line community to warn people about the suspect, and how far the federal agencies should go in trying to exploit the Net to catch criminals. I was checking out one of the newsgroups and I saw Jan had said some interesting things, and we started exchanging private mail." Oh great, I thought. A mutual interest in serial killers. Always a good place to start a relationship. "Then we found out we both hung out in quite a few of the same newsgroups," Gizmo continued. "We'd just never crossed paths before." He stopped dead and took a deep swig of beer. It was possibly the longest speech I'd heard Gizmo make.

"And?"

"And we really hit it off. Loads of stuff in common. Lately, it's been getting more and more intense between us. I . . . I don't think I've ever felt like this before," he mumbled.

"And now you want to do a reality check by getting together in the flesh?"

He nodded. "Why not? Pen friends have been doing it for years."

This wasn't the time to remind him that pen friends had one or two little safeguards, like knowing where each other lived. It also wasn't the time to remind him that it was somehow easier to lie in cyberspace than in meatspace, since right from the beginning the hackers and computer freaks who had hung out on the very first bulletin boards had always hidden behind nicknames. The first time I'd been confronted with Gizmo's real name was years into our acquaintance, when he'd signed his initial consultancy contract with Brannigan & Co. I sipped my drink and raised my eyebrows. "And sometimes it's a big disappointment. Why is it so important that you meet? If things are so excellent between you, maybe it's better to keep it cyber."

He squirmed in his seat. "Sometimes it's too slow, the Net. Even in a private conference room in a newsgroup, you can still only communicate as fast as you can type, so it's never as spontaneous as conversation."

"I thought that was the charm."

"It is, to an extent. You can structure your dialogue much more than you can in a meatspace conversation, where you tend to go off at tangents. But we've been doing this for a while now. We need to move on to the next stage, and that's got to be a face-to-face. Hasn't it?"

I wasn't cut out for this. If I'd been an agony aunt, my column would have invariably read, "For God's sake, get a grip." But Gizmo was more than just another contractor. Less than a friend, admittedly, but somebody I cared about, much as I'd cared about Polly the cocker spaniel I'd grown up with. So I took a deep breath and said, "Where does she live?"

"London. But she comes up to Manchester every two or three weeks on business. I was thinking about suggesting we got together for a beer next time she's up."

It would be a beer, too. Somehow I didn't have this woman pegged as a white-wine-spritzer drinker. "You don't think it might destroy what you've already built up?"

He shrugged, a difficult feat given that he was impersonating a human pretzel. "Better we find that out now, don't you think?"

"I honestly don't know. Maybe the cyber-relationship is the shape of things to come. Communication with strangers, all of us hiding behind a façade, having virtual sex in front of our terminals. Not as replacement for face-to-face stuff, but as another dimension. Adultery without the guilt, maybe?" I hazarded.

"No," Gizmo said, unravelling his limbs and straightening up. "I think it's just another kind of courtship. If you don't take it out of virtuality into reality, it's ultimately sterile because you've no objective standards to measure it against."

Profound stuff from a man I'd never suspected of being capable of love for a sentient being without microchips. "Sounds to me like you've already made your decision," I said gently.

He took a deep breath. His shoulders dropped from round his ears. "I suppose I have."

"So go with your instincts."

I'd said what he wanted to hear. The relief flowed off him like radiation. "Thanks for listening, Kate. I really appreciate it."

"So show me how much, and dig me some dirt on Harry Thompson and the mystery baby."

14

JUPITER TRINE SATURN

Cheerful Jupiter tempers the stern, hard-working nature of Saturn. She is a visionary, but one firmly rooted in the practicalities. She is a good organizer and seldom feels overwhelmed by her responsibilities. She is good at coordinating people to collaborate with her. She has the self-discipline to achieve her goals without getting wound up about it.

From *Written in the Stars*, by Dorothea Dawson

I'd set off early enough to follow the snow-plough down the main road from Oldham through Greenfield. Getting down Gloria's alley was out of the question, but the hacks had moved on to the next big thing, so the only threat to Gloria's wellbeing was the possibility of wet feet. I should have known better.

She emerged in knee-high snow boots and a scarlet ski suit with royal-blue chevrons and matching earmuffs. "Hiya, chuck," she greeted me. "I've never been skiing in my life, but they do great gear, don't they?" she enthused. As usual, I felt underdressed. Wellies over jeans topped with my favourite leather jacket had seemed fine in Ardwick, but somehow they just didn't cut it in the country.

"Got over your hangover?"

"I'll thank you to remember it was a migraine, young lady."
She wasn't entirely joking. "By the way," she said as she settled
into the car, "there's been a change of schedule. Somebody got
excited about the snow, so we're going to do some location shooting instead of studio filming." Gloria explained that because of
the weather, cast members involved in the location shooting had
been told to go directly to Heaton Park on the outskirts of the
city rather than to the NPTV compound. The park was easier
to reach than the studios since it was just off the main motorway network and on a major road. There were various nearby
locations that would be used in the course of the day, but we'd
be based in the main car park with the catering truck, make-
up and wardrobe. And the snow. I could feel myself growing
almost wistful about being a lawyer, cocooned in a nice warm
courtroom with nothing more taxing to do than get a client
off a murder charge.

The one good thing about being away from NPTV was
that we seemed to have escaped the delights of Cliff Jackson's
company. According to Rita, Jackson and his team had been
interviewing cast members in their homes over the weekend,
but they were concentrating on office and production staff at the
studios now. Also according to Rita, who had clearly elected
herself gossip liaison officer, they were no closer to an arrest than
they had been on Friday night. She had managed to get Linda
Shaw to admit that neither Gloria nor I were serious suspects;
Gloria because there were no spatters of blood on the flowing
white top she'd been wearing, me because Linda thought it was
one of the daftest ideas she'd ever heard. I thought she'd probably been telling the truth about me, but suspected she might
have had her fingers crossed when she exonerated Gloria. In her
shoes, I would have.

Gloria went off with Ted so Freddie Littlewood could
work his magic on their faces. I let them go alone since I could
see the short gap between the two vehicles from where I was
sitting in a corner of the cast bus with Rita and Clive. I settled

down, ready to soak up whatever they were prepared to spill. "So who had it in for Dorothea?" I asked. Some people just don't respond to the subtle approach. Anyone with an Equity card, for example.

Clive looked at Rita, who shrugged like someone audition-ing for *'Allo, 'Allo!* "It can't have been to do with her professional life, surely," he said. "Nobody murders their astrologer because they don't like what she's predicted."

"But nobody here really knew anything about her private life," Rita objected. "Out of all the cast, I was one of her first regulars, and I know almost nothing about her. I've even been to her house for a consultation, but all I found out from that was that she must have been doing very nicely. A thatched cottage between Alderley Edge and Wilmslow, if you please."

"Did she live alone?" I asked.

"Search me," Rita said. "She never said a dicky bird about a boyfriend or a husband. The papers all said she lived alone, and they probably know more than the rest of us because they'll have been chatting up the locals."

Clive scratched his chin. "She knew a lot about us, though. I don't know if she was psychic or just bloody good at snapping up every little scrap of information she could get her hands on, but if she'd written a book about *Northerners*, it would have been dynamite. Maybe she went too far with somebody. Maybe she found something out that she wasn't prepared to keep quiet about."

The notion that there was any secret black enough for a *Northerners* star to feel squeamish about using for publicity was hard for me to get my head round. Then I remembered Cassie. Not only what had happened to her, but what she'd said about the prospect of losing a plum role being motive enough for some desperate people. "If that's the case, then the dark secret probably died with her," I said despondently.

"I'm afraid so," Clive said. "Unless she kept the details on her computer along with our horoscope details."

My ears pricked up. "You think that's likely?"

Rita's eyes were sparkling with excitement. "That'll be why the police have taken her computer off to analyse what's on it," she said. "That nice Linda said they'd got someone working on it already, but they've got to call in an expert who knows about astrology because a lot of it's in symbols and abbreviations they can't make head nor tail of."

Another alley closed off to me. Out of the corner of my eye, I saw Ted emerge from the make-up caravan. Time for action, I thought. I didn't want Gloria left alone with anybody connected to *Northerners*, even someone as seemingly innocuous as Freddie from make-up. He was just finishing off painting Gloria's lips with Brenda's trademark pillar-box-red gloss as I walked in. "Don't say a word," he cautioned Gloria. "I won't be a minute," he added, frowning as he concentrated on getting the lipline just right. I closed the door behind me and leaned against the wall. "There," he said with a satisfied sigh. "All done."

Gloria surveyed herself critically in the mirror and said, "Bloody hell, Freddie, that's the most you've said all morning."

"We're all a bit subdued today, Gloria," he said, sounding exhausted. "It's hard not to think about what happened to Dorothea."

Gloria sighed. "I know what you mean, chuck." She leaned forward and patted his hand. "It does you credit."

"It's scary, though," Freddie said, turning away with a tired smile and repacking his make-up box. "I mean, chances are it's somebody we know who killed her. Outsiders don't wander around inside the NPTV compound. It's hard to imagine any of us killing someone who was more or less one of us."

"The trouble is," Gloria said, getting to her feet and pulling her coat on, "that half of us are actors. Who the hell knows what goes on in our heads?"

Neither Freddie nor I could think of anything to say to that one. I followed her out the door and caught up with her and Ted at the edge of the car park. The director was explaining how he wanted them to circle round so that they could walk down the virgin snow of the path towards the camera. It looked like they were set for a while, but I didn't want to go back to the bus and leave Gloria exposed. It wasn't as if I could prevent an attack on her; but I hoped my presence would be enough to give her menacer pause.

I walked over to the catering bus, where Ross was working with a teenage lad I'd not seen before. "I suppose a bacon butty would be out of the question?" I asked. "I left the house too early for breakfast."

Ross served me himself, piling crispy rashers into a soft floury roll. "There you go. Coffee?" I nodded and he poured me a carton. "Mind the shop a wee minute, son," he said, coming out of the side door and beckoning me to join him. "You got anything for me?" he asked.

I shook my head, my mouth full of food. "I'm working on it," I managed to mumble. "Irons in the fire."

"I was doing some thinking myself. You know, nobody knows more about what goes on behind the scenes of *Northerners* than Dorothea did. She had the inside track on everybody. She'd have been perfectly placed to be the mole," he said eagerly.

"Handy for you," I said cynically. "What better way to get yourself off the hook than to blame a dead woman?"

His mouth turned down at the corners and his bright blue eyes looked baffled. "That's a wee bit uncalled for. You know I liked Dorothea fine. It's just with her being in the news this weekend, I couldn't help remembering how she always had everybody's particulars at her fingertips. And she was never backwards about taking advantage of the press for her own purposes. That's all I was getting at."

"I'm sorry," I said. "You might have a point. The only problem I can see is that Dorothea didn't have access to scripts, so she wouldn't have known the details of the future storylines, would she?"

Ross looked crestfallen, his shaggy red hair falling unheeded over his forehead. "I suppose," he said. "I wasn't really thinking it through. My wife says I never do."

Before I could say anything more, the bleat of my moby vibrated in my armpit. I unzipped my jacket and pulled it out. "Hello?"

"All right, KB? Where are you?" It was Alexis, far brighter than she had any right to be on a Monday morning when she was the co-parent of a teething baby.

"Why?"

"I'm out and about making some calls and I thought we could link up. I've got a juicy bit of info for you, and you know how insecure the airwaves are these days. We've probably got half the world's press listening in at your end and the bizzies at mine. Are you down at NPTV?" she asked, her voice all innocence.

"Security be buggered," I said. "You just want to get along-side the *Northerners* cast to see how many exclusives you can dig up about Dorothea."

A throaty chuckle turned into a cough. "You got me bang to rights. Call it the quid pro quo."

I wiggled my fingers at Ross. He took the hint and sham-bled back inside. "I'm not actually at NPTV." I told her where to find me. "They've got some very basic security on the main entrance, but a devious old bag like you should have no problem with that."

"They'll be laying out the red carpet for me, girl, just you wait and see. I won't be long, I'm only down the road in Salford."

I cut across the car park at an angle, ploughing my feet through the dirty slush. It's just as much fun at thirty-one as it is at five. I ended up over near the entrance, but still in a line of sight to Gloria. I was pretty certain by now that she was at no real risk, but being visible was what I was being paid for, so visible I'd be.

Alexis was as good as her word. Within ten minutes of our phone call, she drove authoritatively into the car park. The two elderly security men made a few futile gestures in a bid to get her to stop, but it's hard to argue with something as big as the Range Rover her and Chris had bought to combat the wild weather on the Pennines. Nobody else was interested. I'd soon realized that in a TV production unit, everybody's too busy with their own job to pay attention to anything else short of a significant thermonuclear explosion. That would make Cliff Jackson's job a lot harder. I couldn't resist a shiver of *schadenfreude* at the thought.

Alexis jumped down into the slush and took a few steps towards the security men. "I'm with her," I heard as her arm waved in my general direction. There was nothing wrong with her eyesight. "Brannigan and Co," she added, veering off towards me.

"You really are a lying get," I said when she was close enough for them not to hear.

"Only technically," she said. "I am, after all, here on a mission on your behalf."

"No, you're not, you're here entirely on a fishing expedition to net you tomorrow's front page. So what's this momentous news you have to impart?" I glanced over my shoulder to make absolutely sure we couldn't be overheard.

"Does F. Littlewood mean anything to you? F. Littlewood of fifty-nine, Hartley Grove, Chorlton?"

I tried not to show that more bells were ringing and lights flashing inside my head than on the average pinball machine. The address was unfamiliar, but I had no trouble recognizing the name. Why was Freddie Littlewood the make-up artist betraying his colleagues so viciously and comprehensively? What could he possibly have to gain? And how did he obtain the intimate details of people's past secrets? I'd already seen how casually Gloria let slip information to the charming Freddie, but I couldn't believe her fellow stars would have readily revealed most of the *Northerners* scandals. Alexis had done me a favour, but in the process she'd given me a headache.

I found a pen and notepad in my bag and got Alexis to write down Freddie's address. "You're sure this is the mole?" I asked.

"This is the person who got paid for the story about you bodyguarding Gloria," she said cautiously. "More likely than not, that's your mole. I finally got my hands on the credits book this morning, and that didn't take me a whole lot further forward. What it is, you see, sometimes we need to make irregular payments to regular sources who need to be protected. So then we use code names. The very fact that this Littlewood person has a code name means he or she has done this before."

"So how did you get from the code name to the identity?" I asked. It wasn't important, but I'm a sucker for other people's methods. I'm not such an old dog that I can't learn new tricks.

Alexis winked. "There's this cute little baby dyke in accounts. She thinks being a reporter is seriously the business. She thinks my new haircut is really cool."

I groaned. Forget the new tricks. "And does she also know you're happily married?"

"Let the girl have her dreams. Besides, it made her day to tell me that The Mask is F. Littlewood. Whoever he or she is?"

I shook my head. "That's for me to know and you to find out."

"Oh, I will, believe me. This isn't soft news any more. It's crime, and that's my business. If the newsdesk won't share, I'll just have to help myself." Alexis cupped her hands round a cigarette and lit it. She breathed a smoky sigh of satisfaction. "God, I love the first cigarette of the day. If you need more leverage, by the way, we've paid F. Littlewood five times in the last year. I checked out the back numbers and they were all *Northerners* stories. I'd bet it's the same mole selling the stories to the nationals, because all the ones we've had have either been local interest only or time sensitive. Except for the one about you and Gloria, interestingly enough." Alexis's eyes were flickering round the car park and over towards the distant shrubberies. She'd done her duty and now she was sniffing the air for her story. "You going to tell me who this Littlewood character is?" she asked, not really expecting an answer.

"Just be grateful I've not shopped you. Thanks, Alexis."

"No problem." She was already on the move. "Hang in there, KB. Jackson's so busy getting his knickers in a twist about his missus that he's not got a fucking clue who to arrest. So there's plenty of room for glory."

I watched her trudge through the snow, the ultimate bull-dog when it came to stories. Which reminded me that I had to see a woman about a dog. I checked my watch. Chances were that Ruth would be in court. I decided to call her mobile and leave a message with the answering service. "Ruth, it's Kate," I said. "Can you check for me if Dennis shows any signs of having been in a ruck with Pit Bull's pit bull? Or if the pit bull shows any signs of having been in a ruck with person or persons unknown? I'm ashamed to say it was Debbie's idea rather than mine, but it's worth pursuing."

The second call was to Detective Chief Inspector Della Prentice of the Regional Crime Squad's fraud task force. She should have been Detective Superintendent by now, but a sting I'd set up with her had gone according to someone else's script and Della was still scraping the egg off her face. I knew she didn't blame me, but if anything, that made it worse. Sometimes I looked round the table on our girls' nights out and wondered how Alexis, Ruth, Della and two or three of the others put up with the fact that one way or another I'd exploited each and every one of them and managed to drop most of them in the shit along the way. Must be my natural charm.

I tracked her down in a building society office in Black-pool. She sounded genuinely pleased to hear me, but then she was working her way through a balance sheet at the time. "I doubt you're having a more pleasant time than I am," she said. "I see from the papers that you and Cliff Jackson are too close for comfort again."

"Being on the same land mass as Jackson is too close for comfort. Especially at the moment. Did you hear about his wife?"

"Even in Blackpool," she said drily.

"You should rescue that Linda Shaw from his clutches. She's got the makings of a good copper, but he gives her the shit work every time and sooner or later she's going to get bored with that."

"We'll see. My sources tell me that my promotion's likely to come through soon," Della said. It sounded like a non sequitur, but I figured she was trying to tell me that she was slated for a senior post in the Greater Manchester force. And that Linda might not be Jackson's gofer much longer.

"I can't tell you how relieved that makes me feel. I'm buying the champagne that night."

"I know," Della said without bitterness. "So what's the favour?"

"Does there have to be a favour," I asked, wounded.

"In working hours, yes. You never ring up for a gossip between nine and five."

"You know about Dennis?"

"What about Dennis? I've been stuck in Blackpool since Thursday. I'm praying the snow keeps off so I can get home tonight. What's Dennis done this time?"

"For once, it's what he's not done." I gave her a brief run-down. "I've got a hunch that's so far off the wall I'm not even prepared to tell you what it is," I said.

"What is it you need?"

"A look at the scene-of-crime photos. I don't know any of the team working the case, otherwise I'd ask. The boss cop's a DI Tucker."

"I know Tucker's bagman. He did a stint with me at fraud before he was made up to sergeant. I expect I can persuade him he owes me one. I'll try and sort something out this evening, provided I can get back to Manchester," she promised. I grovelled, she took the piss, we said goodbye.

I automatically scanned the car park, clocking Alexis over by the chuck wagon. She was leaning on the counter, steam rising from the cup of coffee in her hand, deep in conversation with Ross and a couple of the younger cast members who had braved the cold in search of a free bacon butty. I didn't envy their chances of escaping the front page of the next day's *Chronicle*.

I drifted back across the churned-up slush to where Ted and Gloria were rounding some bushes and walking into shot, their body language shouting "argument" at the top of its voice. At the same moment, I heard a commotion behind me. I swung round to see Cliff Jackson loudly lecturing a PA that he was a police officer and this was a public car park and she was in no position to tell him where to stand.

The director's head swung round. "Jesus Christ!" she yelled. "And cut. Who the fuck do you think you are?" she demanded.

"Detective Chief Inspector Jackson of Greater Manchester Police. I'm here to interview Ms Gloria Kendal."

"Are you blind? She's working."

Nothing was calculated to make Jackson's hackles rise faster than anyone who thought the law didn't apply to them. "You can't seriously imagine that your television programme takes precedence over a murder investigation? I need to talk to Ms Kendal, so, if you don't mind, you'll just have to rearrange your filming schedule to accommodate that."

Gloria and Ted had reached us by now. "Accommodate what?" she demanded crossly. She was clearly not thrilled with the prospect of shooting the snow scene again.

"As I've just explained to your director here, I'd be obliged if you would accompany me to the police station for a further interview," Jackson barked. He clearly wasn't star struck like Linda Shaw.

Gloria gave me a panic-stricken look. "I don't want to," she protested.

Time for my tuppenceworth. "You don't have to. Not unless he's arresting you. If you want him to interview you here, that's your right."

Jackson rounded on me. "You're still here? I thought I told you to butt out of this investigation?"

"When you pay my wages you can give me orders," I said mutinously. "My client does not wish to accompany you to the police station, as is her right. She is willing to talk to you here, however. Do you have a problem with that, Inspector?"

Jackson looked around him. "There's nowhere here to conduct an interview," he said contemptuously.

Seemingly out of nowhere, Alexis loomed up at his elbow. "I wouldn't say that, Mr Jackson. I've been doing interviews all over the place. Is there some kind of problem here? Is somebody being arrested?"

"What the hell is the press doing here?" Jackson exploded.

"Press?" the director yelped. "Suffering Jesus, this is supposed to be a closed set. Security!" she bellowed. She pointed at Alexis. "You, out of here." Then she turned to Jackson. "The same goes for you. Look, we've got a people carrier over there. Plenty of room in that. All of you, just fuck off out of my sight, will you?"

Gloria started walking towards the big eight-seater van as two uniformed security guards appeared to escort an unprotesting Alexis back to her car. "Come on, Kate," Gloria called over her shoulder. "I'm not talking to him without you there."

"She's got no right," Jackson protested. "You're not a lawyer, Brannigan."

I shrugged. "Looks like you get to talk to Gloria with me present, or you don't get to talk to Gloria at all. She is one determined woman, let me tell you."

I watched Jackson's blood pressure rise. Then he turned abruptly on his heel and stalked past Gloria towards the people carrier. She followed more slowly and I brought up the rear with Linda Shaw. "I thought Gloria was off the hook," I said mildly.

Linda pursed her lips. Then, so quietly I could have believed I was imagining things, she said, "That was before we knew about the motive."

15

PLUTO IN VIRGO IN THE 5TH HOUSE

She is critical, both of herself and others. She is driven to seek the answers to the world's problems and has an analytical mind which she uses in her pitched battles against injustice. She has a great appetite for life, enjoying a vigorous lust in her sexual relationships.
From *Written in the Stars*, by Dorothea Dawson

I'd barely absorbed the impact of Linda Shaw's bombshell when she delivered the double whammy. "Or the fingerprints on the murder weapon," she added. There was no time for me to find out more; we'd reached the people carrier by then. Funny, I'd never suspected her of sadism before.

Gloria had already climbed into the front row of rear seats and Jackson, predictably, was in the driving seat. I went to sit next to Gloria, but Linda put a hand on my arm and motioned me into the back row before she slid into place next to my client. "I've already told you everything I know," Gloria started before the doors were even closed. Bad move.

"I don't think so," Jackson said brusquely, twisting round to face us. I had a moment's satisfaction at the sight of a painful razor rash along the line of his collar. Couldn't happen to a nicer bloke.

"I didn't kill her. She was still alive when I left her."

"You had reason to want her dead, though." Jackson's words seemed to materialize in the cold air, hanging in front of us like a macabre mobile.

"I beg your pardon, I never did," Gloria protested, her shoulders squaring in outrage.

Jackson nodded to Linda, who took out her notebook and flipped it open. "We've had a statement from a Mr Tony Satterthwaite—"

"That vicious scumbag?" Gloria interrupted. "You're not telling me you wasted your time listening to that no-good lying pig?"

"Your ex-husband has been extremely helpful," Jackson said smoothly, nodding again at Linda.

"Mr Satterthwaite was distressed by Ms Dawson's death, not least because, according to him, it was his affair with her that precipitated the end of your marriage."

I remembered that line about backbenchers resembling mushrooms because they get kept in the dark except when someone opens the door to shovel shit on them. I knew just how they felt. I glared at Gloria. She stared open-mouthed at Linda. It was the first time I'd ever seen her stuck for something to say.

"He suggested that you had never really forgiven Ms Dawson for the affair, and that you were, and I quote, 'the sort of devious bitch who would wait years to get her own back.' We'd be very interested in your comments, Ms Kendal," Linda said coolly.

"You don't have to say a thing, Gloria," I said hurriedly.

"What? And let them go on thinking there's a word of truth in what that money-grubbing moron says? My God," she said, anger building in her voice, "you lot are gullible. I dumped Tony Satterthwaite because he was an idle leech. He couldn't even be bothered to look further than his own secretary when he decided to have a bit on the side. Even though she looked like Walter Matthau. He never even met Dorothea, never mind had an affair with her. I'd kicked him out a good six months before she first turned up at *Northerners.*"

"So why would he tell us a pack of lies?" Jackson sneered.

"Because if he saw a chance to give me a bad time, he'd not let it go past him," Gloria said bitterly. "Especially if he could see a way of turning it into a moneyspinner. You can bet your bottom dollar that the next call he made after he spoke to you was to the *Sun* or the *Mirror.* You've been had, the both of you. What you don't realize is that if he had been having an affair with Dorothea, I'd have bought her a magnum of champagne for giving me a twenty-four-carat reason for ditching the sod. Ask my daughter. Ask anybody that was around me then. They'll tell you the same." She snorted. "Tony Satterthwaite and Dorothea? Don't make me laugh. Apart from anything else, Dorothea had a hell of a lot more taste than to get between the sheets with a snake like Tony."

"You married the man," Jackson pointed out.

"Everybody's entitled to one mistake," Gloria snapped back. "He were mine. Let me tell you, you'll not find a single person can back up his tale and there's a good reason for that."

Linda and Jackson exchanged a look that said they both knew they were backing a loser here. I wasn't so sure. I'd seen how well Gloria acted off screen. But even if the tale of the affair was true, I couldn't see Gloria nursing her bitterness for all those years. She was far too upfront for that. If she'd had a bone to pick with Dorothea, it would have been lying bleached in the sun a long time since.

"At the end of the day, we don't have to prove motive in a court of law," Jackson pointed out. "Most people think detectives have to prove means, motive and opportunity. But we don't. All we need is evidence. And we've got evidence against you. There's circumstance—you're the last person known to have seen her alive, and more often than not the last person to see a victim alive is also the first person to see them dead."

I opened my mouth to speak and he waved a hand at me. "You'll get your say in a minute. Let me finish first. But we've got more than that, Gloria. We've got fingerprints. To be precise, we've got your fingerprints on the murder weapon."

There was a long silence. Gloria stared impassively at Jackson, then lit a cigarette with a hand that showed no tremor. "The crystal ball?" she asked.

His smile was as thin as the line of the new moon. "The crystal ball," he confirmed.

It was obviously my week for fingerprints. All I needed now was for one of DI Tucker's merry band to find Gloria's prints inside Dennis's shop and then I could swap client for buddy behind bars. Then something occurred to me. "Excuse me, but I don't remember anyone taking my client's fingerprints. Where exactly has the comparison set come from?" I asked belligerently.

Linda's eyes widened and I could see her forcing her body not to react. Jackson scowled. "That's neither here nor there. Take my word for it, the prints on the murder weapon are a perfect match for Gloria's here."

I shook my head. "You'll have to do better than that." I glanced at my watch. "Otherwise I'm going to call Ruth Hunter and get this whole shooting match on the record. And I don't have to tell you how much Ruth hates having her lunch interrupted." I knew the last thing Jackson wanted now was to get to the "lawyers at dawn" stage. He was relying on Gloria being confident enough to think she could handle this alone, and even with me along to stick a spoke in his wheel, he still thought he was the one holding all the cards. You'd think he'd have known by now. "So where did you get a verified set of my client's prints?" I demanded again.

"You gave her a glass of water in the green room on Friday night when we had our initial interview," Linda said. Jackson glared at her, but he must have known they'd reached the point of put up or shut up.

"And you helped yourself to it after we left," I said, shaking my head in a pretence of sorrow at their deviousness. "So how do you know it's not my prints on the murder weapon?"

Linda allowed herself a small moment of triumph. "Because you were still wearing your leather gloves."

OK, so I'd forgotten. I didn't think Gloria was going to sue me. At least the conversation had provided enough of a diversion for my client to pull herself together. "Of course my fingerprints were on the crystal ball," she said. All three of us turned to stare at her.

"Gloria," I warned, stifling a momentary panic that she was about to confess.

"It's all right, chuck. There's a simple explanation."

My favourite kind.

"I'd just had a consultation, hadn't I? I'd been sat opposite Dorothea, with my fingertips touching the crystal ball. That's what we always did. I suppose she did it with everybody, but she must have buffed it up between times because it was always sparkling, that crystal. She'd lay her fingertips on one side and I'd match her on the other side. To form a psychic bond," she added, as if stating the obvious.

I grinned. Usually when I'd been present to watch Jackson get shafted, I was the one doing the shafting, which meant the pleasure was always tinged with a degree of apprehension. This time, the delight was entirely unadulterated. Jackson looked like a man whose cat just ate his prize canary.

"I bet it was just my fingertips on that crystal ball, wasn't it? Not my whole hand," Gloria said. She sounded as if she was half teasing, half scolding a naughty schoolboy. "You've been trying to get me going, haven't you? You've been stretching the truth to try and get me to confess." She wagged her finger at him. "I don't like people that think they're smart enough to get clever with me. Brenda Barrowclough might have come up the ship canal on a bike, but I'm not so daft. I'm not talking to you again, Mr Jackson, not without I've got my solicitor with me."

"I can't believe you tried that on, Jackson," I said. "Wait till Ruth Hunter hears about this. You better thank your lucky stars that you didn't drag us down the nick for this bag of crap."

Jackson turned dark red, his eyes narrowing as I'd seen them do too many times before. Just before the geyser of his rage erupted over us, the door behind him jerked open, nearly tipping him backwards towards the slushy car park.

John Turpin stepped back, not prepared to stand between Jackson and a nasty fall. At the last minute, Jackson grabbed the steering wheel and hauled himself back into the seat. "Jesus," he exclaimed. "You nearly had me on the floor there, Mr Turpin."

Turpin's broad face was wearing a scowl that matched most of the tales I'd heard about him. "I'm very disappointed in you," he said, his voice as sharply clipped as a topiary peacock. "I had thought we'd reached an accommodation. We've bent over backwards for you and your team. We've given you space to work in, we've offered you full access to our site and to all NPTV staff. The one thing I asked was that you didn't disrupt filming." He shook his head sorrowfully.

Jackson was at a major disadvantage, stuck in the van seat well below Turpin's superior height. "I'm conducting a murder inquiry," he retorted, pushing himself clear of the steering wheel and out into the car park. He was still four inches shorter than Turpin, but that didn't seem to worry him. "When evidence presents itself, I have to act on it. I said we'd do our best not to disrupt your filming schedules, but as far as I'm concerned, better your film crew stands about idle than a murder suspect slips through the net."

Turpin snorted and jerked his thumb at Gloria. "That's your murder suspect?" he said, his voice a suppressed laugh. "My God, man, you must be grasping at straws. This is the woman who's so timid she's hired a private detective because she's had some hysterical hate mail. Even if she had the nerve to commit murder, I don't think she'd be doing it when she's got a minder on her tail. Unless of course you think Gloria hired Brannigan and Co to commit murder for her?" I couldn't repress my smile. Linda broke into a spasm of tactical coughing, but Jackson couldn't see the funny side. He probably thought Turpin's sarcastic suggestion was a promising line of inquiry. "It wouldn't have hurt to have waited for a natural break in filming. I mean, she's hardly dressed to go on the run, wearing Brenda Barrowclough's wig," the TV executive continued with genial sarcasm. "Did you think she was going to take a cameraman hostage with her handbag?"

"This is a police inquiry," Jackson said obstinately. "Only the case dictates the timetable I work to."

Turpin gave Jackson a thoughtful look. When he spoke, his voice had a kindly tone at odds with his words. "The press is always interested in anything that affects *Northerners* and this company is a notoriously leaky sieve. You might think your murder investigation is the most important thing in this city, but there are far more people interested in the outcome of Monday night's episode of *Northerners* than in who killed some stargazing charlatan. You might want to think about how dumb you could be made to look by some news-hungry journalist." Without waiting for a reply, Turpin bent forward, head and shoulders into the van, forcing Jackson to step hastily aside, with the cavalier lack of concern most big men display.

"Gloria, my dear," he said coldly. "Time to earn your grossly inflated salary. Mustn't keep Helen waiting, must we?"

Gloria squared her shoulders, gathered her coat around her and made a nimble exit. "Ta-ra, Linda, chuck," she said, leaning back into the van. "I won't be talking to you again without a lawyer, but I don't hold that sneaky trick with the glass against you. You were only doing your job, and we both know what it's like to work for complete shits, don't we?"

Turpin's stare was surprisingly malevolent. "The people you have to deal with in this job," he sighed, including us all in his comprehensive glower.

"Never mind," I said sweetly. "If NPTV sell out to cable or satellite, you'll be able to retire to the South of France on your profits."

His calculating eyes made the snow look warm and welcoming. "You really shouldn't believe actors' gossip," he said. He turned on his heel, brushing past Jackson, and made for the catering truck. I didn't envy Ross if the coffee was stewed.

Jackson spun round to close the door, his face still scarlet with rage. It was clear he regarded my continued existence on the planet, never mind in his eyeshot, as pure provocation. Rather than wait to be arrested for behaviour likely to cause a breach of the peace, I slid along the seat and out of the opposite side of the van. Sometimes, bottling out is the sensible course of action.

I gave the catering van a wide berth too and trudged across to the knot of people round the director. Gloria and Ted were already heading back across the snow to begin their long tracking shot again. At this rate it was going to take all day to film one scene. I didn't have to be an accountant to work out why that would piss Turpin off, especially if he was obsessed with making the balance sheet look good to possible bidders for the show.

I switched my phone to mute, not wanting to risk the rage of the director if it rang during another take. When the shot was finally in the bag, I followed Gloria to the wardrobe truck. While she changed into her own clothes, I checked for messages. To my surprise, Della had called back already. I found a quiet and sheltered corner behind the make-up trailer and dialled her number. "Good news," she said.

"I could use some."

"I'm on my way back to Manchester now. I managed to get hold of my contact, and he's meeting me around three in La Tasca. If you want to swing by there around half past three, I should have what you need."

"And I can buy you both some tapas?" I said with resignation.

"Just me," she said firmly. "I'm not having you corrupting any more police officers."

"As if. See you." I hung up and checked my watch. If the roads were still as clear out in Saddleworth as they'd been earlier, I could get Gloria back home and still make it to the tapas bar in time for my meeting with Della.

Forty minutes later, outside my house, I handed Gloria's car keys to a nervous Donovan. "Do I have to stay over?" he asked, glancing apprehensively at Gloria, who was giving him flirtatious waves and winks through the windscreen.

"She's got no personal appearances this evening, but she wants to visit her daughter for dinner. I'd like you to drive her there and take her home afterwards. I've told her I think she's in no danger and she should pay us off, but she's adamant that she wants us to carry on."

"She's after my body, more like," he grumbled.

"You should be so lucky. I think pretending she's trying to get into your knickers is a more acceptable motive to her than admitting she's scared shitless. Just because she doesn't like doing vulnerable doesn't mean she's not afraid," I told him. "So it might not be a bad thing if you do stay over. It also saves me having to drive to Saddleworth in arctic conditions at the crack of sparrowfart, and if I was you, I'd be happy to store up a few Brownie points with the boss."

He grinned. "You going to tell my mum, then?"

Suckered again. "I'll tell her. At least you're not going to get arrested for taking care of Gloria."

He didn't look as if he thought it was much of a consolation. I waved them off, then walked across to Upper Brook Street and caught a bus down to Deansgate. Even public transport was better than trying to get into town and parked legally when the snow was falling three weeks before Christmas. I ducked into the steamy warmth of La Tasca with five minutes to spare. I was glad Della had suggested it; with its wood panelling, nicotine-coloured paintwork and salsa music, it feels enough like the real thing to hold a Manchester winter in abeyance.

I spotted Della right away, sitting at a round table near the back. She was sitting with a young Asian bloke who I guessed was her former colleague, now DI Tucker's bagman. I helped myself to one of the tall wooden bar stools and ordered a Corona. It came with the obligatory slice of lime, which always made me feel like an amateur teenage drinker again, fourteen and down the pub with a half of lager and lime. These days, I need all the help I can get.

Ten minutes later, her companion left and I picked up my beer and threaded my way across the room. "You look good," I said, meaning it. Her copper hair had started to show a few silver strands, but somehow it only made it look richer. Her skin was still glowing from the month she'd just spent in Australia; the old shadows under her eyes hadn't reasserted themselves yet. A Cambridge-educated economist, Della had one of the most devious financial minds I'd ever encountered. Way too smart for the Serious Fraud Office, she'd carved out her own niche in the north, unrivalled when it came to unravelling the sordid chicanery of the sharks in sharp suits.

"You look knackered," she said. "Have some chorizo. I just ordered more prawns and the aubergine with grilled cheese."

My mouth watered and I remembered how long it had been since breakfast. As I made uncouth sandwiches with French bread and the meltingly rich sausage, I filled Della in on my day. She winced at the encounter between Turpin and Jackson. "I wouldn't like to be Linda Shaw this afternoon," she said. She pushed a large manila envelope towards me as I finished the last of the chorizo. "One set of crime-scene photographs. I've had a quick look myself, and I didn't see anything to excite me. But then, murder has never interested me much."

I didn't bother opening them. There would be a better time and place soon. Besides, food was due any minute, and I didn't want to lose my appetite. "Thanks."

Della smiled. "I said it might tie in with a long firm fraud I
was working on, but I didn't want to go public on it yet, hence
the unofficial request. I don't think he believed me, but I don't
think he much cared. So, no big deal."

"I owe you," I said. I meant it; but what I owed Della was
nothing compared to the debt Dennis would face if my hunch
worked out. I couldn't wait to see his face when I told him he
was in hock to a DCI.

16

SUN CONJUNCTION WITH URANUS

*She has an independent, progressive and original mind, backed
with a strong and forceful personality. Individuality is important
to her and she thrives on breaking patterns. She can be a breath
of fresh air or a devastating tornado. In the 5th house, friends will
be important in helping her to secure success.*

From *Written in the Stars*, by Dorothea Dawson

The gods had finally started to smile on me, I decided when I
arrived at the office to find Shelley temporarily absent from her
desk. Before she could emerge from the loo, I slipped into my old
office, where I found Gizmo hunched over one of the computers.
I recognized the program he was running, a basic template for a
computer-controlled security system for a medium-sized building split into a mix of large and small rooms. It looked like one of
the privately owned stately homes whose owners had turned to
us after we'd scored a spectacular success in closing down a ring
of specialist art thieves. It was a case that I didn't like thinking
about, for all sorts of reasons, so I was more than happy to have
Gizmo around to take care of that end of the business.

He grunted what I interpreted as a greeting. "I've been
thinking, Giz," I said. "I know you probably think I'm being

paranoid, but if you're going ahead with a meeting with the cyberbabe . . ." I caught his warning look and hurriedly corrected myself. "I mean Jan, sorry. If you're going to arrange a meeting with her, you should have somebody to cover your back. Just in case she turns out to be a nutter. Or the whole thing is some terrible set-up."

He did that thing with his mouth that people use to indicate you might just have something. "I guess," he said. "It'd have to be somebody I could trust. I don't want the piss taking out of me from now till next Christmas if it's a meltdown."

"How about me?"

"You don't mind?"

I sat down and made meaningful eye contact. "Gizmo, you need someone who can suss this woman out at a hundred yards. Your anorak friends would be about as much use as a cardboard barbecue. Besides, this is self-interest. The last thing I need right now is the human equivalent of the Pakistani Brain Virus eating up my computer genius. Just check the date and time with me, and I'm all yours."

"Sound," he said, his eyes already straying back to the screen.

"There is, of course, a price to pay," I said.

He closed his eyes and raised his face towards the ceiling. "Suckered," he said.

I spread out the contents of the envelope Della had given me and explained what I wanted. "It's a freebie," I said. "For Dennis. Can do?"

He scratched his chin. "It won't be easy," he said. "I'll have to take it home with me. I don't have the software loaded here. But yeah, it should be doable. When do you need it for?"

"The sooner the better. The longer it takes you, the longer Dennis is going to be behind bars."

He shuffled the photographs together, giving each one a glance as he fed them back into the envelope. "I'm still working on the Dorothea information," he said. "I farmed one end of it out to a lad I know who's shit hot on adoption records. But there are some more avenues I can pursue myself. Which is the priority—this stuff or the Dorothea material?"

I had to think about it. All my instincts said that I should be pulling out all the stops to help Dennis. But whoever killed Dorothea might have other victims in mind so the sooner I got to the bottom of that can of worms, the better. Besides, I was being paid for finding out who had murdered the astrologer. If there had been only me to consider, the decision would have been easy. But being the boss isn't all about strutting your stuff in jackboots, especially with wages day approaching on horseback. "Dorothea," I said reluctantly.

Gizmo had the look kids get when they're told they can't play with the new bike until Christmas morning. "OK," he said. "By the way, I think Shell wants a word."

I bet she did. Short of abseiling out of the window, I didn't see how I was going to be able to avoid letting her have several. I took a deep breath and walked into the outer office. Shelley was sitting behind her desk. It looked as if she was balancing the cheque book, a manoeuvre I find slightly more daunting than walking the high wire. "Hi, Shelley," I said breezily. "I'm glad you're back. I wanted to tell you Donovan will be doing an overnight, so you won't have to bother cooking for him tonight."

If glares had been wishes, the genie would have been on overtime that day. "I've been wanting to talk to you about my son," Shelley informed me.

The words alone might not have seemed menacing, but the tone put them on a par with, "Has the prisoner a last request?" Ever since she had her hair cut in a Grace Jones flat top, I've been expecting her to batter me. Sometimes when I'm alone, I practise responses to the verbal challenges I know she's storing up to use against me. It doesn't help.

I smiled and said brightly, "Don's settling in really well, isn't he? You must be well proud of him."

Her eyes darkened. I waited for the bolts of black lightning. "I was proud of his A level results. I was proud when he made the North West schools basketball team. I was proud when he was accepted at Manchester University. But proud is not the word for how I feel when I find out my son's been arrested twice in the space of a week."

"Ah. That." I tried edging towards the door, but noticed in time that she'd picked up the paperknife.

"Yes, that. Kate, I've been against this right from the start, but I gave in because Donovan wanted so badly not to be dependent on me and not to get deep into debt like most of his student friends. And because you promised me you wouldn't expose him to danger. And what happens? My son, who has managed to avoid any confrontation with the police in spite of being black and looking like he can take care of himself, gets arrested twice." She banged her fist on the desk three times, synchronizing with her last three words. I've watched enough natural history documentaries to understand the mother's passion for her young. I wondered whether I'd make it to the door before she could rip my throat out.

"You can't hold me responsible for police racism," I tried.

"Suddenly it's a secret that the police are racist?" Shelley said sarcastically. "I can hold you responsible for putting him in places where he's exposed to that racism."

"We're working on a way to deal with that," I said, trying for conciliation. "And the work he's doing tonight couldn't be less risky. He's protecting Gloria Kendal against a nonexistent stalker."

Shelley snorted. "And you don't think that's dangerous? I've seen Gloria Kendal, remember?"

Time for a different approach. "Gimme a break here, Shelley. People pay money in encounter groups for the sort of experience Don's getting here. He's not complaining, and he's making good money. You've done a great job with him. He's solid as a rock. He can handle himself, he knows how to take responsibility, and it's all because he's your son. You should believe in him. And it's about time you let him go. He's a man now. A lot of lads his age are fathers. He's got more sense, and it's down to the way you've brought him up."

Shelley looked astounded. I couldn't remember the last time I'd stood up to her like that either. We faced off for a good thirty seconds that felt more like minutes. "His name's Donovan," she said finally. "Not Don."

I nodded apologetically. "I'm going home now," I said. "I need to have a bath and a think. I've done some background checks for Toronto and San Juan, I'll e-mail you the billing details." I made for the door. On my way out, I turned back and said, "Shelley—thanks."

She shook her head and returned to the cheque book. We hadn't actually built a bridge, but the piers were just about in place.

✿

I got home to two messages on the answering machine. Richard had called to tell me he'd be home around nine with a Chinese takeaway, which was more warning than I usually get from him. I'd been thinking about going round to Freddie Littlewood's to ask him why he was leaking such destructive stories to the press, but just for once, I was tempted to let pleasure beat business into second place. Richard and I hadn't had much time alone together lately, and the fact that he'd taken the trouble to phone ahead with his plans indicated he was missing it as much as I was. I decided to leave Littlewood until the morning.

The second message was from Cassie, asking me to call her when I could. She sounded concerned but not panicky, so I fixed myself a drink and ran a hot bath that filled the air with the heady perfume of ylang-ylang and neroli essential oils. I was determined to make the most of a night in with Richard. I slid into the soothing water and reached for the phone. Cassie picked up on the second ring.

"Thanks for getting back to me, Kate," she said.

I could feel the water soothing me already. "No problem. How can I help?"

"Well . . ." She paused. "It could be something and nothing. Just a coincidence. But I thought you might be interested."

"Fire away," I said. "I'm always interested in coincidence."

"I've just had a reporter round. A freelance that does a lot for the national tabloids. She was waving the cheque book, trying to get me to dish the dirt on Dorothea and the *Northerners* cast. Scraping the bottom of the barrel, I thought, but I suppose everybody who's still on the show has closed ranks. They'll have been warned, reminded that their contracts forbid them to talk to the press without the agreement of NPTV. So the hacks have to dredge through their contacts books to see if they can find anybody who might talk."

"And because you sold your story at the time, they think you might be tempted to spill some more beans?"

"Exactly. But I said everything I was ever going to say back then. And that's what I told this reporter. The thing is, though, I recognized her name. Tina Marshall. It's her by-line that's been on most of the really big *Northerners* scandal stories. She's obviously somebody that has a direct relationship with the mole."

"That's certainly worth knowing," I said, trying to sound interested. I couldn't figure out why Cassie felt the need to phone me up to tell me something I could have worked out for myself. Discovering who the mole was talking to wasn't going to get me any further forward, not even if this Tina Marshall and Alexis went way back. No journalist, especially not a freelance, was going to give up a source who was the fountainhead of her bank balance.

"But that's not all I recognized," Cassie continued. "I recognized her face, too. A couple of months back, a friend of mine took me to dinner at the Normandie. Do you know it?"

I knew the name. Alexis and Chris always went there for their anniversary dinners. Alexis claimed it was one of the best restaurants in the region, but I wasn't likely to be able to verify that for myself as long as I stayed with a man who believes if it hasn't come from a wok it can't be food. "Not personally," I sighed.

"Well, it's not cheap, that's for sure. Anyway, when I went to the loo, I noticed this woman. I didn't know then that she was Tina Marshall, of course."

I was sceptical. A quick glance in a restaurant a couple of months previously wasn't the sort of identification I'd want to base anything on. "Are you sure?" I asked. The fragrant warmth had clearly activated my politeness circuit.

"Oh, I'm sure. You see, the reason I noticed her in the first place was her companion. She was dining with John Turpin." Cassie mistook my silence for incredulity rather than stupefaction. "I wouldn't make any mistake about Turpin," she added. "He's the bastard who gave me the bullet, after all. So seeing him wining and dining some woman in the kind of sophisticated restaurant where he's not likely to run into *Northerners* regulars was a bit like a red rag to a bull. I paid attention to the woman he was with. When she turned up this afternoon on my doorstep, I knew her right away."

"Turpin?" I said, puzzled. The man had no possible motive for leaking stories about *Northerners* to the press, least of all to the woman who had plastered scandal after scandal over the nation's tabloids. I pushed myself up into a sitting position, trying not to drop the phone.

"Turpin. And Tina Marshall," Cassie confirmed.

"Unless . . . he was trying to get her to reveal her source?" I wondered.

"It didn't look like a confrontation," Cassie said. "It was far too relaxed for that. It didn't have the feel of a lovers' tryst, either. More businesslike than that. But friendly, familiar."

"You got all this from a quick glimpse on the way to the loo?" I asked doubtfully.

"Oh no," Cassie said hastily. "Turpin had been sitting with his back to me, but once I realized it was him, I kept half an eye on their table." She gave a rueful laugh. "Much to the annoyance of my companion. He wasn't very pleased that I was so interested in another man, even though I explained who Turpin was."

"Did Turpin see you?" I asked.

"I don't think so. He was far too absorbed in his conversation."

"I'm surprised Tina Marshall didn't clock you. Women check out other women, and you must have been familiar to her," I pointed out.

"I look very different from my Maggie Grimshaw days," Cassie said. "Nobody stops me in the street any more. Thank God. And like I said, the Normandie isn't the sort of place you'd expect the *Northerners* cast to be eating. It's not owned by a footballer or a rock star," she added cynically. "So, do you think there's something going on between them?"

I groaned. "I don't know, Cassie. Nothing makes sense to me."

"It's very odd, though."

I was about to tell her exactly how odd I thought it was when my doorbell rang. Not the tentative, well-mannered ring of a charity collector, but the insistent, demanding, lean-on-the-bell ring that only a close friend or someone who'd never met me would risk. "I don't believe it," I moaned. "Cassie, I'm going to have to go." I stood up. It must have sounded like a whale surfacing at the other end of the phone.

"Are you OK?" she asked anxiously.

"Somebody at the door. Sorry. I'll call you when any of this makes sense. Thanks for letting me know." As I talked, the phone tucked awkwardly between dripping jaw and wet shoulder, I was wrapping a bath sheet round me. I switched off the phone and drizzled my way down the hall.

I yanked the door open to find Gizmo on the doorstep. "Hiya," he said, not appearing to notice that I was wrapped in a bath sheet, my damp hair plastered to my head.

"What is *wrong* with the telephone, Gizmo?" I demanded. Remarkably restrained in the circumstances, I thought.

He shrugged. "I was on my way home from the office. You know, going home to sort out Dennis's little problem? And I thought you'd like to see what I found out about Dorothea's mysterious past."

I shivered as a blast of wintry air made it past him. There goes snug, I thought. "Inside," I said, stepping back to let him pass. I followed him into the living room. "This had better be good, Giz. I'd only just got in the bath."

"Smells nice," he said, sounding surprised to have noticed.

"It was," I ground out.

"Any chance of a beer?" Spoken like a man who thinks "considerate" is a prefix for "done."

"Why not?" I muttered. On the way, I collected my own glass and topped it up with the Polish lemon pepper vodka. I grabbed the first bottle that came to hand and relished the look of pained disgust that flashed across Gizmo's face when his taste buds made contact with chilli beer—ice-cold liquid with the breathtaking burn of the vengeful vindaloo that curry shops serve up to Saturday-night drunks. "You were saying?" I asked sweetly, enjoying the sudden flush on his skin and the beads of sweat that popped out across his upper lip.

"Jesus, Mary and Joseph," he gasped. "What in the name of God was that?"

"I didn't know you'd been brought up Catholic," I said. That should discourage him from the space-invading that was threatening to become a habit. "It's a beer, like you asked for. Now, what did you want to tell me about?"

He fished inside his vast parka and produced a clear plastic wallet. Wordlessly, he handed it over. I took the few sheets of paper out of the sleeve and worked my way through them. By the time I reached the end, I knew when Dorothea had been born and who her parents were, when she'd married Harry Thompson and when they'd been divorced. I knew the date of Harry's death, and I knew the date of Dorothea's release from the mental hospital.

Most importantly, I knew who the mystery baby was. And I had more than the shadow of a notion why the relationship might have led to murder.

I opened my mouth to try out my idea on Gizmo. Of course, the phone rang. "I don't believe this," I exploded, grabbing the handset and hitting the "talk" button. "Hello?" I barked.

"It's me," the familiar voice said. "I'm in Oldham police station. I've been arrested."

17

MOON TRINES MERCURY

She concentrates best on matters she's emotionally involved with. She expresses herself fluently and clearly and has a quick grasp of what is being said, easily picking up facts and drawing apt conclusions. Shrewd and intuitive, she sometimes lacks a sense of direction, shooting off in different directions at the same time. She has a good memory and is naturally inquisitive.

From *Written in the Stars*, by Dorothea Dawson

The desk sergeant at Oldham police station was obviously having about as good an evening as I was. His waiting area was clogged with hacks who'd heard there had been an arrest involving Gloria Kendal. Somewhere inside the station, the three photographers and two reporters were being treated as witnesses. Somewhere else, my part-time process-server and bodyguard was under arrest for breach of the peace and assault. Berserk student batters mob-handed team of journos. Yeah, right.

I pushed my way through the representatives of Her Majesty's gutter press, waving an ineffectual hand against the cigarette smoke and wondering if force of numbers was the only reason why they were allowed to ignore the "no smoking" notices that everybody else was told to obey. "You're holding an employee of mine," I said to the sergeant, trying to keep my voice down. "His solicitor is on her way. I wonder if I might have a word with the arresting officer?"

"And you are?"

"Kate Brannigan." I pushed a business card across the counter. "Donovan Carmichael works for me. I think we can clear all this up very easily if you could arrange for me to talk to the arresting officer."

He picked up the card as if it contained a communicable disease. "I don't think so," he said dismissively. "We're very busy tonight."

"I was hoping to reduce the burden of work on your officers," I said, still managing sweetness. "I'm sure there has been some misunderstanding. I don't know about you, Sergeant, but I hate paperwork. And just thinking about the amount of paperwork that a racism case against GMP would generate gives me a headache. All I want to do is chat to the arresting officer, explain one or two elements of the background that might show the evening's events in a different light. I really don't want to spend the next two years running up legal bills that your Chief Constable will end up paying." I could feel the smile rotting my molars. For some reason, the desk sergeant wasn't smiling.

"I'll see what I can do," he said.

That was clearly my cue to go and sit down. I just carried on smiling and leaning on the counter. "I'll wait," I said.

He breathed heavily through his nose and disappeared through a door behind the counter. One of the hacks casually wandered across to me and offered his cigarettes. "I don't do suicide," I said. "Quick or slow."

"Sharp," he said, slotting in beside me at the counter with a swagger designed to show off his narrow hips and expensive suit. "What's a spice girl like you doing in a place like this?"

"Just a little local difficulty to sort out," I said. "What about you? You don't look like Oldham Man to me."

He couldn't resist. "I'm a reporter."

"Ooh," I said. "That sounds exciting. Who do you work for?"

I got the full CV, ending with the most notorious national tabloid. He shrugged his shoulders in his jacket, just to make sure I hadn't missed how gorgeous he was. In his dreams.

"Wow," I said. "That's impressive. So what's the big story tonight?"

"Are you a *Northerners* fan?" I nodded. "You'll have read about Dorothea Dawson getting murdered on the set, then?" I nodded again. "Well, a couple of my colleagues got a tip-off from the police handling the murder inquiry that Gloria Kendal's fingerprints were plastered all over the murder weapon."

I couldn't believe what I was hearing. I had no doubts where this particular leak had come from. That bastard Jackson was getting his own back for being made to look a pillock first by me and Gloria and then by John Turpin. "No!" I gasped, struggling to keep up the pretence in the teeth of my anger.

"I'm telling you, that's what we heard. So we send out a pic man and a reporter to Gloria's place, out in Greenfield. She comes out in the car, and our lads are standing at the entrance to her lane, just doing their jobs, trying to get a picture or a story. Then this big black lad comes jumping out of the car and weighs into our lads. One of the reporters calls the police, Gloria shoots off God knows where in the car, and the rest is history."

"The bodyguard started it?" I couldn't keep the scepticism out of my voice.

My new friend winked. "Five words against one. Who do you think the cops will believe?"

Not if I had anything to do with it they wouldn't. But before I could let him know what I thought of the credibility of the press, the door to the station swung open and Ruth sailed in like a Valkyrie on ice, her blonde hair loose for once, falling in a cascade over the silver fake fur. At once, the journalist forgot all about chatting me up and scuttled towards her. "Ruth," came the cry from several throats. "Tell us what's going on!"

She swept past them, a snow leopard scattering fleas in her wake. "Later, boys and girls, later. Let me at least speak to my client. Kate," she greeted me, putting one arm round my shoulders and turning me so that we formed an impenetrable wall of backs as she pressed the button for the desk officer. "You know I can't take you in with me?" she said, her voice low but audible against the clamour behind us.

"I know. But I want to talk to the arresting officer first, before you all get embroiled in interviews. I want him to know that if they charge Don, I'm filing a racial harassment suit first thing in the morning. I told you about their antics last week, didn't I?"

"Oh yes. I'm sure we're not going to have a problem with them."

"It's Jackson that's behind this." I told her briefly what I'd just learned. There was no time to discuss it further, for the desk officer reappeared.

"I'm Ruth Hunter," she said. "Here to see my client, Donovan Carmichael. His employer also has some relevant information to place before the arresting officer if you would be so good as to get him here?"

The desk man nodded to a door at the side of the reception area. "He'll be right out."

The journalists were still hammering us with questions when the door opened moments later. The uniformed sergeant who emerged looked harried and hassled, his short red hair sticking out at odd angles as if he'd been running a hand through it. His freckles stood out like a rash on skin pallid with tiredness. "Ms Brannigan?" he asked, looking at Ruth.

"I'm Ruth Hunter, Donovan's solicitor," she said. A gentle shove in the small of my back propelled me towards the door. "This is his employer." Ruth continued her forward movement, sweeping all three of us back through the door and neatly closing it behind us. "A moment of your time before I see my client, Sergeant?"

He nodded and led us into an interview room that looked freshly decorated but still smelled inevitably of stale smoke, sweat and chips. I think they buy it in an aerosol spray. "I'm Sergeant Mumby," he said, dropping into a chair on one side of the table. "I'm told Ms Brannigan wanted a word."

"That's right," I said, glad I'd had the chance to forearm myself with information from the smoothie outside. "I don't want this to sound threatening, but if you charge Donovan tonight, Ms Hunter's firm will be making a complaint of racial harassment against GMP. He's already been arrested twice in the last week for nothing more than being black in the wrong place. Now he's facing serious charges because five white people who were blocking my client's private road wouldn't get out of the way and they didn't like being told what to do by a young black lad. That's about the size of it, isn't it?"

He sighed. "I've got five witnesses saying he came at them like a madman, pushing them and shoving them, and that he punched one of them in the back. Believe me, I sympathize with your point of view. When we turned up, it was all over bar the shouting. But Mr Carmichael had made no effort to get away from the scene. And he's actually the only one with any visible injury."

I caught my breath. "What happened?"

"Just a split lip. He says one of the photographers swung his camera at him; the photographer says Mr Carmichael tried to head butt him and the camera got in the way."

I shook my head incredulously. "This is outrageous. Some scummy paparazzo smacks Donovan in the face with a camera then turns round and says he started on them? And Don's the one facing charges? What has Gloria got to say about all this?"

The sergeant's lips compressed in a thin line. "We've not been able to contact her yet."

"I bet she'll have plenty to say. Not least about the fact that this whole thing happened because one of your colleagues decided to leak confidential evidence in a murder inquiry to the press. Evidence which has already been totally discredited," I said bitterly.

Ruth leaned forward. "There is, of course, one way to make all of this go away. You can let my client go without charge. Give him police bail if you must. He's not going anywhere. He's a student at Manchester University, he lives at home with his mother and sister, he has no criminal record and he has a part-time job with Ms Brannigan. I'm certain that once Ms Kendal has outlined the real course of events you'll realize the only charge that should be brought is one of wasting police time, and not against my client. What do you say, Sergeant? Shall we all have an early night?"

He rubbed a hand over his chin and cocked his head on one side. "And if I do what you suggest, it'll be all over the papers that we let a black mugger walk free."

"Probably," Ruth agreed. "But that's a story that will be history by the weekend, whereas a racial harassment action will rumble on for a very long time. Especially one that's supported by Gloria Kendal."

"And the *Manchester Evening Chronicle*," I added. "Donovan's mother is a very close friend of the *Chronicle*'s crime correspondent, Alexis Lee. They love a good campaign at the *Chron*."

He smiled, a genuine look of relief in his eyes. "You talked me into it, ladies. Between ourselves, I never saw it the way the journalists were telling it. For one thing, a lad built like your client would have done a hell of a lot more damage if he'd had a serious go. But what can you do? You've got witnesses saying one thing and not much evidence pointing the other way. At least now I can let you take Mr Carmichael home secure in the knowledge that I've got good reasons to put in front of my inspector." He got to his feet. "If you'd just wait there a minute, I'll get it sorted."

He left us alone to exchange gobsmacked looks. "I'd always heard the police out here were a law unto themselves, but I didn't think that'd ever work in my favour," I said faintly.

"I know," Ruth said, sounding somewhat baffled. "I must tell all my clients to make a point of getting arrested in Oldham."

"I can't believe that scumbag Jackson," I said.

"You'll never nail him on it. He'll have got one of his min-
ions to do the dirty work. Go after Jackson and you'll probably
end up with Linda Shaw's head on a stick." Ruth leaned back
in her seat and lit one of her long slim cigarettes. "By the way,
I made those inquiries you suggested about Pit Bull Kelly's dog.
Dennis has no marks anywhere on his body that correspond to
dog bites. And the dog himself showed no signs of having been
in a fight. Care to tell me where this is going?"

"I've got Gizmo working on something. An idea I had. It
came from a case I read about on the Internet a while back. An
American case. I'd rather wait till I've got something concrete
to show you, because it sounds so totally off the wall."

Ruth gave me the hard stare, but she could see I wasn't
going to budge. "How long?"

"Probably tomorrow? I'll need you to set up a meeting
with DI Tucker. Preferably at my office. I'll let you know when
I'm ready. Is that OK?"

"The sooner the better," Ruth said. "Normally, Dennis
takes custody in his stride, but this time he's not handling it
well. Probably because he's genuinely innocent," she added drily.

The door opened and Sergeant Mumby stuck his head into
the room. "Your client's ready to leave now. I think the back
way would be better, in the circumstances."

I left Donovan climbing reverently into the Bentley, Ruth
promising to drop him at his girlfriend's so we could avoid
letting his mother know about his latest brush with the law. I
looked at the dashboard clock and realized there was no point
in going home. Richard would have eaten the Chinese; it takes
more than irritation at being stood up to disturb his appetite.
Then, if habit held, he'd have decided to show me how little he
needed me by jumping a taxi back into town and partying the
night away. I couldn't honestly blame him.

I sat in my car and rang the number Gloria had given me
for her daughter's house. The voice that answered was familiar

in its inflexions, but twenty years younger in its tones. "I'm looking for Gloria," I said. "Can you tell her it's Kate?"

"Hang on, love, I'll just get her."

Moments later, I heard the real thing. "All right, chuck?"

"I am now," I said severely. "Now I've got Donovan out of jail."

She chuckled. "That poor lad's having a proper education, working for you. I knew you'd have it sorted in no time. Whereas if I'd hung around, it would just have got more and more complicated."

"He got a smack in the mouth from a journalist's camera," I said coldly.

There was a short pause, then, serious, she said, "I'm really sorry about that. Is the lad OK?"

"He'll live. But the police need a statement from you, otherwise they're going to have to believe that bunch of scumbag hacks claiming Donovan set about them without any provocation."

She gasped. "Is that what they're saying?"

"What else do you expect paparazzi to be saying, Gloria? The truth?" I demanded sarcastically. "They've got bosses on the newsdesk who aren't going to be well impressed if they tell them they didn't get a story or pictures because a teenage lad told them to bugger off. If they don't get a proper story, they make one up."

"Aye well, at least you got it sorted," she said, sounding chastened for once.

"It'll be sorted once you've given Sergeant Mumby a statement and half his colleagues an autograph. Now, are you staying at your daughter's tonight?"

"I better had, I suppose. And I'm not filming tomorrow, so I'll probably take her shopping."

"Not in town," I said firmly.

"Harvey Nicks, chuck," she said. "In Leeds. I'll bell you in the morning once we've decided what's what. Thanks for sorting it all out, Kate."

The line went dead. Nothing like a grateful client. Given that the wheels were well and truly off my evening, I figured I might as well go for broke and see what Dorothea Dawson's child had to say about her murder. It was, after all, what I was being paid for. I drove through the virtually deserted streets of Oldham, south through Ashton, Audenshaw and Denton, past rows of local shops with peeling paint, sagging strings of dirty Christmas lights, sad window displays and desperate signs trying to lure customers inside; past the narrow mouths of terraced streets where people sprawled in front of gas fires denying the winter by watching movies filled with California sunshine; past down-at-heel pubs advertising karaoke and quiz nights; past artificial Christmas trees defiant in old people's homes; past churches promising something better than all of this next time round in exchange for the abandonment of logic.

It was a relief to hit the motorway, hermetically sealed against the poverty of the lives I'd driven past. Tony Blair said a lot about New Labour giving new Britain new hope before he was elected; funny how nothing's changed now he's in power. It's still, "get tough on single mums, strip the benefit from the long-term unemployed, close the mines and make the students pay for their education."

I cruised past Stockport, admiring the huge glass pyramid of the Co-op Bank, glowing neon green and indigo against the looming redbrick of the old mills and factories behind it. It had stood empty for years, built on spec in the boom of the Thatcher years before the Co-op had rescued it from the indignity of emptiness. I bet they'd got a great deal on the rent; wish I'd thought of it.

I took the Princess Parkway exit, almost the only car on the road now. Anyone with any sense was behind closed doors, either home writing Christmas cards or partying till they didn't notice how cold it was outside while they waited for the taxi home. Me, I was sitting in my car opposite the other deadheads in the vast expanse of the Southern Cemetery. Only one of us was using the *A-to-Z*, though.

The street I was searching for was inevitably in the less seedy end of Chorlton, one of those pleasant streets of 1930s semis near the primary school whose main claim to fame is the number of lesbian parents whose children it educates. To live comfortably in Chorlton, you need to have a social conscience, left-of-centre politics and an unconventional relationship. Insurance salesmen married to building society clerks with two children and a Ford Mondeo are harder to find around there than hen's teeth.

The house in question was beautifully maintained. Even in the dead of winter, the garden was neat, the roses pruned into symmetrical shapes, the lawn lacking the shaggy uneven look that comes from neglecting the last cut of autumn. The stucco on the upper storey and the gable gleamed in the streetlight, and the stained glass in the top sections of the bay window was a perfect match for the panel in the door. Even the curtain linings matched. I walked up the path with a degree of reluctance, knowing only too well the kind of mayhem I was bringing to this orderliness.

Sometimes I wish I could just walk away, that I wasn't driven by this compelling desire for unpicking subterfuge and digging like an auger into people's lives. Then I realize that almost every person I care about suffers from the same affliction: Richard and Alexis are journalists, Della's a detective, Ruth's a lawyer, Gizmo's a hacker, Shelley's never taken a thing at face value in all the years I've worked with her. Even Dennis subjects the world around him to careful scrutiny before he decides how to scam it.

The need to know was obviously too deeply rooted in me to ignore. Sometimes it even seemed stronger than the urge for self-preservation. Driven as I was by the prospect of finding out what lay behind the string of recent strange events, I had to remind myself that I might be knocking on the door of a murderer. It wasn't a comfortable thought.

I took a deep breath and pressed the bell. A light went on in the hall, illuminating me with green and scarlet patterns from the stained glass. I saw a dark shape descend the stairs and loom towards me. The door opened and Dorothea Dawson's genetic inheritance stood in front of me. I should have seen it, really. The features were so similar.

"Hi," I said. "I've come for a chat about your mum."

18

SATURN OPPOSES URANUS

Whenever she seems about to carve out a destiny or even a destination, Uranus steps in to force her to kick over the traces and express her individuality. Something always disrupts her best-laid plans; she is forever having to include new elements in her arrangements. The rest of her chart indicates capability; she will succeed in a conventional world by unconventional means.

From *Written in the Stars*, by Dorothea Dawson

Freddie Littlewood blinked rapidly, dark eyes glittering. His thin lips twitched. It was hard to tell if he was furious or on the point of tears. I figured he was deciding whether to brazen it out or to deny all knowledge of what I was talking about. It was possible, after all, that I was only guessing. "My private life is no concern of yours," he said eventually, sitting firmly on the fence.

I sighed. "That's where you're wrong, Freddie. I'm very concerned with the relationship between you and Dorothea. The nature of my concern rather depends on whether you killed her or not. If you did, it puts my client in the clear and it probably means Gloria isn't the next target of a killer. If you didn't, you can probably tell me things that would help me to protect her.

Either from false accusation or from murder. So my concern is legitimate."

"I've nothing to say to you," he said, closing the door in my face.

I hate bad manners. Especially when it's late and there are almost certainly more interesting things I could be doing with my time. I took out my mobile phone and pushed open the letterbox. "The police don't know Dorothea was your mother." I started to press numbers on the phone, hoping the beeping was evident on the other side of the door. "Want me to tell them now?"

Before I could have pressed the "send" button if I'd been serious, the door opened again. "There's no need for this," Freddie snapped. "I didn't kill Dorothea. That's all you need to know. And it's all you're getting from me. I don't care if you tell the police she was my birth mother. It's not like it was news to me. I've known for ages, and I can prove it. Even the police aren't stupid enough to take that as a motive for murder." He was probably right. The bitterness in his voice spelled motive to me, but acrimony's never been grounds for arresting someone.

I leaned against the doorjamb and smiled. "Maybe so. But if you factor in the stories you've been selling to the papers, the picture looks very different. Intimate details that people have revealed to Dorothea, spiced with the snippets you've picked up, that's what's been tarted up in the tabloids. Maybe Dorothea decided she didn't need a partner any more?"

His eyes widened and he flashed a panicky glance to either side of me, as if checking whether I was alone. "You're talking rubbish," he said, his voice venomous.

I smiled. "Have it your own way. But you didn't get paid in cash. Somewhere there's a paper trail. And one thing the stupid old plod is very good at is following a paper trail. Freddie, if what you're saying is true, and you didn't kill Dorothea, I've got no axe to grind with you. John Turpin isn't paying me to find out who the *Northerners* mole is." I refrained from mentioning

that Ross Grant might be. There was no point in complicating
things that were already difficult. "All I'm interested in is protecting Gloria. You *like* Gloria, for God's sake, I know you do.
I've seen the way you are with her. Can we not just sit down
and talk about this? Or do I have to blow your life out of the
water with NPTV as well as the cops?"

One side of his mouth lifted in a sneer. "Gloria said you
were smart," he said, opening the door wide enough to let me
enter. He shooed me ahead of him into a small square dining
room. There was an oak table with four matching chairs, all
stripped back to the bare wood, oiled and polished till they
gleamed in the soft glow of opalescent wall lights. A narrow
sideboard in darker oak sat against the far wall. The only decoration came from the vibrant colours of the Clarice Cliff pottery
ranged along a shelf that ran round the room at head height. If
it was genuine, selling the collection would have bought him a
year off work. Freddie waved me to a chair and sat down with
his back to the door.

"How did you find out she was my birth mother?" he asked.

I raised one shoulder in a shrug. "There's not much a good
hacker can't find out these days. How did you find out?"

He ran his thumb along the sharp line of his jaw in a
curious stropping gesture. "A mixture of luck and hard work,"
he said. "The first time I got into a serious relationship, when
I was in my twenties, I decided I wanted to know where I'd
come from. It hadn't seemed important before, but the idea of
being with someone long term, maybe even having kids with
them, made me curious. I searched the records, and found out
my father was already dead. Killed by a heart attack." He gave
a bitter cough of laughter. "Not bad for a heartless bastard. I
carried on looking and I discovered my mother was Dorothea
Thompson, née Dawson. But the trail went cold." His eyes were
alert, never leaving my face. I suspected he was watching for
any signs that he was breaking new ground, revealing things I
didn't already know.

"I know about the breakdown," I said. "Was that where the trail petered out?"

He nodded. "She was released from the hospital still using her married name, and she disappeared without trace. I found a cousin, the only other member of the family still alive, but he had no idea what had happened to her. The only useful thing I got from him was a copy of her wedding picture. I even hired one of your lot, but he never found her. Then one day I was sitting in the staff canteen at NPTV and Edna Mercer walked in with her latest fad. It was like someone took my stomach in their fist and squeezed it tight. I didn't need to hear her name to know who she was. That was just confirmation of what I knew the minute I saw her face. All those years later, she was still the spitting image of her wedding picture."

"But you didn't rush across the room and reveal you were her long-lost son."

He gave a twisted smile. "When I started out looking for my past, I don't think I'd thought it through. In a way, it was almost a relief not to have found her. You see, I blamed her. My childhood was a nightmare. I never knew what it was to be held with love. I was bullied because I was small. I was beaten black and blue by one sadistic bitch of a foster mother because I was still wetting the bed when I was seven. I was gang-raped in a children's home when I was eleven by three older boys and a so-called care worker. I never got to choose my own clothes or my own toys. I was supposed to be grateful for what I was given. I never even got to keep my own name. My father changed it by deed poll before he dumped me." He stopped, apparently choking on the bile of memory.

I couldn't think of anything to say that wasn't offensively trite. My childhood was breathtaking in its comforting and confident normality. When I'd fallen over, there had been someone there to pick me up and stick a plaster on my knee. I'd fallen asleep with stories, not nightmares. There had always been arms to hold me and faces to reflect pride in my achievement. I could barely imagine the yawning gap of such an absence, never mind the agony of having it filled with such poisonous viciousness. "You must have come to hate her," I said, surprised by the huskiness of my voice.

He shifted in his chair so his face was obscured by shadow, his spiky hair emphasized in a dark fragmented halo. With his black polo neck and black trousers, he looked like a satanic ghost. "I wanted to make her life a misery too," he said. "I wanted her to understand something about the pain and misery she'd given me."

"I don't think she had a lot of choice in the matter."

"More choice than I did," he blazed back at me. "She could have come looking for me. It couldn't have been that hard to find a child in care. But she made the decision to leave me in whatever hell I happened to be in."

In the silence that swallowed his outburst, I thought of how it must have been for Dorothea. Tainted with the stigma of mental illness, abandoned by her husband, wrenched from her child, without resources. She couldn't go home for she had no home to go to. The village where she'd grown up was the one place she'd never be allowed to forget or escape. She had no formal training, no professional skills to fall back on, yet she had to find a way to scrabble together enough to live on in a town where she had not one friend to turn to. It must have taken every ounce of guts she had just to survive. She probably saw it as a kindness to her son to leave him be. "Maybe she did try," I suggested. "Maybe they wouldn't give you back to her."

"*She* tried to get me to fall for that line," he said scornfully. "No way. She never came after me. She left me to it. And my problem is that I'm not stupid. I know I'm fucked up. And I know exactly how and why. I'm fucked up because she left me to rot, to be abused, to be fucked over. And that's why I didn't murder her. I hated her far too much to give her the easy way out. I wanted her to go on suffering a whole lot longer. She still had years to pay for."

Strangely, I believed him. The vitriol in his voice was the real thing, so strong it made the air tremble. "So you didn't let on when you realized Edna Mercer's latest discovery was your mother?"

He shook his head. "I didn't say a word. I just watched her, every chance I got. I listened to the actors talking about her when I made them up. At first, I was confused. It was like part of me desperately wanted to love her and be loved back. And another part of me wanted revenge. I just sat it out, waited to see which side would win." Freddie shifted in his chair, folding his arms across his stomach and bending forward. Lit from above, his eyes were impenetrable pools in shadowy sockets. "It was no contest, not really. The more they went on about how lovely she was, the more I resented what she'd deprived me of. I wanted revenge."

"But you ended up in business with her. Earning money together," I said, trying not to show how baffled I was by that. I suspected that he still harboured a determination not to tell me any more than I already knew.

He looked up then and stared into my face. He gave a strange barking cough of laughter. "Don't you get it? That was my revenge. One night, I waited till her last client had gone and I walked into the van. I told her my date, time and place of birth and watched the colour drain out of her face. I didn't have to tell her who I was. Sure, she'd seen me around the place, but now it was like she was looking at me for the first time. But even then, her head was right in control of her heart. Nearly the first thing she said to me was, 'Who have you told about this?'

"You see, if she revealed that I was her son, it wouldn't just be another happy tabloid reunion story. She'd have to explain how she came to give me up in the first place. She'd have to tell the world she was a nutter. Most people find mental illness frightening. She was convinced that she'd lose her contracts, lose her clients at *Northerners* and end up back where she was all those years ago when she came out of the mental hospital. I think she was wrong, but it suited me that she believed it. That way, I had leverage. I made her tell me people's secrets and then I sold them. She had this phoney reverence thing about her psychic gift. She was always going on about being like a priest or a doctor, the repository of people's confidences." His contemptuous impersonation was frighteningly accurate; if I'd been the superstitious type, I'd have sworn I could see Dorothea's ghost rising up before me.

"In that case, why did she tell you?"

"I was her son," he said simply. "She wanted to please me. It helped that she was desperate to keep our relationship secret, so she needed to keep me sweet."

"So you put together what she winkled out from her clients with what people let slip in the make-up chair, and with the overlap between two sources you were able to expose all those people who probably think of you as a friend?" I said.

"Don't make me laugh," he said bitterly. "I'm not a friend to them. I'm a servant, a convenience. Oh sure, they treat me like I'm their best buddy, but if I died tonight I doubt if more than three of them would make it to the funeral, and then only if they knew the photographers were going to be there. The programme's last publicist, he made the mistake of thinking they were his friends. He had a breakdown—too much stress. One cast member sent him a get-well card. One sent him a bunch of flowers. And that was it. He'd been working his socks off to cover their backs for the best part of five years, and the day he went sick, it was as if he'd never existed. So don't do the betrayal number on me. The only person I betrayed was my mother, and that was deliberate. And she knew it."

"Wasn't it a bit of a risk, revealing secrets people knew they'd told Dorothea? Didn't anybody put two and two together?"

He shook his head, a smirk on his narrow mouth. "I always waited a few months. I used the time to do a bit more digging, see if I could come up with extra information, stuff my mother hadn't been told about. Once you know where to look, it's amazing what you can find out."

Tell me about it, I thought, feeling a strange pity for this damaged man who'd subverted the tricks of my trade and used them to generate misery. "I suppose leaking the storylines as well helped to cover your tracks."

He frowned. "Storylines? That wasn't me. I never really know the storylines in advance. Just bits and pieces I pick up from what people say. I'd heard it's supposed to be somebody in the location catering company doing that. Turpin's giving them the heave, and they're getting their own back. That's what I'd heard."

I couldn't help believing him. He'd been so honest about the other stuff, and that painted him in a far worse light. Besides, he was completely off-hand on the subject. I'd begun to realize that Freddie Littlewood was intense about the things at the heart of his life. Anything else was insignificant. "Did you make her take some of the money too?" I asked.

"I tried. But she wouldn't cash the cheques. I even paid cash into her bank account once. The next week, she gave me a receipt from Save the Children for the exact same amount."

It would have been so simple if I could have persuaded myself Freddie had killed his mother. All the pieces were there: a racket selling stories to the press that worked primarily because their relationship remained secret; a falling out among thieves, aggravated by the emotional charge of their relationship; a spur of the moment act of shocking violence. The only problem was that it wasn't true. And if I gave Cliff Jackson the pieces, he'd force them to fit the pattern his closed mind would impose.

But if it wasn't Freddie, who else? Who else would benefit from Dorothea's death? Whose purpose would be served? "I don't suppose you know what was in her will?" I asked.

"I know I wasn't," he said decisively. "When I told her I was going to start selling the stories to the papers, she said that if I needed money, all I had to do was ask. She said that as soon

as she'd satisfied herself that I really was her son, she'd changed
her will in my favour. She said I might as well have the money
now, while she was still alive and we could enjoy it together. I
told her I didn't want her money, that wasn't the point. I wasn't
selling the stories to make a few bob. I was doing it to hurt her.
The money was just a bonus. She told me if I went ahead with
it, she'd change her will back again and leave all her money to
mental health charities."

"I bet she didn't do it," I said.

He moved his head almost imperceptibly from side to side,
rubbing his thumb along his jaw again. "You didn't know Dorothea. The week after the first story was published, she sent me
a photocopy of her new will. Dated, signed, witnessed. Apart
from a few small legacies to friends, everything she owns goes
to charity."

"It could have been a bluff. She might also have made a
second will leaving it all to you."

He shook his head. "I don't think so. If she had, I think
the police would have been round. Either that or the solicitor
would have been on the phone. No, she meant it. I don't mind,
you know. I've never expected anything good from life. That
way, you're not disappointed." Freddie pushed his chair back, the
legs squeaking on the parquet floor. He looked down anxiously,
checking the polished surface wasn't scarred.

I stood up. "I'm sorry," I said.

His wary look was back. "Why? I wasn't part of her life.
I don't know who her friends were outside *Northerners*. I don't
even know if she had any lovers." He sighed. "In all the ways
that count, we were strangers, Kate." It was the first time he'd
used my name.

I followed him to the door. As we emerged into the hall,
a woman was coming downstairs wrapped in a fluffy towelling
dressing gown. I don't know who looked more startled, me or
her. I hadn't registered any sounds to indicate there was anyone
else home. She looked uncertainly from me to Freddie, her soft

features concerned rather than suspicious. "This is Kate," Freddie said. "She's from work. She just bobbed round to tell me about a change of schedule for tomorrow's filming. Kate, this is Stacey, my fiancée."

I took my cue from Freddie and grinned inanely at the woman who continued down the stairs and gave me a trusting smile. She had a disturbing resemblance to Thumper the rabbit but with none of his street smarts. "Hello and goodbye, Stacey," I said, noticing that she looked a good ten years younger than Freddie.

"Maybe see you another time, eh?" she said, standing back to let me reach the front door.

"Maybe," I lied, suddenly feeling claustrophobic. I turned the knob on the lock and let the night in. "See you, Freddie."

"Thanks, Kate."

I looked back once, as I turned out of the gate. His slim frame was silhouetted dark against the light spilling out of the hallway, Stacey a white blob beside him. I didn't fancy her job one little bit.

⚔◆⚔

My stomach hurt. Not because of the nagging sense of failure but because it was a very long time since I'd last eaten. I stopped at the first chippie I came to and sat in the car eating very fishy cod and soggy chips, watching tiny stutters of snow struggling to turn into a blizzard. They were getting nowhere fast, just like me. So far, I had no idea who'd been sending hate mail to Gloria Kendal, or why. I had no idea who had killed Dorothea Dawson, or why, or whether they posed a threat to Gloria or anybody else. I couldn't even clear my sort-of other client, Ross Grant, because the only mole I could substitute for him in Turpin's firing line was someone who had even more to lose. My assistant had been arrested more times than I'd had hot dinners all week, my computer specialist was in love with somebody who might not even exist and one of my best friends was in jail.

It was just as well none of the women's magazines were thinking about profiling me as an example of Britain's thrusting new businesswomen.

I scrunched up the chip papers and tossed them into the passenger footwell. I hoped I'd remember to dump them when I got home, otherwise the car would smell of fish and vinegar until the first sunroof day of spring. Home seemed even less appetizing, somehow. The idea of an empty house and an empty bed felt too much like film noir for my taste.

I had a reasonably good idea where Richard might have gone. Since he'd planned a romantic night in, he wouldn't have made any plans to listen to a live band. That meant he'd have chosen somewhere he could sit in a corner with a beer and a joint and listen to techno music so loud it would make his vertebrae do the cha-cha. I knew he wouldn't have ventured further afield than the city centre when the roads were so treacherous and there was no one to drive him home. There were only a couple of places that fitted the bill.

I gave the matter careful thought. Frash was the most likely. He'd been raving about the new midweek DJ there. The way my luck was running, that meant he was almost certainly not grooving in Frash. It had to be the O-Pit, a renovated die-cast works down by the canal that still smelled of iron filings and grease. To add insult to injury, there was a queue and I didn't have enough energy left to jump it. I leaned against the spalled brickwork, shoulders hunched, hands stuffed deep into my pockets. I might not be dressed for the club, but I was the only one in the queue who stood a chance against hypothermia. Eventually, I made it inside.

It was wall to wall kids, fuelled with whizz and E, pale faces gleaming with sweat, clothes sticking to them so tight they appeared to be wearing body paint. I could spot the dealers, tense eyes never still, always at the heart of a tight little knot of punters. Nobody was paying them any mind, least of all the bar staff, who could barely keep pace with the constant demand for carbonated pop.

I found Richard where I'd expected, in the acoustic centre of the club, the point where the music could be heard at maximum quality and volume. Unlike the dancers, he went for the drug that slowed down rather than speeded up. His eyes had the gently spaced look of the benevolently stoned. A half-litre bottle of Czech Bud hung from his right hand, a joint from his left. A copper-haired teenager wearing a lot of stripy Lycra and young enough to be his daughter was giving him covert come-on glances. I could have told her she was wasting her time. He was lost in the music.

I moved into his line of vision and tried an apologetic smile. Instead of a bollocking, he gave me that slow, cute smile that had first reeled me in, then drew me into his arms and gently kissed the top of my head. "I love you, Brannigan," he shouted.

Nobody but me heard. "Let's go home," he yelled in my ear.

I shook my head and took a long swig of his beer, leading him to the dance floor. Sometimes sex just isn't enough.

19

NEPTUNE IN SCORPIO IN THE 6TH HOUSE

She loves research and investigation, particularly if it is done secretly. She uses her discoveries to assert her power in the workplace. She is subtle, fascinated by secrets and their revelation and loves to expose hidden wickedness, especially if they feed her sense of social justice.

From *Written in the Stars*, by Dorothea Dawson

I remember a Monty Python sketch where a character complains, "My brain hurts. I've got my head stuck in the cupboard." I knew just how he felt when the opening chords of Free's "All Right Now" crashed through my head. It felt like the middle of the night. It was still dark. Mind you, in Manchester in December, that could make it mid-morning. I dug Richard in the ribs. It was his house, after all. He made a noise like a sleeping triceratops, rolled over and started snoring.

I stumbled out of bed, wincing as my aching feet hit the ground and gasping at the stiffness in my hips as I straightened up. Richard's "Twenty Great Rock Riffs" doorbell blasted out again as I rubber-legged my way down the hall, wrapping my dressing gown around me, managing to tie the belt at the third fumbling attempt. I knew I shouldn't have had that last treble Polish hunter's vodka on the rocks. I yanked the door open and Gizmo practically fell in the door, accompanied by half a snowdrift.

"I've done it," he said without preamble.

I wiggled my jaw in various directions, trying to get my mouth to work. "Oh God," I finally groaned through parched lips. I leaned against the wall and closed my eyes while the floor and ceiling rearranged themselves in their normal configuration.

"You look like shit," Gizmo observed from the living-room doorway.

"Bastard," I said, gingerly pushing myself away from the wall to test whether I could stand upright. Nothing seemed to collapse, so I put one foot in front of the other until I made it to the living room. "My place," I croaked, leading the way through the conservatory to the life support system in my kitchen.

"It's not that early," Gizmo said defensively. "You said it was important."

The clock on the microwave said 07:49. "Early's relative," I told him, opening the fridge and reaching for the milk. "So's important." I poured a glass with shaking hand and got the vitamins out. Four grams of C, two B-complex tablets and two extra-strength paracetamol. I had a feeling it was going to be one of those days when ibuprofen and paracetamol count as two of the four main food groups. I washed the pills down with the milk, shuddered like a medieval peasant with the ague and wished I'd remembered to drink more water when we'd finally got home the wrong side of four o'clock.

"Did you come on the bus?" I asked. Gizmo has the same affection for public transport as most obsessives. He's the sort who writes to TV drama producers to complain that they had the hero catching the wrong bus on his way to his rendezvous with the killer.

"The one-nine-two," he said. "Single decker."

"Do me a favour? I left my car at the O-Pit. If you get a cab round there and pick it up for me, by the time you come back I'll be able to listen to whatever you've got to say."

His mouth showed his discontent. "Do I have to?" he asked like a ten-year-old.

"Yes," I said, pointing to the door. "Call a cab, Giz."

Half an hour later, I'd kick-started my system with a mixture of hot and cold showers followed by four slices of peanut-buttered toast from a loaf that had been lurking in the freezer longer than I liked to think about. I even managed a smile for Gizmo when he returned twirling my car keys round his trigger finger.

"Thanks," I said, settling us both down in my home office with a pot of coffee. "Sorry if I was a bit off. Rough night, you know?"

"I could tell," he said. "You looked like you needed a new motherboard and a few more RAM chips."

"It's not just the brain, it's the chassis," I complained. "This last year I've been starting to think something terrible happens to your body when you hit your thirties. I'm sure my joints never used to seize up from a night's clubbing."

"It's downhill all the way," he said cheerfully. "It'll be arthritis next. And then you'll start losing nouns."

"Losing nouns?"

"Yeah. Forgetting what things are called. You watch. Any day now, you'll start calling everything wossnames, or thing-umajigs, or whatchamacallits." He looked solemn. It took me a few seconds to realize I was experiencing what passed for a joke on his planet. I shook my head very slowly to avoid killing off any more neurones and groaned softly.

Gizmo reached past me and switched on my computer. "You've got Video Translator on this machine, haven't you?"

"It's on the external hard disk, the E drive," I told him.

He nodded and started doing things to my computer keyboard and peripherals too quickly for my hungover synapses to keep up. After a few minutes of tinkering and muttering, he sat back and said, "There. It's a bit clunky in places, not enough polygons in the program to keep it smooth. The rendering's definitely not going to win any awards. But it's what you asked for. I think."

I managed to get my bleary eyes to focus on the screen. Somehow, the colours looked brighter than they had on the original crime-scene photographs. If I'd been alone, I'd have been reaching for the sunglasses, but my staff has little enough respect for me as it is. I leaned forward and concentrated on what Gizmo had put together.

We both sat in silence as his work unfolded before us. At the end, I clapped him on the shoulder. "That's brilliant," I enthused. "That must have taken you hours."

He tilted his head while shrugging, regressing to awkward adolescent. "I started soon as I got home. I finished about two. But I did have a little break to talk to Jan. So it wasn't like I blew the whole night on it or anything." He scuffed his feet on the carpet. "Anyway, Dennis is your mate."

"He owes you," I said. "Don't let him forget it. There must be somebody out there you want menacing."

Gizmo looked shocked. "I don't think so. Unless he knows where to find the moron who sent me that virus that ate all my .DLL files."

I said nothing. It wasn't the time to point out that if the lovely Jan was a hoax, he might want Dennis's talent for terror sooner than he thought. "I'm going to be half an hour or so on the phone. You can either wait or head on into the office."

"I've got my Docs on. I'll walk over," he said. "I like it in the snow. I'll let myself out."

I reached for the phone and called Ruth. Within ten minutes, she'd rung back to tell me she'd set up a meeting with DI Tucker at our office later that morning. "He's not keen," she warned me. "I think your fame has spread before you. He did ask if you were the PI involved with the Dorothea Dawson case."

"Did you lie?"

"No, I told him to check you out with Della. Apparently his bagman used to work for her, so it's a name that meant something to him."

"Ah."

"Is that a problem?"

"Not for me, but it might be for the bagman," I said. Tucker wouldn't have to be much of a detective to work out where I'd gained my access to the crime-scene photographs. "My fault. I should have warned you."

"I don't like the sound of this," Ruth said warily.

"Don't worry. I'll see you later."

It took another twenty minutes to sort out Donovan and Gloria. We finally fixed that he would pick up her and her daughter, take them to the police station and hang on while Gloria gave the statement that would get him off the hook. Then he'd take them shopping. I hoped they'd stick to the plan of going a very long way away from anywhere policed by the Greater Manchester force. If they were going to be arrested for shoplifting, I didn't want to be involved.

I took a fresh pot of coffee out into the conservatory. The sun had come back from wherever it had been taking its winter holiday. The reflection on the snow was a killer. I fished a pair of sunglasses out of the magazine rack and stared at the blank white of the garden. Some days I could do with being a Zen master. The sound of one hand clapping was about all my tender nerve endings could cope with, but I still had a murder to solve and no apparent prospects for the role of First Murderer. Somebody must have wanted to murder Dorothea, because what had happened to her definitely hadn't been suicide. But I still couldn't figure out who or why.

I wasn't any nearer a solution by the time I had to leave for my meeting with Tucker and Ruth. Richard was still asleep, flat on his back, arms in the crucifixion position. I considered nails but settled for sticking an adhesive note to his chest suggesting lunch. When all else fails, I've found it helps to enlist another brain. Failing that, I'd make do with Richard and his hangover.

If Shelley had heard about the previous night's debacle, the atmosphere in the office was going to be frostier than it was outside. I stopped off at the florist on the way in and bought the biggest poinsettia they had. It would act both as peace offering and office decoration. There were three weeks to Christmas, and even with my chlorophyll-killer touch the plant had to stand a good chance of making it into the New Year.

I placed the poinsettia on her desk, a tentative smile nailed on. She looked up briefly, surveyed the plant and savaged me with fashion folk wisdom. "Red and green are never seen except upon a fool," she said. "Gizmo was right. You do look like shit."

"And a merry Christmas to you too, Scrooge," I muttered.

"I don't have to work here," she sniffed.

"Nobody else would put up with you now the war's over," I told her sweetly and swept into my office. Gizmo had already set everything up. All I needed now was a cop with an open mind. If they could get miracles on 34th Street, I didn't see why we couldn't have them on Oxford Road.

Ruth was first to arrive. "I hate surprises," she grumbled, dropping her fake fur in a heap in the corner. Maybe Tucker would take it for a timber wolf and be cowed into submission.

"Nice outfit," I said, trying to change the subject.

"Mmm," she said, preening her perfectly proportioned but extremely large body in its tailored kingfisher-blue jacket and severe black trousers. "You don't think it's a bit Cheshire Wife?"

"Sweetheart, you *are* a Cheshire Wife."

She bared her teeth in a snarl. If she'd still been wearing the coat I'd have dived out of the window. "Only geographically," she said. "I thought you needed me on your side this morning?"

Before we could get too deeply into the banter, the inter-com buzzed. "I have a Detective Inspector Tucker for you," the human icicle announced. I made a big production of crossing my fingers and opened the door.

If the man standing by Shelley's desk had been any taller, we could have dipped his head in emulsion and repainted the ceiling. He was so skinny I bet he had to make a fist when he walked over cattle grids. He had a thick mop of salt and pepper hair, skin cratered from teenage acne and a thousand-watt smile that lit up the kind of grey eyes that can resemble granite or rabbit fur. "I'm Kate Brannigan," I said. "Thanks for coming. Would you like to come through?"

Close up, my eyes were on a level with the breast pocket of his jacket. I flashed Ruth a "why didn't you tell me?" look and ushered him in. He exchanged ritual greetings with Ruth and folded himself into the chair I pointed him towards. I swung the monitor screen round till it was facing them both. "I'm sorry I was so mysterious about this," I said. "But if I'd told you what I had in mind, you'd have laughed in my face. You certainly wouldn't have taken it seriously enough to come and see for yourself."

"I'm here now, so let's cut to the chase. We're all busy people," he said, with no trace of hostility. He obviously didn't go to the same Masonic dinners as Cliff Jackson.

"It's not a long preamble, I promise you. Last week, you found Pit Bull Kelly dead inside a shop that had previously been squatted by Dennis O'Brien. Pit Bull had told his brothers he was going down to the shop to sort Dennis out and take over the pitch for himself. Next morning, Pit Bull was found dead from a sub-arachnoid haemorrhage, an unusual injury and one that's hard to inflict. You decided, not unreasonably given what you know about Dennis, that he'd used a commando karate blow to kill Pit Bull. But given what I know about Dennis, I know it couldn't have happened like that." I held my hands up to ward off the objection I could see Tucker about to make.

"But putting prejudice aside, there's a key piece of evidence that tells me Dennis didn't kill Pit Bull. I've known Dennis a long time, and the one thing he won't have anything to do with is guard dogs. Back when he was burgling, he'd never touch a house that had a guard dog. If Pit Bull Kelly had turned up with his dog in tow, Dennis wouldn't even have opened the door. But just supposing he had, that dog is a trained killer. He was Pit Bull Kelly's private army, according to his brothers. If Dennis had lifted his hands above waist level, the dog would have gone for him. He'd never have got as far as laying a hand on the master without the dog ripping his throat out."

Tucker nodded sympathetically. "I've already heard this argument from Ms Hunter. And if this crime had taken place out in the open, I might have been forced to agree. But what you tell me about O'Brien's dislike of fierce dogs doesn't mean he didn't kill Patrick Kelly. I could make the argument that the fact the dog was separated from its master by the back door of the shop lends weight to the notion that O'Brien was in fact in the shop and agreed to talk to Kelly on the sole condition that the dog stayed in the service corridor."

"If so, how did he escape? There's no way out through the front without being filmed by security cameras and breaking through a metal grille," I pointed out.

Tucker shrugged. "O'Brien's a professional burglar. If he put his mind to it, I'm sure he could find a way out that neither of us would come up with in a month of Sundays."

"That's not an argument that will carry much weight with a jury in the absence of any evidence to the contrary," Ruth chipped in drily. Tucker's eyebrows descended and his eyes darkened.

"What I want to show you," I interrupted before the good-will melted, "is an alternative hypothesis that answers all the problems this case presents. It should be relatively easy to make the forensic tests that will demonstrate if I'm right or wrong. But for now, all I want the pair of you to do is to watch."

I tapped a couple of keys and the screen saver dissolved. The corridor behind Dennis's squat appeared. A few seconds passed, then a jerky figure with Pit Bull Kelly's face and clothes walked towards us. Even with the limited resources of time and software that Gizmo had been working with, he managed to convey that Kelly was under the influence of the drink and cannabis that, according to his brothers, he'd indulged in before he had the courage to face Dennis. Beside Kelly, a boisterous pit bull terrier lurched, its movements twitchy and not very well coordinated. Every few steps, the dog would jump up towards its master's chest and Kelly would slap it down. Gizmo had even overlaid a soundtrack of a barking dog.

"Two of his brothers confirmed that the dog was always jumping up at Pit Bull. It's still not much more than a pup. It's full of energy," I said, forestalling any protest from Tucker when he saw where this was heading.

"It's impressive," was all he said.

We watched Kelly and the dog arrive at the door to Dennis's squat. He reached out a hand for the doorknob and clumsily turned it. Expecting it to be locked, he stumbled as it opened under his hand. As Kelly lurched forward, the dog yanked on its leash, jerking Kelly off balance and spinning him half around so that the vulnerable angle under his jaw cracked into the door-jamb, accompanied by a thud courtesy of Gizmo.

The screen went black momentarily. Then the point of view shifted. We were inside the shop, behind the door. Again, we saw Kelly topple into the doorjamb, the dog skittering back from its master. The leash dropped from Kelly's fingers and the dog scampered back into the service corridor as Kelly collapsed sideways to the floor, the weight of his body slamming the door shut as he fell. The final scene dissolved into the starkness of the crime-scene photograph that had been the starting point for the whole process.

I heard Tucker's breath leak from him, the first sign that he'd been taking seriously what he saw. "I suppose I'd be wasting my time if I asked you where exactly your source material came from?"

I nodded. "I'm afraid so. All I will say is that it wasn't the obvious route," I added in an attempt to give Della's contact a little protection.

"I take it I can expect the immediate release of my client, in the light of this?" Ruth said, leaning back expansively and lighting a cigarette. Noel Coward would have loved her.

Tucker shook his head. "A very convincing performance, Ms Brannigan, but you know as well as I do that it doesn't change anything."

"It should, because it explains everything a damn sight better than any hypothesis you've been able to come up with," I said. "The door was unlocked because Dennis didn't want to be responsible for the landlord having to cause any damage getting into the premises. Dennis's alibi holds water. It also explains why the dog didn't get into a fight with the killer, because there was no killer. I know it's bad for your clear-up statistics, but this wasn't a murder, it was the purest of accidents."

Tucker sucked his lower lip in between his teeth. "You make a good case. But O'Brien's wife has given him false alibis before, and he did have a strong reason for falling out with the dead man."

"You will be running full forensic checks on the doorjamb, won't you, Inspector?" Ruth said ominously.

"I'm not sure that's justified," Tucker said cautiously. "Besides, the crime scene has been released."

"Because if you don't," Ruth continued as if he hadn't spoken, "I will. I'll be getting my own expert witness down there this afternoon. And when he finds fragments of skin and maybe even a bit of blood with Patrick Kelly's DNA all over that doorjamb at precisely the height where his jaw would have hit it, Mr O'Brien will be suing you for false imprisonment. Won't that be fun?"

"A lovely Christmas present for the Chief Constable," I added. I was starting to get the hang of threatening the police. I could see why Ruth got such a buzz out of her job.

Tucker sighed then chewed his lower lip some more. "I will get someone to take a look at the door," he eventually said. "And I will also have a word with the pathologist." He stood up, his long body unfolding to its unnerving height. "It's been an interesting experience, Ms Brannigan. I'm sure we'll meet again."

Ruth extracted a promise that he'd call her as soon as he had any information, and I shepherded him out.

"Tell me, what set you off on this train of thought?" Ruth demanded the moment the door closed.

"I wish I could say it was some brilliant intuitive leap. But it wasn't. I'm on the Internet mailing list of a forensic pathology newsgroup," I said, feeling slightly sheepish. "Mostly I'm too busy to do much more than skim it, but every now and again, some bizarre detail sticks in my mind. I read about a similar case and I remembered it because the reporting pathologist described it as, 'Man's best friend and worst enemy.'"

If Ruth had had four paws and a tail, her ears would have pricked up. Instead, she settled for leaning forward with an intent gaze. "You've got a copy of this?"

I shook my head. "I don't save the digests. But I could put out a request for whoever filed the original case report to get in touch with me. I've managed to track down a couple of references to it, and that should be enough to get me heading in the right direction."

Ruth got to her feet, stubbing out her cigarette in the soil of the dying Christmas cactus on the windowsill. "Do it," she said decisively, reaching for her coat. "You did a great job there," she added. "I shall tell Dennis he owes his freedom entirely to you. Send me a bill, will you?"

"I thought Dennis was on Legal Aid?"

"He is."

"But the Legal Aid Board won't pay for this," I protested.

Ruth's smile matched the timber-wolf coat. "No, but Dennis will. You're running a business, not a charity. There's favours for friends, and there's charges for professional services. This is one he pays for."

"But . . ."

"No buts. You're no use to either of us if you can't make this business pay. Send me a bill."

I would have argued. But she's bigger than me. Besides, it always takes forever to argue with a lawyer. And I had a lunch appointment.

20

JUPITER TRINES NEPTUNE

She is idealistic, and enjoys discussion on a theoretical or philo-sophical level. She can be excessively generous and will go out of her way to help others. She does not always manage to meet her own high standards.

From *Written in the Stars*, by Dorothea Dawson

The Yang Sing was Manchester's most famous Chinese restaurant until it burned down, and it suffered accordingly. Trying to get a table at a busy time of day or night, especially near Christmas, was about as rewarding as waiting for a night bus. What the tourists didn't know was that just round the corner is the sister restaurant, the Little Yang Sing, where the cooking is at least as good and the decor leans more towards the clean lines of sixties retro than the traditional fish tanks and flock wallpaper of most Chinese restaurants.

Richard was already there by the time I arrived. So were a couple of bottles of Tsing Tao, a plate of salt and pepper ribs and a tidy little mound of prawn wontons. I dropped into my seat and reached for the beer. If the morning had taught me anything, it was that the only way to get through the day was going to be by topping up the alcohol level in my bloodstream at regular intervals. I didn't have time to suffer today; I'd have my hangover when I was asleep and not before.

As I swigged beer, I checked out Richard. Even allowing for the fact that he'd had four hours more sleep than me, he had no right to look so untouched by the excesses of the night before. His hazel eyes looked sleepy behind his new rimless glasses, but then they always have that fresh-from-the-bedroom look. The light dusting of stubble was sexy rather than scruffy, and his skin stretched tight over his broad cheekbones. I swear he looks no older than the night we first bumped into each other six years ago. I wish I could say the same, but one look in the mirrors that line the back wall of the restaurant and I knew it was a lie. The unforgiving light glinted on a couple of strands of what might have been silver in my dark-auburn hair. To dye or not to dye was a decision that was closer than I liked.

"How was your morning?" he asked just as I got a spare rib to my lips. Typical; he always asks questions when there's food to be fought over.

I shook my head and stripped the bone with my teeth. "Tough," I said. "But it looks as if Dennis is going to be back on the streets for Christmas."

"That's one less thing for you to worry about, then. And Gloria? Has she had any more hate mail?"

"Nothing. I've got Donovan taking her and her daughter shopping today. I keep waiting for the phone call."

Richard grinned. "Switch the phone off. You need both hands for what I've ordered."

He wasn't wrong. We ate our way through half a dozen dim sum and appetizers, a double helping of hot and sour soup and four main-course dishes. My capacity for food after a heavy night never ceases to astonish me. I'll probably need a stomach transplant when I'm forty. By then, they'll probably be able to give me one.

I picked up the last king prawn with my chopsticks then laid it regretfully back on the plate. "I can't do it," I said.

"Me neither," Richard admitted. "So where are you up to with this murder?"

I brought him up to speed on my meeting with Freddie Littlewood. It felt like half a lifetime ago, but it was only the night before. "So I seem to have tracked down the source of most of the tabloid stories," I said. "At least, the ones involving personal scandal rather than storyline revelations. But I don't know how to use the information to clear Ross Grant without dropping Freddie in the shit. I don't really want to do that if I can help it, because, to be honest, he seems to have had a pretty raw deal from life anyway."

"And you're sure he didn't kill his mother? He'd have had the opportunity, and he freely admits to hating her."

"I just don't think he did it. Why should he? He was making a nice little earner out of their story selling, and he got the added bonus that it really upset her. Profitable revenge. There's not many of us manage that."

Richard poured himself a cup of Chinese tea and stared into it consideringly. "Maybe she'd had enough," he said at last. "Maybe she was going to blow the whistle on the whole racket and throw herself on the mercy of her clients."

I snorted. "She certainly wouldn't have got much change out of them. And even supposing the cast members were prepared to forgive and forget, John Turpin would never let her back on NPTV property again. Which reminds me . . ." I drifted off, remembering what Cassie had told me.

"I said," Richard commented in the tones of a man repeating himself, "who is John Turpin?"

"He's the Administration and Production Coordinator at NPTV," I said absently. "One of those typical telly executives. You know the kind. About as creative as a sea slug. They're great at counting beans and cutting expenses. You must have them in journalism."

"Editorial managers," he said glumly.

"And he's obsessed with uncovering the mole who's leaking the *Northerners* stories. He's even threatening to end the location caterers' contract because he suspects one of them of being guilty."

"Nice guy. So what is it about this Turpin that sent you off the air just now?" Richard asked.

"I was just remembering a conversation I had yesterday with Cassie Cliff."

"Maggie Grimshaw as was?"

"The same."

Richard smiled reminiscently. "I loved Maggie Grimshaw. The woman who put the 'her' in *Northerners*. The sex goddess of soap." His smile slipped. "Until the truth came slithering out. So what did Cassie have to say about John Turpin?"

I told him the tale about Turpin and Tina Marshall in the Normandie. "I can't figure it out at all," I said.

"He might have been wining and dining her on the off-chance that she'd let something slip about her mole."

I pulled a face. "I don't think he's that stupid."

"He might be that vain," Richard pointed out. "Never underestimate a middle-aged executive's opinion of himself."

I sighed. "Well, if that's what he was after, he obviously didn't succeed, since he's still making a huge performance out of flushing out the mole."

"Has he got shares in NPTV?" Richard asked.

"I think so. *Northerners* is up for contract renegotiation. One of the actors was talking about how much money Turpin would make if NPTV got into a bidding war between the terrestrial and the pay channels over *Northerners*. So I guess he must have some financial stake."

Richard leaned back in his seat, looking pleased with himself. "That's the answer. That's why Turpin was cosying up to Tina Marshall. John Turpin's the *Northerners* mole." He signalled to a passing waiter that we wanted the bill.

Sometimes I wonder how someone who never listens makes such a good living as a journalist. "Richard, pay attention. I already told you who the mole is. Freddie Littlewood was using Dorothea to dig the dirt then he was dishing it."

"I *was* paying attention," he said patiently. "Freddie was pulling skeletons out of cupboards, courtesy of Dorothea's privileged information. What you didn't tell me was who's been selling out the storylines. From what you say, Turpin must have access to them."

"But why? What does he gain by it?"

Richard shook his head in wonderment. "I can't believe you're being so slow about this, Brannigan," he said. "You're normally so quick off the mark where money's concerned. It's viewing figures, isn't it? The more notorious *Northerners* becomes, the more people watch. The more people watch, the higher the value of the show when it comes to negotiating any satellite or cable deal because there are people who will shell out hundreds of pounds for satellite dishes and cable decoders and subscription charges rather than be parted from their regular fix of *Northerners*."

"I know that," I protested. "But it's different with storylines that get leaked before transmission. That makes people turn off."

The waiter dumped the bill on the table between us. Automatically, we both reached for our wallets. "Says who?" Richard demanded as his plastic followed mine on to the plate.

"Says the actors. When the punters know what happens next, they don't mind missing it. And they get hooked on something else so they drop out altogether."

The waiter removed the bill and the credit cards. "Two receipts, please," we chorused. He nodded. He'd served us enough times to know the routine of two self-employed people who liked to eat together. "That's bollocks, you know," Richard said. "That might be what Turpin's telling them, but it's bollocks. If you leak upcoming storylines, what happens is you get a buzz going. First one paper breaks the story, then all the rest follow it up, then the TV magazines pick it up and run with it and before you know it, everybody's buzzing. Don't you remember the whole 'Who shot JR?' thing back in the eighties? Or the furore over Deirdre Barlow and Mike Baldwin's affair on *Coronation Street*? The whole nation was watching. I bet Turpin got the idea when Freddie's exclusives started hitting the headlines and the viewing figures rose along with them."

"He wouldn't dare," I breathed.

"Where's the risk? He's in charge of hunting for the source of the *Northerners* stories. Turpin knows there's a real mole as well as himself, so if he does uncover anything, he can pin all the guilt on the other one. There's no way Tina Marshall is going to expose him, because he's the goose that lays the golden eggs. She's probably not even paying him much."

I leaned across the table and thrust my hand through his thick butterscotch hair, pulling his head towards mine. I parted my lips and planted a warm kiss on his mouth. I could still taste lemon and ginger and garlic as I ran my tongue lightly between his teeth. I drew back for breath and said softly, "Now I remember why I put up with you."

The waiter cleared his throat. I released Richard's head and we sheepishly signed our credit card slips. Richard reached across the table and covered my hand with his. "We've got some unfinished business from last night," he said, his voice husky.

I ran my other thumbnail down the edge of his hand and revelled in the shiver that ran through him. "Your place or mine?"

Just before we slipped under my duvet, I made a quick call to Gizmo, asking him to arrange for some background checks into the exact extent of John Turpin's financial involvement with NPTV. Then I switched the phone off.

Sometime afterwards, I was teetering on the edge of sleep, my face buried in the musky warmth of Richard's chest, when his voice swirled through my mind like a drift of snow. "I'll tell you one thing, Brannigan. If a few juicy stories can push up the ratings, just think what murder must have done."

Suddenly, I was wide awake.

❦

Sandra McGovern, née Satterthwaite, had inherited her mother's flair for ostentation. The house where she lived with her husband Keith and their daughter Joanna had definite delusions of grandeur. Set just off Bury New Road in the smarter part of Prestwich, it looked like the one person at the party who'd been told it was fancy dress. The rest of the street consisted of plain but substantial redbrick detached houses built sometime in the 1960s. Chateau McGovern had gone for the Greek-temple makeover. The portico was supported by half a dozen ionic columns and topped with a few statues of goddesses in various stages of undress. Bas reliefs had been stuck on to the brick at regular intervals and a stucco frieze of Greek key design ran along the frontage just below the first-floor windows.

They might just have got away with it on a sunny summer day. But the McGoverns clearly took Christmas seriously. The whole house was festooned with fairy lights flashing on and off with migraine-inducing intensity. Among the Greek goddesses, Santa Claus sat in a sled behind four cavorting reindeer, all in life-sized inflatable plastic. A Christmas tree had been sawn vertically in two, and each half fixed to the wall on either side of the front door, both dripping with tinsel and draped with flickering-light ropes. A vast wreath of holly garlanded the door itself. I pressed the doorbell and the chimes of "Deck the Halls with Boughs of Holly" engulfed me. Sometimes I felt Scrooge had had a point.

There was a long silence. I was steeling myself to ring again when I saw a figure looming through the frosted glass. Then Donovan opened the door. But it was Donovan as I'd never seen him before, swathed in a plum silk kimono that reached just below his knees. A fine sheen of sweat covered his face and he looked extremely embarrassed. "Bah, humbug," I muttered. He seemed baffled, but what else could I expect from an engineering student?

"Hiya, Kate," he said.

I pointed to his outfit. "I hope this isn't what it looks like," I said drily.

He rolled his eyes heavenwards. "You're as bad as my mother. Give me some credit. Come on in, let me get this door shut. We're through the back," he added, leading the way down the hall. "You think the outside is over the top, wait till you see this."

I waded after him through shag pile deep enough to conceal a few troops of Boy Scouts. I tried not to look too closely at the impressionistic flower paintings on the walls. At the end of the hall was a solid wooden door. Donovan opened it, then stood back to let me pass.

I walked from winter to tropical summer. Hot, green and steamy as a Hollywood rainforest, the triple-glazed extension must have occupied the same square footage as the house. Ferns and palms pushed against the glass and spilled over in cascades that overhung brick paths. Growing lamps blazed light and warmth everywhere. The air smelt of a curious mixture of humus and chlorine. Sweat popping out on my face like a rash, I followed the path through the dense undergrowth, rounded a curve and found myself facing a vast swimming pool, its shape the free form of a real pond.

"Hiya, chuck," Gloria screeched, raucous as an Amazonian parrot.

She was stretched out on a cushion of wooden sunbed, wearing nothing but a swimsuit. Beside her, a younger version reclined on one elbow like a Roman diner, a champagne glass beaded with condensation hanging loosely from her fingers. Gloria beckoned me over, patting the lounger next to her. "Take the weight off," she instructed me. I sat, slipping off my leather jacket and the cotton sweater underneath. Even stripped to jeans and cotton T-shirt, I was still overheating. "Don, sweetheart, fetch us another sunbed, there's a love," Gloria called. "This is our Sandra," she continued. "Sandra, meet Kate Brannigan, Manchester's finest private eye."

We nodded to each other and I told a few lies about the house and swimming pool. Sandra looked pleased and Gloria proud, which was the point of the exercise. Donovan reappeared carrying a fourth lounger which he placed a little away from our grouping. Self-consciously, he peeled off the robe, revealing baggy blue trunks, and perched on the edge of the seat, his body gleaming like a Rodin bronze. "No problems today?"

Gloria stretched voluptuously. For a woman who was fast approaching the downhill side of sixty, she was in terrific shape. It was amazing, given what I'd seen of her lifestyle. "Not a one, chuck. Nowt but pleasure all the way. We went to Oldham police station and I spoke to a lovely young inspector who couldn't see what all the fuss last night had been about. Any road, young Don's in the clear now, so we don't have to worry about that. And then we went shopping for Christmas presents for Joanna. We had to get a robe and some trunks for Don and all, because our Keith's a tiddler next to him. We've not seen a journalist all day, and there's nobody more pleased than me about that. What about you? Any news?"

"I wanted to ask you about something," I said, side-stepping the question. "You remember when I came to fetch you from Dorothea's van the night she was killed? Well, I was busy wrestling with the umbrella and keeping an eye out in case anybody jumped us, so I wasn't really paying attention to individuals. Besides, I don't really know anybody at NPTV, so even if I had noticed who was around, it wouldn't mean anything to me. But you . . ."

"You want me to think about who I saw in the car park?"

"It might be important."

Gloria leaned back, closing her eyes and massaging her temples. "Let's see . . ." she said slowly. "There were two women getting into a car a couple of bays down from Dorothea's. I don't know their names, but I've seen them in the accounts office . . . Valerie Brown came out of the admin block and ran across to production . . . I saw that red-haired film editor with Maurice Warner and Maurice's secretary. They were legging it for Maurice's car . . . John Turpin was standing in the doorway of the admin block, like he couldn't decide whether to make a run for it . . . Freddie and Diane and Sharon from make-up, they were getting in Sharon's car, that lot always go to the pub in town on a Friday . . . Tamsin from the press office, she came out the admin block and went across towards the security booth, but she wasn't running because of them daft shoes she wears." She opened her eyes and sat up. "There were one or two other folk about, but either they were too muffled up for me to see who they were or else I didn't know them. Does any of that help?"

I reached for my sweater. "More than you can imagine, Gloria. Much more than you can imagine."

"So what's going on?" she demanded. "Do you know who killed Dorothea?"

"I've got an idea," I said. "I don't want to say too much yet. I've got stuff to check out. But if you get Donovan to bring you to the office first thing tomorrow morning, I think I might be able to give you your money's worth."

Donovan gave me a look of resignation. "You want me to stick with Gloria?"

"Oh, I think so," I said. "You make such a lovely pair."

21

SATURN IN PISCES IN THE 11TH HOUSE

She is comfortable with her own company and works best alone. Her friends are valued as much for their experience as for their personal qualities. She has a single-minded concentration on objectives, but has a flexible and sympathetic mind. She is intuitive and imaginative. She can be moody.

From *Written in the Stars*, by Dorothea Dawson

When Freddie Littlewood got home from work, I was waiting for him. Stacey of the big eyes and trusting soul had made it back fifteen minutes ahead of him and she'd let me in without a moment's hesitation. She'd shown me into the dining room again, presumably because that was where Freddie and I had spoken before. She'd been back inside five minutes with a tray containing teapot, milk, sugar and a china mug with kittens on it.

"It can't have been easy for Freddie, the last few days," I said sympathetically.

She gave me an odd look. "No more than usual," she said. "Why would it be difficult?"

Until that moment, the idea that Freddie might not have mentioned his mother's murder to Stacey hadn't occurred to me. People have called me cold in my time, but I don't think I could plan to spend the rest of my life with someone I trusted so little. "I meant, with the police everywhere," I improvised hastily, remembering I was supposed to work for NPTV too. "It's been really disruptive. They walk around as if they own the place, asking all sorts of questions. And it's not even as if Dorothea Dawson worked for NPTV."

Seemingly satisfied, Stacey drifted off, saying she was going to get changed and get the dinner on, if I didn't mind. I also couldn't imagine marrying someone with so little curiosity about a strange woman who turned up looking for her fiancé twice in such a short space of time. I sipped my tea and wished there was a large lemon vodka in it. The sound of the front door opening and closing was immediately followed by Stacey's footsteps in the hall and the low mutter of conversation.

Freddie stepped into the doorway, looking grey-faced and exhausted. "What's so urgent it couldn't wait for work tomorrow?" he asked brusquely. More for Stacey's benefit than mine, I suspected.

"I needed the answer to a question," I said. "I won't be at NPTV first thing in the morning, so I thought you wouldn't mind if I caught up with you at home."

He closed the door behind him and leaned against it. "Have you never heard of the telephone?" he said, exasperation in his voice.

"It's much harder to tell when people are lying," I said mildly. "Sorting out the truth is difficult enough as it is."

Freddie folded his arms over his chest and glared. "Since you're here, I'll answer your question. But in future, if you want to talk to me, see me at work or call me on the phone. I don't want Stacey upset by this, OK?"

"That's very chivalrous of you," I said. "There's not many men who are so concerned for their future wives' wellbeing that they don't even tell them their prospective mother-in-law's just been murdered."

"What goes on between Stacey and me is none of your business. You said you had a question?"

"You told me that it wasn't you who leaked the advance storylines to the press, and I believe you," I said. "But somebody did. I was wondering if Dorothea had ever indicated to you that she knew who the mole was?"

He gave me a long, considering stare, running his thumb along his jaw in the unconscious gesture I'd already become familiar with. "She once told me that it wasn't hard to work out who the mole was if you looked at the horoscopes. She said there weren't that many people connected with *Northerners* who had the right combination of features in their charts. If you excluded people who didn't really have access to advance stories, she said, it narrowed right down."

"Did she mention anybody's name to you?"

He shook his head. "Not then. She said she didn't seem to have much choice about passing me other people's secrets but that she wasn't going to ruin somebody when she had no evidence except her own instinct. But then later . . ." His voice tailed off.

"What happened, Freddie?" I asked urgently.

"Turpin was in make-up one day and somebody said something about one of the stories in the paper and was it true he was going to get rid of the caterers because they were the moles. Turpin said he wasn't convinced that would solve the problem. I turned round and he was staring at me. I thought maybe he suspected me. So I went round to Dorothea's house and told her. I said she'd probably be glad if Turpin did find out, because then she'd be off the hook and wouldn't have to break her precious client confidences any more."

"She wasn't though, was she?" I said gently.

He shook his head and cleared his throat. "No. She said she wouldn't let Turpin destroy my career. She said she was as certain as she could be that he was the storyline mole and she was going to confront him."

"She was going to expose him?" I couldn't believe Freddie was only revealing this now.

"No, she wasn't like that. I told you, she was obsessed with trying to do her best for me, supposedly to make up for all the bad years. No, she said she'd do a deal with Turpin. If he stopped hunting the mole, she'd keep quiet about her suspicions of him."

"But she didn't have any evidence apart from an astrological chart," I protested.

"She said that if she was right, there had to be evidence. All it needed was for someone to look in the right place and Turpin would realize that once she'd pointed the finger, he'd be in trouble. So he'd have to back off and leave me alone. Except of course she wasn't going to come out and say it was me, not in so many words. She was just going to tell him that she was acting on behalf of the mole."

"When was this?" I asked, trying to keep my voice nonchalant.

Freddie shrugged. "A couple, three weeks ago? She told me afterwards he'd agreed to the deal. That he'd seen the sense of what she was saying. You don't think that had anything to do with why she was killed, do you?"

"You don't?" I asked incredulously.

"I told you, it was weeks ago."

I couldn't get my head round his naiveté. Then I realized he wasn't so much naive as self-obsessed. "There's a lot at stake," I pointed out. "You know yourself you'd never work in TV again if I told NPTV what you've been doing. And there are a lot of people involved with *Northerners* who have a lot more to lose than you do. If somebody thought Dorothea was a threat . . ."

Freddie stared at the floor. "It wasn't like she was blackmailing him. She was too straight for that."

"She let you blackmail her," I pointed out.

"That was different. That was guilt."

"Looks like it killed her, Freddie."

I got up and put a hand on his arm. He pulled away. "Don't touch me! It's meaningless to you. You never knew my mother."

There was nothing more to say. I'd got what I came for and Freddie Littlewood was determined to need nobody's sympathy for the death of a mother he'd barely come to know. I walked back to the car, glad I wasn't living inside his skin.

I'd barely closed the door when my moby rang. "Hello?"

"Hey, Kate, I'm out!" Dennis's voice was elated.

"Free and clear?" I could hardly believe it.

"Police bail pending results from the lab. Ruth says you played a blinder! Where are you? Can I buy you some bubbly?"

If anyone deserved champagne, it was the long-suffering Debbie. But female solidarity only stretches so far, and I needed Dennis more than she did. I was glad I hadn't done as Ruth suggested and submitted a bill, because tonight I needed payment in kind. "Never mind the bubbly," I said. "I need a favour. Where are you?"

"I'm in the lobby bar at the Ramada," he announced. "And I've already got the bottle in front of me."

"Take it easy. I'll be there in half an hour." I needed to make a quick detour via a phone book. I started the engine and fishtailed away from the kerb. The roads had iced up while I'd been indoors. It was going to be another treacherous night. And I was quite sanguine about contributing to the total.

If you walk out of Strangeways Prison up towards town, the Ramada Hotel is probably the first civilized place to buy a drink. It's certainly the first where you can buy a decent bottle of champagne. Following the IRA bomb, its façade reminded me of those mechanical bingo cards you get on seaside sideshow stalls where you pull a shutter across the illuminated number after the caller shouts it out. So many of the Ramada windows were boarded up, it looked like they'd won the china tea service. I found Dennis on a bar stool, a bottle of Dom Perignon in front of him. I wondered how many "Under a Pound" customers it had taken to pay for that.

He jumped off the stool when he saw me, pulling me into a hug with one arm and handing me a glass of champagne with the other. "My favourite woman!" he crowed, toasting me with the drink he retrieved from the bar.

"Shame we're both spoken for," I said, clinking my crystal against his.

"Thanks for sorting it," he said, more serious now.

"I knew it wasn't down to you."

"Thanks. This favour . . . we need a bit of privacy?"

I gestured towards a vacant table over in the corner. "That'll do." I led the way while Dennis followed, a muscular arm embracing the ice bucket where the remains of the champagne lurked. Once we were both settled, I outlined my plan.

"We know where he lives?" Dennis asked.

"There's only one in the phone book. Out the far side of Bolton. Lostock."

He nodded. "Sounds like the right area."

"Why? What's it like?"

"It's where Bolton folk go when they've done what passes for making it. More money than imagination."

"That makes sense. I looked it up on the *A-Z*. There's only houses on one side of the road. The other side's got a golf course."

"You reckon he'll be home?"

I finished my champagne. "Only one way to find out." I pointed to his mobile.

"Too early for that," Dennis said dismissively. Then he outlined his plan.

≈✦≈

An hour later, I was lying on my stomach in a snowdrift. I never knew feet could be that cold and still work. The only way I could tell my nose was running was when the drips splashed on the snow in front of me. In spite of wearing every warm and waterproof garment I possessed, I was cold enough to sink the *Titanic*. This was our second stakeout position. The front of the house had proved useless for Dennis's purposes and now we were lying inside the fence surrounding an old people's home, staring down at the back garden of our target. "Is it time yet?" I whimpered pathetically.

Dennis was angled along the top of the drift, a pair of lightweight black rubber binoculars pressed to his eyes. "Looks like we got lucky," he said.

"Do tell me how."

"He's not bothered to pull the curtains in the kitchen. I've got a direct line of sight to the keypad that controls the burglar alarm. If he sets that when he goes out, I'll be able to see what number he taps in."

"Does that mean we're going to do it now?" I said plaintively.

"You go back round the front. I'll give you five minutes before I make the call. Soon as he leaves, you shoot up the drive and start working on the front-door lock. I'll get to you fast as I can." He turned and waved a dismissive hand at me. "On your bike, then. And remember, we're dressed for the dark, not the snow. Keep in the shadows."

That's the trouble with living in a climate where we only get snow for about ten days a year. Not even serious villains bother to invest in white camouflage. Neither Dennis's lock-up nor my wardrobe had offered much that wouldn't blend in with your average dark alley. I slunk off round the edge of the shrubbery and down the drive of the old people's home. I nipped across the road and on to the golf course, where I waded through knee-high snow until I was opposite the double-fronted detached house we were interested in. A light shone in the porch, and the ghost light from the hall cast pale oblongs on the ceilings of upstairs rooms. The rooms on either side of the front door had heavy curtains drawn.

I checked my watch. A couple of minutes before, Dennis would have rung the house and explained that there had been a break-in at the administrative core of NPTV and that the police wanted Mr Turpin to come down right away to assess the damage. A quick call to Gloria had already established that he was divorced and as far as she knew, unattached. We were taking a gamble that Turpin was alone. As I watched, the front door swung open and he appeared, shrugging into a heavy leather coat over suit trousers and a heavy knit sweater. On the still night air, I could hear the high-pitched whine of an alarm system setting itself. He pulled the door to behind himself, not bothering to double lock it, and walked briskly to his car. A security light snapped on, casting the drive into extremes of light and shade.

Ignition, headlights bouncing off the garage door, reversing lights, then the big Lexus crunched down the icy drive and swung into the road. I watched the tail lights as far as the junction, then scrambled over the banking, across the road and up Turpin's drive, dodging in and out of shadow and blinding light. The porch was brighter than my kitchen. I'd never broken the law in quite so exposed a way before. I fumbled under my jacket and fleece, fingers chill in latex probing the money belt I was wearing until they closed around my lock-picks. At least I'd be able to see what I was doing.

Oddly enough, it didn't really speed up the process. Picking a lock successfully was all about feel, not sight, and my fingers were still clumsy from the cold. Dennis was hovering impatiently by my shoulder by the time I got the right combination of metal probes, muttering, "Come on, Kate," in a puff of white breath.

The door opened and he was past me, running down the hall to the alarm panel, tapping in the code to stop the warning siren joining forces with the klaxon that would deafen us and, in an area like this, have the police on the doorstep within ten minutes. I let him get on with it and checked out the downstairs rooms. A living room on one side of the hall, a dining table on the other. Kitchen at the rear. I ran up the stairs. Four doors, three ajar. The first was Turpin's bedroom, an en suite bathroom opening off it. The second, closed, was the guest bathroom. Third was a characterless guest room. Last, inevitably, was the one I was looking for. As I walked in, the alarm went quiet, the silence a palpable presence.

Luckily, Turpin's study overlooked the back garden, so I felt safe enough to switch on the desk lamp. I took a quick look around. There was one wall of books, mostly military history and management texts. On the opposite wall, shelves held file boxes, stacks of bound reports and fat binders for various trade magazines. A PC squatted on the desk and I switched it on. While it booted up, I started on the drawers. None of them were locked. Either Turpin thought himself invincible here or we were doing the wrong burglary.

Suddenly, Dennis was standing next to me. "Do you want me to do the drawers while you raid the computer?" he asked.

"I'd rather you kept an eye out the front," I said. "I know it should take Turpin an hour to get to NPTV and back, but I'd rather be safe than sorry."

"You're probably right," Dennis said. He went out as silently as he'd come in. At least now I didn't have to worry about being caught red-handed. I checked out the computer. It looked as if Turpin used Word for all his documents, which suited me perfectly. I took a CD-ROM out of my money belt and swapped it for the encyclopaedia currently residing in the drive. It had taken all my powers of persuasion to get Gizmo to lend me this disk and I hoped it had been worth it. It was a clever little piece of software that searched all Word files for particular combinations of words. I typed "Doreen Satterthwaite," and set the program running.

Meanwhile, I started on the desk. Not surprisingly, Turpin was an orderly man. I flicked through folders of electricity bills, gas bills, council-tax bills until I found the phone bills I was looking for. Domestic and mobile were in the same file. A quick glance around revealed that I wasn't going to have to steal them. Turpin had one of those all-singing, all-dancing printers that also act as a computer scanner and a photocopier. I extracted the itemized bills for the last six months and fed them through the photocopier.

When the phone rang, I jumped. After three rings, the answering machine kicked in. A woman's voice floated eerily up from the hall. "Hi, Johnny. It's Deirdre. I find myself unexpectedly at a loose end after all. If you get this message at a reasonable time, come over for a nightcap. And if I'm not enough to tempt you, I've got sausages from Clitheroe for breakfast. Call me." Bleep.

I glanced at the screen and discovered that there were two files containing "Doreen Satterthwaite." I was about to access them when Dennis's yell made my heart jolt in my chest. "Fuck!" he shouted. "We're burned, Brannigan!"

22

MARS IN LEO IN THE 4TH HOUSE

*She has combative strength and brings her ambitious plans to frui-
tion. She is honourable and takes responsibility for her actions. She
has a temper, acts with audacity and is often prone to involvement
in incidents that embrace violence. She has a powerful sense of
drama that can verge on the melodramatic. Generous, she hates
small-mindedness.*

From *Written in the Stars*, by Dorothea Dawson

The adrenaline surge was like being plugged into the mains.
Dennis was almost screaming. "Switch off. Spare room. Now!"
No time to exit properly from Windows. I stabbed my finger
at the computer power button. I grabbed the photocopies and
stuffed the originals back into their folder, thrusting them into
the drawer without checking I was returning them to the right
place. I leapt to my feet, switching off the desk lamp.

Three paces across the room, I heard the wail of the alarm
siren as Dennis reset it. I dived across the hall and into a spare
room bathed with light from the security lamps outside. I skidded round the door to stand against the wall. Seconds later I
heard Dennis pounding up the stairs. Then he was beside me,

his chest heaving with the effort of silent breathing. "There's a sensor in the corner," he said. "Under the bed. Quick!"

I dropped to the floor and rolled, aware of him following me. As I hit the bedside table on the far side of the bed the alarm finished setting itself and silence fell once more. I heard the slam of a car door. Then the front door opened and the warning siren went off again. By now, every nerve in my body was jangling, and I suspected Dennis was no better. I was going to wake up sweating to the nightmare sound of that burglar alarm for months to come, I could tell. "How the fuck do we get out of this?" I hissed.

"Worst comes to worst, we wait till he goes to sleep. Just relax. But not too much. Don't want you snoring," Dennis muttered, clutching my hand in a tightly comforting grip. We endured a few more seconds of aural hell, then blessed silence apart from the thudding of two hearts under John Turpin's spare bed. If he'd had parquet floors instead of carpet, we wouldn't have stood a chance. Then a click, a bleep and a replay of Deirdre's attempt at sultry seductiveness, thankfully muffled. I heard the clatter of a handset being picked up and the electronic stutter of a number being keyed in. Amazing how certain sounds travel and others don't. At first all I could hear of Turpin's voice was a low rumble. Then, as he mounted the stairs and walked into his bedroom, I could hear every word.

". . . halfway down the motorway when it dawned on me. When I'd asked this supposed security man if he'd called Peter Beckman, he'd said Peter was already on his way in. But Peter's taken a couple of days off this week to go to some stupid Christmas market in Germany with his wife. So I rang him on his mobile, and he's only having dinner in some floating restaurant on the bloody Rhine." I heard the sound of shoes being kicked off.

"Well, I know," he continued after a short pause. "So I rang studio security and they denied any report of a break-in or any

call to me . . . No, I don't think so. It'll be some bloody technicians' Christmas party, some idiot's idea of a joke, let's bugger up
Turpin's evening . . ." Another pause. "Oh, all right, I'll check,
but the alarm was on . . . Yes, I'm just going to get changed, and
I'll be right over. You know how I feel about Clitheroe sausages
for breakfast," he added suggestively. I was going to have serious
trouble with sausages for a while, I could tell.

I strained my ears and picked up the sound of sliding doors
open and close, then faint sounds like someone doing exactly
what Turpin had said. I heard the bathroom door open, the
sound of a light cord being pulled once, twice, and the door
closing. A door moved over carpet pile, a light switch snapped
twice. The study. He was checking, just like he'd told Deirdre he
would. My throat constricted, my muscles went rigid. Gizmo's
CD-ROM was still in Turpin's drive. Where had I left the CD
I'd taken out of it? Dennis's hand clamped even tighter over
mine. All round the bed was suddenly flooded with light, but
only momentarily. Then twilight returned.

I felt the tension slowly leaking out of my body. We'd got
away with it. Turpin was going out again. The terrible irony
was that if we'd waited quarter of an hour longer before Dennis
had made his hoax call, Deirdre would have saved us the trouble
and I'd not have lost five years off my life expectancy. Dennis
let go of my hand. I patted his arm in thanks.

Finally, the alarm was reset and the low thrum of Turpin's
car engine dimmed in the distance. "Now what?" I asked.

"He's gone for the night. You've got hours to play with,"
Dennis said cheerfully.

"The alarm's on. As soon as we move out from under the
bed, Lostock calls the cavalry. And for all we know, Clitheroe
sausages is only a couple of hundred yards away."

Dennis chuckled. "The trouble with you, Kate, is you
worry too much. Now me, I've got the advantage of a commando training. Cool under pressure."

I poked him sharply in the ribs, enjoying the squeal that accompanied the rush of air. "You can't get the staff these days," I said sweetly. "I'll just lie here and meditate while you get it sorted." It's called whistling in the dark.

In the dim gleam from the landing, I watched as Dennis rolled on to his stomach and propelled himself across the floor using toes, knees, elbows and fingers for purchase. Keeping belly to the carpet made it a slow crawl, but it was effective. The little red light on the passive infrared detector perched in the corner of the room stayed unlit. He disappeared round the corner of the door and my stomach started eating itself. I badly needed to go to the loo.

Time stretched to impossible lengths. I wondered if Dennis was going downstairs head first or feet first. I wondered whether the keypad itself was covered by an infrared detector. I wondered whether it was possible to install detectors that didn't show they'd been activated. I even wondered if Turpin was paranoid enough to have installed one of those silent alarms that rang in a remote control centre staffed by battle-hungry security guards. I wondered so much about burglar alarms that night that I was beginning to consider a new profit centre for Brannigan & Co.

Suddenly the main alarm klaxon gave a single whoop. Shocked, I cracked my head on the underside of the bed in my manic scramble to get out from under there. "It's all right," Dennis shouted. "It's off."

He found me sitting on the landing carpet gingerly fingering the egg on my forehead. "Don't ever do that to me again," I groaned. "Jesus, Dennis, if I was a cat I'd be on borrowed lives after tonight."

"Never mind whingeing, let's get done and get out of here," he said. "I fancy a night in with the wife."

"I didn't realize you'd been banged up that long," I said tartly, getting to my feet and heading back into Turpin's study, this time via the loo. I was amazed we'd got away with it; directly in the line of sight from the doorway was a CD gleaming like a beacon on Turpin's desk.

Ransacking his secrets took less time than I expected. Less time, certainly, than I deserved, given how overdrawn my luck must have been that night. We let ourselves out of the front door just after midnight. I dropped Dennis outside his front door half an hour later and drove home on freshly gritted roads. For once, Richard was home alone, awake and ardent. Unfortunately I felt older than God and about as sexy as a Barbie doll so he made me cocoa and didn't say a word against me crashing alone in my own bed. It must be love.

I think.

><

I was constructing the fire wall between me and the evidence when Gizmo stuck his head round my office door next morning. "What's happening?" he asked.

"I'm trying to make this stuff look like it came through the letterbox," I said, waving a hand at the pile of material I'd amassed from John Turpin's office. "It's all sorted now, except for the computer files. All I can do is enclose a floppy copy with a printed note of where to find the original files on Turpin's hard disk. But it's not conclusive."

Gizmo sidled into the room, looking particularly smart in one of the suits I'd chosen. He'd even had a haircut. I wondered if today was the day. I'd find out soon enough, I reckoned. He placed a thin bundle of papers on the desk in front of me and said, "I think this might be."

The top sheet revealed John Turpin's present shareholding in NPTV as well as details of his future potential share options. I whistled softly. Even a movement in share price of a few pence could make a significant difference to Turpin's personal wealth. Next came what were clearly commercially sensitive details of NPTV's current negotiations with a cable TV company. I didn't even want to know where this stuff had come from. What was clear from the terms of the deal was that if certain levels of viewing figures were reached in the twelve months either side of the deal, senior executives of NPTV—among them John Turpin—were going to be a lot richer than they were now.

The last sheet was the killer. Somehow, Gizmo had got his sticky fingers on the details of a transaction carried out by John Turpin's stockbroker on his behalf. The order for a tranche of NPTV shares had been placed on the day of Dorothea Dawson's murder. According to the computerized time code on the order, Turpin had instructed his broker in the short space of time between Gloria and me leaving the camper van and the police arriving in response to my call.

I looked up at Gizmo. "I suppose he thought he'd be too busy later on to get his order in. And then he'd have lost the edge that killing Dorothea had given him."

"You mean he killed her just to push up the programme ratings and make himself richer?" Gizmo said, clearly shocked.

"I think that was just a bonus. He actually killed her because she'd sussed that he was the mole leaking the storylines to the papers. Ironically, she had powerful reasons for keeping quiet about his involvement, but he didn't believe her. He thought she was going to blackmail him or expose him, and he wasn't prepared to take that risk. He just bided his time till he found the right opportunity."

Gizmo shook his head. "It never ceases to amaze me, what people will do for money. People always say shit like it buys you privacy, or it lets you live the life you want. But I don't know. I've got all the privacy I need, and I'm mostly skint. But I live the life I want. I reckon most people that chase money only do it because they don't really know what it is they do want."

Philosophy for breakfast now. It had to be better than Clitheroe sausages, I thought with a bitter smile. I hoped Turpin was making the most of it. He'd be a fair few years older before he tasted anything other than prison food. With a sigh, I picked up the phone and managed to persuade the police switchboard to connect me to Linda Shaw. "Hi, Sergeant," I said. "It's Kate Brannigan."

"Oh yes," she said, her voice guarded.

"I've something at the office I think you might like to see," I told her.

"Oh yes? And what would that be?" She sounded neutral. I guessed Jackson was within hearing range.

"You need to see it to get the full effect. I can promise you it'll help your clear-up rate."

"I'd heard you've already contributed to that this week," she said tartly. "I can't say I'd like to share the experience."

"This is different," I said firmly. "Please, Linda. I'm trying to do us both a favour here. You know and I know that if I approach Jackson his first instinct will be to rubbish what I've got. And that could mean a murderer walking. You don't want that any more than I do. So will you come round?"

"Give me an hour," she said, a noticeable lack of enthusiasm in her voice.

It couldn't have suited me better. An hour was perfect for what I had to do.

❧

Given the grief I'd already had over the Perfect Son, I'd expected Shelley to rip Gloria's face off and send her home with it in a paper bag. Instead, Gloria got the star treatment. Apparently, according to Shelley, if her boy was with Gloria, he couldn't be getting into the kind of trouble I organized especially for him on a daily basis. But Gloria, being a mother herself, would understand Shelley's concerns. Gloria patted Shelley's hand, sympathized and told her what a credit to his mother the Perfect Son was. Donovan shifted from foot to foot, faintly embarrassed but relieved not to be on the receiving end of another maternal diatribe. Excuse me, I wanted to shout. Who's the one with frostbite and coronary heart disease and a major sleep deficit and a bump on the head the size of Rochdale as a result of this case?

Eventually, I managed to shoo Gloria into my office. She did a double take when she saw Freddie perched uncomfortably on the edge of the sofa. I'd promised him there was no reason why anyone had to know he was Dorothea's son or that he'd been the major mole, but his body language didn't actually indicate conviction. When Gloria walked in, his face spasmed in panic. "Gloria," he stammered, jerking to his feet and taking an involuntary sideways step away from her.

"Hiya, chuck," she said warmly, collapsing on to the sofa. "You another one of Kate's mystery witnesses, then?"

"Er . . . yes. She never mentioned you were coming . . ." He shot me a look that said he'd never trust a private eye again. I wouldn't have minded so much if I'd lied to him, but I hadn't. Well, not so's you'd notice.

We didn't have long to wait for Linda. She came in with more attitude than a rap band. "This better be good," she said even before she got across the threshold. I waved her to a chair and leaned against my desk.

"Since you're all so thrilled to be here, I'll keep it short as I can. There's been a mole at NPTV making a small fortune out of selling scandal stories and advance storylines to the press. Dorothea Dawson thought she had worked out the identity of that mole by studying her astrological charts and matching what they told her against the names of people who had access to advance stories and who were in a position to find out about the murky pasts of the cast." I nodded towards Freddie.

"You might remember Freddie here. He works in the make-up department at *Northerners*. Freddie witnessed an encounter between Dorothea and a senior management figure at NPTV. Freddie, can you tell DS Shaw what you told me last night?"

He was so overwhelmed with relief that I hadn't after all revealed either of his secrets that he told the story we'd agreed on eagerly and openly, with none of his awkward mannerisms to make Linda wonder if there was more going on than met the eye. "Dorothea had come over to the make-up studio looking for one of the actors so she could rearrange an appointment, but she'd just missed him. Anyway, Turpin came in just as she was leaving. She asked if he was still wasting his time on the mole hunt. Then she said she had a pretty good idea who the mole was, and she'd tell him if the price was right."

"What did Turpin say?" I asked.

"He went bright red. He told her if he wanted to waste the company's money, there were plenty of perfectly good charities. Then he just stomped out without doing whatever it was he'd come in for."

"Turpin might well have interpreted Dorothea's comments as an indirect blackmail threat," I pointed out.

Linda had listened with her head cocked to one side, critically appraising Freddie's words. Then she gave a slight nod. I was about to say more, but she raised one finger and made a series of notes in her pad. "Interesting," she said.

"There's more."

"I'm sure," she said.

"You've already taken a statement from Gloria about the events of the evening when Dorothea was killed. I don't know if you remember, but she had a far better opportunity than I did to take notice of who else was in and around the car park at the same time. Among the people she saw was that same NPTV executive, John Turpin. Maybe you'd like to confirm that for us, Gloria?"

My client nodded avidly. "That's right, chuck," she said eagerly. She was loving every minute of it, just as I'd expected. I hadn't really needed her there, but she was paying the bill, and I figured a bit of grandstanding might just be worth a Christmas bonus. "I saw John Turpin standing in the doorway of the admin block. He looked as if he was wondering whether it was worth chancing getting his good suit wet in the sleet."

"Thanks for confirming that, Ms Kendal. But we did know that already, Kate," Linda pointed out, not even bothering to make a note this time.

"I'm just sketching in the background, Linda," I said apologetically. "I became involved in this case because Gloria here was getting death-threat letters. She hired me to take care of her."

"Which you and yours have done admirably," the irrepressible Gloria chipped in.

"Thank you, Gloria. I may need that testimonial before long," I said. "This morning, when I unlocked the office, there was a padded envelope in the mailbox." I produced an envelope from the desk behind me.

"Inside was an assortment of papers and a floppy disk. The disk contains what I believe are the originals of the letters sent to my client. A note attached to the floppy claims that the originals are to be found on the hard disk of John Turpin's home computer. I'd have thought that might be grounds for a search warrant?"

Linda grunted noncommittally, frowning at the disk and the note I handed her. "Why would he target you specifically, Gloria?" she asked.

"I haven't a clue, chuck," she said. "The only thing I can think of is that I'm the only one of the show's really big names who lives alone, so maybe he thought I'd be easiest to scare. Mind you, he's never entirely forgiven me for our Sandra giving him the elbow all those years ago."

"What?" Linda and I chorused.

"He took our Sandra out for a few weeks, years ago now. Before she met Keith. Any road, she decided he wasn't for her and she chucked him. He wasn't best pleased. He's never had a civil word for me since."

All I could do was stare at her and shake my head. I love clients who go out of their way to make the job easier. I just don't seem to get many. I took a deep breath while Linda took more notes.

"Also in the envelope." I placed more papers in front of her. "A photocopy of Turpin's phone bills, home and mobile. A photocopy of what looks like a Rolodex card, giving the number of Tina Marshall. She's the freelance journalist who

broke a substantial number of the *Northerners* stories in the
press. Check out the number of calls to her number. I think
you'll find most of them were made a few days before a big
Northerners story broke."

Linda was now sitting upright, totally focused on the papers
in front of her. Her finger flicked to and fro. Then she looked
me straight in the eye. "This fell through your letterbox," she
said flatly.

"That's right. It seemed to be my civic duty to pass it on
to you, Sergeant." I rummaged inside the envelope. "There is
more." I handed her the material Gizmo had culled from his
electronic sources. More for Gloria and Freddie's benefit than
Linda's, I ran through the contents.

"And at the time when he placed that order for NPTV
stock," I wound up, "only the killer could have known that the
viewing figures were about to climb sky-high on the back of
Dorothea Dawson's murder."

"Hellfire, Kate, you've done wonders," my grateful client
said. "I can sleep easy in my bed at night now."

"I'm glad," I said. Not least because I could get Donovan
back on the work he was supposed to be doing. I turned back
to Linda. "Taken together, it's a hard conclusion to resist."

"It'd be easier for my boss to swallow if the information
came from somewhere else," she said resignedly.

"Howsabout if it does?" I asked. "It won't take five minutes for Gizmo to walk down to Bootle Street and leave it in
an envelope at the front counter with your name on it. You can
tell Jackson you've been out taking a statement from Freddie
about Dorothea's conversation with Turpin and then when you
got back to the office, hey presto! There it was. You can leave
me out of it altogether."

"Are you sure?" she said. I could tell she was weighing up
how much my generosity might cost her in the future.

I shrugged. "I don't need my face all over the *Chronicle*
again. Besides, there is one thing you could do for me."

Her face closed like a slammed door. "I thought it was too good to be true."

I held my hands up. "It's no big deal. Just a word with your colleagues in uniform. Donovan is going to be serving process for me for at least the next eighteen months. I'd really appreciate it if you could spread the word that the big black guy on the bicycle is wearing a white hat."

Linda grinned. "I think I can manage that." She got to her feet and took some folded sheets of A4 out of her shoulder bag. "As it happens, I've got something for you too. I'll see myself out."

Curious, I unfolded the bundle of paper. There was a Post-it stuck on one corner in Linda's handwriting. "Printed out from Dorothea Dawson's hard disk. It gave us all a laugh." I pulled off the note and started to read: **Written in the Stars for Kate Brannigan, private investigator.**

Born Oxford, UK, 4th September 1966.

* *Sun in Virgo in the Fifth House*
* *Moon in Taurus in the Twelfth House*
* *Mercury in Virgo in the Fifth House*
* *Venus in Leo in the Fourth House*
* *Mars in Leo in the Fourth House*
* *Jupiter in Cancer in the Third House*
* *Saturn retrograde in Pisces in the Eleventh House*
* *Uranus in Virgo in the Fifth House*
* *Neptune in Scorpio in the Sixth House*
* *Pluto in Virgo in the Fifth House*
* *Chiron in Pisces in the Eleventh House*
* *Ascendant Sign: Gemini*

Sun in Virgo in the 5th House: On the positive side, can be ingenious, verbally skilled, diplomatic, tidy, methodical, discerning and dutiful. The negatives are fussiness, a critical manner, an obsessive attention to detail and a lack of self-confidence that can disguise itself as arrogance. In the Fifth House, it indicates a player of games . . .

"What is it, chuck? You look like you've seen a ghost," Gloria said, concern in her voice.

I shook my head, folding the papers away. "It's nothing, Gloria. Just some sad twisted copper's idea of a joke."

EPILOGUE

SATURN TRINES NEPTUNE

*She loses her own apprehensions through her profound and pen-
etrating investigative interest in others. She has a strong sense of
how her life should be arranged, often bringing order to chaos.
She follows her feelings and is sensitive to the subtext that lies
beneath the conversation and behaviour of others. She can harness
irrationality and factor it into her decision-making.*

From *Written in the Stars*, by Dorothea Dawson

If I hadn't known how thoroughly Dorothea Dawson researched
her clients, I'd probably have been impressed with her astrological analysis of my character. I wouldn't have minded betting that
the minute Gloria told Dorothea she'd hired me, the astrologer
had started digging. I wasn't exactly a shrinking violet. For a
start, I'd appeared in Alexis's stories in the *Chronicle* more times
than I was entirely comfortable with. So it wouldn't have been
too hard for Dorothea to pick up a few snippets about me and
weave them into an otherwise standard profile.

What she missed completely was my sense of humour. I
mean, if I didn't have a world–class sense of humour, why else
would I be sitting in the Costa Coffee forecourt at Piccadilly
Station drinking moccachino and reading my horoscope when I

could be at home, snug as a bug in a phone, working out how to solve my latest computer game with a Stoly and pink grapefruit juice on the side?

The reason why I was lurking among the sad souls condemned to travelling on Virgin Trains was shuffling from foot to foot a few yards away, like a small child who needs to go to the toilet but doesn't want to miss some crucial development in his favourite TV show. Gizmo had clearly had a hard time deciding between style and comfort and he'd ended up wearing one of the suits I'd chosen for him. The trouble was, the only outer garment that went with it was his mac, which wasn't a lot of use in the lowest December temperatures on record. Neither were the thin-soled Italian shoes. Sometimes I wonder what real Italians wear in winter.

As well as hopping from one foot to the other, Gizmo was clutching a copy of Iain M. Banks's cult sci-fi novel, *Feersum Endjinn*, the agreed recognition signal. He'd arranged to meet Jan off the London train at half past eight and he'd been dancing his quaint jig since a quarter past. Imagine expecting a train to be early. I'd sat comfortably sipping my brew and dipping into Dorothea's digest of my personality.

There was an indecipherable announcement over the Tannoy and Gizmo stopped jigging. He leaned slightly forward, nose towards the platforms like a setter scenting the breeze. I followed his gaze and watched the dark-red livery of the London train easing into platform six with a rumble and a sigh. I couldn't help crossing my fingers. If this went pear-shaped, I'd get no proper work out of him for weeks.

The carriage doors were opening the length of the train and people spilled on to the platform. First past us were the smokers, carrying with them a miasma of overflowing ashtray after two and a half hours sitting in stale tobacco smoke. Then the usual Friday-night mixture of day-trip shoppers, students coming to Manchester for a groovy weekend, senior citizens exhausted from a week with the grandchildren, sales reps and educational consultants in cheap suits crumpled by the journey and, finally, the first-class passengers in sleek tailoring with their identikit suit carriers and briefcases, men and women alike.

Gizmo bobbed like a ball on the tide of humanity streaming past him, his eyes darting from side to side. The crowd swelled, then steadied, then thinned to the last stragglers. His head seemed to shrink into his shoulders like a tortoise and I saw him sigh.

Last off the train was a blond giant. His broad shoulders strained a black leather jacket that tapered to narrow hips encased in tight blue denim. They didn't leave much to the imagination, especially with his swivel-hipped walk. As he reached the end of the platform, he turned his head right, then left, a thick mane of blond hair bouncing on his collar. He looked like a Viking in the prow of a longship, deciding which direction held America.

He settled for left and moved in our direction. As he grew nearer, I could see the book clutched in the massive hand that wasn't carrying the black leather holdall. I closed my eyes momentarily. Even Dennis might have a bit of bother menacing his way out of this one. Gizmo would have no chance.

When I opened them, Jan was looming over Gizmo. "You're Gizmo," he boomed. I couldn't quite place the accent.

Gizmo half turned towards the café, panic in his eyes. "I never . . . she never said anything about anybody else," he stammered desperately.

Typical, I thought. Great with silicon, crap with carbon-based life forms. Does not compute.

Jan frowned. "What do you mean?" I figured he wasn't sure if Gizmo had missed the point completely or if there was a language problem.

Gizmo took a hasty step backwards. "Look, I never meant to cause any trouble, I didn't know anything about you. Whatever she's said, there's been nothing between us, this would have been the first time we'd even met," he gabbled.

Jan looked even more puzzled. He waved the book at Gizmo. "I brought the book. So we'd know each other," he said in that pedantic way that Germans and Scandies have when they're not sure you've understood their impeccable English.

Gizmo swung towards me. "Tell him, Kate. Tell him it's all a misunderstanding. She never said anything about having a bloke. I thought she was unattached."

With a sigh, I got to my feet. "You're Jan, right?" I said, giving the J its soft Y sound. Gizmo's mouth fell open and the Iain M. Banks tumbled to the concourse floor. Then, suddenly, he whirled round and ran for the escalator down to the tram terminus below. Jan made a half-hearted move to step around me and give chase but I blocked him. "Leave it," I said. "He's not the one, Jan."

He frowned. "Who are you? What's going on?" He craned past me, peering anxiously towards the escalators, as if he expected Gizmo to reappear. Fat chance.

"I'm Kate. Gizmo and I work together."

"Why has he run off? We arranged to meet," Jan said, sounding puzzled. "We have been e-mailing each other for months. Getting to know each other. We both figured it was time to meet." He made the inverted commas sign in the air that pillocks use to indicate they're quoting. "'Time to take things further,' Gizmo said."

"Don't you think it might have been sensible to mention that you were a bloke?" I said, unable to keep the sarcasm out of my voice. "He thought you were a woman. Jan with a J, not Jan with a Y."

Jan's fair skin flushed scarlet. "What does that matter? I'm still the same person. Because I am a man suddenly it's different?"

"Of course it's different," I protested. His disingenuousness was really winding me up. "He's not gay, for one thing. I can't believe you never made it clear you're a man. It can't be the first time someone's made that mistake."

He glared at me. "Why should I? I'm not responsible for someone else's assumptions. You British are so terrified of anything that is different, that challenges your sad little conventions."

By now, the entire coffee shop was enthralled, waiting for my response. "Bollocks," I said contemptuously. "Tell that to Julian Clary. Don't try and pretend that deceiving Gizmo was some kind of heroic act of sexual liberation. It was cowardice, that's what it was. You were scared to admit you were a man because you thought Gizmo would end your cyber-relationship."

"And I was right," he shouted.

"No, you were wrong," I said quietly. "He might have rejected you as a lover, but he would still have been your friend. And I've got good cause to know just how much that signifies." Three women sitting round a table in the coffee shop gave me a ragged round of applause.

Jan's laugh was harsh. "In cyberspace, he didn't need a woman to fight his battles." Then he turned on his heel and stalked off towards the taxi rank.

I gave the women a sardonic bow and walked out into a heavy drizzle. Underneath the entrance canopy, the Salvation Army band was playing "In the Bleak Midwinter." A beggar with a dog on a string was trying to sell *The Big Issue* to people with a train to catch. A traffic warden was writing a ticket to stick on some poor sucker's windscreen.

I couldn't see Gizmo turning up for work on Monday morning as if nothing had happened. It looked like Brannigan & Co had just lost their computer expert. And when I got back to my car, the back tyre was flatter than my spirits.

If this was what was written in the stars, there was a script-writer somewhere who'd better watch his back.